ALWAYS
AN EATON

ROCHELLE
ALERS

ALWAYS
AN EATON

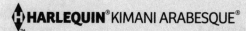
HARLEQUIN® KIMANI ARABESQUE®

ALWAYS AN EATON
ISBN-13: 978-0-373-09155-3

This edition published April 2014
Copyright © 2014 by Harlequin Books S.A.

The publisher acknowledges the copyright holders of the individual works as follows:

SWEET DREAMS
Copyright © 2010 by Rochelle Alers

TWICE THE TEMPTATION
Copyright © 2010 by Rochelle Alers

PLEASE RECYCLE • THIS PRODUCT IS RECYCLABLE

Recycling programs for this product may not exist in your area.

Printed in U.S.A.

HARLEQUIN®
www.Harlequin.com

CONTENTS

Dear Reader,

Welcome back for yet another Eaton family reunion. This time it is Chandra Eaton and her cousin Denise Eaton who will take center stage in *Always an Eaton*.

First let me warn you that the title *Sweet Dreams* may be a bit misleading, as Chandra's dreams are anything but sweet. In fact, they are downright erotic. They are so vivid that she records them in a journal. Then the unthinkable happens. She leaves her journal in a taxi and Preston Tucker, Philadelphia's prize-winning playwright, finds it. But before returning Chandra's property, he reads each and every detailed account. Though, once he meets the sexy author, he is unable to differentiate between reality and fantasy, as he and Chandra become actors in a sensual journey to bring her dreams to life.

In *Twice the Temptation,* Denise is given a second chance at love when she is reunited with the man she'd given her heart to in college. She never stopped loving Rhett Fennell, but what she fears most is his inability to be faithful to her. What she doesn't know is that Rhett never forgave her walking out on him, so he decides to turn the tables. He plans to seduce her and then leave her without a word as she'd done to him years ago. But even as an astute businessman, Rhett couldn't have predicted the outcome of his carefully crafted scheme when he loses his heart a second time to the Eaton woman he's loved forever.

Here's to hoping you'll enjoy the Eatons as much I did creating these characters that remind us of our very own family.

Happy reading,

Rochelle Alers

www.RochelleAlers.org

SWEET DREAMS

Let him kiss me with the kisses of his mouth; for thy love is better than wine.
—*The Song of Solomon 1:2*

Prologue

The sound of labored breathing competed with the incessant whirring of the blades of the ceiling fan overhead. The crescendo of gasps and moans overlapped with the rhythmic thrum of the fan as it circulated the humid tropical night air coming through the screened-in jalousie windows.

It was a scene that had played out nightly countless times since Chandra Eaton had come to Belize to teach. Her right hand cupped her breast while the other fondled her mound, as she surrendered to the surging contractions rippling through her thighs. Arching her back, she exhaled as the last of the orgasm that had held her in the throes of an explosive climax left her feeling as if she'd been shattered into a million pieces.

She lay motionless, savoring the aftermath that made it almost impossible to move or draw a normal breath.

When she did move, it was to reach over and turn on the lamp on the bedside table. The soft golden glow cast shadows over the sparsely decorated bedroom.

Biting her lip, Chandra sat upright and picked up the pen lying atop her cloth-covered journal. Unscrewing the top, she closed her eyes for several seconds. The tip of the pen was poised over a clean page before she sighed and collected her thoughts.

Dream #139—October 2

I could smell him, feel him, taste him, but as usual he wouldn't let me touch his face.

His hand feathered over my leg, moving up slowly until it rested along my inner thigh. My breathing quickened, filling the bedroom with hiccuping sounds. I was so aroused that I hadn't wanted prolonged foreplay. I'd screamed and pleaded for him to make it quick. His response was to place one hand over my mouth, while he used his free hand to guide his engorged erection inside me. The heat from his body, the rigid flesh moving in and out of my body made my heart stop beating for several seconds.

He was relentless, pushing and receding. And then, slowing just before I climaxed, I'd pleaded with him to make love to me and then I begged him to stop. I felt faint. But he didn't stop. And I let go, abandoning myself to the pleasure of a sweet, explosive orgasm. Instead of lying beside me on the mattress, he got up and left. It was as if he knew it would be our last time together.

Chandra reread what she'd written, and then smiled. It was uncanny the way she was able to remember her dreams with vivid clarity. They'd begun the first week she arrived in Belize, and had continued for more than two years. They didn't come every night. But when they did, they served to assuage the sexual tension that came from not sharing her body with a man in nearly three years.

The dreams came without warning. She had begun to see them as a release for her stress and frustration. She didn't know who the man was who came to her when she least expected it, and she didn't care as long as he provided the stimulation needed to give her the physical release so necessary for her sexual well-being.

Smiling, Chandra closed the journal, capped the pen, turned off the lamp and slid under the covers, lying on the pillow that cradled her head. Minutes later she closed her eyes. This time when she fell asleep, there were no erotic dreams to disturb her slumber.

Chapter 1

Chandra Eaton slumped against the rear seat in the taxi as the driver maneuvered away from the curb at the Philadelphia International Airport. She felt as if she'd been traveling for days. Her flight from Belize to Miami was a little more than two hours. But it was the layover in Atlanta that had lasted more than eight hours because of violent thunderstorms that left her out of sorts. All she wanted was a hot shower, a firm bed and a soft, fluffy pillow.

As a Peace Corps volunteer, she'd spent more than two years teaching in Belize. She'd returned to Philadelphia twice: once to attend the funeral of her eldest sister and brother-in-law, and three months ago to be a bridesmaid in the wedding of her surviving sister, Belinda. Now, at the age of thirty, she'd come home again. But this time it was to stay.

Her father called her his gypsy, and her mother said she was a vagabond, to which she had no comeback. What no one in her family knew, her parents in particular, was that she'd been running away from the tragedy that had befallen one of her students, followed by her own broken engagement.

Thankfully, her previous homecoming and this one would be more joyful occasions. Belinda had married Griffin Rice in June and two months ago her brother Myles had exchanged vows with Zabrina Mixon-Cooper after a ten-year separation. She also looked forward to meeting her nephew for the first time.

"What the…"

She opened her eyes and sat up straighter, her heart slamming against her ribs. The cabbie had swerved to avoid hitting another vehicle drifting into their lane. Her purse and leather tote slid off the seat and onto the floor with the violent motion, spilling their contents. Bending over, she retrieved her cell phone, wallet, passport and a pack of mints. Then she checked the tote to make certain her laptop was still there.

"Are you all right back there, miss?" the driver asked over his shoulder.

Chandra exhaled audibly. "I'm good," she lied smoothly.

She wasn't good. If she'd been a cat, she would've used up at least one of her nine lives. It was going to be some time before she would be able to adjust to the fast pace of a large urban city. Living in Philadelphia, even in one of its suburbs, was very different from living and teaching in a small town in Northern Belize.

The cabdriver took a quick glance in the rearview

mirror. "Let me try and get around this clown before I end up in his trunk."

Settling back again, Chandra closed her eyes. When she'd called her mother to tell her that her flight had been delayed, Roberta Eaton had offered to drive to the airport to pick her up. But she'd told her mother she would take a taxi to the subdivision where her parents had purchased a two-bedroom, two-bath town house. Aside from her purse and tote bag, she had checked only one piece of luggage. The trunk with most of her clothes was scheduled to arrive in the States at the end of the month.

It appeared as if she'd just fallen asleep when the motion stopped, and she opened her eyes. Chandra missed the six-bedroom, four-bath farmhouse where she'd grown up with her sisters and brother. She understood her parents' need to downsize now that they were in their sixties. They didn't want to concern themselves with having someone shovel snow or mow the lawn, or deal with the exorbitant expense of maintaining a large house.

What she'd missed most was opening the door leading from the main house and into the connecting space that had been Dr. Dwight Eaton's medical practice. Her father didn't schedule patients between the hours of twelve and one; the exception was in an emergency. It had been her time to have her father all to herself. Gathering her purse and tote, she paid the fare, opened the rear door and stepped out of the taxi as the driver came around to retrieve her luggage from the trunk, setting it on the front steps.

Roberta Eaton stood in the entryway. The smile that parted her lips caused the skin around her eyes to crinkle. She prayed that this homecoming would be Chandra's last. She thought she knew all there was to know about her youngest child, but Chandra's mercurial moods kept her guessing as to what she would do or where she would go next.

What she'd found so off-putting was that there was usually no warning. It was if her daughter went to sleep, then woke with a new agenda, shocking everyone with her announcements. First it was her decision not to attend the University of Pennsylvania, but Columbia University in New York City. Then she'd declined an offer to teach at a Philadelphia elementary school and instead taught at a private all-girls' school in Northern Virginia. The most shocking, and what Roberta thought most devastating, was when Chandra announced she'd joined the Peace Corps and decided to teach in Belize. Although she'd become accustomed to her daughter's independent nature, it was her husband, Dwight Eaton, who said his youngest daughter had caused him many sleepless nights.

Roberta approached Chandra with outstretched arms, the tears she'd tried vainly to hold back overflowed. "Welcome home, baby."

Her mother calling her *baby* was Chandra's undoing. She could deal with any and everything except her mother's tears. Roberta was openly weeping—deep, heart-wrenching sobs that made Chandra unleash her own flood of tears.

Pressed closer to Roberta's ample bosom, she tightened her hold around her mother's neck, savoring the warmth of the protective embrace. "Mama, please don't cry."

Roberta's tears stopped as if she'd turned off a spigot. "Don't tell me not to cry when I've had too many sleepless nights and worn out my knees praying that you'd make it home safely."

Easing back, Chandra stared at her mother. Roberta Eaton hadn't changed much over the years. Her body was fuller and rounder, and there was more salt than pepper in her short natural hairstyle. Her face had remained virtually unchanged. Her dark brown complexion was clear, her skin smooth.

"I'm home, Mama."

"You're home, but for how long, Chandra Eaton? I was talking to your father last night, and we have a wager that you won't hang around for more than three to six months before you start getting itchy feet again."

"I'm not going anywhere. I'm home to stay."

Roberta gave her a look that said *I don't believe you,* but Chandra was too tired to get into an argument with her mother. She'd been up since two that morning for a 5:00 a.m. flight to Miami, with a connecting flight to Atlanta. Sitting in Hartsdale for hours had tried her patience, and that meant she had no intention of engaging in a conversation where she had to defend herself or convince her mother that she didn't plan to leave home again. Once she'd completed her tour with the Peace Corps she'd promised herself that she would stop running away, that she would come home, face her fears and reconcile her past.

"May I please go into the house and shower before going to bed?"

As if she'd come out of a trance, Roberta leaned forward and kissed Chandra's cheek. Within seconds she'd morphed into maternal mode. "I'm sorry, baby. You have to be exhausted. Did you eat?" she asked over her shoulder as she stepped into the spacious entryway.

"I ate something at the airport."

Picking up her luggage, Chandra walked into the house and made her way toward the staircase to the second floor guest bedroom. Methodically, she stripped off her clothes, leaving them on the bathroom floor, and stepped into the shower stall. Her eyelids were drooping by the time she'd dried off. She searched through her luggage for a nightgown and crawled into bed. It was just after six. And even though the sun hadn't set, within minutes of her head touching the pillow she was asleep.

Preston Tucker ducked his head as he got into the taxi and gave the driver the address to his duplex in downtown Philadelphia. He'd spent the past twenty-four hours flying to Los Angeles for a meeting that lasted all of ten minutes before returning to Philadelphia after flying standby from LAX.

He'd told his agent that he had reservations about meeting with studio executives who wanted to turn one of his plays into a movie with several A-list actors. But all Clifford Jessup could see were dollar signs. Preston knew if he sold the movie rights to his play he would have to relinquish literary control. But he was unwilling to do so at the expense of not being able to recognize his play, something he'd spent more than two years writing and perfecting, breathing life into the characters.

He was aware of Hollywood's reputation for taking literary license once they'd optioned a work, but the suits he'd spoken to wanted to eviscerate his play. If he'd been a struggling playwright he probably would've accepted their offer. But fortunately for him, his days of waiting for a check so that he could pay back rent were behind him. What made the play even more personal is that it was the first play he'd written as a college student.

Slumping in the rear seat, he tried to stretch his long legs out to a more comfortable position under the seat in front of him. His right foot hit something. Reaching under the passenger seat, he pulled out a slim black ostrich-skin portfolio with the initials *CE* stamped on the front in gold lettering. Looking at the driver's hack license, he noticed the man's first and last names began with an *M,* so he concluded a passenger had left it in the taxi.

Preston debated whether to open it or give it to the taxi driver, who most likely would turn it in to Lost and Found or discard the contents and keep the expensive-looking portfolio for himself. He decided to unzip it and found a cloth-bound journal. Judging from the mauve color of the book, he knew it belonged to a woman.

His suspicions were confirmed when he saw the neat cursive writing on the inside front cover: "If found, please return to Chandra Eaton." What followed was a telephone number with a Philadelphia area code and an e-mail address. Reaching into the breast pocket of his suit jacket, he took out his cell phone to dial the number, but the first sentence on the first page caused him to go completely still.

Dream #9—March 3
I opened my eyes when I heard the soft creaking sound that told me someone had opened my bedroom door. Usually he came in through the window. I held my breath because I wasn't certain if it was him. But who else would it be? I didn't know whether to scream or reach under the bed for the

flashlight I kept there in the event of a power failure. I decided not to move, hoping whoever had come would realize they were in the wrong room and then leave.

The seconds ticked off and I found myself counting slowly, beginning with one. By the time I'd counted to forty-three, there was no sound, no movement. I reached under the bed for the flashlight and flicked it on. I was alone in the bedroom, the sound of the runaway beating of my heart echoing in my ears and the lingering scent of a man's cologne wafting in the humid tropical air coming in through the open windows. I recognized the scent. It was the same as the one I'd given Laurence for our first Christmas together. But, he's gone, exorcised, so why did I conjure him up?

Preston slipped the cell phone back into his pocket as he continued to read. He was so engrossed in what Chandra Eaton had written that he hadn't realized the taxi had stopped and his building doorman had opened the rear door.

"Welcome home, Mr. Tucker."

His head popped up and he smiled. "Thank you, Reynaldo."

Preston returned the journal to the leather case, paid the driver and then reached for his leather weekender on the seat next to him. He'd managed to read four of Chandra Eaton's journal entries, each one more sensual and erotic than the one before it. As a writer, he saw scenes in his head before putting them down on paper, and he was not only intrigued but fascinated by what Chandra Eaton had written.

Clutching his weekender, he entered the lobby of the luxury high-rise, which had replaced many of the grand Victorian-style mansions that once surrounded Rittenhouse Square. He'd purchased the top two floors in the newly constructed building on the advice of his financial planner, using it as a business write-off. His office, a media room, gourmet kitchen, formal living and dining rooms were set up for work and entertaining. The three bedrooms with en suite bathrooms on the upper floor were for out-of-town guests.

There had been a time when he'd entertained at his Brandywine Valley home, but as he matured he'd come to covet his privacy. Lately, he'd become somewhat of a recluse. If an event wasn't work-related, then he usually declined the invitation. His mother claimed he was getting old and crotchety, to which he replied that thirty-eight was hardly old and he wasn't crotchety, just particular as to how he spent his time and more importantly with whom.

Preston was exhausted and sleep-deprived from flying more than six thousand miles in twenty-four hours. His original plan was to shower and go directly to bed, but Chandra Eaton's erotic prose had revived him. He would finish reading the journal, then e-mail the owner to let her know he'd found it.

He didn't bother to stop at the concierge to retrieve his mail, and instead walked into the elevator and pressed the button for his floor. The elevator doors glided closed. The car rose smoothly and swiftly, stopping at the eighteenth floor. The doors opened again and he made his way down a carpeted hallway to his condo.

It was good to be home. If he'd completely trusted Cliff Jessup to represent his interests, he never would've flown to L.A. What bothered him about his agent was that they'd practically grown up together. Both had attended Princeton, pledged the same fraternity, and he'd been best man at Cliff's wedding. Something had changed. Preston wasn't certain whether he'd changed, or if Cliff had changed, or if they were just growing apart.

Inserting the cardkey into the slot to his duplex, Preston pushed open the door and was greeted with a rush of cool air. He'd adjusted the air-conditioning before he left, but apparently the drop in the temperature outside made it feel uncomfortably chilly. It was mid-October, and the forecasts predicted a colder and snowier than usual winter.

He dropped his bag on the floor near a table his interior decorator had purchased at an estate sale. It was made in India during the nineteenth century for wealthy Indians and Europeans. It was transported from India to Jamaica at the behest of a British colonist who'd owned one of the largest sugarcane plantations in the Caribbean. Not only was it the most extravagant piece of furniture in the condo, but Preston's favorite.

Emptying his pockets of loose change, he put the coins in a crystal dish on the table along with his credit card case and cardkey. Floor lamps illuminated the living room and the chandelier over the dining room table sparkled like tiny stars bathing the pale walls with a golden glow. Preston worked well in bright natural sunlight, so he'd had all of the lamps and light fixtures programmed to come on at different times of the day and night.

There was a time when he'd thought he had writer's block, since he found it very difficult to complete a project during the winter months. It was only when he'd reexamined his high school and college grades that he realized they were much higher in the spring semester than the fall. When he mentioned it to a friend who was a psychologist, she said he probably suffered from SAD, or seasonal affective disorder. Knowing this, he developed a habit of beginning work on a new script in early spring.

Walking past the staircase leading to the upper level, he entered the bathroom that led directly into his office. He undressed, brushed his teeth, leaving his clothes on a covered bench before stepping into the shower stall. The sharp spray of icy-cold water revived him before he adjusted the water temperature to lukewarm. Despite his jet lag, Preston was determined to stay awake long enough to read more of the journal.

He didn't know why, but he felt like a voyeur. But instead of peeking into Chandra Eaton's bedroom, he had read her most intimate thoughts. He smiled. Either she had a very fertile imagination, or an incredibly active sex life.

After wiping the moisture from his body with a thick, thirsty towel, he slipped into a pair of lounging pants and a white tee from a supply on a shelf in an alcove in the bathroom suite. Fifteen minutes later, Preston settled onto a chaise lounge in his office with a large mug of steaming black coffee and the cloth-covered journal. It was after two in the morning when he finally finished reading. His eyes were burning, but what he'd read had been too arousing for him to go to sleep.

Turning on the computer, he waited for it to boot up. He e-mailed Chandra Eaton to inform her that he'd found her portfolio in a taxi and where she could contact him to retrieve it.

Chapter 2

Chandra opened one eye, then the other, peeking at the clock on the bedside table. It was after nine. She couldn't believe she'd been asleep for more than twelve hours. It was apparent she was more exhausted than she'd originally thought. And there was no doubt her body's time clock was off. If she were still in Belize she would've been in the classroom with her young students.

Stretching her arms above her head, she exhaled a lungful of air. Chandra was glad to be home and looked forward to reuniting with her family. Sitting up, she swung her legs over the side of the twin bed and walked into the bathroom. She had a laundry list of things to do before the weekend: get a complete beauty makeover—including a haircut, mani/pedi and a hydrating facial. Despite using the strongest sunblock and wearing a hat to protect her face, the rays of the Caribbean sun had dried out her skin. She also had to go online to search for public schools in the Philadelphia area. It was too late to be assigned a full-time teaching job, but she could find work as a substitute teacher. Her sister, Belinda, who'd moved to Paoli after she married Griffin Rice, still taught American history in one of the city's most challenging high schools.

After a leisurely shower, Chandra left the bathroom to prepare for her day. It felt good not to have to shower within the mandatory three-minute time limit, to avoid using up the hot water for the next person. She'd gotten used to taking short, and sometimes cold, showers. But it wasn't just soaking in a bathtub that made her aware of what she'd had to sacrifice when she'd signed up for the Peace Corps.

Her cousin Denise had offered to sublet her co-op to Chandra after she relocated to Washington, D.C. to accept a position as executive director of a child care center. Purchasing furniture for the co-op was another item on Chandra's to-do list. But her list and everything on it would have to wait until she had something to eat. She knew she wouldn't get to see her father, who had patients booked, until later that evening. Her mother divided her time between volunteering several days a week at a senior facility and quilting with several of her friends. The quartet of quilters had completed many projects for homebound and chronically ill children.

It was after eleven when Chandra returned to the bedroom to make the bed and clean up the bathroom. Bright autumn sunlight came in through the blinds when she sat down at the corner desk and opened her laptop. When she went online she saw e-mails from her sister, brother and her cousin Denise. Without reading them, she knew they were welcoming her home. There was another e-mail with an unfamiliar address and the subject: Lost and Found, that piqued her interest. She clicked on it:

Ms. Eaton,
I found your portfolio in a taxi. Please contact me at the following number to arrange for its return.
P. J. Tucker

Chandra stared at the e-mail, thinking it was either a hoax or spam. But how would the person know her name? And what portfolio was he referring to? She picked up her tote bag, searching through it thoroughly. The leather case her brother had given her as a gift for her college graduation wasn't there.

"No!" she hissed.

P. J. Tucker must have found her journal. It had to have fallen out when the taxi driver swerved to avoid hitting another vehicle. The journal was the first volume of three others she'd filled with accounts of her dreams. She was certain she'd packed all of them in the trunk until she found one in a drawer under her lingerie. Mister or Miss P. J. Tucker had to open the journal to find out where to contact her. Chandra prayed that was all he or she had looked at. The reason she'd put the journals in the trunk, which was stowed on a ship several days before she left Belize, was that she hadn't wanted custom agents to read it when they went through her luggage.

Reaching for her cell, she dialed the number in the e-mail. "May I please speak to Mister or Miss P. J. Tucker," she said when a deep male voice answered.

"This is P. J. Tucker."

Please don't tell me you read my journal, she prayed. "I'm Chandra Eaton."

"Ms. Eaton. No doubt you read my e-mail."

"Yes, and I'd like to thank you for finding my portfolio."

"It's a very nice case, Ms. Eaton. Is it ostrich skin?"

Chandra chewed her lip. It was apparent P. J. Tucker wanted to talk about something other than the material her portfolio was made from. She wanted to set up a time and place, so that she could retrieve her journal.

"Yes, Mr. Tucker, it is. I'd like to pick up my portfolio from you. But of course, whenever it's convenient for you."

"I'm free now if you'd like to come and pick it up."

"Where are you?" Reaching for a pen, Chandra wrote down the address. "How long are you going to be there?"

"All day and all night."

She smiled. "Well, I don't have all day or all night. What if I come by before noon?"

"I'll be here."

Her smile grew wider. "Goodbye."

"Later."

Chandra ended the call. She punched speed dial for a taxi, then quickly changed out of her shorts and T-shirt and into a pair of jeans that she paired with a white men's-tailored shirt, navy blazer and imported slip-ons. There wasn't much she could do with her hair, so she brushed it off her face, braided it and secured the end with an elastic band. She heard the taxi horn as she descended the staircase. Racing into the kitchen, she took the extra set of keys off a hook, leaving through the side door.

The address P. J. Tucker had given Chandra was a modern luxury condominium in the historic Rittenhouse neighborhood. One of her favorite things to do as a young girl was to accompany her siblings when their parents took them on Sunday-afternoon walking tours of Philadelphia neighborhoods, of which Rittenhouse was her personal favorite. It had been an enclave of upper-crust, Main Line, well-to-do families.

Dwight and Roberta Eaton always made extra time when they walked through Rittenhouse, lingering at the square honoring the colonial clockmaker, David Rittenhouse. Her father knew he had to be up on his history whenever Belinda asked questions about who'd designed the Victorian mansions, the names of the wealthy families who lived there and their contribution to the growth of the City of Brotherly Love.

Unlike her history-buff sister, Chandra never concerned herself with the past but with the here and now. She was too impulsive to worry about where she'd come from. It was where she was going that was her focus.

She paid the fare, stepped out of the taxi and walked into the lobby with Tiffany-style lamps and a quartet of cordovan-brown leather love seats. Although the noonday temperature registered sixty-two degrees, Chandra felt a slight chill. In Belize she awoke to a spectacular natural setting, eighty-degree temperatures, the sounds of colorful birds calling out to one another and the sweet aroma of blooming flowers, which made the hardships tolerable.

The liveried doorman touched the brim of his shiny cap. "Good afternoon."

Chandra smiled at the tall, slender man with translucent skin and pale blue eyes that reminded her of images she'd seen of vampires. The name tag pinned to his charcoal-gray greatcoat read Michael.

"Good afternoon. Mr. Tucker is expecting me."

"I'll ring Mr. Tucker to see whether he's in. Your name?"

"It's Miss Eaton."

Michael typed her name into the telephone console on a shelf behind a podium. Then he tapped in Preston Tucker's apartment number. Seconds later *ACCEPT* appeared on the display. His head came up. "Mr. Tucker will see you, Miss Eaton. He's in 1801. The elevators are on the left."

Chandra walked past the concierge desk to a bank of elevators, entered one and pushed the button for the eighteenth floor. The doors closed as the elevator car rose smoothly, silently to the designated floor. When the doors opened she found herself staring up at a man with skin reminiscent of gold-brown toffee. There was something about his face that seemed very familiar, and she searched her memory to figure out where she'd seen him before.

A hint of a smile played at the corners of his generous mouth. "Miss Eaton?"

She stepped out of the car, smiling. "Yes," she answered, staring at the proffered hand.

"Preston Tucker."

Chandra's jaw dropped. She stared dumbfounded, looking at the award-winning playwright whose critically acclaimed dramas were mentioned in the same breath as those of August Wilson, Eugene O'Neill and Tennessee Williams. She'd just graduated from college when he had been honored by the mayor of New York and earned the New York Drama Critics' Circle Award for best play of the year. At the time, he'd just celebrated his thirtieth birthday and it was his first Broadway production.

Preston Tucker wasn't handsome in the traditional

way, although she found him quite attractive. He towered over her five-four height by at least ten inches and the short-sleeved white shirt, open at the collar, and faded jeans failed to conceal the power in his lean, muscular physique. Her gaze moved up, lingering on a pair of slanting, heavy-lidded, sensual dark brown eyes. There was a bump on the bridge of his nose, indicating that it had been broken. It was his mouth, with a little tuft of hair under his lower lip, and cropped salt-and-pepper hair that drew her rapt attention. She doubted he was forty, despite the abundance of gray hair.

She blinked as if coming out of a trance and shook his hand. "Chandra Eaton."

Preston applied the slightest pressure on her delicate hand before releasing her fingers. Chandra Eaton was as sensual as her writings. She possessed an understated sexiness that most women had to work most of their lives to perfect. He stared at her almond-shaped eyes, high cheekbones, pert nose and lush mouth. Flyaway wisps had escaped the single plait to frame her sun-browned round face.

"Please come with me, Miss Eaton, and I'll get your portfolio." Turning on his heels, he walked the short distance to his apartment, leaving her to follow.

Chandra found herself staring for the second time within a matter of minutes when she walked into the duplex with sixteen-foot ceilings and a winding staircase leading to a second floor. Floor-to-ceiling windows brought in sunlight, offering panoramic views of the city. The soft strains of classical music floated around her from concealed speakers.

Her gaze shifted to the magnificent table in the foyer. "Oh, my word," she whispered.

Preston stopped and turned around. "What's the matter?"

Reaching out, Chandra ran her fingertips over the surface of the table. "This table. It's beautiful."

"I like it."

"You like it?"

"Yes, I do," he confirmed.

"I'd thought you'd say that you love it, and because you didn't I'm going to ask if you're willing to sell it, Mr. Tucker?"

"Preston," he corrected. "Please call me Preston."

"I'll call you Preston, but only if you stop referring to me as Miss Eaton."

His eyebrows lifted. "What if I call you Chandra?"

She smiled. "That'll do. Now, back to my question, *Preston.* Are you willing to sell the table?"

He smiled, the gesture transforming his expression from solemn to sensual. "Chandra," he repeated. "Did you know that your name is Sanskrit for *of the moon?*"

"No, I didn't." A slight frown marred her face. "Why do I get the feeling you're avoiding my question?"

Preston reached for her hand, leading her into the living room and settling her on a sand-colored suede love seat. He sat opposite her on a matching sofa.

"I'd thought you'd get the hint that I don't want to sell it."

Her frown deepened. "I don't do well with hints, Preston. All you had to say was no."

"*No* is not a particularly nice word, Chandra."

She wrinkled her nose, unaware of the charming quality of the gesture. "I'm a big girl, and that means I can deal with rejection."

Resting his elbows on his knees, Preston leaned in

closer. "If that's the case, then the answer is no, no and no."

Chandra winked at him. "I get your point." She angled her head while listening to the music filling the room. "Isn't that *Cavalleria Rusticana*—Intermezzo from *Godfather III?*"

An expression of complete shock froze Preston's face. He hadn't spent more than five minutes with Chandra Eaton and she'd surprised him not once but twice. She'd recognized the exquisite quality of the Anglo-Indian table and correctly identified a classical composition.

"Yes, it is. Are you familiar with Pietro Mascagni's work?"

"He's one of my favorites."

Preston gestured to the gleaming black concert piano several feet away. "Do you play?"

"I haven't in a while," Chandra admitted half-truthfully. She had played nursery rhymes and other childish ditties for her young students on an out-of-tune piano that had been donated to the school by a local church in Belize. Some of the keys didn't work, but the children didn't seem to notice when they sang along and sometimes danced whenever she played an upbeat, lively tune.

"Do you have any other favorites?" Preston asked.

"Liszt, Vivaldi and Dvorak, to name a few."

"Ah, the Romantics."

"What's wrong with being a Romantic?" Chandra knew she came off sounding defensive, yet she was past caring. As soon as she retrieved her things, she would be on her way.

"Nothing."

"If it's nothing, then why did you make it sound like a bad thing?" she asked.

"It's not a bad thing, Chandra. It's just that I'm not a romantic kind of guy," Preston countered with a wink.

She felt a shiver of annoyance snake its way up her spine. "Anyone can tell that if they've read or seen your plays. They're all dark, brooding and filled with pathos."

Preston realized Chandra Eaton had him at a disadvantage. She knew about him and he knew nothing about her, except what she'd written in her journal. And, he wasn't certain whether she'd actually experienced what she'd written or if it was simply a fantasy.

"That's because I'm dark *and* brooding."

"Being sexy and brooding works if you're a vampire," Chandra shot back.

"You like vampires?"

"Yes. But only if they are sexy."

"I thought all vampires were sexy, given their cinematic popularity nowadays."

"Not all of them," she said.

"What would make a vampire sexy, Chandra?"

"He would have to be…" Her words trailed off. She threw up a hand. "What am I doing? Why am I telling you things you probably already know?"

"You're wrong, Chandra. I don't know. Perhaps you can explain what the big fuss is all about."

She stared, speechless. "Are you blowing smoke, or do you really want to know?"

Quickly rising from the sofa and going down on one knee, Preston grasped her hand, tightening his grip when she tried to pull free. "I'm begging you, Chandra Eaton. I need your help." He was hard-pressed not to laugh when Chandra stared at him with genuine concern in her eyes. He didn't need her help with character development as much as he wanted to know what motivated her to write about her dreams.

"You're serious about this, Preston?"

"Of course I'm serious."

"Get up, Preston."

"What?"

"Get up off your knees. You look ridiculous."

"I thought I was being noble."

"Get up!"

"Yes, ma'am." Preston came to his feet and sat down again.

Chandra rolled her eyes at him. "I'm not old enough to be a ma'am."

"How old do you have to be?"

"At least forty," she said.

"Don't worry, I'm not going to ask your age."

"It's not a deep, dark secret," she said, smiling. "I'm thirty."

"You're still a kid."

"I stopped being a kid a long time ago. Now, back to my helping you develop a sexy character. What are you going to do with the information?"

"Maybe I'll write a play about two star-crossed lovers."

"That's already been done. *Romeo and Juliet, Love Story* and *West Side Story.*"

"Has it been done on stage as a musical with vampires and mortals?"

Unexpected warmth surged through Chandra as her gaze met and fused with Preston Tucker's. She didn't want to believe she was sitting in his living room, talking to the brilliant playwright.

"But you don't write musicals."

"There's always a first time. It could be like *Phantom of the Opera,* or *Evita.*"

"Where would it be set?"

Closing his eyes, Preston stroked the hair under his lower lip. "New Orleans." When he opened his eyes they were shimmering with excitement. "The early nineteenth-century French Quarter rife with voodoo, prostitution, gambling and opium dens and beautiful quadroons with dreams of becoming *plaçées* in *marriages de la main gauche.*"

Chandra pressed her palms together at the same time she compressed her lips. How, she thought, had he come up with a story line so quickly? Now she knew why he'd been awarded a MacArthur genius grant. The plot was dark, but with a cast of sexy characters and the mysterious lush locale, there was no doubt the play would become a sensation.

"Would you also write the music?" she asked Preston.

"No. I know someone who would come up with what I want for the music and lyrics."

"What about costumes?"

"What about them, Chandra?"

"Women's attire changed from antebellum-era ball gowns to the flowing diaphanous dresses of the Regency period. Are your characters going to be demure, or will they favor scandalous décolletage?"

Staring at the toes of his slip-ons, Preston pondered her question. "I'd like to believe the folks in the French Quarter didn't always conform to the societal customs of the day. Remember, we're talking about naughty *Nawlins.*"

"It sounds as if it's going to be just a tad bit wicked."

When she smiled, an elusive dimple in her left cheek winked at him.

"Just a tad," he confirmed. "When do you think we can get together to talk about developing a sexy vampire story?"

Chandra narrowed her eyes at Preston. Was he, she thought, blowing smoke, or was he actually serious about needing her input? "I'll be in touch." She wasn't going to commit until she gave his suggestion more thought.

"You'll be in touch," Preston repeated. "When? How?" Chandra stood up, as did Preston.

"I have your e-mail address, so whenever I clear my calendar I'll e-mail you."

The seconds ticked as they stared at each other. "Okay. Let me go and get your portfolio."

Walking over to the window, Chandra stood and stared down at the street. She couldn't wait to tell her cousin Denise that she'd met Preston Tucker. After graduating from college, she and Denise had regularly traveled to New York to see Broadway plays. Every third trip they would check into a New York City hotel and spend the night. A few times they were able to convince their dates to accompany them, which worked out well since the guys always wanted to hang out at jazz clubs in and around Manhattan.

She turned when she heard footsteps. Preston had returned with her portfolio and handed it to her. Myles had given it to her along with a lesson plan book for her college graduation, and she had continued to use it while in Belize.

"Thank you for taking care of this for me," she said. Chandra valued Myles's gift as much as she did the contents of her journal.

Preston cupped her elbow and escorted her to the door. "I'll see you downstairs."

She gave him a sidelong glance. "I think I can make it downstairs all right."

"I'll still go down with you, because I need to pick up my mail."

Chandra and Preston rode the elevator in silence, parting in the lobby. She felt the heat from his gaze boring into her as she walked out into the bright autumn sunlight. She strolled along a street until she found a café with outdoor seating.

She ordered a salad Nicoise and a glass of white zinfandel and then called her cousin at the child care center. It rang three times before her voice mail switched on. "Denise, Chandra. Call me back tonight when you get home. I just met your idol. Later."

She ended the call, smiling. If anyone knew anything at all about Preston Tucker, it was Denise Eaton. Chandra decided she would wait until she heard from her cousin before she agreed to meet Preston again.

Chapter 3

Preston silently chastised himself for forgetting his manners. He hadn't offered Chandra Eaton anything to eat or drink. It was apparent that his annoyance with his agent sending him on a six-thousand-mile wild-goose chase had affected him more than he wanted to admit. If Clifford had been in the room with him during the negotiations, there was no doubt he would've fired the man on the spot. Wanting to avoid a fight, he decided to wait, wait until Clifford contacted him.

He retrieved his mail and then returned to the apartment. A smile tilted the corners of his mouth when he recalled his conversation with the young woman who'd recorded dreams so erotic, so sensual that he felt as if he'd actually entered the dream and it was he who'd made love to Chandra. He'd taken one shower, then hours later he was forced to take another one. Standing under the spray of ice-cold water was the antidote to an erection that had him thinking of doing what he hadn't done since adolescence.

Preston hadn't lied to Chandra when he told her he wasn't romantic in the true sense of the word. Yet he'd never mistreated or cheated on any woman he was seeing. He'd grown up witnessing his father passively and aggressively abuse his mother until she'd become an emotional cripple. Craig Tucker had never raised his voice or hit him or his sister, Yolanda. But whenever he drank to an excess, he blamed his wife for his failures, of which there were a few. A two-pack-a-day cigarette habit and heavy drinking took its toll, and Craig suffered a massive coronary at forty.

Walking into his home office, Preston put the pile of letters and magazines on his desk. The idea of writing a dramatic musical was scary *and* exciting. And, although he'd mentioned using a vampire as a leading character, the truth was he knew nothing about them. Sitting in a leather chair, he reached for a pencil and a legal pad and began jotting down key words.

The sun had slipped lower in the sky, and long and short shadows filled the room when he finally glanced up at the clock on a side table. It was after five. He'd spent more than four hours outlining scenes for his untitled musical drama. What kept creeping into his head were the accounts of the dreams he'd read the night before.

A knowing smile softened the angles in his face. He suddenly had an idea for a plot.

Chandra spied her father's car when the taxi driver maneuvered into the driveway. She hadn't expected her father to come home so early. She paid the fare, and clutching the case to her chest, got out and walked to the door. It opened before she could insert her key into the lock.

She didn't have time to react before her father held her in a bear hug, lifting her off her feet. Wrapping her arms around his neck, she kissed his cheek. "Daddy, stop! You're crushing my ribs."

Dwight set his daughter on her feet. "I'm sorry about that, baby girl."

Chandra smiled at the man against whom she measured every man she'd met in her life. Her father was soft-spoken, patient and benevolent—and that was with his patients. He was all that and then some to his children. He'd always been supportive, telling them they could do or be anything they wanted to be.

It was her father she'd gone to when she contemplated going into the Peace Corps. He encouraged her to follow her dream *and* her heart, while Roberta had taken to her bed, all the while complaining that her youngest was going to be the death of her.

She smiled at her father. He looked the same at sixty-three as he had at fifty-three. His dark face was virtually wrinkle-free and his deep-set brown eyes behind a pair of rimless glasses reminded her of chocolate chips. His thinning cropped hair was now completely gray.

"What are you doing home so early, Daddy?"

Dwight tugged at the thick braid falling midway down his daughter's back. "My last two patients canceled, so I thought I'd come home early and take my favorite girls out to dinner."

"Do you mind if we postpone it to another time?"

Eyes narrowing, Dwight led Chandra into the entryway. He cradled her face between his palms. "Aren't you feeling well?"

"I'm well. It's just that I stopped to eat a little while ago. I'm certain Mama would appreciate you taking her to a restaurant with dining and dancing."

"You know your mother was quite the dancer in her day."

"She still is," Chandra said. Roberta had danced non-stop at Belinda and Griffin's wedding. She kissed her father's cheek. "I have to go online and look for a job."

"I thought you were going to take some time off before you go back to teaching."

"I'd really like to, Daddy, but I have to buy some furniture before I move into Denise's co-op."

"You should talk to Belinda before you buy anything. She told your mother that she has a buyer for her house, and expects to close on it before Halloween."

Myles had stayed in Belinda's house during the summer, and then returned to Pittsburgh where he taught constitutional law at Duquesne University School of Law. Despite the uncertainty in the real estate market, Belinda was fortunate enough to find a buyer for her house.

Chandra couldn't see herself purchasing property at this time in her life. Although she'd told her parents she hadn't planned to live overseas again, she still wasn't certain of her future.

"I'll call her later," she said to her father. "You and Mama have fun, and if you two can't be good, then be careful," she teased.

He chuckled and was still chuckling as she climbed the staircase. She walked into her bedroom, slipped out of her shoes and blazer and then sat down at the desk. Turning on her laptop, Chandra searched the Philadelphia public schools Web site for openings. Surprisingly, she found ten—eight of which were in less-than-desirable neighborhoods. Her heart rate kicked into high gear. Instead of substituting she would apply for a full-time position. The one school that advertised for a Pre-K, third and fifth grade teacher was about a mile from Denise's co-op and close to Penn's Landing and to public transportation.

Chandra was so engrossed in copying down the names of the schools, their addresses and principals that she almost didn't hear her cell phone. She retrieved it from her handbag, glancing at the display. "Hello, cousin."

"Hello, yourself. When did you get back?"

"Yesterday. I called you because I had the pleasure of meeting Preston Tucker today." She held the phone away from her ear when a piercing scream came through the earpiece. "Denise! Calm down."

"You've got to tell me everything, and I do mean everything, Chandra."

Settling down on the bed, she told her cousin about leaving her portfolio in the taxi and Preston e-mailing her to let her know he'd found it. She was forthcoming, leaving nothing out when she related the conversation between her and the playwright, including that he wanted her to work with him to develop a vampirelike character for a new play.

"Are you going to do it?" Denise asked, her sultry contralto dropping an octave.

"That's why I called you. What do you know about him?"

"He's brilliant, but you probably know that. And he's never been married. There were rumors a little while back that he was engaged to marry an actress. But the tabloids said she ended it. He rarely gives interviews and manages to stay out of the spotlight. I've seen every one of his plays, and if I were given the chance to work with him, I'd jump at it."

"I'm flattered that he asked for my help, but why, Denise? Why me?"

"Maybe he likes you."

Chandra shook her head.

"I don't think so."

"What did you say to him?"

"What are you talking about, Denise?"

"You had to say something to Preston for him to ask you to develop a character for his next play."

A beat passed. "I told him that all his plays were dark and brooding, and he admitted that he was dark and brooding. I suppose when I said brooding works if he were a vampire, he took it as a challenge."

"There you go, Chandra. You just said the operative word—*challenge*. Preston Tucker's bound to have an ego as large as the Liberty Bell, so he expects you to put your money where your mouth is."

"It's either that or…"

"Or what?" Denise asked when she didn't finish her statement.

"Nothing."

Chandra had said nothing, although there was the possibility that Preston had read her journal. He hadn't mentioned that he'd read it, and she didn't want to ask because she didn't want to know if he had. The only way she would be able to find out was to work with him.

"I'm going to do it, Denise. I'm going to help the very talented P. J. Tucker develop a vampire character for his next play."

"Hot damn! My cousin's going to be famous."

"Yeah, right," Chandra drawled. "I'll let you know how it turns out."

"You better," Denise threatened. "I'd love to chat longer, but I have a board meeting in ten minutes."

"Are you coming up to Paoli this weekend?"

"I plan on being there. I'll see you in a couple of days. Later."

"Later," Chandra repeated before she ended the call.

She sat, staring at the sheers billowing in the cool breeze coming through the open windows. To say she was intrigued by Preston Tucker was an understatement. Something told her that he didn't need her or anyone's help with character development. Did he, as Denise claimed, like her?

Chandra shook her head as if to banish the notion. She knew she hadn't given off vibes that said she was interested in him. After her yearlong liaison with Laurence Breslin she had sworn off men. Whenever she affected what could best be described as a "screw face" most men kept their distance. The persistent ones were greeted with, "I'm not interested in men," leaving them to ponder whether she didn't like them or she was only interested in a same-sex liaison. She liked men—a lot. It was just that she wasn't willing to set herself up for more heartbreak.

She went back to the task of researching schools. All she had to do was update her résumé and submit the applications online. Flicking on the desk lamp, she scrolled through her old e-mails until she found the one from Preston, her fingers racing over the keys:

Hi Preston,
I'm available to meet with you Friday. Please call or e-mail to confirm.—CE

    She didn't have to wait for a response when his AIM popped up on the upper left corner of the screen.

PJT: Hi CE. Friday is good with me. What time should I pick you up?

CE: You don't have to pick me up. I'll take a taxi to your place.

PJT: No, CE. You tend to lose things in taxis.

CE: You didn't have to go there.

PJT: Sorry.

CE: Apology accepted.

PJT: Will call tomorrow to let you know when driver will pick you up.

CE: O.K. I'll see you Friday. Meanwhile, think of a name for your vampire.

PJT: He's not my vampire, but yours. So, you do the honor.

CE: O.K. Good night.

PJT: Good night.

Chandra logged off. She mentally checked off what she had to do before meeting with Preston. She still had to unpack, call her sister Belinda and update her résumé. During lunch she'd called the salon and was given an appointment for Thursday at eleven. The Eatons had planned a get-together at Belinda and Griffin's for Saturday to celebrate Sabrina's and Layla's thirteenth birthday. She wasn't certain what her nieces wanted or needed, but decided to give them gift cards. Then, there was her ten-year-old nephew whom she would meet for the first time. Aunt Chandra would have to buy him something, too.

Chandra waited for the driver to come around and open the rear door for her. As promised, Preston had arranged for a driver to bring her to his apartment building. He'd also arranged for them to have brunch.

She gave the doorman her name and three minutes later she came face-to-face with Preston Tucker for the second time when the doors to the elevator opened.

Preston stared, completely surprised. He almost didn't recognize Chandra. She'd changed her hair. The braid was gone, replaced by a sleek style that framed her face and floated over her shoulders. It made her look older, more sophisticated.

"You look very nice."

Chandra couldn't stop the pinpoints of heat pricking her face. She'd lightly applied a little makeup and changed outfits twice before deciding on a tailored charcoal-gray pantsuit, white silk blouse and black patent leather pumps.

"Thank you."

Preston not only looked good, she thought, but he also smelled good. He wore a pair of black slacks and matching shirt and the stubble on his chin gave him a slightly roguish look. He'd admitted to being dark and brooding and his somber attire affirmed that. She didn't have to go very far to find the inspiration for her vampire. Preston Tucker was the perfect character.

"Have you come up with a name for your vampire?" Preston asked as he led Chandra down the hallway and into his apartment.

"I have," she admitted.

He closed the door and turned to stare at her. "What is it?"

"Pascual."

Preston angled his head. "Pascual or Paschal?"

"Pascual. It's Spanish and Hebrew for *Passover*. The name is somewhat exotic and implies that he's passed through a portal from another world to ours."

"If the setting is New Orleans, shouldn't you give him a French name?"

Chandra drew in a breath, held it and then let it out slowly. They hadn't even begun to work together and already he was questioning her. "I thought you said Pascual is *my vampire*."

"He is, Chandra."

"Then, please let me develop him the way I want, Preston. And that includes giving him a name that's Spanish. Remember, France lost control of New Orleans to Spain, then regained it before it was sold to the U.S."

Preston looked sheepish. "Unfortunately, history and languages weren't my best subjects."

"I have you at a disadvantage because my sister teaches American history to high school students."

"What do you teach?"

"How do you know I'm a teacher?"

Reaching for her hand, he gave her fingers a gentle squeeze. "Today you look and sound like a teacher. Besides, you didn't deny it. By the way, are you on sabbatical or are you playing hooky?"

Chandra's lips twitched as she tried not to smile. She knew she had to remain alert with Preston. He probably processed everything she said within seconds. "I'm in between jobs."

"Come with me to the kitchen. We can talk while I cook."

Her eyebrows lifted. "You write, direct and cook. I'm impressed. What other talents are you hiding?"

Throwing back his head, Preston let loose genuine laughter. He'd found Chandra Eaton cute and very talented. What he hadn't counted on was that she could make him laugh.

"I don't know. You'll have to tell me."

"Maybe I should ask your girlfriend."

Preston's expression changed suddenly. He glared at her under hooded lids. "I don't have a girlfriend."

"What about a wife?" Chandra asked. Denise had said Preston was a bachelor, but she needed him to confirm his marital status.

"I also don't have a wife."

"Is it because you're not romantic?" Chandra asked, knowing she was treading into dangerous territory. She really didn't want to know any more about Preston than what Denise had told her. Whatever she would share with him was to be strictly business.

"Not being romantic has nothing to do with whether I'm married or involved with a woman."

"Are you a misogynist?"

"Of course not."

"Don't look so put out, Preston. I've read about a lot of high-profile men who date women, but detest them behind closed doors."

"Well, I'm not one of those down-low brothers." He hadn't lied to Chandra. It had taken many years and countless therapy sessions for him to let go of the enmity between he and his father. "Women should be loved and protected, not physically or emotionally abused."

"Spoken like a true romantic hero."

"Give it up, Chandra. It's not going to work."

"What's not going to work?"

"You're not going to turn me into a romantic hero."

She wrinkled her nose in a gesture Preston had come to appreciate. "You think not, Preston?"

"I know not, Chandra."

"We'll see," she drawled.

His eyes narrowed. "What are you hatching in that very cute head of yours?"

Chandra ignored his referring to her being cute. "Wait until I develop Pascual's character and you're forced to breathe life into what will become a vampire who's not only sexy but very romantic. You'll be the one who has to come up with the dialogue whenever he interacts with his romantic lead."

"We'll see," Preston said.

"Have you thought of a name for your new play?"

Taking a step, he dropped Chandra's hand, pulling her to his chest. Lowering his head and fastening his mouth to the column of her scented neck, Preston pressed a kiss there. He increased the pressure, baring his teeth and stopping short of nipping the delicate flesh.

"Death's Kiss," he whispered in her ear.

Chandra turned her head, her mouth inches from Preston's, breathing in his warm, moist breath. "You can't kill your heroine, Preston." Her gaze caressed the outline of his mouth seconds before he kissed her cheek.

"We'll see, won't we?" he said, smiling.

"What would I have to do to convince you to include a happy ending?"

"I'll think of something."

Bracing her hands against Preston's chest, Chandra sought to put some distance between them. "I don't like the sound of that."

Preston winked at her. "Not to worry, Chandra. You're safe with me."

Chandra recoiled when his words hit her like a stinging slap. "The last man I was involved with said the very same words to me. But in the end I was left to fend for myself. Thanks, but no thanks, Preston. I can take care of myself."

"Was he your husband?"

"No. Thank goodness we didn't get that far. But we were engaged."

"Do you want to talk about it?"

"No. Not because I don't want to. It's just that I can't."

Preston dropped a kiss on her fragrant hair. "Then you don't have to. Are you ready to eat?" he asked, changing the subject.

"What's on the menu for brunch?"

Resting a hand at the small of her back, he escorted Chandra toward the kitchen. "You have a choice of fresh fruit, pancakes, waffles, an omelet or bacon, sausage, ham and grits. To drink, there's herbal tea, regular and hazelnut coffee, orange, grapefruit or cranberry juice. As for cocktails you have a choice between a Bloody Mary and a mimosa."

"I prefer a mimosa." Chandra flashed an attractive pout. "I'm really impressed with you, Preston. I've never hung out with a guy who could cook."

Preston gave Chandra a sidelong glance, his gaze lingering on the tumble of hair falling around her face. "I'm no Bobby Flay or Chef Jeff, but I can promise you won't come down with ptomaine poisoning."

"I think I'm going to enjoy working with you."

And I promise not to like you too much, she added silently.

It was what Chandra told herself every time she met a man to whom she felt herself attracted. It'd worked in the past and she was certain it would work with Preston Tucker.

Chapter 4

Chandra followed Preston into an expansive state-of-the-art stainless-steel-and-black gourmet kitchen outfitted with Gaggenau appliances. "Very nice," she crooned.

"Should I take that to mean you like my kitchen?" There was a note of pride in Preston's voice, as if he were talking about one of his children who'd aced an exam.

She met his questioning gaze with a wide smile. "Did you think I was talking about you?"

"I was hoping you'd think I'm nice."

Chandra sobered. "Does it matter what I think of you, Preston?"

"Of course it does. After all, we're going to be collaborating."

"Hold up, dark and brooding. First you want me to develop a paranormal character, and now you're talking about collaboration."

"Pascual is yours, beautiful, and that means we'll have to collaborate to make him a powerful *and* memorable character. I need for him to mesmerize the audience the second he walks on stage. Even before he opens his mouth, he must pull them in and not let them go until the final curtain."

"Are you going to include him in every scene?" Chandra asked.

"No. It would make it too intense. Whenever he's offstage I want to build enough tension for the audience to look forward to his reappearance. Enough shoptalk. I don't know about you, but I'm ready to eat."

Chandra was also ready to eat. Aside from the salad she'd eaten the day before, her only intake of food was a cup of coffee earlier that morning. "It looks as if you do some serious cooking in here."

"It works whenever I host a dinner party. There's more than enough room for a caterer and his staff to work without them bumping into one another."

Preston's kitchen was almost as large as the apartment she was renting from her cousin. It was furnished with top-of-the-line cookware and miscellaneous culinary gadgets suspended on hooks from an overhead rack.

"How often do you have dinner parties?" she asked, recalling Denise telling her that Preston usually kept a low profile.

"I always host one before the debut of a new play. I invite the entire cast and production staff."

She watched as Preston rolled back his shirt cuffs, exposing muscular forearms before washing his hands in one of the double sinks. "How long does it usually take for you to write a play?"

He dried his hands on a towel. "It depends on the

subject matter *and* my state of mind. My first one took several years because I'd reworked it half a dozen times. However, there was one I completed in four weeks, but it took its toll on my health because I'd averaged about three hours of sleep each night. I took a couple of months off, checked into a resort and did nothing more strenuous than eat and laze around."

Removing her suit jacket, Chandra hung it on a high-back stool pushed over to the slate-gray granite countertop. "You probably were burned out."

"Probably? I was. It was another year before I was able to focus and write again."

"How long do you project it will take for you to complete *Death's Kiss?*" she asked.

Preston, resting his elbows on the countertop, gave her a long, penetrating stare. "That all depends on my collaborator's availability."

"And that depends on whether I can find a teaching position. I've applied to several schools with vacancies for Pre-K to 6. I'll be available to you until I'm hired."

The schools Chandra had applied to were in designated hard-to-staff districts. Belinda taught at a high school in those districts. Earlier that year one of Belinda's students was arrested and expelled for discharging a handgun in her classroom. Fortunately the incident ended with no casualties.

Teaching in the public school system would be vastly different from what she'd experienced in the exclusive private school in Northern Virginia where the yearly tuition was comparable to private colleges. The most profound difference between the children who attended Cambridge Valley Prep, Philadelphia public schools and her former students in Belize was that the prep school students were the children of elected officials and foreign dignitaries.

Preston stood up straighter. "Where did you teach before?"

"The Peace Corps, and before that I taught at a private school in Virginia."

"You really were in the Peace Corps?" There was a note of incredulity in his query.

"Yes," Chandra confirmed.

"Where were you stationed?" he asked, continuing with his questioning.

"Belize."

Preston never imagined that she had been a Peace Corps volunteer. There was something about Chandra Eaton that projected an air of being cosseted. Now that she'd revealed that she spent two years working in Central America he saw her in a whole new light.

"After you let me know what you want to eat, I want you to tell me about Belize, and if it is as beautiful as the photographs in travel brochures?"

Propping her elbow on the cool surface of the countertop, Chandra supported her chin on her heel of her hand. "I'd like an omelet."

"Would you like a Western, Spanish or spinach?"

"Spinach."

"Blue or goat cheese?"

"I prefer blue cheese." Pushing back from the countertop, Chandra slipped off the stool. "Do you mind if I help you?"

Preston held up a hand. "No. Sit down and relax."

She affected a frown. "I'm not used to sitting and doing nothing."

Preston stared at the slender woman in business attire, realizing they were more alike than dissimilar. Even when he was in between writing projects he always found something to do. He usually retreated to his Brandywine Valley home to catch up on his reading and watching movies from his extensive DVD collection. He also chopped enough wood to feed two gluttonous fireplaces throughout the winter months. And whenever he heard the stress in his sister's voice from having to deal with her four sons—both sets of twins—he drove down to South Carolina to give her and his probation officer brother-in-law a mini vacation. He took his rambunctious nephews on camping excursions and deep-sea fishing. Last year they'd begun touring the many Sea Islands off the coast of Georgia, Florida and their home state.

Preston enjoyed spending time with the seven-and ten-year-olds, becoming the indulgent uncle, yet oddly had never felt the pull of fatherhood. He wasn't certain if it was because of his own father or because he hadn't met that special woman who would make him reexamine his life and bachelorhood status.

Chandra had thought him a misogynist when he was anything but. He liked women. He liked everything about a woman: her soft skin, the curves of her body and her smell. It was the smell of her skin and hair that was usually imprinted on his brain. Whenever he dated a woman, he was able to pick her out in a darkened room because of her scent.

He preferred working in the kitchen without assistance or interference but decided to relent and let Chandra help him. "Let me get you something to cover your clothes. If you want, you can cut up the fruit."

Chandra flashed a dimpled smile. She needed to do more than sit and watch Preston. She wanted to discover what it was like to actually cook in a gourmet kitchen. "Where's your bathroom?"

Preston pointed to a door at the opposite end of the kitchen. "It's the door on the right," he said as Chandra headed toward the bathroom.

He stared at the roundness of her shapely hips until she disappeared from his line of vision. *I like her.* Preston liked everything there was to like about Chandra Eaton: her blatant femininity, natural beauty and the intelligence she made no attempt to hide.

When she'd mentioned the idea of writing a play using a vampire as the central character, it had started a flurry of ideas like a trickle of water that flowed into a stream, then into rapids and finally into a fast-flowing river. It reminded him of the Colorado River rushing through the Grand Canyon.

With his creative imagination going full throttle, he was able to outline the production, design the lighting, costumes and props. He could hear the slow drawling Southern cadence and Creole inflections that were as much a part of New Orleans as its cuisine. *Death's Kiss* had come alive in his mind. All that remained was writing it once Chandra developed Pascual.

Preston had taken a package of frozen spinach, four eggs and a plastic container of blue cheese from the refrigerator/freezer as Chandra returned to the kitchen. She was barefoot and had twisted her hair in a loose chignon at the nape of her neck. He smiled when he saw the bright red color on her toes.

Reaching into a drawer under the countertop, he pulled out a bibbed apron. "Come here," he ordered.

Chandra approached Preston, turning so he could slip the apron over her head. He adjusted the length until it reached her knees, then looped the ties twice around her waist.

Shifting, she smiled up at him. "I'm ready, chef."

Lowering his head, Preston kissed the end of her nose. "Never have I had a more delicious-looking sous chef. If you look in the right side of the refrigerator, you'll find fruit in the lower drawer."

He left Chandra to take care of the fruit salad while he began the task of thawing the spinach in the microwave, placing it in a colander to drain before removing the remaining moisture by squeezing the chopped leaves in cheesecloth. Pausing, he opened an overhead closet and pushed a button on a stereo unit. The beautifully haunting sound of a trumpet filled the duplex.

Chandra shared a smile with Preston as she glanced up from peeling the fuzzy skin of a kiwi, revealing its vibrant green flesh. She found it ironic they had a similar taste in music. Before leaving for Belize, she'd loaded her iPod with music from every genre. Chris Botti's *Night Sessions* had become a favorite.

"You have to have at least one romantic bone in your body if you like Chris Botti," she said teasingly.

Preston stopped mincing garlic on the chopping board. "Okay. I'll admit to having one," he said, conceding.

He didn't know what Chandra meant by being romantic. If it was about sending flowers, telling a woman she looked nice or buying her a gift for her birthday or Christmas, then he would have to say he was. But if a woman expected him to declare his undying love for her then she was out of luck.

He'd asked Elaine to marry him because they'd dated exclusively for three years. It just seemed like the right thing to do. But Elaine wanted more than the flowers, gifts and sex. She wanted his undivided attention whenever she didn't have an acting role. It hadn't mattered if he was working on a new play or directing one slated to go into production. She wanted what she wanted whenever she wanted it.

Preston opened the refrigerator, took out a carafe of freshly squeezed orange juice and a bottle of chilled champagne from a wine storage unit and then returned to the cooking island. There was a soft popping sound when he removed the cork from the bubbly wine. Reaching for two flutes on a rack, he half filled the glasses with orange juice, topping it off with champagne before gently stirring the mixture.

Chandra arranged the fruit in glass dessert bowls. She started with melon balls, adding sliced kiwi, and topped them off with orange sections. The contrasting colors were soft, the fresh fruit inviting.

"Do you want me to set the table?" she asked Preston.

"That can wait until after we toast each other." He handed her a flute, touching his glass to hers. "Here's to a successful collaboration." Their gazes met as they sipped the orange-infused champagne cocktail. She smiled over the rim of the flute.

Chandra let the sweet, tart liquid slide slowly down the back of her throat. "It's delicious."

Preston nodded.

Chandra set down her glass. She didn't want to drink too much before she had a chance to eat. "Where are your dishes?"

"They're in the cabinet over the sink."

"What about coffee or tea?"

"I'll have whatever you have," he said.

"What about juice, chef?"

"I'm not a chef, Chandra."

Preston turned and glared at Chandra, but he couldn't stay angry with her when he saw the humor in her eyes. He was going to enjoy working with her. There was no doubt she was a free spirit if she'd left the States to teach in Belize.

His gaze softened when Chandra swayed to the Latin-infused baseline beats of "All Would Envy" written by Sting and sung by Shawn Colvin.

He took three long strides and pulled her into a close embrace. She fit perfectly within the arc of his arms. They danced as if they'd performed the action count-less times. Preston closed his eyes, listening to the words about a wealthy older man who was the envy of other men, old *and* young, because he'd convinced a beautiful young woman to marry him.

Everything about the woman in his arms seeped into him. She was becoming the heroine in *Death's Kiss*. Chandra was right. The play had to have a happy ending. He knew very little about vampires, but he remembered stories about mortals who were bitten by vampires and needed to feed on human blood in order to stay alive.

"Pascual has to be an incredible dancer," Chandra said softly.

"In other words, he must waltz."

Leaning back, she smiled up at Preston. "Yes, but his dance of choice is the tango."

"Where did he learn to tango?" Preston asked.

"In Argentina, of course."

Inky-black eyebrows lifted a fraction. "So, your vam-pire is from South America?"

"Yes. He's lived there for two centuries, hence his name. He's the son of a noble Spanish landowner and an African slave. Although the tango did not become popular outside of the Argentine ghettos until the early years of the twentieth century, Pascual time travels from one century to another, establishing his reputation as a professional dancer."

Preston angled his head. "I like that you made him mixed race."

"Why's that?" Chandra asked.

"Because Josette is also mixed race, and, like her mother, is a free woman of color. I've decided to make her a quadroon, because the character will be easier to cast when I begin auditions. Josette's mother will present her at one of the balls the year she turns sixteen."

"Isn't she rather young?"

Preston twirled Chandra around and around in an intricate dance step. "Not at all. Josette's mother, who is also *placée,* made certain her daughter was educated in France, so once she completes her education Josette will be ready to marry and set up her own household."

"Will she meet Pascual at the ball?"

He pondered her question. "No. That would be too contrived. She'll see him for the first time two weeks before the ball when she goes to her dressmaker for a final fitting of her gown. He's there with another woman, who is also a vampire, whom Josette believes is his mistress. Then, she sees him again when she goes to the market with her maid to pick up flowers to decorate the house because her father is coming to share dinner with her mother."

"What happens next, Preston?"

Dipping her low, Preston kissed the end of her nose and then straightened. "No more questions. You will see the play once I begin rehearsals."

Chandra pouted the way she'd done as a child when she hadn't gotten her way. "That's not fair."

He stared at her lush lips. What wasn't fair was that he wanted so much to make love to her, but didn't, because he didn't want to send the wrong message. He'd asked Chandra to work, not sleep with him.

"What's not fair is that you're asking me questions I can't answer because you haven't given me enough information to breathe life into Pascual. You've told me he's an Argentinian of mixed blood and an expert dancer."

Tilting her chin and closing her eyes, Chandra thought of the fantasy man from her erotic dreams. He could've easily become Pascual, coming to her in the dark of the night to make the most exquisite love she'd ever experienced or imagined.

"What are you thinking about?" Preston asked in her ear.

Her eyes opened. "I was trying to imagine Pascual making love to Josette for the first time."

"Before or after she becomes *plaçée?*"

A beat passed. "Would it add to the conflict if she offers him her virginity?" Chandra asked.

Preston gave Chandra a conspiratorial wink. "It would. But how is she going to convince her white Creole gentleman that she's a virgin?"

"She will confide in her maid, who in turn will ask a voodoo priestess for help. Perhaps you can show a scene with Josette meeting with the voodoo woman. She has great disdain for the woman, but is forced to give up the priceless necklace she's wearing in exchange for a potion that will cause one to fall asleep, and upon waking not remember anything."

He was impressed. Chandra had come up with a credible rationalization for Josette to protect her reputation. After all, the play was to be set in New Orleans.

"Do you want Josette to continue to sleep with Pascual after she becomes *placée,* Chandra?" Preston asked.

Chandra scrunched up her nose. "I see where you're going with this. I think I want Pascual to become her only lover."

"What about her benefactor? Do you think the man will continue to consort with his *placée?* There's no way he would be respected in his social circle if word got out that he'd been cuckolded by a woman of color."

"A couple of drops of the potion in a glass of wine each time he comes to visit Josette will eventually take its toll on the poor man when he becomes an amnesiac."

Preston stared at Chandra, and then burst out laughing. He didn't give her a chance to react when he swept her up off the floor, fastening his mouth to hers in an explosive kiss that robbed her of her breath. Her arms went around his neck, she melting against his length when he deepened the kiss.

Chandra's lips parted as she struggled to breathe, giving Preston the slight advantage he needed when the tip of his tongue grazed her palate, the inside of her cheek and curled around her tongue as he made slow, exquisite love to her mouth. The dreams that had plagued her within days of arriving in Belize came to life; she was unable to differentiate between her fantasy lover and Preston Tucker. The familiar flutters that began in her belly moved lower. If he didn't stop, then she knew she would beg him to make love to her.

"Please! No more, Preston."

Preston heard the strident cry that penetrated the sensual fog pulling him under with the force of a riptide. His head popped up, he stared down at Chandra as if seeing her for the first time. The sweep hand on a wall clock made a full revolution before he lowered her until her feet touched the floor.

"I'm sorry, baby."

The skin around Chandra's eyes crinkled when she smiled. "I'm not."

Preston froze. "You're not?"

Going on tiptoe, she kissed his cheek. "You have a very sexy mouth, P.J., and I'd wondered if you knew what to do with it."

A shiver of annoyance snaked its way up his body. Chandra was the first woman who'd let it be known that she was testing his sexual skills.

"Did I pass?"

"Just barely."

Preston's mouth opened and closed several times, and nothing came out. "What did you say?" he asked after he'd collected his wits.

"I said you barely passed." Chandra turned so he wouldn't see her grin. She tried but was unsuccessful when her shoulders shook with laughter. "No!" she screamed when Preston lifted her again, this time holding her above his head as if she were a small child.

"Apologize, Chandra."

"I'm sorry, I'm sorry," she chanted until he lowered her bare feet to the cool tiles.

Still smarting from her teasing, Preston's expression was a mask of stone. "One of these days I'm going to show you exactly what my mouth can do."

"Is that a threat, Preston?"

A smile found its way through his stern-faced demeanor. "No, baby. It was a warning that if you tease me again, then I'm going to expect you to bring it."

His arms fell away and Chandra took a backward step. She didn't know what had gotten into her. She'd known girls who had teased boys they liked, but she hadn't been one of them.

Why now?

And why Preston Tucker?

The questions nagged at her until she dropped her gaze. It'd taken only two encounters with the temperamental playwright to know that he didn't like to be teased or challenged. That meant she had to tread softly and very carefully around him.

"Warning acknowledged."

Chapter 5

Chandra sat across the table from Preston in the kitchen's dining area, enjoying an expertly prepared spinach and blue cheese omelet. Sautéed garlic, olive oil and butter enhanced the subtle flavor of the mild blue cheese, eggs and spinach. Preston had warmed a loaf of French bread to accompany the omelet.

She took a bite of the bread topped off with sweet basil butter. "You missed your calling, P.J.," she said after swallowing. "You should've been a chef."

Preston smiled, staring at Chandra under half-lowered heavy lids. His former annoyance with her teasing him was gone. There was something about her that wouldn't permit him to remain angry. Perhaps it was her lighthearted personality that appealed to his darker, more subdued persona. He was serious, as were his plays which seemed to appeal to the critics. But for the first time since he'd begun writing he was considering one that was fantasy-driven *and* a musical. Since when, he'd asked himself, had he thought of himself as an Andrew Lloyd Webber?

"I'd seriously thought about becoming a chef," he admitted.

"Before you decided to become a playwright?" Chandra asked.

"No. I always wanted to write. I'd like it to be a second or backup career when I decide to give up playwriting."

"Do you think you'll ever stop writing?"

Preston traced the design on the handle of the knife at his place setting with a forefinger. Chandra had asked what he'd been asking himself for years. He loved the process of coming up with a plot and character development. It was sitting through casting calls, ongoing meetings with directors and producers and daily rehearsals before opening night that usually set his teeth on edge. He'd written, directed and produced his last play, thereby alleviating the angst that accompanied a new production.

"That's a question I can't answer, Chandra. I suppose there will become a time when the creative well will dry up."

"Let's hope it's not for a very long time."

"That all depends on my collaborator."

He'd told himself that he would take the next year off and not write—but that was before he found Chandra Eaton's journal in the taxi, and definitely before he met her.

Chandra studied the man sitting opposite her, recognizing an open invitation in his enigmatic dark eyes. "Are you referring to me?"

Preston leaned over the table. "Who else do you think I'm talking about?"

"Did you go to culinary school?" she asked, deftly shifting gears to steer the topic of conversation away from *them* as a couple.

What she and Preston shared was too new to predict beyond their current collaborative project. She'd returned to the States to teach, reestablish her independence and reconnect with her family, not become involved with a man, and especially if that man was celebrity playwright Preston Tucker.

"Why didn't you answer my question, Chandra?"

"I've chosen *not* to answer it because I don't have an answer," she countered with a slight edge to her tone. "Did you go to culinary school?" she asked again.

Preston fumed inwardly. *The stubborn little minx,* he mused. She'd chosen not to answer his query not because she didn't have an answer, but because she hadn't wanted to answer it. He'd never collaborated with another person only because he hadn't had to. *Death's Kiss* was her idea, derived from her suggestion to use a vampire as a central character *and* from her erotic dreams. There was no doubt the play would cause a stir, not only because of the pervasive popularity of vampires in popular fiction, but also because it would be the first time his play would include a musical score.

He would write the play, produce and direct it, which would give him complete control. And if Hollywood wanted to option the work for the big screen then he would make certain his next literary agent would negotiate the terms on his behalf and adhere to his need for creative control.

"I didn't attend culinary school in the traditional sense," he said, answering Chandra's query. "However,

I've taken lots of cooking courses. I spent a summer in Italy learning to prepare some of their regional dishes."

Chandra touched a linen napkin to the corners of her mouth. "Do you speak Italian?"

Preston shook his head. "The classes were conducted in English. How about you? Do you speak another language?"

"I'm fluent in Spanish."

"Did you learn it in Belize?"

"No. I took it in high school and college, and then signed up for a crash course before going abroad. English remains Belize's official language, but Kriol, a Belizean Creole, is the language that all Belizeans speak."

Preston took a sip of herbal tea, enjoying its natural subtle, sweet flavor. He'd enjoyed cooking for Chandra as much as he enjoyed her company. She appeared totally unaffected by his so-called celebrity status. What he'd come to detest were insecure, needy women who wanted him to entertain them, and the woman sitting across from him appeared to be just the opposite.

"What does Kriol sound like?"

"It's a language that borrows words from English, several African languages, a smattering of Spanish and Maya and the Moskito Indian indigenous to the region. *Good morning* in Spanish is *buenas dias.* Creole would be *gud mawnin.* And African-based Garifuna is *buiti binafi.* If you visit the country you'll also hear German and Mandarin."

"It sounds like a real melting pot."

"It is." While staring at Preston, Chandra went completely still. The distinctive voice of Josh Groban filled the kitchen. "He sings beautifully in Spanish."

Preston realized Chandra was listening to the song's lyrics. "What is he saying?"

"*Si volvieras a mi,* means *if you returned to me.*"

"Why do songs always sound so much better when sung in a foreign language?" Preston asked.

"Most songs sound better when you don't understand the words. The love theme from the *Crouching Tiger, Hidden Dragon* sound track is more romantic sung in Chinese than English."

"What are you trying to say?"

Chandra's mind was churning with ideas. "Have your lyricist write at least one song for the play that will be sung in English and Spanish with only a guitar as an accompaniment."

"Should it be a love song?"

She smiled. "But of course."

Preston realized he'd hit the jackpot when he found the journal containing Chandra's erotic dreams. *Death's Kiss* would be a departure from his plays about dysfunctional families and societal woes. He'd won a Tony for the depiction of a psychotic killer who morphs into a sympathetic, repentant character but is denied a stay of execution before the curtain comes down for the final act. Theater critics praised the acting and minimal set decoration, but took the playwright to task for his insinuation of political propaganda in the drama.

His gaze lingered on Chandra, roving lazily over her soft, shining hair to the sweetest lips he'd ever tasted. Her conservative attire artfully disguised a curvy body and a passion he longed to ignite. And there was no doubt Chandra Eaton was a passionate woman as gleaned from the accounts of her dreams. She'd numbered and dated each one, leaving him to ponder how many others she'd had and he hadn't read.

He'd admitted to her that he wasn't a romantic only because he wasn't certain how she'd interpret the word. However, he'd read more than six months of dreams that he could draw upon to make Chandra's vampire a passionate lover.

"How difficult is it to write a play?"

Chandra's query pulled Preston from his reverie. "I thought we were talking about Belize."

She waved a hand. "We can talk about Belize some other time. I want to know about scriptwriting."

"Why? Do you plan on writing one?" he teased with a wide grin.

"Maybe one of these days I'll try my hand at either writing a novel or a play—whichever is easier."

Leaning back in his chair, Preston angled his head. "Anyone can be taught the mechanics of writing, but no one can give an aspiring writer an imagination." He tapped his head with his forefinger. "You have to conjure up plots and characters in your head before you're able to bring them to life on paper."

Chandra thought she detected a hint of censure in Preston's words. Had he believed she wanted to compete with him? "I am not your competition, Preston." She'd spoken her thoughts aloud.

A shadow of annoyance hardened his features. "Do you actually believe I'd think of you as a competitor?"

"If not, then why all the secrecy about not telling me how to write a script?"

"There's no secrecy. And as to competition, the only person I compete with is Preston Japheth Tucker, so don't get ahead of yourself, Miss Eaton."

Chandra sucked her teeth. "Don't start with the bully attitude, P. J. Tucker, because I don't scare easily. Now, are you going to tell me or not?"

Preston stared, unable to form the words to come back at Chandra. She was the complete opposite of any woman he'd ever interacted with. She was as strong and confident as she was beautiful.

"Well, if you put it that way, then I suppose I'd *better* tell you. There's no way I'd be able to explain to my mother that I'd allowed a little slip of a woman to jack me up."

A wave of heat stole its way across Chandra's cheeks. "I wouldn't hit you. In fact, I've never hit anyone in my life." The seconds ticked, and her heart beat a rapid tattoo against her ribs as Preston glared at her.

A slow smile parted Preston's lips, he pointed at her. "Gotcha!"

Pushing back her chair, Chandra came around the table, launching herself at him. He caught her in a split-second motion too quick for the eye to follow. She was sprawled over his knees when his head came down. Covering her mouth with his, Preston robbed her of her breath. The passionate, explosive kiss ended quickly, as quickly as it'd begun.

"Either you have a problem with your short-term memory or you want me to take you upstairs and show you just how romantic I can be. I'm not making an idle threat when I tell you that when I'm finished with you it won't be today, tomorrow or even the next day. I will…" His words trailed off when the telephone rang.

"Excuse me," Preston said as if nothing had passed between him and the woman in his arms.

He stood up, bringing Chandra with him. Instead of

releasing her, he held on to her upper arm as he walked over to the wall phone; he tightened his grip when she attempted to extricate herself. Chandra wasn't going anywhere until he settled something with her.

He picked up the receiver. "Hello."

"What's up with you, P.J.?"

Preston took a deep breath, holding it until he felt a band of constriction across his chest. It had taken his agent four days to contact him. "That's what I should be asking you, Cliff. Why the hell did you send me three thousand miles across the country when you knew I wouldn't agree to what the studio heads were proposing? Stop wiggling," he hissed at Chandra.

"Who are you talking to?" Clifford Jessup asked.

"None of your damn business. Now, answer my question, Clifford."

There came a pause. "I thought you would change your mind when you heard what they were offering."

"I thought I told you that the deal wasn't about money, but creative control," Preston said through clenched teeth. "I don't have the time or the inclination to fly to the West Coast for BS. I pay you twenty-five instead of the prevailing fifteen and twenty percent as my literary agent to protect my interests. But apparently you haven't this time. And if I were completely honest, then I'd have to say you haven't looked after my interests in some time."

"What the hell are you trying to say, P.J.?"

"I'm firing you as my literary agent, effective immediately. You'll receive a letter in a few days confirming this. Good luck, Clifford." He replaced the receiver in its cradle with a resounding slam. "What?" he asked Chandra when she stared him. Her mouth had formed a perfect O, and her breasts rose and fell heavily under the silk blouse.

"Are you always so diplomatic?"

"Don't comment on something you know nothing about."

"You're pissed off with me, so you take it out on someone else."

Preston exhaled a breath. "I'm not pissed off with you, Chandra."

Her gaze shifted from his face to his hand clamped around her arm. "No? Then why the caveman grip on my arm, Preston?" He loosened his hold, but not enough for her to escape him.

"I don't want to know anything about the men you're used to dealing with," Preston said in a soft voice that belied his annoyance, "but at thirty-eight I'm a little too old to play games. Especially head games." He leaned in closer. "I like you, Chandra. And it's not about you collaborating with me. You're pretty and you're smart—a trait I admire in a woman, and you're sexy. Probably a lot more sexy than you give yourself credit for. I want to work with you *and* date you."

Chandra couldn't stop the smile stealing its way over her delicate features. "You don't mince words, do you, P.J.?"

"Nope. Too old for that, too, C.E."

Chandra didn't know how to deal with the talented man whose moods ran hot and cold within nanoseconds. "Why should I date you, Preston?"

"Why?" he asked, seemingly shocked by her question. "Didn't I tell you that I'm a nice guy?"

"So you say," she drawled, deciding not to make it easy for him. She wanted to go out with Preston Tucker.

In fact, she'd be a fool to reject him. It'd been a long time, entirely too long since she'd found a man with whom she could have an intelligent conversation without watching every word that came out of her mouth. Chandra knew she'd shocked Preston with her off-the-cuff remarks, but she had to know how far she could push him before he pushed back.

It hadn't been that way with Laurence Breslin. They'd dated for a year before he asked her to marry him. However, when she met his parents for the first time they were forthcoming when they expressed their disapproval. They'd always hoped that Laurence would eventually marry the daughter of a couple within their exclusive social circle. To add insult to injury, they'd demanded she return the heirloom engagement ring that had belonged to Laurence's maternal grandmother. Laurence compounded the insult when he forcibly removed the ring from her finger.

"Okay, Preston," she said, smiling, "I'll go out with you."

His eyebrows lifted a fraction. "Why does it sound as if you're doing me a favor?"

"Don't let your ego get the best of you, P.J."

"What are you talking about?"

"You're probably not used to women turning you down."

"Whatever," he drawled.

"Yes or no, Preston?"

"I'm not going to answer that."

Standing on tiptoe, Chandra touched her lips to Preston's. "You don't have to," she whispered, "but there's one question I do expect you to answer for me."

"What's that?" Preston asked, as his lips seared a sensual path along the column of her neck.

Baring her throat, she closed her eyes, reveling in the warmth of his mouth on her skin. "Can I trust you?"

Preston froze as if someone had unexpectedly doused him with cold water. His arms fell to his sides as he glared at Chandra. "You think I'm going to be with you *and* another woman at the same time?"

"I'm not talking about infidelity."

"What are you talking about?"

She stared at a spot over his broad shoulder before her gaze returned to meet his questioning one. "It's about you not lying to me."

"I'd never—"

"Don't say what you won't do," she interrupted. "Just don't do it, Preston."

A beat passed. Preston knew without asking that something had occurred between Chandra and her former fiancé that caused her not to trust him and probably all men. He hadn't slept with so many women that he couldn't remember their names, but whenever they parted it was never because they didn't trust him, and it wouldn't be any different with Chandra.

A sensual smile tilted the corners of his mouth upward. "Now that we've gotten that out of the way, I'd like to take you out to Le Bec-Fin tomorrow night."

Chandra lashes fluttered as she tried to bring her fragile emotions under control. *Maybe he likes you.* Denise's words came back with vivid clarity. Maybe Preston did like her, and not because she was collaborating with him. And despite his literary brilliance and celebrity status she wasn't ready to completely trust him.

Dating Preston Tucker openly would no doubt thrust

her into the spotlight for newshounds and the paparazzi, and she had to prepare herself for that. Denise had also revealed that Preston tended to keep a low profile, yet he wanted to take her to a restaurant long considered the best in fine dining. Being seen with him at a fancy, four-star Philadelphia restaurant was hardly what she would consider maintaining a low profile.

"Would you mind if we go another time?"

"Of course I don't mind," he said. "We'll go whenever it's convenient for you."

Chandra decided to flip the script. "How would you like to go out with me tomorrow?"

Preston's eyes narrowed. "I thought you weren't available?"

"I can't have dinner with you because I have a prior engagement. I'm going to Paoli to join my family in celebrating my twin nieces', Sabrina's and Layla's, thirteenth birthday."

"You want me to go to a teenage birthday party?"

"No, Preston. You just fired your literary agent, which means you're going to have to replace him. I just thought if you talk to my brother-in-law, perhaps he'll consider representing you."

The impact of his firing his friend and agent weighed heavily on Preston. He hadn't wanted to do it, but Cliff had left him no alternative. If his friend was having personal problems, then he should've confided in him. After all, there were few or no secrets Preston kept from his agent.

But, on the other hand, business was business, and he'd entrusted Clifford to handle his career without questioning his every word or move. Unfortunately, the man had screwed up—big-time and with dire consequences.

"Who is your brother-in-law?"

Chandra flashed a sexy moue, bringing Preston's gaze to linger on her lips. "You'll see tomorrow."

His eyebrows shot up. "You expect me to go with you on a whim?"

"Is that how you see me, Preston?" she spat out. "Now I'm a whim?"

"No, no, no! I didn't mean for it to come out like that."

Crossing her arms under her breasts, Chandra pretended to pout. "Well, it did."

"I'm sorry, Chandra."

She bit back a smile. "Say it like you mean it, Preston."

Preston took a step and pulled her into the circle of his embrace. "I'm sorry, baby." His mellifluous voice had dropped an octave.

Why, Chandra asked herself, hadn't she noticed the rich, honeyed quality of his voice before? It was the timbre of someone trained for the stage.

"Apology accepted. I don't want to tell you my brother-in-law's name because I want you to trust me."

"So, we're back to the trust thing?"

She smiled. "It will always be the trust thing, Preston."

"I thought most women concerned themselves about the love *thang*," he said, teasingly.

"Not with you, P.J. Why would I take up with a man who professes not to be romantic? Women don't need sex from a man as much as they want romance and courtship."

"Maybe I'm going to need a few lessons in that department."

"You're kidding, aren't you?" Chandra asked. "You're thirty-eight years old and you don't know how to romance a woman?"

"What I'm not is romantic," he retorted.

Lowering her arms, she rested her hands on his chest. *"Porbrecito."*

"Which means?"

"You poor thing," she translated.

Preston winked at her. "Now, don't you feel sorry for me?"

"Only a little. However, I'm willing to bet if you follow Pascual's lead you'll do quite well with the ladies."

He wanted to tell Chandra that he was only interested in one lady: her. Not only had she intrigued him but also bewitched him in a way no other woman had. "What time do we leave for Paoli tomorrow?"

"Everyone's expected to arrive around three."

"What time do you want me to pick you up?"

"I'll pick you up at two," Chandra said. Her father would drive her mother in his car, and she would take her mother's car.

"Okay. I want you to relax while I clean up the kitchen. Then we'll go to the office and talk about the play."

"Wouldn't it go faster if I help you?"

Preston glared at Chandra. He'd learned quickly that she wanted to control situations. Well, she was in for a rude awakening. When it came to control of his work he'd unquestionably become an expert.

"Sit down and relax."

She held up her hands. "Okay. You didn't have to go mad hard," she whispered under her breath.

"What did you say?"

"Nothing," Chandra mumbled.

She walked around Preston and sat down at the table. She knew working with him wasn't going to be easy, especially if, without warning, his moods vacillated from hot to cold. What she didn't intend to become was a punching bag for his domineering and controlling personality.

Chandra Eaton was not the same woman who'd left her home and everything familiar and comfortable to work with young children in a region where running water was a priceless commodity.

She'd promised Preston she would help him with his latest play, and she would follow through on her promise—that is until he pushed her to a point where she would be forced to walk away and not look back. It'd happened with a man she'd loved without question, and it could happen again with a man she had no intention of loving.

Chapter 6

Chandra sat between Preston's outstretched legs on a soft leather chaise in a soft butter-yellow shade, wishing she'd worn something a lot more casual. He'd changed into his work clothes: jeans, T-shirt and sandals.

When he'd led her into the home/office Chandra was taken aback with the soft colors, thinking Preston would've preferred a darker, more masculine appeal. Instead of the ubiquitous black, brown or burgundy, the leather sofa, love seats and chaise were fashioned in tones of pale yellow and orange, reminiscent of rainbow sherbet. The citrus shades blended with an L-shaped workstation in a soft vanilla hue with gleaming cherrywood surfaces.

Two walls of floor-to-ceiling built-in bookcases in the same vanilla bean hue were stacked with novels, plays, pamphlets and biographies. Several shelves were dedicated to the many statuettes and awards honoring Preston's theatrical achievements. She smiled when she saw two Tony awards.

The third wall, covered with bamboolike fabric, was filled with framed citations, diplomas and academic degrees. The last wall was made of glass, bringing in the natural light and panoramic views of the Philadelphia skyline.

Reclining against Preston's chest seemed the most natural thing to do as he explained the notations he'd put down on a legal pad. Chandra squinted, attempting to read his illegible scrawl.

She pointed. "What is that word?"

Preston pressed a kiss to the hair grazing his chin. "You got jokes, C.E.?"

Tilting her chin, Chandra smiled at him over her shoulder. "I'm serious, Preston. I can't decipher it."

He made a face. "She can't decipher *conflict*," he said sarcastically.

"Hel-lo, P.J. It looks like *confluent* to me."

"I can assure you it *is conflict*. Writing a play is no different from writing a novel or a script for a film or television. It all begins with an idea or premise, a sequence of events, characters and conflict. As the writer I must touch upon all of these elements not only to entice theatergoers to come to see the stage production, but keep them in their seats until the final curtain."

"What's the difference between writing a script for the screen and one for the stage?" Chandra asked.

"Stage plays are much more limited when it comes to the size of the cast, number of settings and the introduction of characters. Whereas with films there can be many, many characters and locales. I try and keep the page count on my plays around one hundred."

"Have you ever exceeded that number?"

"Yes," Preston replied. "But it should never go beyond one hundred twenty pages. The story should concentrate on a few major characters who reveal themselves through dialogue, unlike a film actor who will utilize dialogue and physical action."

Shifting slightly, Chandra met Preston's eyes. "When do you know if your premise is a play or a film?"

"The key word is physical action. If I imagine a story and I see it as frames of images, then it's a play. But, if the images are filled with physical action, then it's a film script."

"So, you see *Death's Kiss* as a play?"

"It can go either way. As a film it probably would be darker, more haunting, the characters of Pascual and Josette more complex, and there would be more physical action than on the stage."

"What would the rating be if you wrote the screenplay?"

"Probably a PG-13," he said.

His response surprised Chandra. "Why not an R rating?"

"An R rating would be at the studio's discretion. I always believe you can sell more tickets with a PG-13 rating than one that's rated R or NC-17."

"Is that why you insist on literary control?" she asked, continuing with her questioning.

Preston nodded. "That's part of it. What you and I have to decide on is the backstory for *Death's Kiss*."

"Would I need a backstory for a mythical character?"

"Do you want Pascual to feed on blood in order to

survive? If not, then what are his family background, education, social and political beliefs? Is he in favor or opposed to slavery?"

A look of distress came over Chandra's face. "I don't want the play to focus on slavery, because it's a too-painful part of our country's history."

"It will *not* focus on slavery, but a peculiar practice germane but not limited to New Orleans and the descendants of *gens de couleur*. I've done some research," Preston continued, "uncovering that it was acceptable behavior for a white man to take a slave as young as twelve as his lover. It would prove beneficial to the woman if she produced children. She would be emancipated along with their offspring. Josette's mother is a free woman of color, thereby making her free."

"Where does Josette's father live?"

"Etienne Fouché has a plantation twenty miles outside of New Orleans where he lives with his white family, and he also has an apartment within the city where he entertains his friends. Then, there's a Creole cottage he'd purchased for his *plaçée* and Josette only blocks from his apartment. He will spend a few months with his legitimate wife, but most of his time will be spent within the city.

"France has declared its independence and the Louisiana territory has been ceded to the United States. The first act will open with Josette returning to the States from France and her mother telling her she must prepare for the upcoming ball. However, the Josette who returns at sixteen isn't the same naive and cosseted girl who'd cried incessantly when she boarded a ship to take her to Paris four years before. She is also educated, while it was illegal to teach blacks to read and write in the

States. She doesn't believe in *plaçage,* wants to choose her own husband, and her opposition results in conflict because her mother has promised her to the son of one of the largest landowners in the region. Within minutes of the opening act…"

Preston's words trailed off when he saw that Chandra had closed her eyes, while her chest rose and fell in an even rhythm. "Chandra," he said softly, "did you fall asleep on me?"

"No. I was listening to you. Champagne always makes me drowsy."

"We can stop now if you want to."

Chandra smiled, but didn't open her eyes. "Do you mind if we don't move?"

Shifting slightly, he settled her into a more comfortable position. "We can stay here all night if you want."

She opened her eyes. "No, Preston. I'm not ready to sleep with you."

Preston twirled several strands of her hair around his finger. "I wasn't suggesting we sleep together. The bedrooms on the second floor are for my guests."

"Where do you sleep?" Chandra asked quickly, hoping to cover up her faux pas. Preston had kissed her twice and she'd assumed that he wanted to sleep with her. If she could have, at that moment she would've willed herself totally invisible.

"Here on the chaise. The sofa converts into a bed, but half the time I end up sleeping on it instead of in it."

"I hope you have a chiropractor." Preston's height exceeded the length of the sofa by several inches.

"I happen to have one on speed dial. Sitting for hours in front of a computer takes a toll on the neck, back and shoulders."

"You should practice yoga or tai chi," Chandra suggested. "I find it works wonders whenever I have trouble sleeping."

Preston was hard-pressed not to smile. Chandra had just given him the opening he needed to delve into her dreams without letting her know he'd read and committed to memory what she'd written in the journal he'd found.

"What would keep you from sleeping?" he asked.

"It's usually anxiety or a very overactive imagination."

"What do you have to be anxious about, Chandra?"

She exhaled an audible sigh. "A couple of weeks before I was scheduled to leave for Belize, I discovered I couldn't sleep. I'd go to bed totally exhausted, but couldn't sleep more than one or two hours. My dad, who is a doctor, offered to write a scrip for a sedative, but I refused because I didn't want to rely on a controlled substance that could possibly lead to dependency.

"I was losing weight and when I ran into a friend from college I told her about my problem. She was on her way to a yoga class so I went along just to observe. I joined the class the following day, and also signed up for tai chi."

"How long did it take for you to get rid of your insomnia?"

Chandra stared at the vivid color on her toes. "It took about two weeks. By the time I'd arrived in Belize I was sleeping soundly, but then something else happened."

Lowering his head, Preston pressed his nose to her hair, inhaling the sweet fragrance. "What happened?"

The seconds ticked, bringing with them a comfortable silence. "I began dreaming."

The admission came from a place Chandra hadn't known existed. Her dreams were a secret—a secret she never planned to divulge to anyone. She'd recorded her dreams in journals, believing she would one day re-read them. She'd thought about publishing them under a pseudonym, because some of them were more than sensual. They were downright erotic.

"Were they dreams or nightmares?"

"Oh, they were dreams."

Preston smiled. Her dreams had become his night-mares because they'd kept him from a restful night's sleep. "How often did you dream?"

"I had them on average of two to three a week."

"Whenever I dream I usually don't remember what they were," Preston admitted.

"It's different with me," Chandra said. "Not only do I remember, but they were so vivid that I was able to write them down."

"What do you think triggered your dreams?"

"I don't know, Preston."

"Are your dreams different, or all along the same train of thought?"

Chandra didn't know how much more she could di-vulge about her dreams before Preston realized that she was sexually frustrated, that it had been years since she'd slept with a man. And she didn't need a therapist to tell her that she'd used her dreams to act out her sexual fan-tasies.

"They were the same," she finally admitted.

"That sounds boring, C.E."

She rolled her eyes. "My dreams were hardly bor-ing, P.J."

"Do you want to tell me about them?" Preston whis-pered in her ear.

"No!"

Preston fastened his mouth to the side of her neck. "Why not?"

Chandra shivered slightly when Preston increased the pressure along the column of her neck. A slight gasp escaped her parted lips with the growing hardness pressing against her hips. It took Herculean strength not to move back to experience the full impact of Preston's erection.

"What are you doing, Preston?" Chandra questioned, not recognizing the strangled voice as her own.

Closing his eyes while swallowing a groan, Preston tried to think about any and everything except the soft crush of Chandra's buttocks pressed intimately to his groin.

"I'm committing your scent to memory."

Chandra closed her eyes. "I'm not talking about you nibbling on my neck."

"What are you talking about?"

"Pascual would never hump Josette."

"I'm not humping you, baby. This is humping." Preston gyrated back and forth, pushing his erection against her hips.

Waves of desire swept over Chandra like a desert sirocco, stealing the breath from her lungs and stopping her heart for several seconds. The sensations holding her in an erotic grip were similar to what she'd experienced in her dreams. Her breasts were heavy, the area between her thighs moist and throbbing with a need that screamed silently to be assuaged.

The man who came to her in her dreams was a fantasy, a nameless, faceless specter she'd conjured up from the recesses of her overactive imagination, but Preston Tucker was real, as real as his heat *and* arousal.

"Please don't move." Chandra was pleading with him,

but she was past caring, because if he didn't stop then she would beg him to make love to her. It was one thing to fantasize about making love with a faceless specter and another to have an actual live, red-blooded man simulating making love to her.

Preston went still, but there was little he could do to still the pulsing sensations in his groin. He didn't know what it was about Chandra Eaton that had him so lacking in self-control. He'd wanted to rationalize and tell himself it was because of her erotic dreams, but he would be lying to himself. He'd told Chandra that he liked her. The truth was he liked her *and* wanted her in his bed; however the notion of sleeping with Chandra was shocking and totally unexpected.

"What were we talking about before you decided to hump me, Preston?"

The soft, dulcet voice broke into his reverie. "We were talking about your dreams."

"Even before that," Chandra said in an attempt to change the topic. Preston had asked what she'd dreamed about, and how could she tell him that her dreams were *all* about sex, that they were continuous frames of R- and X-rated films with her in the leading role.

"We were discussing Josette's father."

"Will he have legitimate children?"

Wrapping an arm around Chandra's waist, Preston shifted her to a more comfortable position. His erection had gone down and her body was more relaxed, pliant. "No. His wife gave him a daughter, but she died from a fever before she turned two. Since then she has had several miscarriages, thereby leaving him without a legitimate heir."

"Is Etienne Fouché wealthy?"

"Very," Preston confirmed. "He'd bought out a neighboring planter and is now the owner of the largest sugarcane plantation in St. Bernard parish."

"How is Etienne's relationship with his wife?" Chandra asked.

"They're cordial. Theirs is a marriage of convenience. Madame Fouché is what one could call homely, so her father offered Etienne a sizable dowry to marry his daughter. Madame Fouché, who has an aversion to sex, is overjoyed when her doctor tells her that her husband must not share her bed again. She spends most of her free time entertaining the wives of other planters and/or spending the summers in Europe to escape the heat and fevers that claim thousands of lives each year."

Sitting up straighter, Chandra turned to stare up at Preston. "You've made Etienne a gentleman farmer who derives his wealth from slaves who grow and process white gold."

"The geographic location and family background are key elements of the backstory. I could've easily made him a professional gambler, but how would that work for Josette and her mother? A gambler who could win or lose a fortune with the turn of a single card. And if he found himself without funds, then he would use their home as collateral. I know you don't want to touch on the slavery issue, but remember we're dealing with free people of color.

"As the writer I'm totally absorbed in the lives of the characters until the play is completed. Then it becomes the director's responsibility to get his actors to bring them to life on stage."

Chandra swiveled enough so that she was practically facing Preston. "Do you know who you want to direct

Death's Kiss?" A smile softened his mouth, bringing her gaze to linger on the outline of his sensual lower lip. "What are you smiling about?"

"I'm going to write, direct *and* produce *Death's Kiss*."

"Total control," she whispered under her breath.

Preston's eyebrows lifted. "Do you have a problem with my decision, C.E.?"

Silence filled the room as Chandra boldly met his eyes. Missing was the warmth that lurked there only moments before. "It's your play, Preston, so you can do whatever you want with it."

"It's not only my play, Chandra."

"Who else does it belong to, if not you, Preston."

"Pascual is your character."

"And *Death's Kiss* is your play," she countered. Chandra pushed to her feet. "I'm going to head home now. Based on what you've told me about Etienne and Josette, I'm going to have to revise my first impression of Pascual."

Preston knew Chandra was smarting about his decision to write, direct and produce the play. What she didn't understand was that he knew his characters better than anyone, and he hadn't wanted to explain their motivation to a tyrannical director who insisted on having his way. He'd lost count of the number of times he'd had to bite his tongue so as not to lose his financial backing.

He moved off the chaise. "Don't stress yourself too much. It will probably be another month before we flesh out the entire cast of characters."

Nodding, Chandra turned and walked out of the office. "I'll see you tomorrow at two."

"I'll be downstairs."

She entered the kitchen, pushing her feet into her

shoes before reaching for her suit jacket. "Dress is casual."

Resting his hands on her shoulders, Preston turned Chandra around to face him. "Thank you for coming. I really enjoyed your company."

Chandra was momentarily shocked into speechlessness. Preston thanking her for her company spoke volumes. Despite his brilliance, fame, awards and financial success, Preston J. Tucker was a private and a lonely man.

A hint of a smile parted her lips when she stared into his fathomless dark eyes. "Thank you for inviting me."

Preston didn't want Chandra to leave, but he didn't want to embarrass himself and communicate that to her. "I'll call the driver and have him bring the car around."

Going on tiptoe, Chandra touched her lips to his. "Thank you."

They shared a smile as she slipped her hand into his. They were still holding hands during the elevator ride to the building lobby and out onto the sidewalk where the driver stood with the rear door open.

She slid onto the rear seat and waved to Preston. He returned her wave before the driver closed the door and rounded the Town Car to take his place behind the wheel.

Chandra turned to stare over her shoulder out the back window to find Preston standing on the sidewalk. His image grew smaller and smaller then disappeared from view when the driver turned the corner.

A knowing smile softened her mouth when she shifted again. *I like him.* "I like him," she repeated under her breath, as if saying it aloud would make it more real.

Chapter 7

Chandra maneuvered her car to the curb of the high-rise, tapping lightly on the horn to garner Preston's attention. He was dressed in a lightweight, navy blue suit, white shirt and black slip-ons. Her eyebrows lifted slightly when she spied the two small colorful shopping bags he held in his left hand.

He rounded the car to the driver's side and dipped his head to peer through the open window. "I'll drive. I do know how to get to Paoli," Preston added when Chandra gave him a quizzical look. Reaching in, he unlocked the door, opened it and helped her out. Three inches of heels put the top of her head at eye level. His penetrating gaze took in everything about her in a single glance: lightly made-up face, luxurious dark brown hair secured in a ponytail, black stretch tank top, matching stretch cropped pants and high-heeled mules. He brushed a kiss over her cheek. "You look very cute."

Heat feathered across her face with his unexpected compliment. She'd changed her outfits twice. When she'd gotten up earlier that morning, the mercury was already sixty-eight, and meteorologists were predicting temperatures to peak in the mid-eighties. Chandra much preferred the Indian summer weather to the near-freezing temperatures because she knew it would take her a while to adjust to the climate change.

Her eyes met Preston's as the skin around his penetrating gaze lingered briefly on her face before slipping lower to her breasts. "Thank you."

Preston's lips parted in a smile as he reached over with his free hand and tugged gently on her ponytail. "You're quite welcome." He led her around the Volvo, seated her and then retraced his steps once she'd fastened her seat belt.

He took off his suit jacket, placing it and the shopping bags on the rear seat. Sitting behind the wheel, he adjusted the seat to accommodate his longer legs, noting that Chandra had already programmed her trip into the GPS.

"What's in the shopping bags?" Chandra asked when Preston maneuvered into the flow of traffic.

"It's just a little something for your nieces."

She frowned. "You didn't have to bring anything."

Preston's frown matched hers. "I couldn't show up empty-handed."

"Yes, you could, Preston. You're my guest."

"That may be true, but I feel better bringing something. After all, it's not every day someone turns thirteen. Your nieces are no longer tweens, but bona fide teenagers. And I'm willing to bet they'll be quick to re-mind everyone of that fact."

Chandra's frown disappeared. "You're right. When I spoke to my sister earlier this morning, she told me that was the first thing they said."

"Do you remember being thirteen?" Preston asked.

She shook her head. "No. Every year was a blur until I turned eighteen."

"What happened that year?"

"I left home for college."

"Where did you go?"

"Columbia University."

"Was Columbia your first choice?"

Chandra stared through the windshield. "No. I was seriously considering going to the University of Penn-sylvania, then decided an out-of-state school was a bet-ter choice if I wanted to stretch my wings."

Preston gave Chandra a sidelong glance before re-turning his gaze to the road. "Mom and Dad didn't want their baby to leave the nest? Yes or no?" he asked when she glared at him.

"No," she said after a prolonged pause. "I decided to go away because my brother and sisters went to in-state colleges. I wanted to be the one to break the tradition."

"Where did—" The chiming of the cell phone at-tached to his belt preempted what he intended to say. Preston removed the phone, taking a furtive look at the display. "Excuse me, Chandra, but I need to take this call."

She nodded, smiling. "It's okay."

He pressed a button, activating the speaker feature. "Hey, Ray. Thanks for getting back to me."

"What's up, P.J.?" asked a raspy voice.

"How's your schedule?" Preston asked.

A sensual chuckle filled the car. "What do you need, P.J.?"

"I need a score for a new play with an early nine-teenth-century New Orleans setting." He shared a smile with Chandra when she winked at him. "It's a dramatic musical."

A pregnant silence filled the interior of the vehicle. "Did you say musical?"

"Yes, I did."

"Hold up, prince of darkness," Ray teased, laughing. "Don't tell me you're going soft."

"It's nothing like that, Ray."

"What happened?"

"I'm collaborating with someone who convinced me to leave the dark side for my next project."

"Good for her."

"How do you know it's a she?" Preston asked.

"I know you too well, P.J. If she was a *he,* and if it's a musical, then it wouldn't have been about nineteenth, but twenty-first-century New Orleans." His *New Orleans* sounded like *Nawlins.*

Preston wanted to tell Ray that he didn't know him *that* well. It had been the same with Clifford Jessup. Cliff had felt so comfortable managing his business affairs that he'd found himself with one less client.

"Can you spare some time where we can get together to talk about what I want?" he asked instead.

"I'm free tomorrow. I'd rather get together at your house. Beth isn't due for another two weeks, but she's been complaining about contractions. I don't want to be too far away if and when she does go into labor."

The reason Preston had moved into the city was not to

conduct business out of his home, but with Ray's wife's condition he would make an exception. "That's not a problem. Better yet, bring Beth with you. If the warm weather holds, we can cook and eat outdoors."

The lyricist met his artist wife when they were involved in a summer stock production written by a Bucks County playwright. Ray had written the songs, while Beth designed the set decorations. It was love at first sight, and they married two months later. They'd recently celebrated their tenth wedding anniversary, and now were expecting their first child.

"It would do Beth good to get out of the house," Ray remarked.

"How does one o'clock sound to you?" Preston asked.

"One is good. We'll see you tomorrow."

Preston smiled. "One it is." He ended the call, placing the phone on the console between the seats. Following the images on the GPS, he made a left turn on the road leading to Paoli. "Will you join me tomorrow?"

Preston's query was so unexpected that Chandra replayed it in her head. She stared at his distinctive profile for a full minute. "You want me to join you where?"

"I have a house in Kennett Square, and I'd like you to be present when I meet with Ray Hardy."

She sat up straighter, all of her senses on full alert. "Are you talking about *the* Raymond Hardy?"

"Yes. Since you suggested a musical, then I'll leave the music portion of the play up to you."

Chandra felt her pulse quicken. Raymond Hardy had been compared to British lyricist Sir Tim Rice, whose collaboration with composer Sir Andrew Lloyd Webber had earned them countless awards and honors in the States and across the pond.

She gave Preston a skeptical look. "You're kidding, aren't you?"

"No. My task will be to write the dialogue, while the music will be at your discretion."

"But…but I can't write music or lyrics," she sputtered.

"That will be Ray's responsibility. What I want you to do is tell him what you want. Ray is amazing. Give him an idea of what you want, and within a couple of hours he will have a song written in its entirety."

Chandra chewed her lower lip. She was being thrust into a situation where there was no doubt she would be in over her head. And it had all begun with her leaving her journal in a taxi where Preston Tucker had found it. If she'd retrieved her journal and not remarked about Preston's work, then she wouldn't be faced with the quandary of whether she wanted to become inexorably entwined in the lives of an award-winning dramatist and lyricist.

"You're going to have to let me know a little more about the plot," she said, stalling for time.

"We'll either discuss it tonight or tomorrow morning."

"When are we going to have time tonight, Preston? We probably won't leave my sister's house until at least eight or nine. And, remember it's at least an hour's drive between Philly and Paoli."

Reaching over, Preston rested his right arm over the back of Chandra's seat. "Don't stress yourself, baby. You can spend the night with me, which means we can stay up late."

Chandra looked at him as if he'd taken leave of his senses. "I can't spend the night with you."

A soft chuckle began in Preston's chest before it filled the interior of the Volvo. "Don't tell me you're worried about your virtue, Miss Independent. Didn't I tell you that you're safe with me, Chandra?"

His teasing her made Chandra feel like a hapless ingenue instead of a thirty-year-old woman who'd left home at eighteen to attend college in New York. When she returned it wasn't to put down roots in her home state, but in Virginia. Then she'd left the States to teach in a Central American country for a couple of years. She was currently living with her parents but that, too, was temporary; she was estimating she would move into her cousin's co-op before the end of the month.

She rolled her eyes at Preston. "Nothing's going to happen that I don't want to happen."

"There you go," he drawled. "After we leave Paoli I'll drive back to my place to pick up my car, then I'll follow you back home, so you can get what you need for a couple of days."

"A couple of days, Preston! When did overnight become a couple of days?"

"There's no need to throw a hissy fit, Chandra." His voice was low, calm, much calmer than he actually felt. "I need as much of your input as possible before you go back to work."

He didn't want to tell her that he wanted to begin working on the play before the onset of winter—his least productive season when there were days when his creative juices literally dried up.

"Okay," Chandra agreed after a comfortable silence. She was committed to helping Preston with the play, and she planned to hold up her end of the agreement. "But I'm going to have to use your computer to check my e-mail."

"That's not going to present a problem. I have both a

laptop and desktop at the house. Do you have to ask your parents if you can stay out overnight?"

Chandra rolled her eyes, then stuck out her tongue at Preston. "Very funny," she drawled sarcastically.

He smothered a grin. "You better watch what you do with that tongue."

"What are you talking about?"

"I have the perfect remedy for girls who offer me their tongues."

She rolled her eyes again. "I *ain't* scared of you, P. J. Tucker."

"I don't want you to be, C.E., because I intend for us to have a lot fun working together."

"I hope we can."

Preston gave her a quick sidelong glance. "Why do you sound so skeptical?"

"You're controlling, Preston."

"And you're not?" he countered.

"A little," Chandra admitted.

"Only a little, C.E.? You're in denial, beautiful. You are very, very controlling. If it can't be your way, then it's no way."

Resting a hand on her hip, Chandra shifted, as far as her seat belt would permit her, to face Preston. Her eyes narrowed. "Do you really think you know me that well?"

Preston longed to tell Chandra that he knew more about her than she realized, that he knew she was a passionate woman with a very healthy libido.

"I only know what you've shown me," he stated solemnly. "There's nothing wrong with being independent or in control as long as you let a man be a man."

"In other words, you expect me to grovel because you're the celebrated Preston Tucker."

Preston shook his head. "No."

"Then, what is it you want?"

"I want us to get along, Chandra. We may not agree on everything, but what I expect is compromise. I grew up hearing my parents argue every day, and I vowed that I would never deal with a woman I had to fight with. It's too emotionally draining. I began writing to escape from what I had to go through whenever my father came home.

"He would start with complaining about his boss and coworkers, and then it escalated to his nervous stomach and why he didn't want to eat what my mother had cooked for dinner. Most times she didn't say anything. She'd take his plate and empty it in the garbage before walking out of the kitchen. My sister and I would stare at our plates and finish our dinner. Then we would clear the table, clean up the kitchen and go to our respective bedrooms for the night. I always finished my homework before dinner, so that left time for me to write."

"Did your father have a high-stress job?"

"He was an accountant, who'd had his own practice but couldn't keep any employees."

Chandra couldn't remember her parents arguing, and if they did then it was never in front of their children. Between his office hours, house visits and working at the local municipal hospital, Dwight Eaton coveted the time he spent with his family.

"Did he verbally abuse his employees?"

A beat passed. "Craig Tucker was what psychologists call passive-aggressive. Most people said he was sarcastic. I thought of him as cynical and mocking."

Now Chandra understood why Preston sought to avoid acerbic verbal exchanges. "Are your parents still together?"

Another beat passed as a muscle twitched in Preston's lean jaw. "No. My dad died twenty-two years ago. He'd just celebrated his fortieth birthday when he passed away from lung cancer. He'd had a two-pack-a-day cigarette habit. My mother may have given in to my father's demands in order to keep the peace, but put her foot down when she wouldn't let him smoke in the house or car. He would sit on a bench behind the house smoking whether it was ninety-five degrees or twenty-five degrees. I found it odd that my mother didn't cry at his funeral, but it was years later that I came to realize Craig Tucker was probably suffering from depression."

Preston's grim expression vanished like pinpoints of sun piercing an overcast sky. "He did in death what he wouldn't do in life. He gave my mother a weekly allowance to buy food, while he paid all the bills. If she ran out of money, then she had to wait for Friday night when he placed an envelope with the money on the kitchen table. He was such a penny-pincher that my sister called him Scrooge behind his back. Well, Scrooge had invested heavily *and* wisely, leaving my mother very well off financially. He'd also set aside monies for me and my sister's college fund. Yolanda went to Brown, while I went to Princeton.

"After I graduated, my mother sold the house and moved back to her hometown of Charleston, South Carolina, enrolled in the College of Charleston and earned a degree in Historic Preservation and Community Planning. Then, she applied to and was accepted into a joint MS degree in Historic Preservation with Clemson. With her education behind her, she opened a small shop selling antiques and reproductions of Gullah artifacts. Her basket-weaving courses have a six-month waiting list."

Chandra's mouth curved into an unconscious smile. Preston's mother had to wait to become a widow to come into her own. Her adage was always Better Late Than Never.

"I remember my parents driving down to Florida one year, and when we went through South Carolina I saw old women sitting on the side of the road weaving straw baskets. I'm sorry we didn't stop to buy at least one."

"That's too bad," Preston remarked, "because the art of weaving baskets has been threatened with the advance of coastal development. Those living in gated subdivisions wouldn't let the weavers come through to pluck the sweetgrass they coil with pine needles, bulrushes and palmetto fronds used to make the baskets. Thankfully the true center of sweetgrass basket weaving is flourishing in Mount Pleasant, a sea island near the Cooper River."

"It sounds as if your mother has found her niche," Chandra said in a soft voice, filled with a mysterious longing.

"If not her niche, then her passion. Last year she met a man who teaches historical architecture and sits on the Charleston Historic Preservation and Community Planning board. I've never known my mother to laugh so much as when she's with him. She moved in with him at the beginning of the year."

"Good for her."

A wide grin creased Preston's face. "If you're talking about a romance novel, then Rose Tucker is truly a heroine."

"Is she going to marry her hero?"

"I don't know. I think she's still a little skittish about marriage, because she hasn't sold her condo. They divide their time living at his house during the week, and come into the city to stay at her condo on the weekend. It doesn't bother me or Yolanda if they never marry, as long as they're happy."

"Where does your sister live?" Chandra knew she was asking Preston a lot of questions, but she'd come to appreciate the sound of his sonorous baritone voice.

Settling back against the leather seat, she closed her eyes when he talked about his older sister, his brother-in-law and two sets of identical twin nephews. Again, she wondered why he hadn't married and fathered children when he told of the outings with his nephews. She opened her eyes when he patted her knee.

"Tell me about your family so I know what to expect."

Chandra recognized landmarks that indicated they were only blocks from her sister's house. "Too late. We're almost there."

Preston groaned aloud when the voice coming from the GPS directed him to turn right at the next street. He'd wanted Chandra to brief him as to her relatives. "Did you tell your folks you were bringing a guest?"

"Nope."

Decelerating, he maneuvered into a parking space across the street from a three-story Colonial. "Did they expect you to bring a guest?"

Chandra unbuckled her seat belt. "If you're asking whether I normally attend family functions with a man, then the answer is no. It's been more than three years since I've had a serious boyfriend."

Smiling, Preston rested his right arm over the back of her seat. "So, I'm your boyfriend?"

She flashed an attractive moue. "No, P.J., you're a friend."

He leaned closer. "Do you think I'll ever be your boyfriend?"

Chandra leaned closer until she was inhaling the moist warmth of Preston's breath. "You can if…"

"If what?" he whispered.

"You can if I can trust you."

Preston froze. "What's with you and the trust thing?"

"It's very important to me, Preston. Without trust there can be no boyfriend, girlfriend, no relationship."

He smiled. "Are you amenable to something that goes beyond platonic?"

Chandra blinked. "I am, but only—"

"If you can trust me," he said, completing her sentence.

"Yes."

Preston angled his head, pressing his mouth to Chandra's, reveling in the velvety warmth of her parted lips. It had been years since he'd sat in a car kissing a woman but there was something about Chandra Eaton that made him feel like an adolescent boy. First it was the unexpected erection after reading her erotic dreams and now it was having her close.

"You have my solemn vow that I will never give you cause to mistrust me."

Chandra quivered at the gentle tenderness of the kiss, and in that instant she wanted to trust Preston not because she wanted to but needed to. Every man she'd met after Laurence had become a victim of her acerbic tongue and negative attitude whenever they'd expressed an interest in her.

She'd loved Laurence, expecting to spend the rest of her life with him, but when he caved under pressure from his family, her faith in the opposite sex was shattered—

almost beyond repair. However, Preston Tucker was offering a second chance. She didn't expect marriage, not because he was a confirmed bachelor, but because it didn't figure into her short-term plans.

Chandra wanted to secure a teaching position, settle into her new residence, and dating Preston would become an added bonus. "I believe you," she whispered, succumbing to the forceful, drugging possession of his lips. It was with supreme reluctance that she ended the kiss. "Let's stop before one of the kids see us. I don't want to send my nieces the wrong message, that it's okay to make out in a car."

Preston's lids lowered, he successfully concealed his innermost feelings from the woman he wanted to make love to with a need that bordered on desperation. He knew it was her beauty, poise, intelligence and sensuality that fueled his obsession.

"The curtain just came down on the first act."

Chandra smiled up at him through her lashes. "When do we begin act two?"

"Tonight."

Chapter 8

Tonight. The single word reverberated in Chandra's head as she led the way toward the rear of the house where her sister lived with her husband and their nieces. The sound of voices raised in laughter greeted her and Preston when they walked into an expansive patio overlooking an in-ground pool. Her parents were holding court with their granddaughters and grandson, Myles and Zabrina lay together on a webbed lounger by the pool and Griffin stood at the stove in the outdoor kitchen with an arm around Belinda's waist. A long rectangular table with seating for twelve and a smaller table with half that amount were set up under a white tent.

Chandra stopped short, causing Preston to plow into her back; she saw someone she hadn't expected to see. Sitting under an umbrella with Denise was Xavier Eaton.

The last time she'd seen her cousin was days before he was to begin his tour of duty in Afghanistan.

"I'll introduce you to everyone after I talk to some-one," she whispered to Preston.

Arms outstretched and grinning from ear to ear, she walked into Xavier's embrace when he stood up. She found herself crushed against a rock-hard chest. "Wel-come home, Captain Eaton."

"It's now Major Eaton. I'd pick you up, but I have a bum leg."

Pulling back, Chandra saw that he was supporting himself with a cane. She hadn't realized her cousin, dressed in civilian clothes and looking more like a male model than a professional soldier, had sustained an in-jury. She'd lost count of the number of women who'd asked her to introduce them to Xavier. He was always po-lite to them, while smoothly rejecting further advances. He had also earned the reputation of remaining friends with his former girlfriends.

What they didn't know was that he had a mistress. Xavier Phillip Eaton ate, breathed and slept military. He'd attended military prep school, graduated and then enrolled at The Citadel, The Military College of South Carolina. He continued his military education when he was accepted into the Marine Corps War College. After 9/11 he was deployed to Iraq. He completed one tour of duty before he was sent to Afghanistan.

"Is it serious?"

"It will heal."

"That's not what I asked, Xavier."

Xavier leaned in closer. "If you're asking if I'm going to be a cripple, then the answer is no."

Narrowing her gaze, Chandra decided to drop the

subject. Tiptoeing, she kissed his smooth cheek. "We'll talk later." Shifting slightly, Chandra beckoned Preston closer, reaching for his hand as he approached. "Preston, I'd like for you to meet my cousin, Xavier Eaton. Xavier, Preston Tucker."

Xavier offered his hand. "Why does your name sound so familiar?"

Denise Eaton stood up, looping her arm around her brother's waist. "That's because he's Preston Tucker, the playwright."

Xavier pumped Preston's hand vigorously. "I'm honored to meet you." He gave him a rough embrace, while slapping him on the back with his free hand.

Chandra caught Denise's look of expectation. "Preston, this is Xavier's sister, Denise."

Denise managed to disentangle herself from her brother, shyly extending her hand. Her large dark eyes shimmered like polished jet, while flyaway black curls took on a life of their own whenever she moved her head. A shaft of sunlight fell across her heart-shaped face, highlighting the yellow-orange undertones in her flawless brown face. She was a softer, prettier, feminine version of Xavier.

"Mr. Tucker. I've seen and read every play you've written."

Preston took her hand, squeezing it gently. "Please, no Mr. Tucker. Call me Preston."

Chandra didn't know how, but she knew Preston was uncomfortable with his celebrity status. She rested a hand on his shoulder. "Now I'll introduce you to my sister and brother-in-law."

Preston fell in step with Chandra, feeling the heat of

the eyes that followed him as he walked across the patio. "Is Griffin Rice your brother-in-law?"

Chandra stopped suddenly, staring at Preston as if he were a stranger. She'd wanted it to be a surprise, but apparently he'd turned the tables. "Yes, Griffin *is* my brother-in-law."

Preston dipped his head, brushing a kiss on her mouth. "Good looking out, beautiful." Amid a chorus of coughs and cleared throats his head popped up as a smile softened the angles in his face. "Good afternoon."

Griffin Rice came forward, hand outstretched. Today he wore a white T-shirt, jeans and running shoes. He looked nothing like the man who had graced the cover of *GQ*. As the attorney for some of sports biggest superstars, he had become a superstar in his own right whenever he escorted models and actresses to social and sporting events. His gorgeous face and distinctive cleft chin made him a magnet for women everywhere. When the news got out that he'd married Belinda Eaton the gossip columnists scrambled to uncover everything about the woman who'd snared one of the country's most eligible bachelors.

"P. J. Tucker. You old dog! When did you hook up with my sister-in-law?"

Preston and Chandra shared a smile. "We got together after she got back from Belize." He handed Griffin the colorful shopping bags. "These are for Layla and Sabrina."

"How do you know Preston?" Chandra asked Griffin.

"We worked together on a fund-raiser a few years back. Your boyfriend put the squeeze on some of his well-heeled friends to reach our goal to set up an after-school sports program for some kids in North Philly."

Preston and Griffin shook hands. "I had to do everything short of bringing out a rubber hose to make them dig deep for a good cause. I know some of the guys drop at least ten thousand in a weekend entertaining Vegas showgirls."

Belinda Rice came over to join them, and Chandra made the introductions. Her sister looked wonderful. Her bare face radiated good health. She and Chandra claimed the same eyes and thick dark hair. She then introduced Preston to her parents, nieces, Myles and Zabrina. It was Myles's turn when he introduced her to her nephew for the first time.

It was apparent married life agreed with her brother. His face was fuller than it'd been in years, and the nervous energy that was always so apparent was missing. She'd missed his wedding, but sent a sculpture of a Mayan deity she'd purchased from a local Belizean artisan.

Her anger with Zabrina Mixon for breaking up with Myles two weeks before their wedding had jeopardized her relationship with her brother because he refused to blame Zabrina. What no one knew at the time was that Zabrina was pressured into breaking up with Myles and that she was pregnant with his son.

Myles dropped a proprietary arm around his son's shoulders. "Adam, this lady is your Aunt Chandra. She's been away teaching in Central America. Chandra, this is Adam."

She smiled at the tall, lanky boy who'd inherited his mother's hair and eyes. "Will it be okay if I hug you?" At ten, she wasn't certain whether boys were open to women hugging them. Her question was answered when he stepped forward and put his arms around her waist.

"It's nice meeting you," he said softly.

Chandra squeezed him gently, then lowered her arms. "I've waited a long time for a nephew. You're perfect." Reaching into her tote, she pulled out an envelope with his name written on the front. "I missed your birthday, so this is a little late. Your dad told me you like to draw, so what's in that envelope should help you buy some art supplies. Or, you can put it into a college fund."

Turning to Zabrina, she extended her arms and wasn't disappointed when the attractive woman with the golden skin, black wavy hair and hazel eyes moved into the circle of her embrace. "Congratulations, Brina. It's a little late, but I want to welcome you into the family."

Zabrina Eaton kissed Chandra's cheek. "Thank you. It's been a long time coming, but in the end everything worked out. Once we finish renovating and decorating the house, Myles and I would love to have you come and spend some time with us."

"Trust me, I will."

Her brother had called to tell her that not only was he marrying Zabrina and that he had a ten-year-old son, but he'd bought a house in a Pittsburgh suburb with enough room to have guests stay for an extended period of time. Adam had started classes at a new private school, while Zabrina managed to secure a position in a nearby public school. His own teaching schedule at Duquesne University School of Law had increased, but he'd managed to balance his professional and personal life, giving each equal attention.

"We'll talk later," she said to Zabrina, repeating what she'd told Denise. Chandra wanted to congratulate her nieces and give them their birthday gifts.

Their heads close together, the girls sat on a webbed

lounge chair unwrapping Preston's gifts. Both screamed hysterically when they realized he'd given each of them an iPod touch. They scrambled off the chair and did the happy dance.

Layla whirled like a dervish, her braided hair whipping around her face. "It can hold up to seven thousand songs!"

"We can listen to music and watch movies on it!" Sabrina shrieked excitedly. She executed a dance step where she dropped, popped and locked it.

All of the Eatons exchanged amused glances. Sabrina, the more reserved of the two, had shocked everyone with her effusive enthusiasm.

"Very nice," Chandra whispered to Preston. "How am I going to top that?"

She'd just encountered the same problem as Belinda whenever Griffin gave their nieces and goddaughters more expensive gifts than hers. The unspoken competition continued until they'd become their legal guardians. Becoming parents was very different from being aunt and uncle, and they conferred with each other on every phase of child rearing.

"I'm not competing with you, Chandra," Preston said softly. "When you told me your nieces were turning thirteen, I asked my sister what they would like. I took a chance when I bought the iPod because they could've already had one. And, if they had, then they could take them back to the store and either get a full refund or exchange them for something else. By the way, what did you get them?"

"Electronic readers."

"You're kidding?"

"No, P.J., I'm not kidding. Why?"

"I want one of those."

"Maybe I'll get you one for your birthday."

Preston shook his head. "It passed."

"When was your birthday?"

"March seventeenth. Don't say it. My mother was going to name me Patrick, but changed her mind."

"Maybe I'll get you one for Christmas," Chandra said.

"That'll work. When's your birthday?"

"April twenty-second."

"It's too late to get you something for your birthday, so Christmas will have to do. What do you want for Christmas?"

"Nothing, Preston."

"You're kidding."

Chandra gave him a warm smile. "No, I'm not. I have everything I could ever want."

The minute the admission was out of her mouth she knew she hadn't told the truth. If life could be rewound like a video, then she would've prevented her sister and brother-in-law from getting into their car the day a drunk driver killed them in a head-on collision. But, because life moved forward, not backward, she was grateful that she had her parents, brother, sister and extended family.

Sabrina and Layla screamed again when they opened Chandra's envelope to find gift cards for e-readers and books. Their celebration of becoming teenagers set the tone for an afternoon of casual frivolity. By the time their paternal grandparents, Lucas and Gloria Rice, arrived it was time to sit down and eat. The adults sat at the long table, while Adam, Layla and Sabrina sat at the smaller table. Chandra found herself flanked by Denise and Zabrina. Gloria Rice brought a platter of her celebrated Dungeness crab pot stickers for appetizers, and Roberta Eaton her homemade coconut cake for dessert.

Belinda and Griffin had prepared a smorgasbord of grilled meat and accompanying sides. There were the ubiquitous spareribs, chicken, pulled pork, roasted corn, fried catfish and hush puppies, carrot slaw, slow-smoked brisket, potato salad and baked beans.

Denise pressed her shoulder to her cousin's. "I didn't expect you to come with *him*," she said sotto voce.

Chandra peered through her lashes at Preston. He sat opposite her with Xavier on his left and Roberta Eaton on his right. "I asked him to come along because he wants to discuss business with Griffin."

Denise speared a portion of carrot slaw. "So, you two are not involved."

Cutting into a slice of smoked barbecue brisket, Chandra popped a piece into her mouth, chewing thoughtfully before she deigned to answer Denise's question. "We're not involved the way you think."

"And why not?" Denise's sultry voice had dropped an octave.

"Firstly, I just met him. And, secondly, I think getting involved would make working together more difficult. I need to remain objective when it comes to a professional relationship."

"Is he paying you?"

"No."

"Then it's not professional, Chandra," Denise argued quietly. "And what's up with the kiss? You guys hardly looked professional with your lips locked together."

Chandra picked up her wineglass and took a swallow. She didn't want to argue with her cousin, especially not in front of others. Although two years younger, Denise had always wanted to tell Chandra what she should or shouldn't do. Rather than go on and on about an issue where they'd never agree, she'd developed the practice of tuning her out.

"If you're interested in Preston, then go for it, Denise." She knew she'd shocked the director of a child care center when her mouth opened, but nothing came out except the sound of her breathing.

"He doesn't want me," Denise said between clenched teeth. "Don't look now, but he's not looking but lusting at you, Chandra. I've been without a man longer than you, so if you get the opportunity to sleep with someone you like, then take it."

Chandra went completely still. "Aren't you seeing Trey Chambers?"

"No!" Everyone at the table turned to stare at Denise, who managed to look embarrassed at her outburst. "I'm sorry about that." She pressed her shoulder to Chandra's. "Bite your tongue, cousin. You know how I feel about Trey. If I wasn't afraid of going to prison for the rest of my life, I'd murder the lying bastard."

"Then why did my mother send me a newspaper article with a photo of the two of you together?"

A frown settled onto Denise's features, distorting her natural beauty. "We serve on some of the same boards. If we're photographed together, then it's only for a photo-op. Trey Chambers ruined my life when I lost the only man I've ever loved."

Chandra heard the wistfulness in Denise's voice. "Have you run into Rhett Fennell now that you live in D.C.?"

Denise shook her head, then put her wineglass to her mouth and drained it. "No. And I pray I don't. I know I would lose it completely if I saw him again. It's been six years, Chandra, and I still can't forget him."

"Snap out of it, Denise Amaris Eaton! You're beautiful, smart, and you're the executive director of one of the most progressive child care centers in the country. And I know men are making themselves available to you. Meanwhile you're pining after someone you can't have."

"That's so cruel, Chandra."

Resting an arm over Denise's shoulders, Chandra rested her head on her cousin's. "It's the truth and you know it. When you told me that Laurence was only using me, that although he'd put a ring on my finger you couldn't see me spending the rest of my life with him, I said you were cruel and jealous. But you were spot-on with your observation and assessment of our relationship.

"Necie, you're my cousin. I love you and I want you to be happy. I've lost a student to suicide, sister and brother-in-law to a car accident and a man I loved because he wasn't man enough to stand up to his parents. As far as I'm concerned that's more than enough loss in my thirty years of living. If love comes knocking, then I'm going to open the door and grab it, lip-lock it and hold on so tight it would take the Jaws of Life to pry us apart."

"Either you're blind, or you're in denial," Denise drawled. "What you want and need is sitting across the table as we speak. Don't blow it, Chandra. Remember Grandma Eaton's advice about opportunity? She said it's like a bald-headed man. You have to catch him while he's coming toward you, because if your hand slips off then it's over."

Chandra gave Preston a long, penetrating stare. *"Do you think I'll ever be your boyfriend?"* His query came back with vivid clarity. He wanted more and she wanted more, but only he wasn't afraid to verbalize it. An expression of relief swept over her face. Denise had helped her resolve her own dilemma where it concerned Preston Tucker. She would take their grandmother's advice and grasp the opportunity to love before it slipped past her.

Pillars, votives and floodlights lit up the backyard as the Eaton and Rice clan settled down to relax after eating copious amounts of food. The sun had set, taking with it the heat, and a cool breeze swept over those sitting on the patio.

Chandra and Zabrina helped Belinda put away food, while Griffin cleaned up the outdoor kitchen. Griffin's parents, although divorced, had remained friends. They left after dinner because Gloria had tickets to attend a breakfast fund-raiser at a local chapter of the NAACP. Myles and his family and the elder Eatons planned to stay overnight with Griffin and Belinda.

The young adults sat off in a corner playing board games, while their parents, grandparents, aunt and uncle lay sprawled on loungers talking quietly to the one closest to them. Leaning back on her palms, Chandra splashed her bare feet in the warm pool water. Preston sat beside her, arms clasped around his knees, flexing his bare feet.

"I talked to Griffin."

She stared at his distinctive profile. "What did he say?"

Preston swung his head around to look at Chandra. "He's agreed to represent me." He winked at her. "I owe you, C.E."

"No, you don't, P.J."

"Yes, I do," he crooned. "I'll have to think of something to show my gratitude."

"I'll take a thank-you."

"I will thank you—but in my own way."

Her gaze dropped to his mouth, lingering on the tuft of hair under his lip. "Are you going to give me a hint of what I can expect?"

"No. I want it to be a surprise. Let me know when you're ready to leave."

Chandra withdrew her feet from the water. "I'm ready whenever you are." Pushing to his feet, Preston reached down and pulled her up. They had to drive back to Philadelphia before heading to Kennett Square.

She walked over to her parents, leaning over to give each a kiss. "We're leaving now."

Roberta placed a hand alongside her daughter's cheek. "Get home safely. Dwight and I like your young man."

She wanted to tell Roberta that Preston wasn't her young man. He was her friend. "I like him, too, Mama."

"I'll like him as long as he's good to my baby girl," Dwight drawled, deadpan.

"Daddy!"

Roberta swiped at her husband. "Stop teasing the child."

I'm not a child, Chandra mused. She supposed it was hard for family members not to regard her as the baby of the family, when in reality she'd been the most adventuresome.

"Good night," she said in singsong.

Chandra said her goodbyes, promising Denise she would drive down to D.C. to spend time with her, then hugged and kissed her brother and Zabrina, then Xavier. Belinda and Griffin walked her and Preston to the car, lingering long enough to program dates into their cell phones when they would get together again.

"If you guys want a night on the town, then you can stay over at my place in the city. You can bring your daughters and I'll arrange for a sitter to watch them."

"They can always stay with my parents," Belinda suggested.

"Or my mother," Griffin added.

Chandra smiled. "I guess that means we'll have grown-folk night."

Belinda rested her head on Griffin's shoulder. "We're going to have to get in as many grown-folk outings we can before the baby comes."

"What baby?" Chandra asked, her eyes narrowing.

Griffin smiled at his wife. "We found out yesterday that we're going to have a baby. Lindy and I decided not to say anything until the family gets together again for Thanksgiving. We're telling you, because we want you to be godmother to our son or daughter."

Chandra pantomimed zipping her lips. "I won't say anything, and I'm honored that you've asked me to be godmother." Now she knew why Belinda hadn't drunk anything alcoholic with her meal. "Congratulations to both of you."

After another round of hugs and kisses, Preston assisted Chandra as she slipped into the car. He got in beside her, started the engine, then maneuvered away from the curb, driving down a quiet tree-lined street.

He glanced over at Chandra to discover she'd closed her eyes, her chest rising and falling in a measured rhythm. She'd fallen asleep. He would let her sleep until they reached Philadelphia. Once there, he would retrieve his car from the garage. It would be midnight, barring traffic delays, before they reached Kennett Square.

Chapter 9

Chandra didn't know what to expect when Preston said he had a place in the country. But it certainly was not the sprawling stone farmhouse that reminded her of the English countryside. When she got out of Preston's SUV, she half expected to see grazing sheep.

She stood on the front steps leading to the one-story home, staring out into the autumn night. A near-full moon silvered the countryside. "How long have you lived here?"

Preston moved closer, pulling her against his length. "I moved in six years ago. I used to drive through the Brandywine Valley after I got my driver's license, telling myself if I studied and worked hard I would be able to buy property here."

"Your dream came true." Chandra's voice was soft and filled with a strange longing she couldn't disguise.

Preston pressed his mouth to her hair. "What about you? What do you dream about?"

She closed her eyes, enjoying the sensation that came from the solid body molded to hers. How could she tell Preston of her dreams—dreams that were so erotic that when she woke she could still feel the aftermath of a climax, leaving her completely sated.

After the first few dreams Chandra had told herself she was going through withdrawal, and that her body craved the physical fulfillment she'd had with Laurence. But when the dreams continued she realized something else had triggered them—something more than a physical need. If she'd been in the States, there was no doubt she would've sought out a professional therapist to identify the reason why her dreams were solely erotic in nature. They'd gone beyond filling a sexual void. They had become a sexual obsession.

"My dreams aren't the same as a wish list."

"Can you tell me what's on your wish list?"

Peering up at Preston over her shoulder, Chandra tried making out his expression in the moonlight. Only half his face was visible, and there was something about how the shadows struck his features that reminded her of book covers on paranormal novels. They weren't Preston and Chandra in present Pennsylvania, but Pascual and Josette in early nineteenth-century New Orleans, where he'd come to her under the cover of darkness to make the most incredible love imaginable. The fleeting image of Preston making love to her was one she wanted to be real.

Discussing Preston with Denise had helped her rethink her relationship with him. They were friends *and* were collaborating on writing a play, yet there was sexual attraction that was palpable whenever they shared the same space. Preston was brilliant, gorgeous and inexorably male. He was perfect. Almost too perfect, and it was the perfection that gave her pause.

"There's only one thing on Chandra Eaton's wish list," she admitted. "And that is to do whatever makes her feel happy and complete."

Preston stared at the delicate face with eyes that appeared much too wise for someone as young as Chandra. There were times when she stared at him that made him feel as if she knew what he was thinking. Much to his chagrin, most of his thoughts toward her were purely erotic in nature. It was then he chided himself for reading her journal. Perhaps if they'd met on equal footing, then it would've given him the opportunity to look past what she'd written.

He'd tried to separate Chandra from the woman who'd written about her dreams, but he couldn't. There was so much about the woman in his embrace and the one who'd used her imagination to conjure up the most exquisite lover that they were inseparable. What had shocked Preston was that, although each dream was about making love, she'd approached each one differently. It was as if she'd had a different lover every night.

"Are you happy, Chandra?"

The seconds ticked. "I'm at peace, Preston. I don't feel the need to run away to try and find myself. I've come home and I know this time I'll stay."

Chandra had talked to Belinda about buying the furniture in her house, and after a good-natured back-and-forth Belinda agreed to accept a price well below what the pieces were worth. Chandra had been adamant when she refused to accept the bedroom, living room and kitchen furniture as a housewarming gift.

"I'm thirty years old, and for the first time in my life I know and like who I am. And it's taken me this long to accept that I don't need a man in my life to make me complete."

"Don't you want to get married and start a family like your sister?"

Preston knew he had crossed the line with the question, yet he had to know where Chandra stood on the issue if he found himself in too deep. He didn't know what there was about her, but after spending the afternoon with the Eatons it was as if he'd been struck by a bolt of lightning.

He wanted what they had. He wanted to get together with his mother, his sister and her family, but also for a brief instant he'd imagined having his own wife and children. The Eatons and Rices were representative of most families. They loved one another, but also had their disagreements. What he'd noticed was a fierce loyalty that had extended to the next generation. Layla and Sabrina were as protective of Adam as Griffin was of Belinda.

Chandra pondered Preston's query. There was a time when she'd planned to marry and hopefully have children, yet that dream had ended when Laurence bowed to pressure from his overbearing parents to end their engagement.

"I suppose I do."

"Either you do or you don't, Chandra."

She stared at the beam of headlights from a car in the distance maneuvering around a winding road in the valley below. "I do. But it can't be now."

"Why?"

"I have too many things to do. I'm planning to move into my own place before the beginning of November."

Preston felt a momentary panic. "Where are you moving to?"

"I'm subletting my cousin's Penn's Landing co-op."

He exhaled a breath. He'd thought she was moving out of the state. "That's a nice neighborhood."

"So is Rittenhouse Square," Chandra countered.

"I was looking for something in Society Hill, but there was nothing on the market at the time."

"For someone who appears so contemporary, why do you like old neighborhoods?"

Preston chuckled softly. "There's a certain character in older neighborhoods that I find missing in the ones where all of the buildings are designed like boxes and rectangles. Whether it's the buildings' facades, cobblestone streets or century-old trees, in the historic districts they all have a story to tell. The ones that don't elect to keep their secrets."

Chandra laughed, the rich sound fading in the eerie stillness of the night. "Spoken like a true writer."

Preston's fingers grazed the column of Chandra's neck. "As much as I would love to hang out here with you, we need to go inside and talk about *Death's Kiss*."

"I'd like to take a shower and change into something more comfortable."

"I'll show you to your bedroom, then I'll bring your bag in." Preston had waited in the Eatons' living room while Chandra had gone upstairs to pack a bag. She'd told him that her parents had recently celebrated their forty-second wedding anniversary, and he wondered if his father hadn't died so young whether his parents would've stayed together.

He unlocked the door and walked into the entryway and was met with the subtle scent of fresh roses. The cleaning woman made it a practice of cutting flowers from the garden and arranging them in vases for the entryway and living room.

The flower garden, fireplaces and the house overlooking a valley were what prompted him to purchase the property. The fieldstone house sat on two acres with a copse of trees that provided shade and plenty of firewood. He'd purchased the house several months before he'd proposed marriage to Elaine. His enthusiasm for living in the Brandywine Valley was completely lost on her. She was a city girl who loved living in the city.

"Who arranged the flowers?"

Preston glanced over his shoulder to find Chandra staring at the lush bouquet of late-blooming roses ranging in hues from snow-white to deep purple in a crystal vase resting on a bleached-pine table.

"The woman who comes to dust and vacuum picks them from the garden." The mother of two, who'd come to him asking to clean his house to supplement her income after her husband ran away with his much-younger secretary, had worked for a florist as a teenager, where she'd learned the art of flower arranging.

"You have a flower garden?"

Reaching for Chandra's hand, Preston brought it to his mouth, dropping a kiss on her knuckle before tucking it into the crook of his elbow. "You'll be able to see it tomorrow morning."

"It's already tomorrow," Chandra reminded him with a sly smile.

"And don't tell me you're Cinderella, and at the stroke of midnight you turn back into a chambermaid."

She rolled her eyes upward. "Never happen."

"Did you ever pretend you were a princess when you were a girl?"

"No. My sisters were princesses only because I always insisted on being the queen."

Preston's eyebrows lifted. "They were never the queen?"

"No. I always threw a tantrum and Donna and Belinda knew they had to deal with my father if baby girl came to him crying."

Smiling, he shook his head. "You must have been a hot mess."

Chandra flashed a Cheshire cat grin. "I used whatever I had at my disposal. Being the baby of the family had its disadvantages, and I did whatever was necessary to shift the odds."

"Conniving little wench."

"What…eva," she drawled.

Preston led her into a living room with a massive brick fireplace that opened out to a dining room. If his Rittenhouse Square condo was ultracontemporary, it was the opposite of the farmhouse in the historic Brandywine Valley. A sofa and two facing love seats were upholstered with fabric stamped with flowers, ferns and vines. A coffee table in antique cherry was big enough to double as a place for an informal tea party. Plank cherrywood floors were covered with area rugs that complemented the furnishings. Roses on mochaccino wallpaper and a collection of green crockery and majolica in the dining room evoked the feeling of a Victorian period piece.

"Who decorated your house?" Every piece of furniture and accessories were chosen with the utmost care and consideration.

"My mother."

"She has impeccable taste." Rose Tucker's knowledge of historic preservation was apparent when each item conformed to the design of the updated eighteenth-century farmhouse.

"I'll let her know you said so. This will be your bedroom." Preston stepped aside to let Chandra enter a room with a connecting door to his bedroom. "Mine is through that door." He pointed to a carved mahogany door on the left. "The door on the right is your bathroom."

"Lovely." The single word slipped unbidden between her lips.

Sheltered beneath eaves that reminded her of an attic, Chandra looked at the queen-size bed covered with a quilt pieced with geometric patterns in a mix of plaids, stripes and paisleys. A mound of pillows in soft shades of coffee and cream were nestled against a wrought-iron headboard. An upholstered club chair in a faint brown-and-white pinstripe cradled an off-white chenille throw. She couldn't stop the smile spreading across her face. The charming bedroom had a window seat where one could curl up to read, relax or just stare out the window.

"It reminds me of my bedroom when I was a girl. I grew up in a farmhouse outside Philly," she explained when Preston gave her a questioning look. "My mother never had to go looking for us, because we always played around the house. The best thing about growing up in the suburbs was having a pet. We had dogs, cats, birds, rabbits and baby chicks. But, when the rabbits started multiplying and the chickens grew into hens or roosters, we had to give them away."

Cradling her face, Preston pressed a kiss to Chandra's forehead. "So, you like living in the country?"

She smiled. "I prefer it to the city. Waking up not

hearing car horns or sirens from emergency vehicles alleviates more than fifty percent of one's stress. Which do you prefer? The city or the country?"

"The country."

"Why, then, do you have a place in the city?"

"That's where I entertain and conduct business. I plot at the apartment, but this is where I write because of the natural light." He kissed her again. "Let me get your bag. Knock on my door whenever you're ready."

Chandra stood up in the tub, reaching for a fluffy towel on a stack on a nearby stool. She'd lingered in the bathtub longer than she'd planned because soaking in a tub had become not only a luxury but also a privilege. When she'd entered the bathroom she felt as if she'd stepped back in time. Twin pedestal sinks and a slipper tub harkened back to another century.

The clock on a shelf chimed the hour. It was one o'clock. If she hadn't napped in the car during the ride from Paoli to Philly, there was no doubt she wouldn't have been able to keep her eyes open. Patting the moisture from her body, Chandra stepped out onto a thirsty shag bath mat and moisturized her body with a scented crème before retreating to the bedroom and pulling on a pair of black-and-white-striped cotton lounging pants with a white tank top. Walking on bare feet, she knocked lightly on the connecting door.

She knocked again, listening for movement on the other side. "Preston." Waiting a full minute, she knocked again. "Preston, please open the door." Again, there was no answer, and Chandra placed her hand on the doorknob, turning it slowly.

Pushing open the door, she stuck her head in. A lamp

on a bedside table was turned to its lowest setting, casting a soft glow over the expansive space. A smile replaced her expression of uncertainty when she saw Preston sprawled on a king-size bed. He'd changed out of his suit and into a pair of drawstring white cotton pajama pants.

With wide eyes Chandra moved closer to the bed. Preston had fallen asleep while waiting for her. She felt like a voyeur when she was able to brazenly gaze at his toned upper body. Fully clothed, Preston Tucker was captivating; half-clothed he was mesmerizing.

For a man approaching forty who earned a living sitting behind a desk, she hadn't expected a flat belly, defined abdominals and muscled pectorals. She leaned closer, inhaling the lingering scent of soap on his skin, while staring at the tattooed masks of comedy and tragedy over his heart. Without warning his breathing changed, becoming more ragged, but within seconds it resumed its normal cadence. Turning on her heels, Chandra headed toward the door.

"Where are you going?"

She stopped and turned. Preston had sat up and swung his legs over the side of the bed. "I thought you were asleep."

Preston ran a hand over his cropped hair. "I guess I dozed off waiting for you." He beckoned her, then patted the mattress. "Come and sit down. Come, baby. I'm not going to bite you," he urged, sensing her hesitation.

Chandra took a tentative step, then another, before racing to the bed and launching herself at him. He caught her midair, flipped her onto her back, straddling her.

His gaze lingered on the hair she'd twisted into a knot atop her head, then moved leisurely down to her scrubbed face. "What took you so long?"

Her lids lowered, a dreamy expression softening her delicate features. "It's been a while since I've had the luxury of lingering in a bathtub."

"Did you enjoy yourself?"

Chandra smiled. "Immensely."

Burying his face between her chin and shoulder, Preston breathed a kiss against the column of her scented neck. "That's good."

The heat, the comforting crush of Preston's body and the increasing hardness between his thighs enveloped Chandra as she struggled valiantly not to succumb to the familiar sensations of rising desire. She hadn't been dreaming, or if she had she hadn't remembered, since her return. What she felt was beginning to remind her of the dreams she'd recorded in her journals.

"Preston?"

He groaned in her ear. "What, baby?"

Chandra struggled not to move her hips. "We're supposed to be talking, not making love."

"We're not making love, Chandra."

She closed her eyes when she felt the outline of his erection against her thigh, while the intense heat from his body threatened to swallow her whole. In a motion so quick it caused her to catch her breath, he reversed their positions, she lying between his outstretched legs.

"Preston?"

"What is it, baby?"

"What exactly are we doing?"

Cradling the back of her head in one hand, Preston rested his other one over her rounded bottom. "We're going to talk about Pascual and Josette."

Chandra wanted to tell Preston that she loved it when

he called her baby. It came out in a sensual growl. "What about them?"

"Stop wiggling, or my hard-on will never go down."

Chandra's head popped up, her eyes meeting Preston's. "I was trying to get into a more comfortable position."

"And I'm trying not to spend the rest of the night in pain."

A frown creased her smooth forehead. "Why would you be in pain?"

The seconds ticked as Preston gave her an incredulous look. "Are you a virgin?"

Stunned by his bluntness, her mouth opened, snapped closed, then opened again. "No!"

"No!" he repeated. "If you're familiar with the male anatomy, then you should know men can't sustain an erection for an extended time without a release because it hurts like hell."

"I know that."

"If you know that, then stop teasing me."

Chandra tried to sit up; her efforts were thwarted when Preston held her fast. "Let me go, Preston."

He tightened his hold around her waist. "Now, you know I can't do that, baby. Do you know how hard it's been for me to keep my hands off you?"

"No," she answered truthfully.

"Well, it has. I never imagined how much my life would change when I found your journal in that taxi. My first impulse was to give it to the driver, but I changed my mind."

"So, you opened it and saw my contact information in my journal."

"Yes. And I'm glad I did."

"Do you actually think I believe you were just waiting to meet some anonymous woman?"

Preston glared at Chandra. There were times when he wanted to shake her. He didn't know why she was distrustful. "What the hell did your last boyfriend do to you?"

Chandra averted her gaze while chewing her lower lip. Once she'd gathered her family together to inform them she wasn't marrying Laurence, it was the last time she'd mentioned his name. She'd convinced herself that if she didn't have to retell the story of what went wrong then she wouldn't have to reopen a wound that took years to heal.

"I'd rather not talk about it," she said after a pregnant pause.

"Not talking about it won't make it any less painful."

Her gaze shifted back to Preston as her lips thinned in anger. "There's no pain, Preston, just rage whenever I think about it. The funny thing is that I don't blame Laurence as much as I do his parents. We dated for a year before he asked me to marry him. I accepted, and then the next step was meeting his mother and father, who were quick to tell me I was so wrong for their precious baby boy."

"What do you mean by *wrong?*"

"I didn't have the right *pedigree.*" She spat out the word.

Eyes narrowing, Preston angled his head. Instinctually, he knew it had to go beyond pedigree. The Eatons were one of Philadelphia's prominent African-American families. "You didn't have the right pedigree or the right color?"

The breath caught in Chandra's lungs. "How did you know?"

Preston gave her a look usually reserved for children. "Chandra, please don't insult my intelligence. It was their politically correct way of saying they didn't want their son to marry a black woman. If they had wanted to have you investigated, then the P.I. would've told them that you come from a family of doctors, teachers and lawyers, so it had to be something else. And for me, race was the only other obvious variable."

She shook her head. "I don't know why I didn't think of that."

"It was because you were young and very much in love with someone who didn't deserve your love. If you give me his address I'll pay him a visit."

A frown formed between her eyes. "And do what, Preston?"

"Kick his ass, of course."

"You wouldn't?"

"Hell, yeah. I can promise you he wouldn't look the same after I give him an old-fashion North Philly beat down."

"Don't tell me there's some thug in Philadelphia's famed dramatist."

Preston glared at her under lowered brows. "There's a lot of thug in me. However, I'm able to channel most of it into writing."

"The only time I got a little feisty is when Laurence's mother said it was nothing personal, but she had expected her son would marry someone within his social circle. I told her I understood exactly what she was saying because as a Thoroughbred I should've never hooked up with a jackass."

Throwing back his head, Preston howled, Chandra's laughter joining his as tears ran down their cheeks. She rolled off his body to lie beside him. "I'm glad it turned out the way it did, otherwise I never would've met you."

"Is that a good thing, P.J.?"

He closed his eyes. "It's a very good thing, C.E." Turning on his side, he rested an arm over her belly. "The Tuckers' pedigree can't begin to match the Eatons', but I'd like to hope that I at least have a chance to prove to you that I'm not a jackass."

Chandra shifted, facing Preston, their faces only inches apart. She studied the features of the man who'd managed to scale the wall she'd erected around her in order to protect herself from heartbreak.

She knew he wanted to make love to her, and she wanted to make love with him. Unknowingly, he'd become the nameless, faceless man who'd invaded her sleep and dreams to assuage her sexual frustration.

"You could never be a jackass," Chandra whispered against his parted lips. She tasted his mouth tentatively as if sampling a frothy confection.

Nothing on Preston moved, not even his eyes as he relished her caress of his mouth. "What do you want, Chandra?"

"I want you," she said.

"How?"

The kisses stopped, and she stared at him. "I want you to make love with me."

Preston smiled. She hadn't asked him to make love to her, but with her. His right eyebrow lifted a fraction before settling back into place. "And I want you to make love with me." He pressed a kiss over each eye. "Are you using birth control?"

Pinpoints of heat dotted Chandra's cheeks. In her dreams she hadn't had to worry about conception; but the man in whose bed she lay wasn't a specter or figment of her imagination but flesh and blood and capable of getting her pregnant.

"No."

Preston kissed her again. "I will protect you." And he would. He would protect her from an unplanned pregnancy and protect her from anything and anyone seeking to harm her. It was in that instant that he realized he was falling in love with Chandra Eaton.

Chapter 10

Chandra stared at the flexing muscles in Preston's abdomen when he sat up and swung his legs over the side of the bed. She was certain he could hear the runaway beating of her heart as he opened the drawer in the bedside table. She exhaled a ragged, audible sigh when he placed a condom on the pillow beside her head. It was one thing to sleep with a man she'd known a very short time and another to find herself pregnant with his child.

Her relationship with Preston differed greatly from the ones her sister and brother had with their respective spouses. Belinda had been maid of honor and Griffin best man at their siblings' wedding, and Myles had known Zabrina all his life before finally marrying her last month, while she was preparing to sleep with a man she hadn't met two weeks before.

Preston stood up, untied the cord to his pajama pants,

letting them slide off his waist and hips. His gaze met and fused with Chandra's when he stepped out of them. Her breath quickened. The blood pooled in his groin when he noticed the outline of her hardened nipples against the white tank top.

He stared at her, wanting to commit to memory the cloud of dark curly hair around her face, breasts that were fuller than he'd expected and the look of indecision in the eyes staring back at him in anxious anticipation.

The mattress dipped slightly when he placed one knee, then the other on the bed. Lying beside Chandra, Preston turned to face her. "How are you?"

A tentative smile trembled over her lips. "I'm good, Preston."

He ran the back of his hand over her cheek. "Are you ready for this? If not, then we can sleep together without making love."

Shifting slightly, Chandra draped her leg over his. "I'm ready."

She was more than ready. Preston hadn't even touched her intimately, yet she could feel the trickle of desire coursing through her body.

Preston rose slightly to grasp the hem of Chandra's top, easing it up and over her head. He took his time undressing her, because he had all night in which to make her dreams real. Reading her journal gave him an advantage: he knew what she liked. Ironically, what she liked, he liked, and then some.

He untied her lounging slacks, easing them down her hips. A wide smile split his face when he saw the tiny triangle of black silk covering her mound. Lowering his head, he nibbled at the bows holding up her thong panty. Chandra arched off the bed, and he placed a hand over her belly, preventing her from escaping his marauding mouth.

She'd teased him about his mouth and his ability to kiss and he'd interpreted it as a challenge. He'd become an overachiever because of his father's taunts when he'd revealed he wanted to become a writer. When Craig Tucker told his son he would end up a pauper, Preston had set out to prove his father wrong. Unfortunately, Craig hadn't lived long enough to witness his son's success.

Chandra covered her face with both hands when Preston's moist hot breath seared the apex of her thighs much like the heat from a blast furnace. Delicious spasms made the sensitive flesh of her sex quiver. A rush of moisture bathed her core. In the past it had taken prolonged foreplay to arouse her.

She teased Preston about what he could with his mouth, but that mouth was doing unbelievable things to her, He'd alternated kissing and licking her cropped pubic mound. Without warning, tears flooded her eyes and spilled down her face. His tongue found the swollen bud between the folds. He licked it in an up-and-down motion that made her rise off the mattress.

"No more, Preston. Please stop."

Preston heard her plaintive cry. He would stop, but not before he tasted every inch of her fragrant body. Moving up between her legs, he claimed her mouth in an explosive kiss, his tongue plunging into her mouth.

Everything about Chandra Eaton was intoxicating: her smell, the perfection of her firm breasts, the curvy fullness of her hips, the narrow waist he could span with both hands and the taste of her sex. Her body was a banquet table where he wanted to feast again and again.

With the precision of a cartographer, he charted a

course beginning with her mouth, journeying downward to her bared throat, the column of her scented neck and lower to her breasts. He suckled her like a starving infant, and when drinking his fill he worried the erect nipples with his teeth. The keening coming from Chandra made tiny shivers of gooseflesh on the back of his neck.

Chandra was lost in a web of pleasure so sensual, so wholly erotic that she felt as if she were slipping away to nothingness. Preston's mouth and hands seemed to be everywhere at once.

Preston heard and felt Chandra's breathing quicken, and he knew she was ready to climax. He released her long enough to slip on the condom, then moved between her legs once again. Reaching for her hand, he placed it on his erection.

He kissed her neck. "Let's do this together."

Preston had asked Chandra if she was a virgin, and at that moment she felt like one. In each relationship she'd let her partner take the lead, yet it was different with Preston. They had become equals—in and out of bed.

Her fingers closed around his heavy sex, then Preston's hand covered hers as he positioned his erection at the entrance to her vagina. She gasped slightly as the penetration seemingly took minutes to complete. They shared a smile and a sigh when he was fully sheathed inside her.

Preston did not want to believe the incredible heat that came from Chandra. He wanted to withdraw and pull off the condom just to experience flesh against flesh, heat on heat. Not only was she tight, but she was on fire.

"Oh, baby, I—" Chandra silenced him with a searing kiss that scorched his mouth with its intensity when her teeth sank into his lip. Her hips moved against his, and he was lost.

Her hunger and need was transferred to Preston and he answered. He moved slowly, deliberately. Each time he pulled back it was a little farther, and each time he pushed it was a little harder and deeper.

Chandra's wrapping her legs around Preston's waist was his undoing. Sliding his hands under her hips, he lifted her off the mattress, permitting him deeper penetration. Moans and groans escalated, breathing quickened, then the dam broke. Burying his face against her neck, Preston exploded, his deep moans of ecstasy echoing in her ear.

He's real. What I'm feeling is real. Chandra had waited more than three years to experience why she'd been born female. The flutters that began with his penetration grew stronger. Her muscles contracted around his rigid flesh, pulling him in, holding him fast; she released him before squeezing him again and again.

The walls of her vagina convulsed as a scorching climax hurtled her to a place where she'd never been. Preston Japheth Tucker was the only man she'd slept with able to bring her to climax their first time together.

"I think I'm going to keep you, P.J."

Preston chuckled. "You better, because I don't intend to let you go." He brushed a kiss over her cheek. "I'm going to have to get up." She emitted a small cry of protest when he pulled out.

He left the bed and walked to the bathroom, where he discarded the condom and washed away the evidence of their lovemaking. He'd tried imagining what it would be like to make love to Chandra, but nothing in his imagination could've prepared him for the passion she stirred up in him.

Preston returned to the bedroom to find it shrouded in darkness. Chandra had turned off the lamp. He managed to make it to the bed without bumping into anything. Slipping into bed, he pulled her against his chest. "Are you okay?"

"Yes-s-s," Chandra slurred.

"Do you want to talk about Pascual and Josette?"

"Not now."

"When?"

"Tomorrow morning."

Preston wanted to remind Chandra it was already tomorrow. They had tomorrow and hopefully many more tomorrows.

Ribbons of sunlight from the partially closed drapes threaded their way over the bed where Preston lay, his back to Chandra. He opened his eyes, staring at the door connecting the two bedrooms. A smile softened his mouth when he recalled what he'd shared with Chandra Eaton.

He didn't know why he'd been the one to get into the taxi where she'd left her case, or what had prompted him to read her journal. Whether it was a fluke, serendipity or destiny, he regarded it as a blessing.

He and his younger sister had grown up in a neighborhood where muggings, the sound of gunfire and a heavy police presence were the norm. Some of his boyhood friends never reached adulthood, or if they did then they'd become a statistic in the criminal justice system.

Preston had lost count of the number of times his mother and father preached to him and Yolanda about making something of their lives. The first and only time Craig Tucker asked his son what he wanted to be when he grew up and was told a writer, it elicited a long tirade about how writers were born not made, and very few, if any, earn enough money to support themselves and their families.

Although Craig had passed away years before he walked into Princeton for his first day of classes, Preston couldn't shake off his father's dire warning. Praying his late father was wrong, he majored in English with a minor in mathematics. His rationale was if he couldn't make it as a writer he could always teach math. But he'd proven Craig wrong on two accounts: he hadn't become a victim of the streets, and he *hadn't* failed as a writer.

"Will you share my bath with me?"

Preston's smile grew wider. Hearing Chandra's voice, still heavy with sleep, was the perfect way for him to start his day. He swallowed a groan. She'd pressed her firm breasts against his back.

"What do I get if I say yes?"

"I'll wash your back and any place or anything else you want."

This time Preston couldn't stop the groan escaping his parted lips when his sex hardened with her erotic offer. He curbed the urge to reach between his thighs. He scrambled off the bed and practically ran to the en suite bathroom.

Chandra waited for Preston to return, but when he didn't she left the bed and walked into her bathroom. She turned on the faucets in the bathtub, adjusting the water temperature before adding a capful of scented bath crystals under the flowing water. The tub was half-filled by the time she'd washed her face and brushed her teeth.

She let out an audible sigh when sinking into the lukewarm water. The slight ache between her legs was a reminder of what she'd shared with the man who was now a part of her life as she was his.

What had begun with him returning her case and journal was now a full-blown affair. Resting her arms on the sides of the tub, Chandra closed her eyes and smiled. She was having an affair with P. J. Tucker.

How, she mused, had her life changed in a matter of weeks? She'd had her first sexual encounter during her college sophomore year. He was another student in her study group, and she'd slept with him not because she was in love with him. If the truth were told, then she would have to admit that she barely *liked* him. She'd gone to his apartment to study for a statistics exam, and was forced to spend the night when a winter storm dropped a foot of snow on New York City. She slept with him again a week later, then decided they were better off as friends than lovers.

Then there was Laurence, whom she dated for six months before getting into bed with him. Although she'd found sex with him satisfying, it wasn't exciting. After a while she was resigned to the fact she would marry a man who would provide financial stability for her and their children and do whatever he could to make their marriage a success.

Laurence Breslin may have been what Chandra thought of as benign, but she hadn't been prepared for his reversal of affection. He'd professed she was the love of his life, yet when confronted by *Mommy* he folded like an accordion and sided with his parents against her.

"Do you intend to keep your promise to wash my back?"

She opened her eyes to find Preston lounging against the door frame, arms crossed over his bare chest. He'd put on the pajama pants he'd discarded the night before. Her gaze moved slowly over the stubble on his lean jaw, down to his magnificent upper body, long legs and bare, arched feet.

Sinking lower in the tub, Chandra winked at Preston. "Yes. I always keep my promises."

Lowering his arms, Preston approached the tub, at the same time pushing the pajamas down his hips. It had taken months before his mother was able to locate a slipper tub large enough for two adults. He'd used it once, but preferred taking a shower. It was his sister who used it whenever she came for a visit.

"Scoot forward, baby." Chandra inched toward the opposite end of the tub, and he got in behind her. Scooping up a handful of warm scented water, he poured it over her shoulders. "You know I'm going to smell like a girl," Preston whispered in her ear.

Resting the back of her head on his shoulder, Chandra smiled up at Preston. "There are worse things you could smell like."

His eyebrows lifted. "True. It's a good thing I'm secure about my sexuality or I would be having a few issues."

"I take it you like being a man?"

"Very much. How about you, Chandra? Do you like being a woman?"

"I love being a woman."

Preston's minty breath wafted in her nose. "And what a magnificent woman you are, Chandra Eaton."

Her lids lowered demurely. "Thank you."

"Don't thank me. The thanks go to your parents and their superior gene pool."

"I thought we were going to discuss Josette and Pascual."

"We did, but that was before you distracted me."

Chandra's jaw dropped. "You're blaming me for what happened last night?"

Preston nodded. "If you hadn't come into my bedroom wearing that little skimpy top showing the outline of your nipples—"

"Don't you dare go there, P.J.! You're as much to blame for what took place. Don't," she screamed when his hands cupped her wet breasts, his thumbs sweeping back and forth over her nipples.

"Now, let's talk about Pascual and Josette."

"I can't think with you doing that," Chandra said in protest.

"Is this better?"

She rose several inches when his hand moved from her breast to the area between her thighs. "Preston. If you don't stop, I'm getting out of this tub."

Chandra wanted him to make love to her again, and she also wanted to discuss the play. She didn't know how much more free time she'd have once she began the task of moving into her new residence. Then, there was the possibility that she would be contacted for a substitute or permanent teaching position. Business before pleasure had always been her credo for balancing her life.

Preston didn't have the pressure of looking for a job or a place to live. He owned a condo and a house in the country, while she was subletting from her cousin. She'd saved enough money to sustain her for two years, but only if she continued to live with her parents.

But for Chandra that wasn't an option. She wanted her own place. She wanted to invite whomever she chose to stay over when the mood hit her. Her parents had raised four children, and now that they were in their sixties they could do and go anywhere they chose without having to worry whether their house would be standing when they returned.

Chandra had lived on campus when she attended Columbia, was provided with faculty housing when she taught at the private school in Northern Virginia and during her Peace Corps tenure. She'd celebrated her thirtieth birthday in April, and she still didn't own property or a car.

"Sorry, baby," he apologized, kissing her mussed hair.

She blew Preston an air kiss. "Apology accepted."

Lowering his head, Preston brushed his mouth over hers in a peace offering. "I've plotted the first act of the play."

Settling against his chest, Chandra closed her eyes. "Tell me about it."

Preston wrapped his arms around her waist. "You can interrupt me whenever you need clarification. As I mentioned before, the opening scene will be Josette getting off a ship in New Orleans. She garners a lot of attention not only because she's very beautiful but because she's wearing an Empire-waist gown that is now the rage in Paris."

"Does she look like a woman of color?"

"Her mother, Marie, is mulatto and Josette is a quadroon. Although fair in coloring, she wouldn't be able to pass for white. Her mother meets her at the pier with her household slaves."

Chandra opened her eyes. "Her mother owns slaves?"

"Yes, baby. Many *gens de couleur* owned slaves. Marie, as *plaçée* to a wealthy Creole planter, would have a personal maid and manservant."

"Please continue, Preston."

"Marie is going on about the upcoming quadroon ball and she has arranged for Josette to become *plaçée* to the son of the wealthiest man in New Orleans. Marie overrides Josette's protest when she taps her on the hand with her fan. They arrive home and Josette retreats to her room where she writes a letter to a young man she met in Paris. He is also a man of color, but she knows her mother will not permit her to marry an African. In order to hide her liaison from her mother, she addresses the letter to his sister to give to him.

"The next scene is at the shop of a dressmaker where Josette is to be fitted for a ball gown. She spies a man in the latest European fashion lounging on a chair. When their gazes meet, she suddenly finds herself feeling faint. He gets up to assist, but Marie steps in between them to aid her daughter. The shopkeeper revives her with smelling salts, then leads her into a dressing room.

"Josette suffers through being measured and having to select fabric for her dress. When she emerges from the dressing room she sees the strange man with a woman. I've already established that Francesca is Pascual's sister and a vampire who has to feed, whereas Pascual doesn't."

Chandra smiled. "I like that."

Preston inclined his head. "I thought you would. Josette gets to see Pascual again at the flower market. He buys a nosegay, then presents it to her. She is reluctant to accept it, because her mother has lectured her about talking to men to whom she hasn't been formally introduced. But Josette thinks herself more French than American, and the girls with whom she interacted at her school thought of themselves as libertines. A few of them had become mistresses to wealthy men, while others took lovers by their leave. Pascual gives her a card, asking whether he can call on her. She tucks the card into her reticule, then presents him with her back. When Pascual tells her the woman she saw him with was his sister, she tells him he will hear from her."

"Does she contact him?"

"Yes. She sends the maid with a note to Pascual at the boardinghouse where he's living during his stay in the Crescent City. She invites him to share afternoon tea with her and her mother, a ritual she discovered during a visit to London. I haven't fleshed out the scene between the three of them because you have tell me how Pascual supports himself."

"He's a hide exporter. He has turned vast tracts of land into horse and cattle ranches."

"Nice," Preston complimented. "What does he do to pass his time in New Orleans?"

"He does what most men of leisure during that time did—whore, drink and gamble."

Throwing back his head, Preston laughed. "Damn, baby, you didn't have to say it like that."

"Well, it's true."

"You're probably right."

"I am right," Chandra argued softly. "I did the research. Knowing this, will Marie be receptive to him?"

"She's charmed by him because he appears to be a wealthy foreigner, but she has signed a contract to have

Josette become *placée* to an American. Her dilemma is that the contract is as legal and binding as a marriage certificate. If she permits Josette to become involved with Pascual, then she's risking her future because her daughter's father may withdraw his financial support. *Placée* notwithstanding, she cannot insult or embarrass a white man. Pascual shocks Marie when he offers to make Josette his wife, not his mistress or *placée*. Unfortunately, Marie will not concede, and tells him he can find another quadroon if he attends the ball. Pascual has decided he wants Josette. The scene ends when he tells Francesca he will have Josette. He will go as far as ordering Francesca to turn Josette into a vampire."

Chandra applauded, her heart racing with excitement. "Bravo! Bravo! What have you planned for the second act?"

Lacing his fingers together over her belly, Preston pulled Chandra closer. "You and I will have to work closely together on act two."

"Why?"

"This act will be solely about seduction. It will begin with the ball and the Regency dance, which can be the English Country Dance, the Cotillion, Quadrille, waltz and *your* tango. Of course, I'll have to hire a choreographer. Josette's benefactor will be introduced in this act."

"What does he look like?"

Preston paused. "All I'm going to say is, physically he's the complete opposite of Pascual."

"Don't tell me he's blond, short and frail-looking."

Preston nodded.

"No, Preston! The only thing missing is spectacles and he would be a nineteenth-century nerd."

"What do you want, baby?"

"Make him a worthy competitor. He can be blond, but he can also be gorgeous. Also make him a little older. Perhaps early thirties. Compared to Pascual's two hundred-plus years he's a mere baby."

Preston gave her a long, penetrating look. "Okay. Basil, who will be called Bazz-el, will be Pascual's mirror image."

"Don't forget to include a voodoo ritual replete with drums and dancers. I want everyone in the audience to feel as if they'd been transported to the motherland."

Lowering his head, he nipped the side of her neck. "How would you like to take a trip to the motherland with me?"

"What are you talking about, Preston?"

"Let's go back to bed."

Chandra flashed a saucy grin. "And do what, baby?"

"I don't know, baby," he teased. "Perhaps you can show me what to do."

"Stand up, Preston," she ordered. "Come on, darling. Please stand up."

Deciding it was better to humor Chandra than continue to question her, Preston pushed to his feet. He'd regained his footing at the same time she went to her knees, facing him.

"No!" Preston bellowed like a wounded animal when he felt the heat of her mouth on his sex. Chandra had wrapped her arms around his thighs, holding him fast.

He hardened quickly as he stared, stunned, at his penis moving in and out of her mouth. Eyes closed, fists clenched, he succumbed to the most exquisite pleasure he'd ever had in his life.

Bending over, he forcibly extricated her arms, slid down to the cool water and pushed inside her with one, sure thrust. Between sanity and insanity, heaven and hell, he drove into her like a man possessed. Then without warning, he pulled out at the last possible moment, moaning as he spilled his passion in the water.

"You didn't like it?" she asked innocently.

Preston glared at Chandra, his gaze raking her face like talons. "I loved it, Chandra. But you're driving me crazy," he gasped. He should've known what to expect; what had just occurred was ripped from the pages of her journal.

Moisture dotted Chandra's face when she opened her eyes. "That makes two of us. Now, please let me up. I need to take a shower."

He stepped out of the tub, she feeling the heat from his gaze on her wet body as she headed to a corner shower stall. Closing the door, she turned on the water, then slid down to the tiled floor. Her attempt to live out her fantasy with Preston had nearly met with disaster. He'd entered her without a condom during the most fertile time of her cycle. If he hadn't pulled out, then the risk of her becoming pregnant was more than ninety-nine percent.

The door opened; Preston stepped in and closed the door behind him. Anchoring his hands under her shoulders, he eased her to stand. "We can't do that again. Not unless you want a baby."

Water spiked her lashes when Chandra glanced up at Preston. "It won't happen again."

"I want it to happen again," he crooned. "It just can't happen unless I'm wearing protection."

He pulled her to his chest, rocking her from side to side. They stood under the falling water, rinsing the lingering soap from their bodies. Minutes later they stood on a bath mat drying each other's body.

They'd made love—twice, discussed *Death's Kiss* and had to prepare for Ray Hardy and his wife.

Chapter 11

Chandra knew she'd made an error in judgment when she'd initiated oral sex. Although he'd claimed to have liked it, she wasn't certain whether he appreciated her assertive take-charge approach. Although not as sexually experienced as some of her classmates and/or coworkers—her sum total of liaisons was limited to two—she'd become a participant whenever sex became the topic of conversation. It was those explicit conversations, coupled with pornographic films, that fueled her fertile imagination.

She'd bonded with three single female teachers at Cambridge Valley Prep. When they didn't have dates, they usually got together on either Friday or Saturday nights. If they met in her apartment, then it'd become Chandra's responsibility to provide the food and beverages. In order to avoid a conflict, they'd set up a rotating schedule for their get-togethers.

One night someone rented a pornographic movie, and when the images appeared on the television screen it was to stunned silence. They laughed at most of the antics because the acting was so contrived, but viewing the movie served as a pleasant diversion for their girls' night.

Afterward, they scheduled one day a month as "naughty night." Most times they wound up critiquing the acting, or lack thereof, plot and set decorations.

Chandra pulled on a pair of faded jeans, thick white socks and a cotton sweater with a rolled neckline and cuffs in a soft oatmeal shade. She'd towel-dried her hair, brushed it and pulled it into a ponytail. Preston told her their meeting with the Hardys was casual and informal.

She cleaned up the bathroom, then turned her attention to making the bed.

"I didn't invite you here to do housework."

She turned to see Preston in the doorway, hands folded at his hips. Jeans, a navy blue waffle-weave pullover and running shoes completed his casual look. He'd showered but hadn't shaved.

"I have a thing about unmade beds," she retorted.

"Get over it, Chandra. Now, come eat breakfast."

Chandra didn't move. "Are you pissed with me?"

Preston lowered his hands as his expression stilled, becoming a mask of stone. "What are you talking about?"

"Are you upset because I took the initiative in making love to you?"

Closing the distance between them, Preston stood over her like an avenging angel. "Do you really hear yourself? Did I tell you that I was upset? Do I look upset?"

"I don't know, Preston."

"Well, I'm not. It's not about who initiates what. For me it's about enjoying making love with you. Now if you're talking about unprotected sex, then that's something we can discuss. If I do father a child, then I want it to be by mutual consent. When I asked you whether you want marry or have children, your response was you do, but it can't be now. And to me, that translates into my protecting you."

There was something about the way Preston was looking at her that made Chandra feel as if he could read her mind. "I understand."

"No, you don't understand, baby. You truly have no idea what you are doing to me."

With wide eyes, she asked, "What am I doing to you?"

"You're turning me into a madman. Whenever we're apart I find myself obsessing about you, while trying to come up with any excuse to bring us together. You're beautiful and you're smart. I love the way you smell, how you taste and your feistiness. And I love the fact that you're a tad bit wicked in bed."

Chandra took a step, resting her head on Preston's shoulder. She longed to tell him that she loved everything about him, yet was reluctant because she didn't want a repeat of what she'd had with Laurence. She'd been the first one to bare her soul, confessing that she was in love with him. Only after their breakup did she realize he'd never professed to loving her. He wanted her, adored her, was proud of her, but the dreaded four-letter word was never a part of his verbal repertoire.

"Just a tad?" she whispered in the fabric of his shirt.

Resting his chin on the top of Chandra's head, Preston smiled. "Is there more?"

Easing back, she stared into the velvety dark eyes

of the man who made her feel things she didn't want to feel and made her do "naughty" things to him. "There's a lot more."

Attractive lines fanned out around Preston's eyes when his smile grew wider. "I can assure you that you won't get a complaint from me."

"We'll see."

"Should I be afraid of you, C.E.?"

She patted his chest. "No. P.J. I just want you to enjoy it."

"And I promise you, I will." His eyes caressed her face seconds before he grasped her hand and led her out of the bedroom and into the kitchen.

A cool breeze wafted through screens at the quartet of windows spanning one wall. Roberta Eaton claimed that the kitchen was the heart of any home, and judging from Preston's it wasn't only the heart but also its lifeblood. The generously proportioned space combined classic materials with practical up-to-date amenities.

White cabinetry, stainless steel appliances, black granite countertops afforded the kitchen the appearance of those in the grand estates of a bygone era. A third sink fitted in an oversize island was ideal for several cooks to work at the same time.

Her smile was dazzling. "I like it."

Preston dropped a kiss on Chandra's hair. She liked his kitchen and what he felt for her went far beyond a casual liking. He wondered how Chandra would react if she knew he wanted a commitment from her—that they would see each other exclusively.

After he and Elaine mutually decided to go their separate ways, he'd almost become a serial dater. He'd dated women he liked and the ones he tolerated were there to fill up the empty spaces when he wasn't writing. It took a great deal of soul-searching for him to realize he didn't need to see a different woman every other week, or sleep with a different one every couple of months. Preston knew some of the women wanted more, but he refused to offer more. His work had become a jealous mistress he didn't want to give up.

Whenever he began a new project, he wrote in seclusion, averaging four hours of sleep and eating one meal a day. He'd shower, but wouldn't bother to shave. It was during his marathon writing sessions that he refused all social invitations. With Chandra Eaton he could have both: writing and the woman.

"Will you help me prepare dinner?"

Chandra was caught off guard by the query. The last time she'd offered to help Preston he'd snarled at her before relenting. "Of course I'll help you. What's on the menu?"

"I've planned to roast a rack of lamb with an herb crust, couscous, glazed carrots and homemade ice cream."

"How would you like to be my personal chef?"

"I think we can work out something?"

"How much are you going to charge me?" she asked.

"We'll begin with one kiss three times a day for the first week. Then we'll increase it to two, three times a day, for the following week."

"What happens the third week?"

"Why three, three times a week, and so on and so on."

Chandra flashed a sensual moue. "It sounds as if I'm going to have to hand out a lot of kisses."

"You can't have it both ways, beautiful. I have to charge you something."

Going on tiptoe, she wrapped her arms around Preston's neck. "Can't I at least get the family discount?"

Preston's lids came down, hiding his innermost feelings. This was the Chandra Eaton he'd come to look for: soft, sexy *and* teasing.

"You can't get a family discount until you officially become family."

Chandra knew in which direction the conversation was going, and she wanted no part of it. Fortunately, the distinctive chime from his cell phone preempted her reply.

Preston leaned in closer. "To be continued." Turning on his heels, he walked over to the cooking island to answer the phone, glancing at the name on the display. "Good morning, Ray."

"That it is, P.J.," Raymond Hardy shouted, followed by a gravelly chuckle. "Beth just gave birth to a baby girl!"

"Congratulations! How are Beth and the baby?"

"Paige is doing well, but Beth's going to be in the hospital longer than she'd expected. She had to undergo a Cesarean."

A slight frown creased Preston's forehead when Chandra opened and closed drawers in the island. He knew she was looking for pieces for place settings. She exuded a nervous energy that wouldn't permit her to sit and relax.

"It's going to be a while before she's going to feel like doing anything around the house, I'm giving you guys a gift of a cleaning service for the next month."

There was silence before Ray spoke again. "Thanks, man. That's really going to come in handy, because my bank account is hovering around zero after I had to pay my lawyer to sue my sonofabitch ex-collaborator for selling my songs to that slimy record producer."

Preston knew Ray and his wife were strapped for cash, and paying for a cleaning service was his way of lessening their burden. He'd done the same for his sister after she delivered each of her two sets of twins. He'd also paid for a nanny with the second set, only because Yolanda was overwhelmed having to care for four young boys under the age of four.

Preston nodded although Ray couldn't see him. "There's no need to thank me. I know you can't boil water, and Beth is a little obsessive when it comes to having a clean house." The expression "One hand washes the other and both hands wash the face" came to mind. He'd asked Ray to pen the music and lyrics for *Death's Kiss,* not to offer the man a generous commission but because he was one of the best in the business.

"I'm glad you said it, because whenever I mention it she goes off on me," Ray said, laughing. "As soon as Beth is up and moving around without too much difficulty, I'll call you and we can set up another time to meet."

"Don't rush it, Ray."

"I know you, P.J. Once you get something in your head, you're like a dog with a bone. You just won't let go. Now, if you're stepping out of your comfort zone to come up with a musical drama, I know it's going to be spectacular. Tell me a little about it and I'll begin working on something on this end."

Preston gave him a brief overview of the plot. "I need music for a ball and a voodoo ritual." There was a moment of silence, and he knew Ray's mind had shifted into overdrive.

"Early nineteenth-century music and dance would include the Cotillion, English Country Dance and perhaps a Quadrille."

"Throw in a waltz and tango and you've covered all the dances."

"I can understand a waltz, because it had become quite a dance phenomena about 1790, but the tango didn't become popular outside of the ghettos of Argentina until the early twentieth century."

The reason Preston had selected Raymond Hardy to write the score was not only because the man was a musical genius but also a music history expert. He'd appeared in several documentaries chronicling the history of musical genres.

"Pascual is a vampire who originated in Argentina."

"So, he's a time-traveler," Ray said. The excitement in his voice was evident.

"You've got it," Preston confirmed.

"This is very interesting, P.J. What if I write a love theme in Spanish, French and English?"

"You're a musical genius, Ray." He hadn't told the composer about Chandra's suggestion to have a song sung in English and Spanish. Adding French would be in keeping with early nineteenth-century multicultural and multilingual New Orleans.

"You've given me a lot to work with, P.J. Let me see what I can come up with. By the way, when do you project auditioning and rehearsals?"

"Not until the spring." It would take him that long to complete and fine-tune the dialogue. "I've decided to go local with this production. In other words, I want local raw talent. If I'm going to direct and produce, then I'll have a much smaller budget from which to work. And if Beth decides to go back to work, then I'd like her to design the sets."

"I'm sure she'll do it, even if she has to ask her mother to come up and watch Paige while she's working."

"I don't want to infringe on her time with your daughter, but she is my first choice."

"I'll ask her, and then e-mail you Beth's response. P.J.," he said after a pause, "you've got yourself another winner."

Preston stared at Chandra as she moved around the kitchen in an attempt to find what she needed to set the table in the dining area. Instead of sitting around and waiting for him to wait on her, she'd assumed a take-charge approach.

"Thanks, Ray. Give Beth my best and give Paige a kiss from her Uncle P.J."

Ray laughed again. "Will do. Later, buddy."

Preston ended the call. He'd wanted to tell Ray that he never would've come up with the premise for the play if it hadn't been for Chandra Eaton's erotic dreams and her taunt that all of his work was tragically brooding. With ethereal romantic period costumes, historically correct set decorations and star-crossed lovers, *Death's Kiss* was certain to become a stunningly visual feast, just like the sexy woman moving confidently around the kitchen.

His gaze lingered on the shapely roundness of her hips in the fitted jeans. Her conservative style of dress had artfully concealed a curvy lush body that sent his libido into overdrive.

"Thank you for setting the table. It looks very nice."

Chandra turned to face Preston. She hadn't heard him when he'd come up behind her. "You're very welcome."

"I usually don't use a tablecloth, but it does add a nice touch," he admitted.

She suspected he probably took his meals at the cook-

ing island rather than the table, but held her tongue, because she didn't like verbally sparring with Preston.
Debating an issue was one thing, but arguing over inane
issues tended to upset her emotional equilibrium.

"I suppose you overheard my conversation with Ray.
His wife had the baby, so it's just going to be the two
of us."

"That's okay."

Preston's expressive eyebrows lifted a fraction before
settling into place. "If you don't have anything on your
to-do list, I'd like you to hang out here with me for a few
days so we can flesh out the second act." He was anxious to finalize the plotting process so he could begin
the actual writing process.

"I can't commit until tomorrow."

Belinda had promised Chandra she would let her
know when a moving company would deliver the bedroom, living room and kitchen furniture, and she wanted
to be available if or when a school district contacted her
for an interview.

"No problem." Resting his hands on her shoulders,
Preston steered Chandra to the cooking island. "I want
you to sit down and relax." He settled her on a tall stool.
"After breakfast we'll go on a walking tour of the valley." Resting his elbows on the granite surface, he smiled
at the young woman who'd managed to fill the empty
spaces in his solitary life. "Do you like blueberry but-
termilk pancakes?"

Her eyes brightened like a young child's on Christmas
morning. "You've got to be kidding. They're my favorite." Her eyes narrowed. "Who told you I like blueberry
pancakes?"

"No one."

Chandra sat up straighter. "I don't believe you. Someone in my family *had* to tell you."

"Okay, baby, I'll tell you. It was your mother."

Heat seared her cheeks as if someone had placed a lighted match to her face. "You told my mother I was staying over with you?"

"She wanted to know if we were coming back to Paoli for brunch, so I had to tell her we were going to Kennett Square. Does my telling her upset you?"

"No."

At thirty, Chandra didn't have to rely on her parents for financial support, but she was living at home—even if it was only temporarily. If she didn't come home she didn't have to call and give an account of her whereabouts. Yet she still didn't want to advertise when she was spending the night with a man.

"I assured your mother that you were safe with me."

"Why? Because you're a nice guy?"

"Being a nice guy has nothing to do with it. It's just that I would never consciously hurt you."

The seconds ticked as Chandra's gaze met and fused with Preston's. He'd claimed he would never consciously hurt her and she suspected that neither did Laurence. But it happened. Laurence had to have known of his parents' biases, yet he'd pursued her relentlessly until she finally agreed to go out with him. Her ex-fiancé hadn't hurt her as much as he'd deceived her.

"That's nice to hear," she drawled.

"You still don't trust me, do you, Chandra?"

"I'll trust you until you give me cause not to."

Preston ran a finger down the length of her nose. "Let's hope that never happens."

Chandra flashed a smile she didn't feel. *I pray it never*

happens, she mused. She knew she had to shake off the sense of distrust or she would never enjoy her relationship with Preston. Pulling back her shoulders, she exhaled a breath as her heart swelled with an emotion she'd thought she would never feel again. Despite her decision not to— she knew she was falling in love with Preston Tucker.

Chapter 12

Chandra came to a complete stop. She didn't want to believe she was that tired. Her calves were aching. After a breakfast of the most incredibly delicious pancakes she'd ever eaten, she had retreated to her bedroom where she'd put on a pair of running shoes and joined Preston as he led her on a walking tour.

The exterior of his home was as exquisite as the interior. The boxwood garden, covering a quarter acre, was a riot of exotic ferns and flowers. She'd recognized late-blooming roses, hydrangea in hues ranging from deep purple to snow white, dahlia in various colors and sizes and chrysanthemum—some that were six inches in diameter. There were sections with all white, yellow, pink and red flowers in different varieties she didn't recognize, and if she could she wouldn't be able to pronounce.

A shed several hundred feet from the rear of the house

was filled with cords of firewood, while two dozen stumps that would eventually become firewood were covered with a clear plastic tarp. Preston revealed he chopped wood during the winter months and worked out in his building's health club whenever he stayed over in Philadelphia to keep in shape. She'd had her answer to how he'd maintained a slender, toned physique.

Lowering her head, she rested her hands on her knees. "We're going to have to stop while I rest my legs before we start back."

Preston looped an arm around her waist. "Let's get off the road and sit down under that tree." Of the twenty miles of rolling hills and country roads that made up the Brandywine Valley, they'd covered more than five miles.

They sat down under the sweeping branches of a towering oak tree with leaves of brilliant autumnal colors in orange and yellow. The midmorning temperatures were at least ten to fifteen degrees cooler than they'd been the day before. Preston wondered whether summer was about to take its last curtain call. The next weekend would also signal the end of daylight saving time, and with it came fewer hours of daylight. He wanted to complete his first draft of *Death's Kiss* before Thanksgiving and that would give him the winter months to edit and reedit to his critical satisfaction.

Chandra, sitting between Preston's outstretched legs, rested the back of her head against his shoulder. The view from where they sat was awe-inspiring, ethereal.

"I can't believe I've lived in Pennsylvania most of my life, yet I've never visited this part of the state."

Winding several strands of Chandra's hair around his forefinger, Preston rubbed the pad of his thumb over its softness; he released it, watching as it floated into a corkscrew curl.

"You've never been to Longwood Gardens?"

She shook her head. "Unfortunately I haven't."

"Most Philadelphia schoolchildren visit the gardens at least once during a class trip."

Tilting her chin, Chandra smiled at him staring down at her. "Well, I must have had a deprived childhood."

"Where did you go to school?" Preston asked.

"My brother, sisters and I attended Chesterfield Academy."

Preston wanted to tell her that she was anything but deprived. Dr. Dwight and Roberta Eaton had enrolled their children in one of Philadelphia's most prestigious private schools, while he and his sister took advantage of the best that the public school system had to offer.

"I assume you went to Europe instead of Longwood for class trips."

Chandra placed her hands atop the larger one resting on her belly.

"Only the upperclassmen were permitted to leave the country. I spent the second half of my junior year in Spain studying and occasionally taking side trips to Portugal and France. It was the first time I was bitten by the traveling bug. I could've easily lived in a different country every year." She glanced up at Preston again. "How about you? Are you a vagabond or a homebody?"

He smiled. "I'm definitely a homebody."

"Where's your spirit of adventure?" she teased.

"My spirit of adventure means traveling first class."

Chandra shifted to face Preston, she half on, half off his body. "I think I've found my Pascual."

He frowned. "Say what?"

"You," she said. "I hadn't realized when I began developing Pascual that you and he shared similar physical and psychological characteristics. His mantra is enjoying the best immortality has to offer him."

"That's where you're wrong, Chandra. I'm not immortal."

"Okay. But do you gamble?"

"What do you mean by gamble?" he asked, answering her question with one of his own.

"Do you play cards?"

"Yes. *If* I do play, then it's either poker or blackjack."

Pressing her chest to his, Chandra brushed her mouth over his. "Perfect. Blackjack, or as the French call it, *vingt-et-un,* whist or cribbage were the popular card games during Josette's time. Poker didn't become popular until after 1830. Pascual will become quite the center of attention when he introduces a new card game known as poker."

"Poker and the tango," Preston murmured under his breath. "What other surprises does he plan to spring on the curious inhabitants of the Crescent City?"

Excitement shimmered in Chandra's eyes. "I think that's enough. The men will be caught up in the challenge of learning a new card game and the women either mesmerized or scandalized by the mysterious stranger. Can you imagine their reaction at the ball when Pascual presents himself to Josette, then leads her in a tango? It will be another one hundred years before women show their ankles, but more than an ankle will be on display that night. It will also be leg *and* thigh."

"That is scandalous," Preston concurred.

"Marie is mortified because she believes Pascual has deliberately ruined Josette's chance to become *placée* to the man she has chosen for her. But as the night progresses, she notices many of the mothers are scheming to get Pascual to notice their daughters."

"Does he get to dance with the other young women?"

Chandra nodded. "Yes. But with them he is the perfect gentleman, mouthing the proper greetings and thanking them for permitting him to bask in their beauty. One minute he's there, then as a rush of air comes into the ballroom, causing candles to flicker, he's gone."

Preston went completely still. He could see the scene being played out in his head. Chandra had just given him what he needed to set the stage for the all-important, very dramatic act two.

"When does Josette see him again?"

"He's waiting in her bedroom when she returns from the ball. He hides behind a dressing screen while her maid enters the room to help her ready herself for bed. But Josette orders her out, saying she doesn't need her assistance. After the woman leaves, Josette locks the door and closes the casement windows.

"Pascual emerges from behind the screen. He steps into the role as maid and seducer when he removes the pins from Josette's hair, then removes her dress. This scene must be very sensual, Preston. The actors aren't going to have sex onstage. However, they must give the illusion that they are making love. Perhaps this scene can take place where the audience views it through a sheer curtain as if peering through a bedroom window with a single candle for illumination. The lighting will become as much a character as Josette and Pascual.

"When the scene ends, there shouldn't be a sound in the theater. It will be your test as the director that your actors have hypnotized the audience. Every woman should want to be on the stage and in that bed with Pascual, and the same with every man, who is telling himself that he is *the one* seducing the beautiful young virgin. Once the lighting fades to black and there is stunned silence you'll know immediately that you've hit the mark."

Preston was hard-pressed not to make love to Chandra. The scene she'd just described was exactly as she had written in her journal. She'd prepared herself for bed and instead of a lamp, she'd lit a candle. The candle was about to burn out when her mysterious lover enters the room. Chandra had described the lovemaking scene so vividly that Preston felt not like a voyeur but a participant in the act.

"That's not going to be an easy feat, because I've never directed a love scene."

Chandra placed her fingertips over his mouth. "It's not about the dialogue, darling. It's all about what is visual, and therefore sensual. If I were sitting in the audience I would want to hear the sound of her hairpins when they fall to the floor and the whisper of fabric being removed as they undress."

Capturing her wrist, Preston pulled the delicate hand away from his mouth. "Do you want to hear them make love?"

Chandra's brow flickered with indecision. "No," she said after a lengthy pause. "I think it would cheapen the scene. It's not a porno flick, where the sounds are essential to the movie. I believe it would work better if Josette would gasp aloud when Pascual penetrates her. This will let the audience know that she is indeed a virgin. It could conclude with a sigh of satisfaction—again making the audience aware that the lovemaking was wonderful."

"You've missed your calling, Chandra."

She shook her head. "I've never wanted to act."

"I'm not talking about acting."

"What are you talking about?"

Bringing her hand to his mouth, Preston pressed a kiss to the palm. "Writing."

"Thanks for the compliment, but I've never been interested in writing. I prefer to read."

Preston's gaze narrowed when he saw dark clouds moving in from the west. He stood up, bringing Chandra up with him. "I think we better head back because it looks as if we're in for some rain." He pointed. "Look at those clouds."

Chandra didn't need a second warning when she saw how dark the sky had become. She forgot about the pain in her legs when she jogged alongside Preston when they headed in the direction of the house. She'd been so engrossed in talking about *Death's Kiss* that she hadn't noticed the weather had changed.

The wind had picked up, gusts swirling leaves and twigs. Rain had begun falling when the house came into view, then came down in torrents by the time they reached the back door. The wet clothes pasted to Chandra's body raised goose bumps; her teeth were chattering when Preston unlocked the door and deactivated the security system.

"I'm going to take a shower," she announced as she kicked off her soggy running shoes.

Preston, following suit, slipped out of his running shoes. He stripped off his shirt, jeans and underwear, dropping them in a large wicker basket in the space that doubled as a laundry and mudroom.

Walking on bare feet, he made his way into the half bath off the kitchen. Stepping in the shower stall, he turned on the water, gritting his teeth as icy pellets fell on his head. Then he adjusted the temperature to lukewarm. Preston lingered long enough to shampoo his cropped hair and wash his body.

His mind was a maelstrom of vivid images of what Chandra had suggested for the play's second act as he stepped out and dried himself with a bath sheet. He hadn't lied when he told her she should've been a writer. She was an untapped talent, her fertile mind lying fallow; all that was needed was a kernel of an idea to yield a harvest worthy of a literary feast.

He was Preston J. Tucker, the critically acclaimed dramatist who'd won awards, was the recipient of a McArthur genius grant and who had been compared to some of the most celebrated playwrights of the past century. However, when he compared what he'd written and produced to what he was currently collaborating on with Chandra, it paled in comparison.

Chandra had what he lacked: a highly developed sense of visualization. He relied on strong dialogue, characterization and simplistic costuming and stark sets to tell his message, while Chandra added the element of sensual visuals.

The big screen would be the perfect vehicle for *Death's Kiss*. Love scenes could be performed without the limitations that usually went along with a stage production. Nudity on the stage wasn't taboo, but Preston found it more a hindrance than an enticement to put theatergoers in seats. Once the initial shock of frontal nudity was assuaged—then what? He'd always asked himself whether the production would've stood on its own merits without the nudity. If the answer was yes, then he deleted it.

Wrapping the terry cloth fabric around his waist, he walked out of the bath, heading toward his bedroom. The connecting door was ajar and he could hear Chandra opening and closing drawers. Preston would've suggested they share a shower, but he didn't want a repeat of what had happened earlier that morning.

It took Herculean strength for him to pull out when he realized he was making love to Chandra without a condom. He'd pulled out when it had been the last thing he'd wanted to do, and he knew then he wasn't the same person he'd been before meeting her.

Preston believed that he would eventually marry and father children, but *when* was the question. He'd celebrated his thirty-eighth birthday March seventeenth, and as he'd done since turning thirty-five, he went through a period of self-examination, asking himself if he was satisfied with what he'd accomplished, had he learned not to repeat past mistakes, did he like who he was and what he'd become and finally if he was ready to share himself and what he'd accomplished with someone with whom he would spend the rest of his life. All the questions yielded an affirmative. The exception was the last one.

His passion for writing had become paramount, and jealously guarded his privacy and his time. But that had changed with Chandra Eaton. It was as if he couldn't get enough of her—in and out of bed. She hadn't shocked him when she had taken him into her mouth. It was more of a surprise because he hadn't expected it. He'd suspected she was capable of great passion because of what she'd written in her journal, but he still hadn't known whether her dreams were real or imagined. That no longer mattered because he wanted Chandra Eaton to be the last woman in his life.

Dropping the towel on the padded bench at the foot of the bed, he'd pulled on a pair of boxer-briefs, sweatpants and a long-sleeved tee when he heard a groan. Taking long strides, he crossed the room, opened the door wider to find Chandra writhing on the bed, clutching the back of her leg. She had on a bra and a pair of bikini panties.

His heartbeat kicked into a higher rhythm as he sat on the side of the bed. Reaching for her, he pressed her face to his chest. "What's the matter, baby?"

"My leg," she gasped as the muscle tightened even more.

"Move your hand."

Preston stared at the lump that had come up on the back of her calf. "It looks as if you have a muscle cramp. I'm going to have to massage it to get the blood flowing again."

He'd experienced enough cramps when he'd played football in high school, and then in college, to last him several lifetimes. His interest in competitive sports ended once he broke his nose. After it healed a plastic surgeon wanted to reset it, but he didn't want to have to relive the pain that left his face bruised and swollen for weeks.

Chandra had experienced severe menstrual cramps, but the pain in her leg surpassed any she'd had. "Please don't massage it too hard," she said between clenched teeth.

Preston's fingers grazed the tight area. "I'm going to cover your calf with a warm cloth before I massage it."

She half rose from the bed. "Aren't you supposed to ice it?"

"I'll ice it later."

He entered the bathroom, wet a facecloth under running hot water and returned to the bedroom to place it over Chandra's leg. Lying beside her, he kissed the end of her nose. "Did it just cramp up?"

Chandra's smile came out like a grimace. "It was bothering me earlier."

"Why didn't you say something?"

"I'd asked you to stop so I could rest my legs."

"Resting your legs isn't the same as saying you had a leg cramp."

She closed her eyes, shutting out his thunderous expression. "There's no need to get testy, Preston. It's not that critical."

"That's your opinion."

Chandra opened her eyes and glared at him glaring back at her. "If you're spoiling for a fight, then you won't get one from me, Preston Tucker, because with the pain that's kicking my butt I might say something that wouldn't be very intelligent or ladylike."

Preston counted slowly to three. He wasn't about to get into it with Chandra over something that didn't warrant an argument. If she'd told him that her leg was hurting, then he would've suggested they put off walking for another time.

"I don't fight with women."

"My bad," she drawled. "I meant argue."

"And I don't argue with women."

Another spasm gripped Chandra, preempting her comeback. "Argh-h!"

Galvanized into action, Preston moved to the foot of the bed. Removing the cloth, he kneaded the area gently with his thumbs, alternating applying pressure with massaging her calf. Fifteen minutes into his ministration, the lump disappeared.

"Don't move," Preston said in a soft voice. "I'm going to get some ice."

Chandra couldn't move when she felt him get up off the bed, even if her life depended upon it. She'd endured the most excruciating pain possible, and now that it was gone she feared moving because she didn't know if it would return.

She gasped again, this time when icy cold penetrated her limb. Preston had filled a plastic bag with ice, pressed it against her calf and covered it with a towel to absorb the moisture.

She gave him a dazzling smile when he lay beside her again. "I'm sorry I snapped at you." He stared at her under heavy lids, and she thought he wasn't going to accept her apology.

"Are you really sorry, or are you saying it because you think that's what I want to hear?"

Unbidden tears filled her eyes, shocking Chandra. She was the Eaton girl who rarely cried. Even when she fell and hurt herself she refused to cry. She was the tough tomboy sister who threw tantrums when she had to wear a dress, while Donna and Belinda loved playing dress-up with frilly dresses and high heels.

The first and only time she'd become hysterical was when she'd returned to the States for a family emergency and was told that her sister and brother-in-law had been killed by a drunk driver. Her father had contacted her in Belize, but refused to tell her what the emergency was until she walked through the front door of her parents' house to find everyone waiting for her—everyone but Donna.

Preston froze when he saw the tears well up in Chandra's eyes. Lines of concern etched his forehead. "What's the matter, baby?"

She sniffed back the tears before they fell. "I don't know. I suppose falling in love…" Her words trailed off when she realized what she was about to admit.

Preston's eyes narrowed. "What did you say?"

"Forget it."

"I don't think so, Chandra Eaton. Either you finish what you were going to say or I'm going to hold you hostage until you do."

"That's kidnapping."

His frown deepened. "Am I supposed to be scared?"

"No. I'm just warning you that kidnapping is a crime."

Threading his fingers through her hair, Preston cupped the back of her head in his hand. "It can't be a crime if you willingly come with me. Even your mother knows that." His fingers tightened on her scalp. "Now, who are you in love with?"

Chandra felt as if her brain was in tumult. Her feelings for Preston intensified each time she saw him, which led to ambivalence and confusion. She'd always thought of herself as levelheaded, independent and able to survive without having a man in her life.

She found Preston different from the other men in her life because he was a man in every sense of the word while the others were boys masquerading as men. He was straightforward and not into mind games.

Once she realized who he was, she'd thought his ego would surpass his talent, but it was just the opposite. When she'd introduced him to her family he appeared uncomfortable with his celebrity status.

Preston stared at her without blinking. "I need to

know if there's someone else so I can walk away before I find myself in too deep."

Panic shot through Chandra like a volt of electricity. Preston was talking about walking away when that was the last thing she wanted him to do. She'd admitted to Denise that if love did come knocking, then she was going to hold on to it as if her life was at stake.

"There's no one else." She rolled her eyes upward in supplication. "I swore a vow that I would never fall in love again but…" She pounded his shoulder with her fist.

Mindful of her leg, Preston gathered Chandra until she lay atop him. "It serves you right for making promises you can't keep. I've never said I wouldn't fall in love, so I'm not as conflicted as you."

Her head came up and she met his amused stare. "What are you talking about?"

"I have no problem admitting that I love you."

Chandra froze. "You love me?" The three words were pregnant with uncertainty.

"Yes. Why do you look so startled?"

"I thought we were just friends."

"Yeah, right," he drawled. "You're delusional, baby, if you believe that."

Her smile was dazzling. "How about friends with benefits?"

Preston winked at her. "There you go."

They lay together, each lost in their private thoughts. Chandra couldn't believe she'd confessed to a man she'd known a mere two weeks that she was in love with him.

Each time she left home her parents claimed she'd changed. She may have looked different outwardly, but inwardly she hadn't changed that much. It took living in

Belize for more than two years as a volunteer teacher to change her completely.

She'd left the States a girl and returned a woman.

The dark sky and the rhythmic tapping of rain against the windows lulled both of them into a protective cocoon where any and everything ceased to exist outside their cloistered world reserved for lovers.

Chapter 13

Chandra felt as if she was on the merry-go-round of eternal bliss and that she never wanted to get off.

She'd returned from the Brandywine Valley filled with a joy that prompted her to pinch herself to make certain she wasn't dreaming. She and Preston had stayed over until Monday afternoon, because she had to clean her apartment. The delivery of furniture that had been in Belinda's house was scheduled for Thursday. Preston had offered his cleaning service, but she'd turned him down because she needed to work off the tension that usually accompanied the onset of her menses.

The shipping company contacted her with the news that her trunk had arrived from Belize and wanted to set up a time for a delivery. She gave them her new address, and the trunk arrived an hour after all the other furniture was set up in the one-bedroom co-op with views of the riverside park dubbed Penn's Landing.

She'd just emptied the steamer trunk and covered it with a colorful handwoven Indian rug in the space near the door when the intercom rang, startling her.

Pressing a button, she spoke softly into the speaker. "Yes."

"I have a delivery for Ms. C. Eaton," announced a slightly accented male voice.

"Come on up." She pressed another button, disengaging the lock on the outer door.

Once the furniture was set up in its respective rooms, Chandra realized the space was much larger than she'd originally thought. Denise had had the walls painted a soft oyster-white and the wood floors sanded and covered with polyurethane, so all she had to do was wipe away layers of dust and clean the kitchen, bathroom and refrigerator. Her apartment was one of four on the top floor of a six-story building, which meant she didn't have to deal with someone making noise over her head.

The doorbell chimed Beethoven's Ninth Symphony. Denise had installed a programmable doorbell. Chandra had gone through the selections, deciding on a sample of the classical masterpiece.

She peered through the security eye. "Who is it?"

"Pascual."

Chandra opened the door to find Preston holding a vase filled with a large bouquet of pink and white roses and a bottle of champagne. "You are so crazy." She opened the door wider. "Please come in."

Dipping his head, Preston gave her a searing kiss. "Congratulations. Your place is beautiful." He handed her the bottle of champagne. "Should I take off my shoes?" The light coming from an overhead Tiffany-style hanging fixture reflected off the floor.

She smiled at him. Tonight he wore a pair of gray flannel slacks, navy blue mohair jacket, stark white shirt and purple silk tie. "No."

Preston debated, then slipped out of his slip-ons, walking in sock-covered feet and following Chandra into a living room with a white seating group with differing blue accessories.

"You can put the vase on the dining area table." Chandra indicated a solid oak oval pedestal table with seating for six. She climbed four steps to the kitchen and opened the refrigerator, placing the champagne on a shelf.

She'd gone to the supermarket the day before to fill the pantry with staples and the refrigerator with perishables. She didn't have a car, so she willingly paid to have her order delivered. Chandra wasn't certain how she would be able to get around without a car despite living in the city and having access to public transportation. Turning, she held out her arms and wasn't disappointed when Preston moved into her embrace. It'd been five days since she last saw him, but it could've been fifty-five.

"I have an interview for a position as a fifth-grade social studies teacher."

She'd checked her e-mail and received responses from two school districts. One wanted her to fill in for a special education teacher on leave, despite her not having special education certification, and the other, within walking distance, had advertised for a permanent substitute position. She'd called, setting up an appointment as a substitute.

Picking her up, Preston swung her around. "Congratulations!"

Tightening her hold on his neck, Chandra stared at the man to whom she'd given her love and her heart. How had she forgotten the sensual curve of his sexy mouth, the little tuft of hair under his lip and the hooded, brilliantly intelligent dark eyes. Then there was the body—the lean, muscled physique under tailored attire that made her crave him whether they were together or apart.

"Congratulate me *after* I get the position."

He smiled, the gesture tilting the corners of his mobile mouth upward. "I know you'll get it."

"Because you say so?"

Preston's gaze dropped to her mouth. "Because I know so."

"You're biased, Preston."

"I am when it concerns you."

"Put me down, Preston."

"Why?"

"Because I want to show you the rest of the apartment."

"You can show me the rest of the apartment after we get back."

"Where are we going, Preston?"

"We are going out to dinner."

Chandra stared at Preston as if he'd lost his mind. "I can't go out. Look at my hair. Look at me." She'd made an appointment for a full beauty makeover the day before her interview.

"I am looking at you, and you're beautiful. Remember when I wanted to take you to Le Bec-Fin and we had to postpone until another time?" Chandra nodded. "I tried to get a reservation for tonight, but they were booked. So, I decided to surprise the love of my life and take her to the Moshulu instead."

A smile spread across Chandra like the rays of the rising sun. "Put me down so I can change out of these jeans and into something a little less casual."

Preston kissed Chandra with his eyes before his mouth covered hers in a hot, hungry kiss. "Don't take too long." He lowered her until her feet touched the floor. "Go, before I change my mind and—"

"And what, Preston?"

"And have you for an appetizer, salad, entrée and dessert."

Taking a step, Chandra pressed her breasts to his hard chest. "Start counting. I'll be ready within fifteen minutes."

Preston sat across the table from Chandra in the main dining room on the permanently docked tall ship overlooking the Delaware River. If it had been warmer or earlier in the year, he would've reserved one of the open-air upper decks. He couldn't pull his gaze away from her face.

They'd ordered chilled jumbo shrimp with a horse-radish cocktail sauce from the raw bar and an appetizer of crispy duck wontons filled with hoisin barbecue duck confit and scallions and covered with a sweet soy glaze and chopped cilantro. Both passed on the soup and salad. Chandra's entrée choice was Gulf Coast mahimahi, while Preston selected the Amish chicken breast.

It'd taken her exactly fifteen minutes to change from a pullover and jeans and into a black wool sheath dress ending at her knees, matching sheer hose and suede pumps. A mauve hip-length mohair jacket pulled her winning look together. His gaze caressed her lightly made-up face—a face displayed to its best advantage with her shoulder-length hair fashioned into a classic chignon.

"You look incredibly beautiful tonight," he whispered reverently. "And if you tell me I'm biased I'm going to kiss you until you lose your breath," Preston threatened.

Chandra took a breath and affected a demure smile. Not seeing Preston for several days had afforded her time to step back and assess their whirlwind relationship. At first she'd begun second-guessing herself, believing it was because of her collaborating with him on *Death's Kiss* that Preston felt the need to profess to love her. That it all would come to a screeching halt once he completed the play.

Then she woke one morning, shaking with fear and uncertainty from a disturbing dream. It was upsetting because it was the first dream she'd had since returning from Belize. Unlike the others, in this one she could see a man's face. He was laughing and pointing at her, while others joined in with their own derisive mockery. She hadn't wanted to believe it, but the man was Preston Tucker.

She'd reached for her cell with the intent of calling and telling him she couldn't continue to see him, but her fingers refused to follow the dictates of her brain. Once she recovered from the terrifying nightmare, Chandra knew her distrust of men had reared its ugly head.

However, what she felt for Preston was real, pure. She hadn't fallen in love with Preston J. Tucker, award-winning playwright. She'd fallen in love with Preston, the man.

She loved him, Denise was in awe of him, Griffin had taken on the responsibility of representing him professionally and her parents liked him. Whenever she spoke to Roberta, she always asked about Preston.

"Thank you, Preston."

Chandra wanted to tell Preston he looked deliciously handsome, but couldn't get her tongue to form the words. *What the hell is wrong with me?* She managed to get one of Philly's most eligible bachelors to date her exclusively; meanwhile she was acting like an uptight snob who seemed not to want to give him the time of day.

Reaching across the table, Preston took Chandra's hand. He smiled, but the warm gesture did not reach his eyes. They were cold, his expression a mask of stone. "What's the matter?" he asked perceptively.

"Nothing, darling."

"Don't darling me, Chandra. I know when something is bothering you."

"Have you suddenly become clairvoyant, or have you always been able to read minds?"

Preston decided to ignore her acerbic retort. Something *was* bothering her and he intended to uncover what it was. Perhaps something or someone was bothering her. When he spoke to Chandra on Tuesday, she'd mentioned she had menstrual cramps, and that meant he had to wait to make love to her.

"No, but I grew up in a house with two females, so I'm familiar with them PMSing."

Chandra rolled her eyes. "For your information, I'm finished with my cycle," she whispered.

"If it's not that, then what is it, Chandra?"

She knew she had to tell Preston what had her on edge. "I had a dream the other night."

Preston's impassive expression did not change with her revelation. He'd waited weeks for her to tell him about the dreams that had become the foundation for his latest work. "Do you want to tell me about it?"

Chandra told him—everything. She saw his gaze grow hard, resentful. If they hadn't been in a public place, she knew she wouldn't have been able to rein in her emotions.

Preston signaled for the waiter, then reached into the pocket of his slacks to leave two large bills on the table. Pushing back his chair, he stood, came around the table and helped Chandra to her feet. He'd heard enough.

"Let's get out of here."

Chandra quickened her pace to keep up with Preston's longer legs. "Will you please slow down." She was half jogging and half running, and in a pair of heels. "What's going on, Preston?"

Tightening his grip on her hand, Preston shortened his stride. He had to leave the restaurant, or else cause a scene and bring attention to himself and Chandra. He'd grown up listening to his parents bicker and snipe at each other, and that was something he wanted to avoid, at all costs, with Chandra.

They were steps from her building when he felt composed enough to explain why he'd left the restaurant so abruptly. "When are you going to learn to trust me, Chandra? I'm aware that we've only been together a month, and I don't believe I've ever given you cause to mistrust me. I haven't dated or looked at another woman since we've been together. What is it you want? Tell me, what do I have to do?"

Chandra moved closer to Preston as much to feed off his body's heat as for solace. "I never said you cheated on me."

"You didn't have to," he countered. "What you refuse to do is trust me to love you, protect you, or to be there for you."

"You're overreacting."

"Hell, yeah, I'm overreacting. You can't tell me you weren't bothered by your dream if you keep looking at me sideways and hoping I'll mess up so you'll have an excuse to send me packing."

"That's not true, Preston."

"It has to be true, Chandra."

"Are you calling me a liar, Preston?"

"All I'm saying is that I don't believe you."

Chandra stopped abruptly, causing Preston to lose his footing. However, he recovered quickly, glaring down at her like an avenging angel. The streetlamps threw long and short shadows over his face, distorting his pleasant features.

She threw up her free hand. "I don't know what I can do or say to convince you that I *do* trust you."

Preston's eyes narrowed. "There is one thing you can do."

Pulling back her shoulders, she raised her chin. "What?"

A beat passed. "Marry me."

There came another pause before Chandra asked, "You're kidding, aren't you?"

"Do I look like I'm kidding?" Preston retorted.

Chandra started to walk, but she was thwarted when Preston pulled her back to where he stood. Her temper flared, invisible tongues of red-hot fire sweeping up her chest, scorching her face. "Do not play with me." She'd enunciated each word as if he were hard of hearing.

"I'm too old to play games, Chandra. I'm going to ask you one more time if you want to marry me, and if

I don't get an answer, then I'm going to walk away and never look back."

Chandra swallowed in an attempt to relieve the constriction in her throat. Preston Tucker was asking what every normal woman wanted the man with whom they'd fallen in love to ask: *Will you marry me?* Meanwhile, she stood like a statue on the spot, her tongue frozen between her palate and her teeth. All the while her heart was beating so fast she was certain she was going to faint.

Somewhere between sanity and insanity, good and evil, right and wrong she found a modicum of strength. Preston was right—they'd only known each other a month—four short, intense, passionate weeks in which she was able to communicate—in and out of bed—with a man who treated her as his equal. She didn't know whether it was fate, serendipity or destiny that she'd left her case in that taxi for Preston Tucker to find, but Chandra knew she had to believe something beyond her control deemed that Preston would become a part of her life and her future.

She panicked, a riot of emotions attacking her from all sides when he released her hand.

He was going to walk!

She couldn't let him walk!

"Yes!" The single word was a shriek. "Yes, Preston, I will marry you." She was shaking, tears were flowing, and Chandra wasn't certain how much longer her quivering legs would be able to aid her in remaining upright.

Preston felt his knees buckle slightly before he drew himself up to his full height. He'd gambled *and* he'd won. He hadn't seen Chandra in five days, but it'd taken only one for him to realize why he'd been drawn to her and why he wanted her not only in his life but also a part of his life.

He'd dated women much more beautiful, women who could buy and sell a man with the scrawl of a signature on a bank check and women so eager to please that they'd sell themselves for any price. Women whose names and faces paled in comparison to the one standing before him.

Preston knew Chandra was the *one* within seconds of the elevator doors opening, and he'd come face-to-face with the woman who'd recorded her erotic dreams.

Cradling her face between his hands, he kissed her quivering mouth, then her tears. "Shush-h-h. Don't cry, baby. We're going to have a wonderful life together."

Preston's attempt to console Chandra elicited more tears. Moving closer, she cupped his hands. "I love you so much," she whispered against his parted lips.

"Come home with me, baby." He'd punctuated each word with a kiss at each corner of her mouth.

"Why?"

"I want to make love to you."

Chandra smiled through the moisture shimmering on her lashes like minute raindrops. "We don't have to go to your place. I have protection. And I'll treat you to breakfast in bed if you decide to spend the night."

Preston kissed the end of her nose. "You are incredible."

"Thank you." She wanted to tell the man she'd promised to marry that *he* was incredible, because he'd gotten her to fall in love and agree to marry him within the span of a month.

"We can't sleep in too late tomorrow because I want to take you shopping for an engagement ring."

Chandra nodded numbly. The enormity of what she'd

agreed had become apparent with the mention of a ring. She'd taken a step forward, and now it was too late to backtrack.

"I think there's something very wrong with us, Preston, if we always end up sucking face in public."

Preston smiled. "On that note, we should head upstairs."

Chandra and Preston shared a secret smile as they rode the elevator to the sixth floor. No words were needed. Everything they wanted to say had been said.

After closing and locking the door, Chandra reached for her fiancé's hand, leading him in the direction of her bedroom. She hadn't drawn the silk drapes and sheers at the wall-to-wall windows and the light from a full moon silvered every light-colored object in the room. She took her time undressing Preston: shoes, socks, jacket, tie, cuff links, shirt, belt, slacks and briefs. Smiling, she presented him with her back.

Fastening his mouth to the column of Chandra's scented neck, Preston nipped the delicate skin. He'd become Pascual and Chandra, Josette, he undressing Josette with the intent of claiming her innocence. But instead of a flowing gown with an Empire waistline it was a circa twenty-first-century jacket, dress, stockings and shoes. He searched for the pins in her hair, letting them fall, one by one onto the floor, the sound reverberating in the stillness of the space.

The sound of Chandra's breathing quickened when he removed her bra, followed by her bikini panties. "I love you so much," Preston whispered reverently, pressing his mouth and body to her soft, scented flesh.

Splaying his hands over her back, fingertips tracing, sculpting her ribs, the indentation of her waist and her rounded hips. He pulled her closer to feel the heaviness of his sex stirring between his thighs.

Throwing back her head, Chandra gasped when his rising hardness moved against her mound. Going on tiptoe, she looped her arms around Preston's neck in an attempt to get closer. She was on fire and needed him to extinguish the blaze that threatened to incinerate her.

A shudder ripped through her, bathing the area at the apex of her thighs with a rush of moisture. "Please!"

Preston heard Chandra's desperate cry, echoing his own need to bury his flesh inside her. Bending slightly, he swept her up and carried her to the bed. Supporting his body on his hands, he smiled at the dreamy expression on her face. It was his turn to gasp with the back flow of blood to his penis.

Breathing heavily, he lowered his head and tried to think of anything but the woman under him. "Give… me…the condom, baby," he stammered.

Chandra's response was to grasp his sex and ease it into her moist warmth. She gasped again. The impact of having Preston inside her without the barrier of latex was shockingly pleasurable. Raising her hips, she wound her legs around his waist, allowing for deeper penetration.

Preston rode Chandra like a man possessed, then without warning he reversed their positions. He cupped her breasts, squeezing them gently as an expression of carnality swept over her features.

He'd always liked assuming the more dominant missionary-style position, but having Chandra on top, she setting the rhythm, made it easier to prolong ejaculating.

Chandra stared at her lover as she raised her hips and grasped his testicles, squeezing them gently as he had her breasts. A grin split her face when he groaned and bucked like a wild stallion.

Holding the sac cradling his seed, she slid up and down the length of his sex, quickening and slowing and setting a cadence that kept him completely off balance.

She felt the contractions as the walls of her vagina convulsed, then Chandra didn't remember much after that as she surrendered to the orgasms overlapping one another in their intensity to take her beyond herself.

Preston captured Chandra's mouth as she exhaled the last of her passion. Tucking her curves into his, he reversed their position, his hips pumping as he released his passion inside her wet heat.

They lay together, bodies joined and moist from their lovemaking while waiting for their respiration to resume a normal pace. Supporting his greater weight on his elbows, Preston trailed light kisses over her forehead, cheek and ear.

"I never would've imagined you could feel so good," he murmured in her ear.

"Nor I you," Chandra whispered.

"We better think about setting a date, because I don't want you walking down the aisle sporting a baby bump."

Chandra opened her eyes, trying to make out Preston's expression in the muted light. "That's not going to happen."

"What's not going to happen?"

"I can't get pregnant because I have protection." She explained that she'd been fitted with an intrauterine device that could be easily removed whenever she decided that she wanted to become pregnant. "It can be left in up to five years."

Preston froze. "You want to wait five years before we have a baby?"

"Of course not, Preston. In five years I'll be in the high-risk category."

"And I'll be old as dirt. I don't want white hair by the time my son or daughter goes to school for the first time. The first time some kid asks mine if I'm his or her grandfather I'm going to lose it."

"Don't worry, sweetheart. I don't intend to wait that long."

"When do you want to get married?" he asked.

"How about June?"

Preston smiled. "June sounds good. How long do you want to wait before we start trying for a baby?"

Chandra loved children but she'd found it hard to imagine herself a mother. This was something she'd verbalized to Laurence after he'd proposed. His response was he would leave that decision to her. If she wanted a baby it was okay with him, and if she didn't then he was content not to become a father. His rationale left her unsettled because she'd suspected he didn't want children. But, on the other hand, Preston had let it be known that he wanted a family.

"We can start on our honeymoon."

Preston felt his chest fill with an emotion that nearly overwhelmed him as he tried imagining the joy of becoming a father. "Thank you."

Chapter 14

Chandra and Preston spent more than two hours at Safian & Rudolph Jewelers on Seventh and Sansom Street Sunday afternoon. It took over an hour for her to select a setting, then she had to decide on the cut and clarity of the center stone. She'd watched in amazement as the jeweler set a near-flawless two-carat cushion-cut diamond into prongs that were surrounded by pavé diamonds. The center diamond, pavé and sixty round diamonds on, along and under the platinum band totaled three point twenty carats. Seeing the ring on her left hand made it all real. She was officially engaged to marry Preston Japheth Tucker.

She sat beside Preston in his SUV, her heart beating rapidly when they shared a smile. The light coming through the windshield reflected off the brilliance of the stones on her left hand.

"We're going to have to tell our families."

Preston ran a hand over her hair. "I'll call my mother and sister later. You're going to have to let me know when you can go to Charleston so you can meet my family."

"I can go during the winter recess."

Leaning to his right, Preston kissed her. "I'll call Yolanda and tell her to expect us."

"Do you always stay with your sister?"

"Yes. But only because she's a stay-at-home mom."

"Speaking of mothers. I'm going to call mine to see if she's home so we can give her the good news."

Preston waited in the parking lot while Chandra called her mother. The call lasted less than a minute. The Eatons were home. Shifting into Reverse, he maneuvered out of the lot and into traffic. He found it ironic that he and Chandra had had prior engagements but hadn't married their respective fiancée and fiancé for all right reasons.

"Mama didn't tell me Belinda and Griffin were coming over," Chandra said when Preston maneuvered into the driveway and came to a stop behind the hybrid SUV.

Preston cut off the engine and unbuckled his seat belt. "I spoke to Griffin the other night and he told me to ask you when it will be a good time to get together."

"How about next weekend?"

"Friday or Saturday?" he asked. Preston needed to know, because he wanted to take Chandra and her sister and brother-in-law out to dinner.

"Friday."

Resting his arm along the back of her seat, he angled his head. "What if we ask them to stay over?"

"I'll ask Belinda. And before you ask, I think spending the night in Kennett Square is preferable to the city."

Preston gave her a wink. "I was hoping you'd say that."

Chandra waited for Preston to get out and come around the vehicle to assist her. The front door opened before she rang the doorbell.

Roberta, wearing her perennial apron when at home, smiled at her daughter and the man who no doubt had settled her down. "Please come in. We were just sitting down to eat."

Chandra kissed her mother's cheek. "We didn't come to eat, Mama."

"Why did you come?"

She extended her left hand. "To show you this?"

Roberta pressed a hand to her ample bosom. "Oh, my word! You're engaged. Dwight, come here! Your baby is getting married." Chandra walked around her mother when Roberta began tugging on Preston's arm.

"What is Bertie yelling about?" Dwight Eaton asked Chandra when she met him in the middle of the living room.

"You'll have to ask her, Daddy." She would let her mother break the news of her engagement. "Where's Belinda?"

Dwight gestured over his shoulder. "She is in the kitchen. Griffin and the girls are in the family room watching television."

Chandra kissed her father before she walked into the kitchen. Belinda stood at the stove stirring a pot. The high school history teacher wore a peach-colored cashmere twinset, black wool slacks and matching patent leather slip-ons. Although she'd admitted to being pregnant, her body had not yet begun to show signs that she was carrying a child.

"Hey, sistah!"

Belinda put down the wooden spoon, replacing the cover on a pot of mustard greens. "Hey, yourself. I didn't expect to see you today."

"How are you feeling?" Chandra whispered.

Belinda hugged her sister. "Aside from hurling every morning, I'm good."

"Have you told Mama?"

"Not yet. I told Griffin that I'm tired of hiding and that I'm going to make the announcement today."

Chandra tucked her left hand behind her thigh. "I suppose that'll make two of us making announcements today."

"You're pregnant?" Belinda asked, whispering.

Chandra rolled her eyes, while sucking her teeth. "No!" She extended her hand. "But I am engaged."

Belinda closed her eyes, covered her mouth before screaming into her cupped hands. "Oh, my heavens! I can't believe my sister is going to marry Preston Tucker." She lowered her hands and reached for Chandra's. "Congratulations. Your ring is gorgeous." She glanced around. "Where's your fiancé?"

"Daddy's probably giving him the third degree."

"I suppose he doesn't want a repeat of what happened between you and Laurence Breslin."

"Trust me, Belinda, there is no comparison."

"I hear you," Belinda crooned, raising her hand for a high five handshake.

Preston walked into the kitchen with his future mother- and father-in-law to find Chandra and Belinda laughing and hugging like teenagers.

"What's all the noise about?" Everyone turned to find

Griffin, Layla and Sabrina crowding under the entrance to the kitchen.

Belinda winked at her husband. "Chandra and Preston have some good news."

"They're having a baby, too," Griffin blurted out, then clapped a hand over his mouth.

"What do you mean, 'too'?" Dwight and Roberta chorused.

Layla ducked under Griffin's arm. "Who's having a baby, Uncle Griff?"

"Yes, Griffin," Roberta drawled, "who's having a baby?"

"Belinda and I are having a baby," he announced proudly.

Roberta put up a hand, mumbling a prayer of thanks. "I had to wait twelve years for another grandchild, then we get Adam, and now we can look forward to another one next year. The Lord surely is good."

Sabrina pushed her way into the middle of the kitchen. "Layla and I are going to have a sister or brother, or will it be a cousin?"

Griffin hugged his nieces. "He or she will be whatever you want them to be."

Layla smiled, showing off the colorful bands on her clear braces. "When will we see our sister or brother?"

Belinda's gaze swept over those standing in the kitchen. "May. By the way, I'm not the only one with good news today." Her eyebrows lifted when she looked at Chandra and then Preston. "Sis?"

Chandra took three steps, reaching for Preston's hand. "Preston proposed and I accepted. We plan to marry next June."

Griffin slapped Preston on the back. "Welcome to the family, buddy."

Layla sidled up to Chandra. "Can Brina and I be bridesmaids?"

Chandra kissed her niece. "Of course you can. Lindy, I know we're going to cut it close, but I'd like for you to be my matron of honor."

Crossing her arms over her chest, Belinda gave her sister a long, penetrating look. "That may pose a problem. I'm due to deliver at the end of May, and even if you marry at the end of June, that's not enough time for me to recuperate. And even if I did feel well enough to put up with fittings and rehearsals, I plan to breast-feed."

Chandra bit her lower lip. "I'd planned to ask Denise to be in the wedding party. I suppose she'll have to be my maid of honor."

"We could always change the date." Everyone turned to look at Preston.

Chandra stared at her fiancé as if he'd taken leave of his senses. "Change it to when, Preston?"

"Thanksgiving, Christmas or even New Year's."

"You're kidding?"

"Do I look like I'm kidding?" Preston said, repeating what he'd said the night before.

Roberta stared at her husband, and he nodded. "Everyone, let's go in the family room. Chandra and Preston need to discuss something."

Sabrina balked. "I want to know when the wedding is."

Griffin put an arm around his nieces, leading them out of the kitchen. "Your aunt and her fiancé have to—"

"Discuss grown-folk business," the twins chorused, completing the statement they'd heard countless times.

"How did my favorite girls get so smart?" Griffin teased.

Waiting until they were alone, Chandra gave Preston her undivided attention. "Do you really want to get married before the end of the year?"

Pulling her closer, Preston rested his head on the top of her head. "I'd marry you tomorrow if it were possible."

Chandra listened to the strong, steady beats of his heart. "It's not impossible."

He eased back, staring at her with an expression of shock and astonishment freezing his features. "When, Chandra? Let me know the day, time and place and I'll be there."

"We can get married three weeks from now."

Preston massaged her back. "What's happening in three weeks?"

"It will be the Thanksgiving weekend. It's a family holiday, so it shouldn't pose a problem for our families to get together. We're going to have to send out invitations, decide whether we want something simple or formal. And—"

"Slow down, Chandra. You don't have to do anything. We'll hire a wedding planner."

A feeling of unease shuddered over Chandra as if someone were breathing on the back of her neck. She knew for certain that she loved and was in love with Preston Tucker. She also was certain that she wanted to become his wife and the mother of their children, but something from the nightmare continued to chip away at her confidence.

Shaking off the bad vibes as she would an annoying insect, she forced a smile. "You're right. I'm going to have enough to do when I go back to work."

Dipping his head, Preston placed soft, shivery kisses around her lips, along her jaw and down the column of her neck. "Let me know what you want, and if it's within my power I'll make it happen for you."

Chandra closed her eyes, losing herself in the moment and the man pressed intimately to her heart.

Chandra sat on her bed, cross-legged, the phone cradled between her chin and shoulder. It was her third attempt to procure the services of a wedding planner, and hopefully her last. The first two did not have an opening for the next eight and ten months respectively. Her last hope was Zoë Lang. She'd searched Ms. Lang's Web site and liked what she saw.

"May I make a suggestion, Miss Eaton?"

"Yes, and please call me Chandra."

"Are you opposed to hosting an out-of-state wedding?"

Chandra stopped doodling on the pad resting on her crossed legs. "Where out of the state?"

"Isle of Palms."

She searched her memory as to where she'd heard about Isle of Palms. "Isn't that in South Carolina?"

"Yes, it is. In fact, it's an island off the coast of South Carolina. When you left a message on my voice mail, you said you were willing to assume the expense of lodging out-of-town guests. I've checked with hotels and inns in and around Philadelphia, and most of them are booked up because of the holiday weekend."

"How will Isle of Palms be more convenient?"

"Firstly, Miss…Chandra, it is a summer resort community and after Labor Day many of the vacation properties become available. And secondly, what you'll pay to lodge your guests is considerably lower when compared to a hotel for the Thanksgiving weekend. I'm looking at a listing for an oceanfront villa that will hold a maximum of twenty-two guests for a daily rate of twelve hundred dollars, or a weekly rate of fifty-three hundred. This is far below the average hotel rate of one-fifty a night for three nights. If you were to pay for twenty-two hotel guests for that weekend it would cost you more than twelve thousand dollars."

Chandra jotted down the figures. "I'm going to need more than one villa." Because she wanted a small, intimate wedding, she and Preston had agreed to keep the final count at fifty.

"You're in luck, because I have three properties along the same stretch of beach. There's one with ten bedrooms, ten en suite baths, plus two half baths. There's space for ten cars for a maximum of twenty-six guests."

"How many beds?"

"Six king and four queen beds. The property has three floors, an elevator, high-speed wireless Internet and a boardwalk that leads to a private beach. The total weekly cost for the Thanksgiving week is eighty-three hundred dollars. If you're near a computer I'll send you the link as we speak."

Moving off the bed, Chandra walked out of the bedroom and into the kitchen. Tucked into an alcove was the pantry and a workstation where she'd set up her laptop and printer. "I'm turning on my laptop now." She gave the planner her e-mail address while waiting for her computer to boot; she then logged on to the Internet.

Within minutes she clicked on the link. The seven-thousand-square-foot oceanfront property was exquisite. It was furnished with a large flat-screen TV and DVD/

VCR combo. All of the second floor bedrooms had deck areas. The kitchen opened out to both the dining and living rooms. Photos of the kitchen revealed stainless steel appliances, gas cooktop, double ovens, subzero refrigerator and granite countertops. She liked the fact that each home came with an initial supply of linens and towels, washer and dryer, cable TV, air conditioning and a starter supply of paper products, detergents and local telephone service. The thing that made her consider holding her wedding on a sea island was the twenty-four-hour security in a gated community.

"I like what I see, Ms. Lang," Chandra told the planner. "I know I'm working within a very tight time frame, but I have to talk to my fiancé before I commit to anything."

"When will you get back to me, Chandra?"

"Either tonight or early tomorrow morning." Preston had called to tell her he had a dinner meeting with a friend, and he would come to her apartment later that evening.

"Whatever you decide, I'll put a rush on the invitations. Right now I need you to fax or e-mail the names and addresses of your guests so the envelopes can be printed."

"I'll e-mail them." Chandra didn't have a fax machine, but Preston did. He had one in the office at his condo and another at his home.

"I'm also going to e-mail my contract. Have your attorney look it over. If you agree with the terms, then send it ASAP."

"Okay. Either I'll speak to you tonight or tomorrow."

"Thank you, Chandra."

"You're welcome, Ms. Lang."

Chandra ended the call, staring at the images on the computer monitor. If anyone would've told her that she was going to marry Preston Tucker after a seven-week whirlwind romance, she would've thought them either certifiably crazy, or at best delusional. Well, the joke was on her, because she *was* going to marry Preston and at present the only question was—where.

She pulled up a map for South Carolina. Preston's mother and sister, who lived in Charleston, were only a few miles from Isle of Palms. East of Charleston and across the Cooper River bridge was the town of Mount Pleasant. Driving east on the bridge would take them to Sullivan's Island and the Isle of Palms.

If she and Preston decided to marry on the sea island, their guests could come days before the ceremony and tour the Carolina low country. For some it could serve as an unforeseen vacation filled with centuries of history waiting to be explored.

The beginnings of a smile softened Chandra's mouth when she stared at the ring on her left hand. She'd reached a decision. She was going to have a low-country wedding.

Preston could not believe the man sitting next to him was his fraternity brother. Clifford Jessup had literally blown up his cell phone when he'd left eleven voice mail messages that he *had* to meet with him. When Preston finally returned the call, he agreed to meet Clifford for dinner. His former agent had asked that he pick him up at a motel in an extremely undesirable part of the city.

"What the hell happened to you?" The question had come out before Preston was able to censor himself. Tall, slender, dark, handsome and always fastidiously groomed, Cliff's suit looked as if he'd slept in it, and with his bearded face and shaggy hair he could've easily passed for a homeless person.

Cliff doffed an imaginary hat. "And, good evening to you, too."

Preston's temper flared. "Either you dial down the sarcastic bull, or get the hell out of my car."

Clifford's face crumbled like an accordion. "Look, P.J., I'm sorry."

"Even if you're not sorry, you're a sorry-looking sight. What's up with you?" Preston's tone had softened considerably.

"Can we go someplace and get something to eat?"

"Sure. But there aren't too many places we can go with you looking like one of Philly's homeless."

Running his hand over the sleeve of his suit jacket, Cliff attempted to smooth out the wrinkles. "It is a little wrinkled."

Preston wanted to tell him it was past wrinkled. Shifting into gear, he backed out of the parking lot of the transient establishment known for its rapid turnover of *guests*.

"There's a diner not too far from here where we can eat."

Slumping down in the leather seat, Cliff closed his eyes. "That sounds good."

Preston gave his passenger a quick glance. He drove down a street where most of the streetlights were out, and probably had been out for weeks. If no one called the city to report the outages, then they probably would remain out indefinitely.

What Preston wanted to know was why Clifford was hanging out in a neighborhood with one of the highest crime rates in the City of Brotherly Love instead of at home with his lovely wife and two beautiful children. He arrived at the diner, maneuvering into the last space between two police cruisers.

They walked into the diner and were shown to a booth in the rear. Cliff requested coffee even before he sat down. Music blared from speakers throughout the twenty-four-hour dining establishment, while flat-screen TVs were turned on, but muted. Preston stared at the closed caption on a channel tuned to CNN.

A waitress brought Cliff his coffee, then took their food order. Preston ordered grilled sole, a baked potato and spinach without reading the extensive menu. Cliff ordered scrambled eggs, grits, bacon, home fries and toast.

Waiting until his former agent downed his second cup of coffee, Preston said, "Why all the 9-1-1 calls?"

Cliff ran a hand over his bearded face. "I need you to talk to Jackie."

Preston leaned forward. "You want me to talk to your wife?" Cliff nodded. "Why?"

"Because I know she'll listen to you, P.J."

"Why would *your* wife listen to me, Cliff?"

"Because she likes you."

"And I like her," Preston countered. He continued to stare at the man whom he had regarded as a brother, a brother that went beyond their belonging to the same fraternity.

"I guess you can say I messed up—big-time—and Jackie told me I couldn't stay in the house."

"Is she talking divorce?"

"No."

"It was a woman." Cliff nodded, while Preston shook his head. He couldn't understand why men cheated on their wives. "Does Jackie know who she is?"

"You could say that."

Preston exhaled an audible breath. "I didn't drive all the way over here to play cat and mouse with you when I could be home with my fiancée."

Cliff closed and opened his eyes and gave his fraternity brother an incredulous stare. "You're getting married?"

Preston smiled for the first time. "Yes. Chandra and I will tie the knot over the Thanksgiving weekend."

"That soon?"

"It's not soon enough for me." He waved a hand. "We're here to talk about you, not me, Brother Jessup."

Cliff smiled. Preston calling him brother was a reminder that although they no longer had a business relationship they were still connected. "Do you remember Kym Hudson?"

Grabbing his forehead, Preston swallowed a savage expletive. He couldn't believe Cliff had mentioned her name. The buxom coed slept her way through their fraternity like a virulent plague. Preston was one of a very few who'd refused to feed her voracious sexual appetite.

"Who could forget Kym the Nymph?" He dropped his hand. "Don't tell me you started up with her again?"

Cliff took a deep swallow of the strong black coffee. "Yeah, and Jackie found out."

"How did she find out?"

"Kym told her."

Preston wanted to reach across the table and grab Cliff by the throat. "You're an asshole! If you're going to cheat on your wife, why do it with someone she knows? I don't blame her for kicking your butt out."

"But—it was only once."

"'It was only once,'" Preston mimicked in falsetto. "You expect Jackie to believe that?"

"But it's true. I only did it because I was curious as to whether she was still *that* good, P.J." Cliff chuckled. "The joke was on me, because she wasn't good at all. All that fake moaning and screaming my name turned my stomach. Meanwhile, I risked losing my wife and children because I couldn't forget some adolescent fantasy."

"I can't talk to Jackie."

"Why not?"

"I'm a writer, not a psychologist or marriage counselor. You have to tell her you want to save your marriage, and if it means going into counseling, then you do it. Meanwhile, if you need a place to live, then you can stay with me at the condo until you get your life back on track."

Cliff stared into his coffee mug. "Thanks, man."

"Did you tell Jackie that you're no longer my agent?"

"No."

"Good. Don't tell her. I'm going to send you and Jackie an invitation to my wedding. Let's hope she'll contact you to ask whether you're attending. Tell her you're going to be my best man."

"Am I going to be your best man?"

"Please shut up and let me finish. As my best man you won't be seated together, but at least you'll get to see her. And, knowing Jackie, I doubt whether she'd make a scene."

Cliff scratched his bearded face. Guilt and anxiety had caused him to lose Preston as a client, but nothing could breach the bond they'd taken as fraternity brothers. "Thanks, Brother Tucker."

Preston affected a stern expression. "The first thing

you're going to do when we get back to my place is shave and shower because I don't need an infestation of lice or fleas."

Cliff's teeth shone whitely against his beard. "That's cold, Brother Tucker."

"No, Brother Jessup. That's the deal, or you can continue to live in that turnstile of a cathouse."

Chapter 15

Chandra peered into the adjustable mirror at the back of her wedding gown while the dressmaker tightened the fabric under her armpit, pinning it.

"I'm glad you're getting married in a couple of days, because if not, then I'd have to take your gown in again."

She wanted to tell the talented dressmaker that it was only the second time she'd altered the one-of-a-kind creation. While she was certain that she'd had at least three minor mental breakdowns, her wedding planner was her fairy godmother.

Zoë Lang had arranged for her and Preston to come to Isle of Palms to see the properties where their guests would be housed. She'd mailed off the invitations, monitored the responses by telephone or e-mail, hired local floral and wedding cake designers, DJ and photographer. She and Preston spent two days in Charleston getting acquainted with her future in-laws. Rose Tucker offered her knowledge of regional lore and cuisine when they sat down to plan the menu and decorations.

Chandra was effusive in her thanks when the wedding planner suggested getting married in the South. After an unusually warm autumn, winter had put in an early appearance in the Northeast. Less than a week into the month of November, Philadelphia had more than eight inches of snowfall.

Many of the guests, looking to take advantage of an impromptu vacation, had elected to arrive early and sign up for the many historic tours in and around Charleston.

"Are you certain it's not too tight?" With the strapless, beaded bodice with an Empire-waist and narrow skirt and bolero-style beaded jacket, Chandra looked as if she'd stepped off the pages of a Jane Austen novel. She had become Josette Fouché in every sense of the word.

Irena Farrow narrowed her eyes. "It's perfect—that is if you don't lose another pound between now and Friday."

"I promise you I won't."

"That's what you said last week."

"I had cramps last week, so all I had was tea and soup."

Irena smiled, her bright blue eyes sparkling like precious jewels. "I used to have cramps so bad that I had to take to my bed for the first two days. But, after I had my Seth they stopped."

Chandra wanted to wait for at least six months before she and Preston started trying for a baby. She'd been hired as a substitute teacher and had to cover a third-grade class for two days since her hire. Substituting fit in perfectly with her current lifestyle. There would be no way she'd be able to plan a wedding with three weeks' notice if she'd had the daily responsibility of her own class.

She felt like a traitor when she told Denise that she would have to give up the co-op once she married Preston. Denise was totally unaffected by the abrupt change in plans because she knew someone looking to rent or sublet a one-bedroom in a nice Philadelphia neighborhood.

Denise had agreed to become a bridal attendant, along with Sabrina and Layla Rice. Belinda, who'd only gained two pounds, was to be her matron of honor. Preston had selected a fraternity brother to be his best man, and Griffin, Myles and his brother-in-law as his groomsmen.

She knew the Eatons and Rices would outnumber the Tuckers two-to-one, but holding the wedding in South Carolina seemed the likely compromise. Barring a tropical storm, Zoë planned a beachfront ceremony and reception under a tent. The ceremony was planned for ten in the morning, followed by brunch. Later that afternoon a six-course dinner would be served. The evening would end with dancing and music supplied by a live band and DJ.

Irena undid the hooks on the back of the gown. "You can get dressed while I alter this. Then you can take it with you."

Chandra's attendants had picked up their dresses the week before. In keeping with an autumnal theme, they would wear slip-style street length dresses in a burnt orange. The color would be repeated in the groomsmen's vests.

She'd borrowed Preston's SUV rather than take a taxi to the dressmaker, while he'd hired a driver to take him to Paoli to meet with Griffin. The aborted meeting with the movie studio executives had been rescheduled with Griffin standing in as Preston's agent.

Irena had sewn the dress and put it in a box filled with tissue paper by the time Chandra had put back on her street clothes. "Take it out of the box and hang it in the garment bag I gave you. Thankfully the wrinkles fall out once it hangs for a few hours." She hugged and kissed Chandra's cheek. "Good luck, darling. You're going to be an exquisite bride."

Chandra returned the hug. "Thank you."

"Don't forget to send me a picture of you and your husband so I can brag that Preston Tucker's wife wore an Irena gown."

"Once they're developed I'll personally bring you one," Chandra promised.

Walking to the rear of the shop, she made her way to the parking lot. Late-morning traffic was light and she made it back to the condo in record time. She parked in the underground garage and took the elevator to the eighteenth floor. Once inside, she took the dress out of the box, storing it in the back of a closet in the smaller of the three second-floor bedrooms.

Skipping down the staircase, Chandra went into the kitchen to gather the ingredients for dinner. She and Preston shared cooking duties, but it was always a special treat whenever he cooked. After brewing a cup of chocolate from the single-cup coffee machine, she made her way to the home/office to use the computer. Denise had begun sending her e-mails every day about things she should do before getting married. Some of them were so hilarious that she laughed until tears rolled down her face.

However, it wasn't Denise's e-mail that garnered her

attention, but a draft of *Death's Kiss*. Picking up the un-bound pages of the play, she sat on the chaise and began reading.

The hands on her watch had made two revolutions when she turned down the last page. Chandra hadn't re-alized her hands were shaking uncontrollably until she attempted to gather the pages into a neat pile.

"What are you doing?"

Rising on shaky legs, she saw Preston standing in the doorway. Her shock and rage gave way to a calm-ness that was scary. A brittle smile hardened her gaze. "I was reading *Death's Kiss*."

He walked into the office. "I didn't want you to read it now. It's only the first draft."

Reaching for the pages, Chandra handed them to him when she wanted to throw them in his face. "Why didn't you tell me, Preston?"

Tapping the pages on the surface of the desk, Preston stacked them neatly, then bound them with a wide rub-ber band. "Tell you what?"

"Why didn't you tell me you've read my journal?"

Preston affected a sheepish grin. "I was going to tell you."

"When?" she screamed. "When were you going to tell me that you were using me for your own selfish lit-erary pursuits."

His expression changed, becoming a mask of stone. "That's not true, and you know it."

"What I do know is you used my dreams to write your next masterpiece. How do you know I didn't copyright my journals? Then what you've lifted would be deemed plagiarism."

Preston's hands gripped her shoulders, not permitting movement. "Stop it, Chandra."

"I will not stop until I get the hell out of here and away from you."

"No, you're not. You're going to stand here and listen to me."

"I don't want to hear more lies, Preston. I asked you over and over if I could trust you, and you swore I could. Every time we pretended we were Josette and Pascual you must have been laughing at me. Poor little Chandra. She was so taken with the brilliant playwright that she sold herself for a book of dreams. I—"

"Enough!"

She recoiled as if she'd been struck across the face. It was the first time Preston had ever raised his voice to her. Not even her father had raised his voice when speaking to her.

"No, you didn't yell at me."

Preston tightened his hold on Chandra's shoulders when she narrowed her eyes at him. She looked like a cat ready to come at him with fangs and claws.

"I'm sorry, baby. I'd cut off my right arm rather than yell at you."

"Start cutting, because you did," she spat out.

"Chandra, baby, please let me say something." He felt her shoulders relax. Gathering her to his chest, he pressed a kiss to her forehead. "I was going to tell you once the play was sent to the Library of Congress for a copyright." He released her, walked over to the desk and returned with a single sheet of paper and handed it to her.

Chandra felt her knees buckle as she inched over to sit on the chaise. She read what he'd typed three times before the realization hit her: A Play in Three Acts written by C. E. and P. J. Tucker. He'd included her as the coauthor of *Death's Kiss*.

"Why did you put my name first?" she whispered.

Going to a knee, Preston cradled the back of her head. "Don't you know you come first in my life? I love you, baby. I'd love you even if I never read a word in your journal."

"But you did read it and didn't tell me."

"I didn't want to embarrass you, Chandra, because you'd have to explain if you'd slept with the man in your dreams or if he was an imaginary person you'd conjured up to assuage your sexual frustration."

Chandra demurely lowered her eyes. "It was the latter."

"All I can say is you have a helluva imagination."

She pressed her forehead to his. "What you read is tame. I have three other volumes and most of them are X-rated."

"What I read was X-rated."

"Then double and triple X-rated."

"Dam-n-n. Don't tell me I'm marrying a freak!"

Chandra swatted at him, but missed his head when he ducked. "I'll freak you."

Easing her off the chaise, Preston pressed her down to the floor. "I just happen to like freaks. The freakier the better."

She smiled up at the man she didn't want to trust, and the one with whom she'd fallen inexorably in love. "I'm kind of partial to freaks, too. What do you say we get our freak on before we fly down to Isle of Palms tomorrow."

Chandra would stay in the villa with eighteen other Eatons and Rices. Preston would live in another villa a thousand feet away with his close friends and relatives.

A third villa would accommodate an overflow of friends and family.

She and Preston would remain on the island until Sunday afternoon when they'd fly down to St. Barts for a two-week honeymoon before returning to Philadelphia.

"I'm game if you are," Preston agreed, "but only if you're on top."

"Let's do it, P.J."

Pushing to his feet, Preston swept Chandra off the floor, carried her out of the office and up the staircase to the master bedroom. He took his time undressing her, then himself. There was no need to rush because they had the rest of their lives to live out their sweet dreams.

The weather on Isle of Palms was perfect for an outdoor wedding. A cooling breeze off the river offset the heat of the sun on the bared skin of those who'd come as couples and in groups all week to the sea island to relax and take in the history of the low country.

Pumpkins, stalks of corn and decorative sweetgrass baskets lined the beach as bridesmaids and groomsmen lined the double staircase leading to the two story villa flanked by palmetto trees.

Preston Tucker stood at the foot of the staircases. He was waiting for Dr. Dwight Eaton to escort his daughter through the open French doors. The familiar strains of the "Wedding March" caught everyone's attention, and those sitting under the tent stood up. A lump formed in his throat, he finding it difficult to swallow.

Carrying a bouquet of yellow chrysanthemums, orange blossoms, yellow and orange sunflowers, Chandra carefully navigated the orange runner, the toes of her white satin ballet-type slippers peeking from under the hem of her gown. A light breeze lifted the chapel veil attached to the crown of her head with a jeweled comb.

A minister stood ready to begin officiating. "Who gives this woman in this most sacred rite of matrimony?"

Dwight Eaton appeared to have grown an inch when he pulled back his shoulders. "I do."

It was the second time within four months that he would give away a daughter in marriage, and the third in which he'd witnessed the wedding of his children. All of his surviving children were married, and he and Roberta were looking forward to many more grandchildren.

Chandra smiled at her father. "I love you, Daddy."

He winked at her. "Be happy, baby girl."

She nodded. "I will."

The wedding party descended the staircases to stand opposite one another alongside the carpet when Dwight placed Chandra's hand on Preston's outstretched one.

Chandra focused on the orange blossom boutonniere rather than his face because she didn't want to cry and ruin her makeup. Earlier that morning he'd sent Clifford Jessup to give her a gift. When she'd unwrapped the small package it was to find a pair of Cartier South Sea pearls with yellow oval diamonds. The attached card read:

To be worn on special occasions—weddings, births and award ceremonies. Love always, Pascual.

She glanced up through her lashes to see him staring at her lobes. She'd worn the earrings. A smile trembled over her lips. "I will love you forever."

Preston lowered his head, lightly touching her mouth with his. "Thank you, darling."

The minister cleared his throat as a ripple of laughter came from the assembled. "The groom usually kisses his bride *after* I pronounce them husband and wife."

"Sorry about that."

The minister straightened his tie under his black robe. "Let's get started, so you can get to kiss your wife instead of your bride."

"I'm ready," Preston said softly.

And he was ready to love and live out all the sweet dreams his wife recorded in her journals.

An exchange of vows, followed by an exchange of rings and they were now husband and wife.

When Chandra Eaton came home she'd planned to stay. What she hadn't planned on was becoming Mrs. Chandra Eaton-Tucker, wife of celebrated playwright Preston Tucker.

Life was not only good.

It was sweet.

* * * * *

Twice the Temptation

A time to love and a time to hate;
A time for war and a time for peace.
            —*Ecclesiastes 3:8*

Chapter 1

"Denise? Oh, I didn't realize you were on the phone."

Denise Eaton's head popped up and she waved away the woman who'd come into her office. She couldn't talk to the social worker, because if she didn't resolve what had become a dilemma there would be nothing to discuss.

"Are you certain I have no recourse, Myles?" she asked, continuing with her telephone conversation.

After she'd opened the certified letter, reading it not once but twice, she'd called her cousin, Myles Eaton, who taught constitutional law at Duquesne University School of Law, before she'd faxed the letter.

"I'm sorry, Denise. I wish I could give you more encouraging news, but the new owner *can* legally raise the rent. You approved the clause in your original lease that allows him to do it."

"He had to have known he was going to sell the build-ing when I signed the lease. What I can't understand is why the new owner wants to double the rent. He has to be aware of prevailing rents for this neighborhood."

Denise had chosen the less-than-desirable D.C. neigh-borhood because the working parents who lived there needed the services she offered, and the rent for the building where she'd set up her business was one she could afford.

"Maybe he knows something you don't, Necie."

"Like what, Myles?"

"Perhaps the area is targeted for gentrification and he wants you to vacate so he can use the property for some-thing other than a child care center. Do you know anyone in D.C. who can advocate on your behalf?"

She rubbed her forehead with her fingers as she felt the beginnings of a tension headache. "Like who?"

"Like someone with political connections."

Denise did know someone, but there was no way she wanted to be beholden to Trey Chambers. "No," she lied.

"If you were my client, I'd recommend you contact the owner and see if you can negotiate a deal that would be reasonable for both parties."

"What's reasonable is I can't afford even a hundred-dollar increase in rent. I'm barely breaking even."

"Call the new owner of the property, Denise, and if you're unable to talk to him, then call me back. I'll look up some of my old law school buddies who practice in the District and see if they'll represent you."

"How am I going to pay them, Myles?" She only had three months of budgeted funds for New Visions Child-care and less than a thousand dollars available for legal expenses.

"Don't worry about paying them. I'll cover the fees."

Denise panicked. There was no way she was going to let her cousin subsidize her business. She hadn't accepted any monetary support from her father and mother, deciding instead to take out a business loan to set up the progressive child care center in a D.C. neighborhood where poor and working-classes families desperately needed the services.

Her delicate jaw hardened when she clenched her teeth. "No, you won't."

"Stop being so muleheaded, Necie."

"Thank you, cuz. I'll call and let you know how everything turns out."

"Necie, don't…"

Denise cut off whatever Myles was going to say when she hung up. She wasn't completely destitute. Instead of subletting or renting the one-bedroom Philadelphia co-op her cousin had given her when she moved out after marrying celebrated playwright Preston Tucker, Denise had decided to sell it. After several deals had fallen through, she was finally set to close on the property. But that was three weeks away.

She had to decide whether she wanted to invest the money in the business. The profit she stood to make was enough to cover salaries, utilities, rent and other essentials for operating the child care center. The first year, New Visions had made a modest profit, but this year it was projected to increase by ten percent.

Drumming her fingers on the top of the desk, Denise stared at the framed prints of children from around the world in their native dress. She'd fulfilled a childhood dream of becoming a teacher, but hadn't stopped there. Setting up the child care center was the second stage of her plan and the third and final component was to eventually establish a school for at-risk, underprivileged boys.

However, everything she'd sacrificed and worked so hard for was about to implode. The new owner of the property had given her ninety days to accept the terms of the rental renewal agreement or vacate the property. And there was no way she could find another building, renovate it and secure the necessary permits to run a similar facility in three months.

She stared at the letter for a full minute. Reaching for the telephone, she picked up the receiver and dialed the number on the company's masthead. "Capital Management. How may I direct your call?" asked the woman who'd answered the telephone.

Denise sat up straighter. "May I please speak to Ms. Henderson."

"Who's calling?"

"Denise Eaton, executive director of New Visions Childcare. I received a certified letter this morning signed by Ms. Henderson. I'm calling to set up an appointment to meet with her to discuss the terms of the renewal lease agreement."

"Please hold on, Ms. Eaton. I'll see if Ms. Henderson is available."

Denise continued drumming her fingers, her heart beating rapidly against her ribs, while mumbling a silent prayer that she would be able to appeal to Camilla Henderson's maternal instincts—that was if the woman had any.

"Camilla Henderson," she said in a strong, no-nonsense, businesslike tone. "How may I help you, Ms. Eaton?"

"I'd like to set up an appointment to meet with you to discuss—"

"The letter you received outlining the terms of the rent increase," she said, interrupting Denise.

"How did you know?"

"I'm not clairvoyant, Ms. Eaton." There was a hint of laughter in her voice. "It's just that I've been fielding calls about rent increases all morning." The sound of turning pages came through the earpiece. "Are you available this coming Friday?"

Denise checked her planner. She had a staff meeting at ten. "What time on Friday?"

"I have an opening for Friday morning and another one for late afternoon."

"I'd prefer late afternoon."

"My assistant will call you Friday morning to set up a time and place where we'll meet."

"We won't meet at your office?" Denise asked.

"No, Ms. Eaton. We're currently renovating our offices and conference room."

"Okay. I'll wait for the call. And, thank you, Ms. Henderson."

"I'll see you Friday, Ms. Eaton."

Denise hung up. Camilla Henderson seemed friendly enough on the phone, so now it was up to her to try to convince the woman to lower the rent for the sake of the children, their parents and the employees of the center.

Camilla Henderson exhaled a breath when she dialed Garrett Fennell's extension. It took less than a minute for his executive assistant to transfer her to the CEO of Capital Management Properties.

"Rhett, Ms. Eaton called. I told her I'm willing to meet with her Friday afternoon."

"Call her back and tell her you're available tonight."

"What if she's not available?"

"If I know Denise Amaris Eaton as well as I believe I do, she *will* make herself available. Tell her to meet you in the lobby of my hotel at seven. That should give her enough time to close the center and make it to the Hay-Adams in time for dinner."

Denise parked her car six blocks from the Hay-Adams. She'd been surprised when Camilla Henderson's assistant called soon after they'd hung up to schedule a dinner meeting at the hotel across the street from the White House for seven that evening. Her plan to wash several loads of laundry was scrapped when she'd left the center at four—two hours earlier than her normal quitting time. She'd gone home to shower and change into something more appropriate for a dinner meeting at the landmark hotel that was a popular choice for policy-making meetings among Washingtonian politicos.

She didn't have time to wash and blow out her hair, so Denise brushed it off her face, pinning it into a loose chignon on the nape of her neck. It had taken three changes before she'd decided on a sleeveless ice-blue linen dress with a squared neckline edged in black. The narrow black belt around her waist matched four-inch pumps and the bolero jacket. She wore pearl studs in her pierced ears, a matching strand around her neck and a gold watch that had been her father's gift to her when she'd earned a graduate degree in educational administration. The outfit was perfect for the warm spring weather.

It felt good wearing the heels, only because her work

attire was relegated to slacks, blouses and sensible walking shoes. It was only on rare occasions that she wore a suit or dress to work. The exception was when she had a meeting outside the center. Although she didn't interact as closely with the children as she had when she was a classroom teacher, coming into contact with sticky fingers or when she picked up a toddler who'd had an accident, Denise had learned to dress for practicality.

"Good evening, miss."

Smiling, she nodded to the well-dressed young man. "Good evening." Although she hadn't turned around, Denise could feel the heat of his gaze on her back when he passed on her right.

"You look very nice," he said.

"Thank you."

Her smile was still in place when she crossed H Street, heading for Sixteenth. His unexpected compliment was an ego-booster. Not only did she need to pump up her ego, but she also needed an additional shot of confidence, and Denise wasn't about to rule out a minor miracle.

She had never been one who'd found herself at a loss for words. In fact her mother had always said she should've been the model for Chatty Cathy. Paulette Eaton claimed her daughter spoke in full sentences before she'd celebrated her second birthday. Her father, Boaz Eaton, said children who were talkative were usually very intelligent. Coming from Boaz, who'd stressed education above all else, it had become the ultimate compliment.

Denise detected a smell in the air that she'd come to associate with Virginia and the Capitol district. Maybe it was chicory or another plant indigenous to the region. Once she'd contemplated moving from Philadelphia to

D.C., she'd met with a real estate agent several times a month to look at vacant properties for her business, and when she'd found the one-story brick building she'd been relieved it hadn't required major renovations. Finding an apartment proved a lot easier for her. She was finally settling into a one-bedroom apartment at the Winston House. It had taken her a year to finalize her move from the City of Brotherly Love to the nation's capital.

The walk was what Denise needed to compose herself when she nodded to the doorman, who'd opened the door to the entrance to the Hay-Adams. "Thank you."

Touching the shiny brim of the hat, the man bowed as if she were royalty. "You're welcome, miss."

She entered the opulent lobby of the building that had been originally designed in the 1920s as a residential hotel. However, Denise felt as if she'd walked into a private mansion on Lafayette Square that featured suites with views of Lafayette Park and the White House.

Her eyes swept around the lobby, searching for a woman wearing a tan pantsuit with a white blouse. She checked her watch. It was six forty-five, fifteen minutes earlier than their appointed time. Walking over to a plush armchair, she sat down and waited for Camilla Henderson.

Rhett Fennell's hands tightened on the arms of the chair as he forced himself not to move. He'd come down to the lobby at 6:30 p.m. to wait for a glimpse of the woman with whom he'd waited six years to exact his revenge. The deep-seated anger that had gnawed at him day in and day out burned as hotly as it had the day Denise Eaton walked out of his life and into the arms of a man who'd gone from friend to enemy.

His mother had pleaded with him to let it go—forget about the two people he'd trusted—but he couldn't. It was the thirst for revenge that fueled the fire to propel him to get up every day to grow the business he would use to inflict Denise Eaton with the emotional pain he'd carried for longer than he wanted to remember, and bring Trey Chambers to his knees.

At exactly seven o'clock, he stood and counted the steps it would take to bring him face-to-face with her. A wry smile tilted the corners of his mouth. It was half a dozen—the same number of years since the fateful day that would forever be branded into his memory.

"Good evening, Ms. Eaton."

Denise froze, her breath catching in her throat and making it impossible for her to move. She heard the roaring in her head, fearful that she was going to faint when she registered the voice of the man she'd feared running into since moving to D.C. Rhett Fennell was the only man she knew who could shout without raising his voice.

Her lips parted and she expelled a lungful of air and the roaring stopped. Her head came up as if pulled by an invisible string. Standing less than a foot away was Rhett Fennell, the man with whom she'd fallen in love, given her heart, virginity and a promise to share her life and future with him.

He'd matured. His face was leaner, his black hair close-cropped and there was an intensity in the deep-set dark eyes that didn't look at her but through her. Rising on shaking knees, Denise extended her hand.

"It's good seeing you again, Rhett."

Rhett reached for the proffered hand, holding it firmly within his large grasp before releasing it. His impassive expression did not change as he stared at the heart-shaped face with the wide-set dark brown eyes, delicate nose and temptingly curved mouth that conjured up memories of what he'd been reduced to after they'd finished making love. It was her mouth and what came out of it that had enthralled him before he'd turned to see her face for the first time.

Denise had been blessed with the voice of a temptress. It was low, sultry and definitely had a triple-X rating. She was the only woman he'd known or met who'd been able to seduce him with *hello*. However, time had been more than kind to her. Although appearing slimmer than she had when they were in college together, nonetheless she was strikingly beautiful.

He forced a smile that stopped before it reached his eyes. "And, it's very nice seeing you again. How long has it been?"

Denise's eyes narrowed. She wanted to tell Garrett Fennell there was no reason to play mind games with her. He was brilliant. Everything he saw, heard or read he remembered, and it was his photographic memory that made him an outstanding student and astute businessman.

And he looked every inch the successful businessman in a tailored charcoal-gray suit, pale blue shirt, purple silk tie and black wingtips. Garrett Mason Fennell was the epitome of sartorial splendor.

She'd admitted to her cousin, Chandra Eaton-Tucker, that if she did run into Rhett again she would lose it. Well, she hadn't—even though she was becoming more uncomfortable with each passing second. She'd also confessed to Chandra that she hadn't gotten over her former lover and if she were completely honest with herself she would have to admit she would never get over him because she hadn't wanted to.

"Six years, Rhett."

Rhett angled his head. "Has it really been that long?"

"Yes, it has," Denise retorted sharply. Either he was feigning ignorance, or what they'd shared was just a blip in his memory. She glanced at her watch again. "I'd like to stay and reminisce with you, but I'm supposed to meet someone for dinner."

Rhett glanced around the lobby. "Is he here yet?"

"It's not a he, but a she."

"I hope you're not waiting for Camilla Henderson."

Denise stared at Rhett as if he'd suddenly grown a third eye. "You know Camilla Henderson?"

Rhett felt like a cat playing with a mouse he'd trapped and stunned, but was reluctant to kill. It was time he put an end to the charade and reveal his intent.

"She works for me. Unfortunately, she had an unforeseen situation where she couldn't be here, so you're going to have to deal with me tonight."

"You're involved with Capital Management Properties?"

"I've just taken over as CEO of CMP."

"You…you're responsible for the one hundred percent increase in rent on *my* child care center?"

Rhett's eyebrows lifted a fraction. "Aren't you being premature?"

"What the hell are you talking about?" Her voice had lowered as her temper escalated.

"Didn't you agree to meet with my chief financial officer to negotiate the terms of your center's lease renewal?"

"Yes, but—"

"Let's talk about it, Denise," Rhett said, interrupting

her. He cupped her elbow, steering her across the lobby. "I've reserved a table in The Lafayette."

Denise attempted to extricate her arm, but encountered resistance. She could not escape the fingers tightening like manacles. "You deceived me!"

Rhett stopped abruptly, as she plowed into his side. He turned toward her. "Spoken like someone who's quite familiar with the word."

"I didn't deceive you, Rhett."

"Save your breath, Denise. You're going to need it after you hear my business proposition."

"What kind of proposition?" Denise asked, unable to ignore the shudder swirling throughout her body. Rhett was making a business proposition when they had nothing in common other than he was now her landlord.

"We'll discuss it over dinner."

Denise went completely still, then managed to relax when Rhett rested his hand at the small of her back. It was as if nothing had changed, as if it'd been six hours instead of six years that had separated them.

Chapter 2

However, if things between them *hadn't* changed she now would've been Denise Fennell and probably would've had at least one, if not, two children. Rhett, who was an only child, always talked about having a big family. When she'd asked him what he felt constituted a big family his reply had been a minimum of four children. They'd argued good-naturedly, she refusing to agree to push out four babies, while Rhett reminded her of how much fun it would be making babies.

Denise knew conjuring up images of the passionate encounters she'd had with Rhett would be detrimental to her emotional well-being. It had taken a long time to recover from his deceit and now that her life was on track she wanted nothing to derail it again.

"Your table is ready, Mr. Fennell."

Rhett's arm went around her waist, holding her close

to his length. Denise was relieved she'd chosen to wear
the stilettos. She was five-four in bare feet, and the additional four inches put her at eye level with Rhett's broad
shoulder.

"How often do you eat here?" she asked him after
he'd seated her.

"Enough," Rhett replied cryptically.

Denise stared across the small space of the table
for two, her eyes taking in everything that made Rhett
the confident man she'd loved selfishly. "How often is
enough?" He'd greeted the maître d' and several of the
waitstaff by name.

Rhett stared at Denise with lowered lids. He didn't
want to believe she was more stunning than he'd remembered. The private investigator on his payroll had
more than earned his salary. He made a mental note to
give the man a generous year-end bonus. The former
police officer had information on the teacher she probably hadn't remembered, or had chosen not to remember.

"I stay at the hotel whenever I have business in D.C."

A slight frown furrowed Denise's smooth forehead.
Whenever she saw Garrett Fennell's name linked with
a D.C.-based company in the business section of *The
Washington Post,* she was under the impression that he
still lived in his hometown.

"Where's home now?" she asked, staring at his firm
mouth.

A hint of a smile found its way to Rhett's eyes. "I have
a little place off the Chesapeake."

Resting her elbow on the table, Denise cupped her
chin on the heel of her hand. "So you got your wish,"
she said in a quiet voice. "You always said you wanted
to live on the water."

Rhett's expression changed, becoming somber. "Unfortunately, not all of my wishes were granted."

"What more could you have wanted, Rhett? You've become a successful entrepreneur, you have the home you wanted and—"

"You don't know what the hell you're talking about," he said, cutting her off.

Denise's arm came down and she sat back, her eyes never leaving the pair pinning her to the chair. He'd done it again. He had yelled at her without raising his voice. "If you talk to me like that again, I'm going to get up and walk out of here."

"You do that and you'll throw away everything you've worked so hard for. And knowing you like I believe I do, you won't do that just because someone said something you don't like."

"You're not someone, Rhett," she countered angrily. "Remember, we're not strangers."

"That's something I'll never forget, because you made certain of that."

Her eyes narrowed. "So, you're still blaming me for something you initiated and let get out of control." Rhett's reply was preempted when the waiter brought menus to the table.

"Would you like to order cocktails before I take your order, Mr. Fennell?"

"We'll have a bottle of champagne."

"Your usual, sir?"

"Yes, please."

Denise did not want to believe Rhett had ordered champagne without asking her beverage choice. "I don't want anything to drink because I'm driving," she said softly after the waiter had walked away.

Rhett smiled. "Don't worry. I'll make certain you get home safely."

"How are you going to do that?"

"I'll drive you home and then take a taxi back here."

"That's not necessary." It was enough that Rhett knew where she worked, and Denise didn't want him to know where she lived.

Picking up the menu, Rhett studied the entrées as Denise seethed inwardly. His success had made him not only arrogant but also rude. When they'd dated she rarely drank. Being underage was a factor and even when she'd reached the legal drinking age she'd discovered one drink usually left her feeling giddy.

"You've changed, Rhett."

"And you haven't?" he said, never taking his eyes off the menu.

"Yes, I have. I'm no longer the wide-eyed young girl who got to sleep with the smartest guy on campus."

Rhett's head came up as he slumped back in his chair. "You think what we'd had was all about sex, Denise?"

"What else was it, Rhett?" she asked, answering his question with her own. "Even you admitted you'd never connected with a woman the way you had with me."

Pressing his palms together, he brought his fingertips to his mouth. He'd fallen in love with Denise Eaton because of her outspokenness, passion *and* her ambition. Of all the women he'd met at Johns Hopkins, she'd been the most focused and driven. Even at eighteen she knew who she was and what she'd wanted for her future.

She was a Philadelphia Eaton, while he was the only child of a single mother who'd looked young enough to pass for his sister. Denise had grown up in a sprawling house on several acres with her attorney father and schoolteacher mother and an older brother. Her brother had attended the prestigious Citadel in Charleston, South Carolina, with the intention of becoming a professional soldier.

Meanwhile, he hadn't known his father, and whenever he'd asked Geraldine Fennell about him, she would say she didn't know. His mother didn't know the man who'd fathered him, and every time he walked the streets in his neighborhood he'd randomly searched the faces of men in an attempt to find one who he thought he looked like.

Gerri, as she was affectionately called by the few friends she'd held on to from her childhood, worked two jobs to send him to a boarding school twelve miles from their blighted neighborhood so he would get a quality education. Her sacrifice had paid off, because he'd been awarded full academic scholarships to Stanford, Howard University, Harvard and Johns Hopkins. Rhett had decided on the latter, because the scholarship included not only tuition but also books, room and board. The university was also close enough to D.C. so he could easily return home during school breaks.

The adage that there is a thin line between love and hate was evident after Denise dashed all of the plans they'd made for their future to crawl into bed with Trey Chambers. He'd wanted to hate her, but couldn't. He'd wanted to hurt her, but hadn't. Now the only thing he wanted was revenge—the sweetest revenge that he would exact in his own time, using his own methods.

"That was then."

"And this is now," she said softly.

"Yes, it is," Rhett said slowly as if measuring his words. "Speaking of now—how is your family?"

Denise, relieved to change the focus of the conversation from her and Rhett, smiled. "Thankfully, everyone's well."

"How's your brother?"

"Xavier has retired from active service. He went to Iraq a couple of years after 9/11 for two tours of duty. He was stateside for a while, and last year he was deployed again, this time to Afghanistan. A month before he was scheduled to return home he took a bullet to the leg that shattered his femur."

"What is he doing now?"

"He just got a teaching position at a military school in South Carolina, much to the relief of my mother, who went to church every day to light a candle that he wouldn't come back in a flag-draped casket."

Rhett had always liked Xavier. The career soldier had become the older brother he'd wished he had. "Are your parents well?"

"Very well," she said, smiling. "Daddy is now a state supreme court judge. Mom put in for early retirement, and now complains that she's bored out of her mind. All she does is cook and bake cakes."

"Your mother missed her calling."

"And that is?"

"She should've become a chef instead of a teacher." Whenever he'd gone to Philadelphia with Denise, her mother had prepared so much food that she'd invited every family member within a twenty-mile radius. Although he and Denise hadn't been engaged, the Eatons had unofficially adopted him into their family.

Denise's smile was dazzling. "I think you just gave me an idea, Rhett. When I speak to my mother I'm going to suggest she take some cooking classes."

Rhett's smile matched Denise's and for a brief moment

he forgot why he was sitting across the table from her in a hotel restaurant. "Your mother is an incredible cook, unlike my mother, who still can't boil water."

A tender expression softened Denise's features when she remembered meeting Rhett's mother for the first time. Her greeting of "you're the daughter I always wanted" had resonated with her long after she and Rhett had driven back to Baltimore after a holiday weekend.

"How is your mother?"

"Believe it or not, she got married last year."

"I don't believe it. Your mother is so beautiful, and what I didn't understand was that men were practically genuflecting whenever they saw her, yet she wouldn't give any of them the time of day."

Rhett chuckled, the warm honeyed sound coming from deep within his chest. "She finally met someone who wasn't intimidated by her hostile glares and sharp tongue. Russ claims he chased her until she caught him. She used every excuse in the book as to why she wouldn't make a good wife, including her inability to cook, until he promised to hire a personal chef."

"Did he?" Denise asked.

"Yes. He made good on his promise and they have a cook who prepares their meals, so the only thing Mom has to do is heat them up in the oven or the microwave."

Denise wanted to tell Rhett his mother didn't have to learn to cook because she'd worked at a restaurant and brought food home. She also didn't tell him that six months ago she'd gone to see Geraldine Fennell, but neighbors told her Gerri had moved and hadn't left a forwarding address.

"I hope she's happy."

"She is," Rhett confirmed. "Once I convinced her to

give up one of her jobs, she got her GED and eventually went online to get a liberal arts degree. She says she doesn't know what she's going to do with it, but earning a college degree is something she'd always wanted."

The sommelier approached the table with two flutes and a bottle of champagne in a crystal ice bucket. He poured a small amount into one flute, handed it to Rhett, and then filled both when he nodded his approval.

Rhett offered Denise the wineglass, their fingers touching. Holding his flute aloft, he gave her a long, penetrating look. "Here's to a successful business arrangement."

With wide eyes, Denise stared at him over the rim. "What business arrangement?" The query was barely a whisper.

He took a sip of the sparkling wine. "Drink up, Denise."

Her fingers tightened on the stem of the glass. "No. I'm not going to toast or drink to something I know nothing about."

Rhett set his glass down. He knew his dining partner well enough to know she wouldn't do anything she didn't want to do. "I want you to stand in as my hostess for the summer."

A soft gasp escaped Denise when she replayed Rhett's *business proposal* in her head. "You need a girlfriend?" There was a thread of incredulity in the question.

"No, Denise, I don't need a girlfriend. I broke up with my girlfriend a couple of months ago, and I'm not looking for another one. Unfortunately I've committed to quite a few social engagements this summer, and I need someone who will stand in as my date and hostess, providing your boyfriend doesn't object."

Clasping her hands together, she concealed their trembling under the table. "I don't have a boyfriend."

"That alleviates one obstacle."

She rolled her eyes at him. "Why don't you contact a dating service, Rhett? I'm certain they can find someone to your liking."

Leaning forward, Rhett's face suddenly went grim. "I don't do dating services."

Denise refused to relent. "Have you been in a monastery since we broke up?"

"Who I've slept with is none of your business," he retorted.

"I didn't ask who you were sleeping with, Garrett Mason Fennell. I said—"

"I know what you said. You have a choice, Miss Eaton. Either it's yes or no." He knew she was upset because she'd called him by his full name.

"What are my options?"

"If you say no, then you'll receive a lease renewal agreement doubling your current monthly rent."

Denise blinked, unable to believe what she'd heard. "That's blackmail!"

"I call it negotiating, Denise. You want something from me, and I'm offering you a way out of your dilemma. I could've said I wanted you to sleep with me."

"That's sexual harassment."

"Call it whatever you want," Rhett said quietly. "You have exactly one minute to give me an answer, or the deal is off the table."

"And if I say yes?" Denise felt as if someone had put their fingers around her throat, slowly squeezing the life out of her.

Rhett knew he had Denise on the ropes when he saw

her shoulders slump. And, like a shark drawn to the smell of blood, he went in for the kill.

"You give me the next three and a half months of your life and I'll offer you a two-year lease with a ten percent increase."

"Make it three years and six percent," she countered.

"Three years, eight percent, and that's my final offer."

Denise felt as if she'd won a small victory. Picking up her flute, she extended it. "Deal," she crooned, touching glasses. She took a sip of champagne. "Why me, and not some other woman?" she asked, seeing his smug expression.

Rhett lowered his gaze, staring at the back of his left hand. "I don't have time to tutor someone about social etiquette and protocol."

"How often will I have to stand in as your hostess?"

"Every weekend."

"Every weekend?" she repeated. "You're kidding me, aren't you?"

"No, I'm not kidding you, Denise. We'll either entertain here in D.C., or on Cape St. Claire."

The waiter's sudden appearance to take their order was the only thing that stopped Denise from spewing the acid-laced response poised on the tip of her tongue. She narrowed her eyes, glaring at Rhett when she wanted to wipe the smirk off his face. Crossing her arms over her chest, she counted slowly in an attempt to control her temper.

"It can't be every weekend," she said when they were alone again.

Rhett angled his head. "Is your business open on the weekend?"

She rolled her eyes at him. "No."

"It can't be because of a man, because you said you didn't have a boyfriend."

"Boyfriend or not, I still have other obligations."

Rhett glanced up, annoyance and frustration welling up within him. If he wasn't careful, his plan would backfire and that was something he wanted to avoid, given the risks he'd taken to exact revenge from Denise Eaton for turning his world upside down. His most ruthless business foes hadn't been able to affect him the way she had.

He'd designed his retribution as carefully as he studied a company on the brink of bankruptcy before he stepped in to take it over. Rhett had been hard-pressed not to shout at the top of his lungs when his investigator uncovered that Denise had opened a child care center in D.C., and on property his company had recently purchased from a developer who'd been forced to abandon his plan to revitalize four square blocks of commercial real estate after the housing market bottomed out. He'd paid the developer a little more than half the fair market value for the property, and the developer took the check and thanked him profusely.

His game plan included seducing Denise back into his bed, then walking out on her as she had walked out on him. The only difference was there wouldn't be a woman waiting for him as there had been for her years ago.

"What type of other social obligations?"

"I have two fund-raisers—one in June and the other in August. I'm also involved in planning my cousin Belinda's baby shower."

Belinda Eaton-Rice was due at the end of the month and the family had decided that a get-together over the three-day weekend would provide an opportune setting for a baby shower.

"Does she know about the shower?"

Denise smiled for the first time since she'd agreed to go along with Rhett's unorthodox proposal. "No. My parents are supposedly hosting the get-together, and that will give Griffin time to drive Belinda to Philly while the rest of us decorate their house in Paoli. Once they arrive, Griffin will have to come up with an excuse why they have to return to Paoli."

Rhett lifted his eyebrows a fraction. "I must say I was quite surprised when I'd heard that Griffin Rice had married Belinda Eaton."

It was Denise's turn to raise her eyebrows. "How did you hear about it?"

"Keith Ennis."

"You know Keith?" Denise asked. The Philadelphia Phillies ballplayer was a sports superstar. As Keith's agent, Griffin had helped the naturally gifted athlete from a poor Baltimore neighborhood to superstar status with a five-year multimillion-dollar contract, along with high-profile endorsement deals.

"We'd shared a table at a Baltimore fund-raiser, and I overheard him tell someone he was going to be a grooms-man in his agent's wedding. When I heard him mention Belinda Eaton I knew then it was your cousin."

"Griffin and Belinda shocked everyone when they announced they were getting married," Denise said, smiling. "I'd always thought they couldn't stand each other." She sobered. "Griffin losing his brother and Belinda her sister brought them closer together after they became guardians for Donna and Grant's twin daughters."

"I've always liked your family, Denise."

She nodded, scrunching up her nose. "I kind of like them, too. In fact, Chandra asked me about you."

"And what did you tell her?"

"She'd asked if I'd run into you now that I'm living in D.C. and I told her I hadn't."

Rhett leaned closer. "That is, until now," he said softly.

Denise stared at Rhett. There was something in his eyes that communicated he was mocking her. A sixth sense wouldn't let her feel comfortable about their reunion. It wasn't coincidental that he'd happened to purchase the building where she'd set up New Visions Childcare. His reputation as a ruthless corporate raider had earned him the reputation as one of thirty under thirty rising stars in *Beltway Business Review*. At twenty-eight, Garrett Fennell was touted as the Warren Buffett of his generation. She knew there was only one way to find out what he was up to, and that was for her to play the same game.

"Do you have anything planned for the Memorial Day weekend?"

Rhett drained the flute. "I have an invitation to a neighbor's cookout on Sunday. Why?"

"Belinda's shower is scheduled for Saturday afternoon, and I'd like you to come with me. After that, I'm all yours for the rest of the weekend." Denise knew she'd shocked Rhett with her suggestion when he stared at her as if he'd never seen her before.

"You want *me* to hang out with your family?"

"Of course," she said flippantly. "I'm certain they'll welcome you back with open arms."

A beat passed before Rhett spoke again. "What did you tell your parents about our breakup?"

Denise closed her eyes, recalling the meeting with her parents. She'd managed not to break down when they'd asked when she and Rhett were getting married.

She opened her eyes, her gaze fusing with the man. Despite her silent protest, she still loved and would always love him. He'd deceived her with another woman and she still couldn't hate him.

"I told them the truth." Her voice was barely a whisper. "I said I'd fallen out of love with you."

Reaching across the table, Rhett took her hand, increasing the pressure when she tried to escape him. "Do you hate me, Denise?" The second hand dial on his timepiece made a full revolution as they stared at each other.

"No, Rhett, I don't hate you."

Exhaling a breath at the same time he let go of Denise's hand, Rhett stared at a spot over her shoulder. "If that's the case, then I'll go with you to Belinda's baby shower."

Chapter 3

Denise unlocked the door to her apartment, tossed her keys and handbag on the side table in the entryway and kicked off her shoes. In her stocking-covered feet, she headed for the bedroom.

Rhett hadn't driven her home, because she'd only drunk half a glass of champagne. However, he'd walked her to her car, waited until she'd maneuvered away from the curb and turned the corner.

She was angry and annoyed. Her anger was directed at Rhett for using what amounted to blackmail to get her to do his bidding. His excuse that he needed her to double as his date and hostess was so transparent she had almost laughed in his face.

She was annoyed at herself for inviting him to her cousin's baby shower. His presence would literally open a Pandora's box of questions to which she had few or no answers.

The blinking red light on the telephone console on the bedside table indicated she had a message. Reaching for the cordless receiver, she punched in the numbers to retrieve her voice mail. The voice of Chandra Eaton-Tucker came through the earpiece:

"Denise, this is Chandra. Please call me when you get this message. I don't care how late it is when you get in. Call me."

Denise dialed the Philadelphia area code, then Chandra's number. The phone rang twice before there was a break in the connection. "This is Chandra."

"Hey. I hope I'm not calling too late."

Denise walked over to the window and drew the drapes. She sat on an off-white upholstered chair, and propped her feet on a matching footstool. She'd decorated the bedroom as a calming retreat. A bay window had become a seating area with the chair, footstool and off-white silk drapery and sheers.

A queen-size bed with white and beige bed linens, a padded bench covered with silk throw pillows in shades ranging from chocolate to cream was set up for an alcove that had become a second seating area. The stenciled floral design on the double dresser and lingerie chest matched the area rug.

"Preston has been locked in his office for the past two days revising his latest play."

"Does he come out to eat?"

"Rarely," Chandra said. "I usually don't intrude when he gets into what he calls the 'zone.' Now, back to why I called you. I got a set of keys from Griffin today, so we'll be able to let ourselves in."

"What time do you want me to meet you?" Denise asked her cousin.

"Meet me in Paoli any time before ten. I know that means your leaving D.C. early, but I want to get everything decorated before one o'clock."

"There's something you should know," Denise said after a pause.

"What, Denise?"

"I'm bringing someone with me."

"Good! The more the merrier."

"You don't understand, Chandra."

"What's not to understand, Denise? You have a date."

An audible sigh filled the room as she stared at the lighted wall sconce in the sitting alcove. "What if my date is Rhett Fennell? Are you still there, Chandra?" she asked when silence came through the earpiece.

"I'm here. When did you start seeing him again?"

"Tonight we had dinner together."

Denise knew she had to alert Chandra that she was coming with Rhett, because not to would prove embarrassing to all involved and knowing Chandra she knew she would tell the other family members that Rhett was back in her life. Although it was just for the summer, he would still be a part of her life until she fulfilled the terms of their business arrangement.

"Do you want me to tell the others that he's coming?"

"There's no need to send out an APB."

Chandra laughed. "I'll try to be subtle."

It was Denise's turn to laugh. "You wouldn't know subtle if it stood on your chest, Mrs. Tucker."

"You know you're wrong, Denise Eaton."

"Hang up, Chandra."

"Good night."

Denise ended the call, pressed her head to the back of the chair and closed her eyes. She couldn't believe she'd allowed herself to be victimized by a man who held the future of her business venture in his grasp. Rhett knew the importance of reliable and quality day care. He'd grown up with latchkey kids who were left home alone because their parents had to work and couldn't afford to pay someone to look after their children. Social workers from children's services made regular visits to his neighborhood to follow up on complaints stemming from abuse and neglect of children who were unsupervised at night and into the early morning hours. Rhett had been one of the luckier children because his aunt babysat him until he was school-age.

She opened her eyes, struggling not to let the tears filling her eyes spill over. She'd accused Rhett of blackmail and sexual harassment, while he'd called it negotiating. The only saving grace was they wouldn't sleep together. Making love to Rhett Fennell was akin to smoking crack. The addiction was instantaneous.

Forcing herself to rise from the comfy chair, Denise went through the motions of undressing. Then she walked into the en suite bathroom to remove her makeup. Twenty minutes later she touched the switch, turning off the wall sconce and floor lamp. Her eyelids were drooping slightly when she pulled back the comforter and slipped between cool, crisp sheets. Reaching over, she turned off the lamp on the bedside table, and this time when she closed her eyes she didn't open them again until a sliver of light poured in through the octagonal window over the sitting area.

* * *

Rhett massaged his forehead with his fingertips as he compared the bottom line for three years of profit and loss statements for Chambers Properties, Ltd. A steady decline in profits was an obvious indicator that the company was ripe for the picking.

After reuniting with Denise Eaton, he'd thrown himself into his work with the voracity of a starving man at a banquet. Work and more work had not diminished his anxiety at being unable to get her out of his head.

During the walk back to the hotel, after having made certain she was safely in her car, Rhett had replayed the two hours they'd spent together. Even when he'd executed what some had called his "sucker punch" takeover, he hadn't felt as ashamed as he had now. His quest for revenge had gone beyond what he deemed ethical. He'd used his money and the power that went along with it to intimidate and bully a woman who'd sacrificed her time and money to provide essential services to a low-income and working-class community.

Although he'd threatened to double the rent for the child care facility, Rhett knew he never would've gone through with it. After all, he wasn't that far removed from his humble roots to ignore the importance of adequate child care. He was luckier than most of the children from his neighborhood because his maternal aunt had looked after him while his mother worked long hours waiting tables.

When he was six years old, Geraldine Fennell had enrolled him in Marshall Foote Academy, a prestigious boarding school in northern Virginia, where he'd returned home during the summer months and holidays. He'd studied harder than any other boy at the prep school, and after a year his mother had been able to qualify for financial aid. For every grade of ninety and above, the tuition for that term had been waived.

Rhett had learned early in life that he was smart. But he hadn't realized how smart he actually was until it had come time for exams. One of his instructors had accused him of cheating because he'd written verbatim the answer he'd read in his textbook. It was only after Geraldine had been summoned to the school for a conference with the teacher and headmaster that they had become aware of his photographic memory. He was able to recall whole paragraphs from textbooks without thinking about it.

It had been the first and only time he'd seen his mother lose her temper. And it had been the only time he'd forgotten some of the words she'd flung at the red-faced men. Once they'd apologized profusely, Geraldine had returned to D.C., Rhett had been escorted back to his dormitory and the headmaster had chastised the instructor for embarrassing him and jeopardizing the academy's reputation with unsubstantiated allegations when he'd accused their best student of cheating.

Attending the academy had afforded him the opportunity for a quality education. He'd also managed to escape the social problems that plagued his poor urban neighborhood.

Yes, he'd made it out *and* he'd made a difference. But the differences were quiet, subtle. And with every company he took over, Rhett always looked after the employees. Those who wanted out he offered a generous severance package. Those who didn't, he created positions for them—even if he had to reduce their salaries. The rationale was at least they had a paycheck.

The buzz of the intercom interrupted his reverie. "Yes, Tracy."

"Your uncle is here."

Rhett smiled. "Tell him I'll be right out." He took a quick glance at the clock on his desk. "I'll probably be gone for the rest of the day. Take messages and if there's anything you can't handle, then call me on my cell."

"No problem, Rhett," said his executive assistant.

He'd hired Tracy Powell when his office had been nothing more than a twelve-by-twelve second bedroom in his apartment after he'd earned an MBA from Wharton business school. He'd purchased two used desks, installed a telephone line separate from his personal one and he and the part-time bookkeeper/secretary/receptionist grew a company from two to fourteen employees.

After two years, Rhett rented space in an office building in downtown D.C., and now he owned a four-story town house blocks from Dupont Circle. The first three floors were occupied by his various holding companies. And when renovations on the fourth floor were completed Rhett would move into what would become his private apartment. His decision to live in the same building where he worked was because he'd found himself spending more time there than he had at his condominium. He'd sold the condo and had temporarily moved into the hotel while the contractor renovated the space.

What he constantly reminded himself was that other than his mother, he had no family. His grandparents were dead and so was the aunt who'd looked after him. There was only he and his mother, who'd found happiness with a sixty-year-old widower who adored her.

Rhett knew his reluctance to settle down with a woman stemmed from his relationship with Denise

Eaton. The first time he'd slept with her he knew he wanted her to be the only woman in his life. What he hadn't known at the time was that she wouldn't be. There had been women after Denise—more than he'd willingly admit—to fill up the empty hours or to slake his sexual frustration.

Then everything had changed when a woman had accused him of leading her on, that she'd expected a commitment that would eventually lead to marriage. He'd made a decision not to date or sleep with women. It was during this time that he'd been forced to reexamine his wanton behavior and acknowledge his selfishness.

Women were not his playthings. They were not receptacles for his lust or frustration. They wanted more than a *slam bam thank you ma'am*. When he'd finally told his mother about the revolving door of women in and out of his life, her comeback had been he should think of them as his sister—did he want a man to treat her with a total disregard for her feelings? The analogy had been enough for him to stop his self-destructive behavior.

Rolling down and buttoning the cuffs of his shirt, Rhett reached for the jacket to his suit and walked out of his office. He nodded in the direction of the man lounging on a leather chair in the waiting alcove outside his office.

Tracy Powell peered over her half-glasses, a profusion of salt-and-pepper braids framing her smooth gold-brown face. She couldn't understand why the rumpled-looking older man hadn't taken a hint from his young nephew and put on something that didn't look as if it had just come out of the washing machine.

"Enjoy your lunch," she called out to the two men.

Rhett gave her a wink. "Thank you."

He walked with Eli Oakes to the elevator, taking it to the street level. Moments after stepping out into the bright sunlight, they exchanged a handshake. Eli wasn't his uncle, but a private investigator. When he'd met Eli for the first time, Rhett thought of him as kind of a black Columbo. Eli even wore a wrinkled trench coat during cooler, rainy weather. The former police officer admitted to being forty-seven, a confirmed bachelor and a recovering alcoholic. Tall and gangly with smooth sable-brown skin, the man's innocuous appearance was a foil for a sharp mind that noted details most people were likely to overlook.

"Where do you want to eat?"

Eli put on a pair of sunglasses, then ran a hand over his stubbly pate. "I had a big breakfast, so I don't need anything too heavy."

Rhett rested a hand on the older man's shoulder. "There's a new restaurant on Massachusetts that features salads and wraps and vegetarian dishes. We can try it if you want."

Eli smiled. "Let's try it."

"What do you have for me?" Rhett asked after he and Eli gave the waitress their orders.

Reaching into the pocket of his jacket, Eli pulled out a folded sheet of paper. "See for yourself." He pushed it across the table.

Rhett unfolded the page of type. His expression didn't change as he read the information the investigator had come up with on Trey Chambers. "He's a busy boy," he murmured. "No wonder his business is in the toilet."

Eli picked up a glass of sweet tea, taking a long swallow. "What I didn't include in that report is that Chambers spends a lot of time at the track."

Rhett digested this information as he counted the number of boards on which Trey Chambers either chaired or was a member. What surprised him was Eli's claim that Trey had a gambling problem. When they were in college together he hadn't remembered the business major gambling. Even when coeds were placing bets during March Madness, Trey hadn't participated.

"Is he winning or losing?"

Eli shrugged his shoulders under his jacket. "Both. He made a bundle betting on the Derby and Preakness, but we'll have to see what he does with the Belmont Stakes."

"Trey was never much of a gambler."

A sly smile parted the lips of the man whose decorated law enforcement career had ended after he'd been injured in a hit-and-run when he'd gone out early one morning to buy the newspaper. He'd lain in a coma for several months; when he'd emerged he submitted his retirement papers and went into private investigation. "Trey's daddy is no longer collecting wives, but horses. That could explain Junior's sudden interest in the ponies."

Rhett wanted to tell Eli that if the Chambers were winning at the track, they weren't putting it back into their real estate business. Chambers Properties owned large parcels of land in Baltimore and D.C., and there was one tract not far from Baltimore Harbor that Chambers wanted. Rhett, also interested in the property, had submitted a bid.

The waitress approached the table, setting down a plate with a tuna salad with sprouts on a bed of lettuce for Eli and a bowl of Caesar salad for Rhett.

Over lunch, the topic of conversation changed to

sports—baseball and the upcoming football season. The two men talked about trades and drafts, becoming more animated when they argued good-naturedly about teams they predicted would win the World Series and Super Bowl. Most of the lunch crowd had thinned out when Rhett paid the check and slid an envelope across the table.

Eli picked up the envelope, peering into its contents. "What's up with the cash?" Rhett usually gave him a check as payment for his services.

"Think of it as a mid-year bonus."

Lines of consternation were etched into Eli's forehead. "A bonus for what?"

Rhett wanted to tell the man to take the money and stop asking so many questions, but he knew once a cop always a cop. He didn't want Eli to think he was trying to set him up, which was why he always paid him with a check and at the end of the year issued a 1099 for his personal services.

"It's a little extra for reuniting me with my old girl-friend."

Eli's expression brightened. "If that's the case, then I'll humbly accept your mid-year bonus."

Backing away from the table, the men walked out of the restaurant, going in opposite directions. Rhett walked back to where he'd parked his car. Instead of driving to the hotel, he headed in the opposite direction. A quarter of an hour later, he maneuvered into the parking lot across the street from New Visions Childcare.

"How long will you be gone?" the attendant asked.

"Less than half an hour," Rhett said, handing the man the keys to his late-model Mercedes Benz sedan.

Crossing the street, he opened the door to the one-story brick building and walked into a reception area. Recessed lighting illuminated the space with a warm glow while the calming green paint with an alphabet border added a festive touch. Rhett had also noticed several security cameras were positioned inside and outside the facility.

A young woman sitting behind a glassed partition was on the phone arguing with someone who wanted to pick up a child, but didn't have authorization. "I'm sorry, Mr. Hawkins, but rules are rules. If you submit official documentation from the court, then we'll be able to release your son to you. You have a good day, too." She stuck out her tongue at the telephone console before realizing someone was watching her.

Rhett smiled as she slid back the glass. "I'm here to see Ms. Denise Eaton."

The receptionist, who had long airbrushed nails, gave him a bored look. "Is she expecting you?"

"No, she isn't. Can you please let her know Garrett Fennell would like to see her?"

"Ms. Eaton usually won't see anyone without an appointment."

"I'm certain she'll see me." There was a ring of confidence in the statement.

"What's your name again?"

"Garrett Fennell."

He stared at the woman's long nails, which reminded him of talons, as she tapped the buttons of the telephone console, and spoke quietly into her headset. She pushed another button. "Please have a seat, Mr. Fennell. Ms. Eaton will be with you shortly."

Rhett sat on a decorative wrought-iron back bench and thumbed through a magazine from a stack on a low side table. He smiled at the picture of an infant staring back at him on the glossy cover. Flipping through the magazine, he found an article about coping with temper tantrums. Halfway through the article, the receptionist told him Ms. Eaton was now available to see him.

He walked toward the door with a sign that said you had to see the receptionist before being buzzed in. He pushed open the door when the buzzer sounded, coming face-to-face with a very different Denise Eaton.

Chapter 4

When Denise left Rhett standing on the curb, she hadn't expected to see him again until Saturday. Less than twenty-four hours later he had surprised her again.

"Have you come to renege on our deal?"

Denise had spoken so softly Rhett had to strain to hear what she was saying. "Is that what you want?" he asked. "You want out?"

"Did I say I wanted out?" Denise found it hard to breathe. She was standing in a hallway, less than two feet from Rhett Fennell, whose presence seemed to suck the air from her lungs. She lowered her gaze rather than let him see her lusting after him. And that was exactly what she'd fantasized about the night before. She'd gone to bed thinking of Rhett, which was enough to trigger an erotic dream. When she awoke, it was to a pounding heartbeat and a pulsing between her legs that left her wet and moaning in frustration.

"Come to my office, and we'll talk."

Denise had invited Rhett to her office when what she'd wanted was to show him the door. They had struck a deal to see each other on weekends only.

Rhett noticed the gentle sway of Denise's hips in a pair of black cropped stretch pants. He knew she was tense because her back was ramrod straight and both hands at her side were balled into fists. The casual slacks, sleeveless white blouse and black sandals with a wedge heel made her look more approachable than she had the night before. The blue dress reminded him of an ice queen—look but don't touch. And he hadn't touched her except to cradle her elbow.

Even her hairstyle was different. Instead of the bun, which he'd found much too severe for her age and delicate features, a narrow headband pulled her glossy curls off her face. When they were in school together she'd always worn a short hairstyle.

Rhett felt the flesh between his thighs come to life when the image of her hair spread across his pillow popped into his head. Just as quickly, it went away, leaving him breathing heavier and with an ache in his groin. A muscle twitched in his jaw as he clenched his teeth. Fortunately for him, Denise was in front of him or she wouldn't have been able to miss his hard-on straining against his fly. As surreptitiously as he could, he buttoned his jacket, concealing the bulge.

"How much work did you have to do to this place before you were able to open?" He had to talk. Say anything to keep his mind off Denise's slim, yet curvy body. They walked past closed doors to offices for the center's social worker, dietician and business manager. Nameplates identified each person and their position.

Denise slowed when she came to an open area with eight round tables, each with seating for six. As in the reception area, she'd decided against chairs, opting instead for benches. Several skylights, potted plants, ferns and ficus trees provided a parklike atmosphere.

"Not too much," she threw over her shoulder as she opened the door to her office. Her name and position were etched on the nameplate affixed to the door. "The contractor had to patch up a few holes before he could paint. The previous owner had replaced the roof three years ago, so that saved me at least thirty grand."

Stepping aside, Denise let Rhett precede her into the room that at one time had been her second home. She'd come in at dawn to let the workmen in and occasionally slept on an inflatable bed she'd put away in a closet. The center was equipped with three full bathrooms, each with a shower and two half-baths in the nursery and classrooms for children, ranging in age from two to five.

"Please sit down, Rhett." Denise gestured toward a love seat in a soft neutral shade. She sat in a matching one facing him. She crossed one leg over the other, bringing his gaze to linger on the rose-pink polish on her toes. "Would you like something to eat or drink? We've just finished giving the children their lunch, so the kitchen is still open."

"No, thank you. I just ate."

He glanced around Denise's office. It reflected her personality with plants lining a window ledge. Her desk was an old oak top from another generation, a Tiffany-style desk lamp, a fireplace mantel filled with different size candles. Three of the four walls in her office were brick, the remaining one covered with framed prints of children from around the world.

Denise stared at Rhett through lowered lashes. To say he looked delicious was an understatement. Today he wore a dark blue suit with a maroon-colored silk tie and white shirt. He looked nothing like the college student who'd favored jeans, pullover sweaters or sweatshirts. At that time, Rhett owned just one suit, which he only wore on special occasions.

"How old is that desk?"

Rhett's question caught Denise off guard. She didn't know why he'd come to the center, but she was willing to bet it had nothing to do with the furnishings. "It's quite old."

He smiled. "How old is quite old?"

"I'm not selling it, Rhett."

His eyebrows lifted. "Why don't you wait for me to make an offer."

"Offer all you want, I'm not selling."

Rhett angled his head, staring at the antique desk. "Have you had it appraised?"

She nodded. "Appraised and insured. It belonged to my grandfather who got it from a client who'd lost all of his assets in the crash of '29. The desk and several other pieces of furniture were payment for a criminal case my grandfather had taken on and won for him. My father inherited it from his father. He gave up his practice once he was appointed to the bench, and I quickly put in my bid for the desk."

"Who else wanted it?" Rhett asked.

"Every lawyer in the family pulled out their checkbooks, claiming it should go to someone practicing law, not a schoolteacher."

"Ouch," Rhett drawled, smiling. "That's definitely a shot across the bow."

Denise sucked her teeth. "Yeah, right. I was quick to tell them the desk belonged to *my* father, and as his baby girl I was entitled to it."

"No, you didn't pull the baby-girl card."

"Whatever works, Rhett."

He sobered. "Speaking of whatever works, I'd like you to give me a tour of the facility."

"Why?" she countered. "Are you thinking of becoming an investor?"

Denise regretted the question as soon as it rolled off her tongue. It was enough that Rhett owned the building and the land on which New Visions Childcare sat, but she didn't need him to own a percentage of her business.

"Do you need an investor, Denise?"

"No," she said much too quickly. "My revenues are enough to support the day care operation."

"Do you have money put aside?"

"Yes." And she did. The monies she would get from the sale of her co-op would become her emergency fund. Denise had promised herself that she wouldn't use her personal funds unless it was a dire emergency. So far, she'd been able to keep that promise.

"Good for you." Rhett stood up, extended his hand and pulled Denise gently to her feet. "My initial reason for coming was to talk to you about this weekend."

"You could've called me, Rhett. After all, I did give you my number."

"I was in the neighborhood, so I decided to drop by."

He hadn't lied to Denise. He'd come to this section of D.C. to tour the neighborhood and see what was needed to upgrade the quality of life for the people who lived there. His company owned four square blocks designated for commercial use; the urban planner on his staff had suggested he drive around the neighborhood to survey the area before he made his decision about redevelopment.

"What are you doing, Rhett? Taking stock of your assets?"

Rhett knew Denise was spoiling for a confrontation because he'd coerced her into being his escort for the summer. She could've called his bluff and said no, but she hadn't. Despite their very intimate past, she still hadn't known him that well. If she had, then she would've believed him rather than Trey when he'd told her that he hadn't been sleeping with other women. And if she had truly believed him when he confessed to loving her, she wouldn't have ended up in bed with Trey.

He hadn't purchased the real estate to jack up the rents, as he'd threatened to do with New Visions, but to improve the property and the quality of life for the residents.

Rhett wasn't *that* far removed from the neighborhood in which he'd grown up not to recognize the importance of adequate child care. It provided a safe haven for the children of working parents and those who were trying to pursue their education and thereby better themselves and their families. However, Denise had fallen into a carefully planned trap.

He took a step, bringing him close enough for her chest to touch his. "Which assets do you speak of?"

Denise hadn't realized the double entendre until it was too late. Her lips parted at the same time Rhett angled his head, brushing his mouth over hers. His hands came up and he took her face, holding it gently as if he feared she would shatter if he let her go.

Slowly, deliberately, he caressed instead of kissing her mouth, seeking to allay her fears that he wanted to dismantle what she'd worked so hard to establish. He kissed her because it was something he'd wanted to do the moment he saw her walk across the lobby of the Hay-Adams hotel.

Tiptoeing, Denise pressed her lips closer. Rhett's mouth brushed hers like a butterfly fluttering over her lips. She wanted more, much more, but she knew they couldn't and wouldn't go back in time.

She and Rhett had been caught up in a magical world where love and passion were indistinguishable. They'd eaten together, studied together, made love to each other and spent countless hours planning a future that included marriage and children.

However, four years of togetherness ended abruptly when the rumor floating around the university that Garrett Fennell was sleeping with her and another student was no longer a rumor but real when Denise opened the door to her boyfriend's dorm room to find a naked woman asleep in his bed. In that instant, the love she'd known and felt for Rhett disappeared. She'd left as quietly as she'd come, walking out of the building and out of Rhett's life.

"Don't! Please, Rhett."

Rhett froze, his gaze meeting and fusing with Denise's. There was something in her eyes he recognized as fear and he wondered whether he'd put it there. He dipped his head to kiss her again, but her hands pressed against his chest stopped him.

"What's wrong, Denise?"

A rush of heat singed Denise's face *and* body when she realized the enormity of what had just taken place. "You coming here unannounced and then kissing me when someone could've walked in on us. That's what's wrong," she spat out.

Smiling, Rhett pushed his hands into the pockets of his suit trousers to keep from reaching for her again. Anger had replaced the fear, and he remembered Denise being most passionate whenever she was angry. Memories of their makeup sex were permanently branded into his head.

"The next time I come I'll make certain to make an appointment beforehand. And I promise never to kiss you again in your office."

Denise saw the beginnings of a smirk. If she was going to be angry at anyone, then it had to be at herself. She'd learned never to challenge Rhett Fennell because he would accept the challenge and win.

He'd waged a silent and bloodless battle when he'd outlined the conditions for renewing her lease—leaving her with little or no recourse, and she was forced to accept his terms. Rhett had called it negotiating, while to her it was still a subtle form of blackmail.

The residents in the neighborhood needed the child care center, she wanted to make certain it remained open, and it wasn't as if she had a horde of men lining up outside her door to take her out.

What Denise hadn't wanted to think about was *if* she had had a boyfriend would Rhett have proposed the same game plan. Then she'd recalled him saying, "I need someone who will stand in as my date and hostess, provided your boyfriend doesn't object," and she'd answered her own question. It would not have made a difference.

"Please give me a few minutes, and I'll take you around to see the facility."

Walking on stiff legs, Denise went into the private bathroom and shut the door. The image staring back at her in the mirror over the sink was one she didn't recognize.

"I don't know if I can do this," she whispered. If Rhett hadn't ended the kiss when he did, she probably would've asked for more—and more translated into her begging him to make love to her.

When she and Rhett shared a bed for the first time it had been *her* first time. Denise knew she'd shocked him, because she hadn't told him she was a virgin. What she hadn't wanted was for him to feel guilty and continue to see her out of a perverse sense of obligation.

However, he did continue to date her. It was another month before they made love again, and she'd experienced her first orgasm. Making love with Rhett was always good. Makeup sex was even better. It was the memories of their lovemaking, the plans they'd made for a life beyond college, that had lingered with her after she'd graduated and returned to Philadelphia.

It had taken more than a year for her to acknowledge what she'd had with Rhett was over and she had to move on with her life. She'd gotten back into the dating scene when she and several teachers at the school where she'd taught met regularly at a downtown Philly club on Friday nights. Denise had refused to date any of the male teachers with whom she worked, but she had met a software analyst at one of the weekly social mixers. They'd played telephone tag for several weeks before connecting.

Denise had liked Kevin enough to go out with him for three months. They'd slept together once. Days later she had been filled with guilt because she'd compared Kevin to Rhett, and the former fell far short of satisfying her. Kevin had seemed to get the picture without her having to connect the dots, and they had mutually agreed to stop seeing each other.

"Denise, are you all right in there?" asked Rhett outside the closed door.

"I'm good. Just give me a few more minutes."

When did you become such an astute liar? Denise mused, as she splashed cold water on her face. She patted her face with a soft towel, then opened the chest over the sink and took out a small jar with powder that matched her skin tone. She shook out a minute amount on a brush and applied the powder to her face. Within seconds her face had a rich, healthy glow. A coat of mascara to her lashes and lip gloss rounded out her mini-makeover. Denise ran her fingers through her hair, fluffing up the curls before she washed her hands.

It's amazing what a new do, a new outfit and a little makeup can do to lift a woman's spirit. Denise smiled in spite of the situation in which she'd found herself. "Thank you, Mom," she whispered.

Paulette Eaton's manifesto had served her well on many occasions. She didn't have a new do or outfit, but a little color on her face had done the trick. When she emerged from the bathroom she was emotionally ready to deal with the likes of Rhett Fennell.

Her eyes were smiling and her step light as she reached for a lanyard with her picture ID, then led him out of her office. "This area of the center is called the administrative section. Whenever we have staff meetings, or something when we invite the parents and siblings of the children enrolled here, we hold them out here."

"It looks like a park," Rhett said.

"We wanted it to look like a park with the trees and benches," Denise explained. "I've ordered an indoor waterfall and one of our board members gave the center a gift of a flat-screen television he'd won in a raffle. A technician is expected in before the end of the week to mount it on that wall." She pointed to a wall where anyone sitting at the tables would be able to view it.

"This place is so quiet. Where are the children?"

"It's nap time, so most of them are probably asleep."

"How long do they nap?"

"From twelve thirty to two. At two we get them up and give them a little snack. From three o'clock on, they're picked up by family members." She swiped her ID along a device on the door leading to the area where the children were sleeping. "Even though we have state-of-the-art security with cameras and an alarm that is connected directly to the local police station, we do everything possible to ensure the safety of our children."

"I have to assume everyone is buzzed in."

Denise nodded. "Employees must swipe in and out, and parents and those designated to pick up their children are buzzed in and out. We tell our parents over and over that if custodial arrangements change, then we must know about it immediately. If a woman breaks up with her boyfriend or husband and she doesn't want them to pick up her child or children, or if there is an order of protection or change in custody, then we must be notified like yesterday."

She stopped at a set of double doors, pushing one open. "This is our kitchen and Miss Jessie is our cook and dietician. Ms. Cox, this is Mr. Fennell."

Rhett nodded to the petite woman wearing a pale

green uniform, hairnet and garish orange clogs. "Ms. Cox."

Jessie Cox smiled, then went back to slicing fruit for the afternoon snack. The industrial kitchen was outfitted with stainless-steel sinks and appliances. The refrigerators and walk-in freezers were also equipped with security devices.

Reaching for his hand, Denise led Rhett out of the kitchen. "Ms. Cox has started a dialogue with the parents about proper nutrition for their children. A few of our children are overweight, but after a few months they begin dropping the pounds."

Rhett noticed Denise always referred to the children as *our children,* and he wondered if she'd substituted the children at the facility for the ones they may have had if they'd stayed together.

"How many meals do you serve here?" he asked.

"Breakfast, lunch and an afternoon snack."

"What time do you open?"

"The facility opens at six, but parents can't drop off their children until seven. We close at six, but will stay open as late as seven. After seven, the parents will have to pick up their children at the police station."

"What if they're delayed?"

"If they call us, then usually someone will stay later than seven. It's something I don't advertise or encourage, but there are always exceptions."

"Why do you take them to the police station? Isn't that traumatic for the child?"

"Of course it is, Rhett. We are day care—not a 24/7 babysitting service. If people don't come and get their children, then they're charged with abandoning their child. I'll explain it at another time," she said, lowering her voice when a teacher from the toddler group walked out into the hallway. "We group the children according to age."

Rhett peered through the large window on the door. The shades were drawn and the lights were out. He saw eight tiny bodies on sheet-covered cots under lightweight blankets. "How old are these little munchkins?"

"Those are our two-and three-year-olds. They're all potty-trained, they can feed themselves and all or most recognize the letters in the alphabet. By their third birthday they know their names and addresses, and some can recite their telephone number."

"Do you teach them to read?"

Denise stared at Rhett's profile as he continued to stare into the room. "I've set up a reading-readiness program for the three-and four-year-olds. Some schools are doing away with their pre-K programs, so we've had to pick up the slack. Child care is basically about socialization, but I've tried to incorporate as much education as I can to give our children a head start. When they leave here and enroll in regular school, all are familiar with the alphabet and most of them are able to read.

"The social worker has made it her personal mission to connect with each parent and guardian. If certain deficits are identified, then Tonya becomes a parent's worst nightmare. She will haunt the woman until she either has the child tested or receives the appropriate counseling."

Rhett listened intently when Denise talked about trying to make a difference, not only in the lives of the children but also their families. The center hosted a bimonthly family night for the parents, guardians and siblings of the children. The gatherings served to support the adage that it takes a village to raise a child.

In keeping with the needs of working parents, New Visions had instituted a wellness clinic where children with colds and low-grades fevers were isolated and treated by a nurse practitioner. The children recovered quicker than they would have at home, and their parents didn't have to miss work and stay home with them.

The center was set up to enroll children from six months to twelve years of age. Some school-age children were dropped off at seven, fed breakfast, then lined up for the buses that would take them to their respective schools.

"I'm currently working on a grant to fund an after-school homework or extra help program for middle- and high-school students."

Rhett stared out at the outdoor recreation area enclosed and protected by a high fence and monitored by cameras. There were the requisite slides, teeter-totters, sandboxes, wading pools and picnic tables and benches. All of the classrooms were spacious, with colorful cutouts pasted on windows, reading and play corners and cubbies where coats and boots were stored during colder weather. He'd smiled when seeing the tiny tables and chairs, unable to remember when he'd been that small.

"How much is the grant?" he asked. Denise quoted a figure and he lifted his eyebrows a fraction when he realized what she wanted was less than he'd paid for his car.

"The homework program wouldn't be run here. I don't want the older children interacting with the younger ones."

Shifting, he turned and stared at Denise. "Where will it be?"

Denise gave Rhett a tender smile. "Hopefully I'll be able to rent the space next door."

Taking his hands from his pockets, Rhett took a step closer to Denise. "Have you talked to the owner about the space?"

She flashed a sexy moue. "Not yet."

"Why haven't you, Ms. Eaton?"

"First, it all depends on a grant I've been working on, so I don't know if I'm going to get the funding."

"And secondly…"

"Secondly, if I did get the funding, I'm not certain whether the owner would be willing to lease the space to New Visions, or what the rent would be."

"Have you completed your budget?"

Denise shook her head. "No. The accountant will do the budget."

"Do you know when you'll submit the grant?"

She nodded. "I have a June fifteenth deadline for submission, and the winners will be announced September fifteenth."

Rhett reached out to touch her hair, but caught himself in time. He remembered Denise's warning about her employees seeing her in a compromising position. "We'll talk about the rent for the space."

"Don't you mean negotiate?" she said.

Attractive lines fanned out around his eyes when he smiled. "Are you willing to negotiate?"

Crossing her arms under her breasts, Denise nodded. "I am if I can get a good deal."

"What do you consider a good deal, Denise?"

"A dollar a month and…"

"And what?" he asked when her words trailed off.

"And I'll make myself available to you more than just weekends."

Rhett narrowed his eyes. "How available is *available?*"

"I'll be your girlfriend."

"You of all people should know what being my girlfriend entails." Denise nodded. Rhett held out his hand. "You've got yourself a deal."

Denise shook his hand. "Deal," she confirmed.

Rhett winked at her. "When do we start?"

"This weekend. I have to get to Paoli by ten, which means we'll have to get on the road early."

"I'll come by and pick you up at six. That should give us plenty of time to get out of D.C. before the traffic builds up. We can stop along the way and have breakfast."

"Pack a bag, Rhett, because I plan to stay overnight in Philly."

"Where are we staying?" he asked.

"I have a co-op in Penn's Landing."

Eli had reported to Rhett that Denise had a buyer for the property and was expected to close on it in a matter of weeks. He never asked the former law enforcement officer how he'd gotten his information, but paid him well for it.

"Okay. We'll spend the night in Philly, but we're going directly to the Cape from there, so you, too, will have to pack enough for two days."

Denise concluded the tour of the facility, walked Rhett back to the reception area and waited until the front door closed behind him. For the second time within two days she chided herself for falling prey to Rhett's charm and her own vulnerability when it came to New Visions. What he hadn't known was that she would agree to almost anything to keep the day care business she built from scratch viable, and that meant sleeping with the man who'd broken her heart.

Chapter 5

Denise felt excitement akin to what she'd experienced during the ribbon-cutting ceremony when she and the staff of New Visions posed for photo ops with the mayor and other local dignitaries. Rhett's offer to charge her a dollar a month rent for the adjacent vacant building propelled her to complete the grant sooner rather than later. Not having to pay rent meant she could hire an additional instructor.

The space, half the square feet of the day care center, would be configured into classrooms with teachers providing tutoring services in science, math, English and history. She'd wanted to include another subject—technology, but that meant she would have to purchase computers. Unfortunately, the amount of the grant would not cover the cost for new computers. She had considered going to a computer show and purchasing several older models, but decided the technology module would have to wait.

She came in at six in the morning, and several nights she was still at her desk when the night janitor arrived to clean the center. She'd taken a three-day course on grant writing and the seminar proved invaluable when she had to navigate the waters of endless red tape, giving the bureaucrats exactly what they wanted to read and disseminate.

"Don't tell me you're going to spend the weekend here."

Denise's head popped up. The nurse was standing in the doorway. She'd changed out of her colorful scrubs and into jeans and a tank top. The children loved Miss Randi, and it'd taken redheaded, freckled-faced Miranda Gannon a while before she realized the ones who'd deliberately fallen down used it as a ruse to go to the infirmary because she had Band-Aids with their favorite cartoon characters.

"Bite your tongue. As soon as I finish this paragraph I'm outta here."

Miranda rested her hip against the door frame. "If you're staying in town and not really doing anything, I'd like to invite you to hang out with me and Harper."

Denise chuckled. "You, Harper and your brother?" Miranda nodded. "Look, Randi, I know Brice likes me, but what he doesn't understand is that I can't give him the attention he wants."

"He just wants to date you, Denise."

"The man wants to get married. He sees you with Harper and he wants what you have."

Miranda's blue eyes narrowed. "Is it because he has red hair?"

A shiver of annoyance worked its way down Denise's back. She'd made it a policy not to socialize with her employees, but that was overlooked whenever they hosted a fund-raiser or open house. During the last bake sale her parents had surprised her when Paulette donated a dozen cakes and twenty pounds of her prize-winning double chocolate chip cookies.

"Call it for what it is, Miranda. If you're skirting around the issue that I don't want to go out with your brother because he's white, then you're dead wrong. FYI—the last man I dated was white, so there goes your theory as to why I won't date Brice. Now, go home and enjoy your gorgeous husband."

A flush crept up Miranda's neck to her hairline. "I'm sorry, Denise. I had no idea you'd dated out of your race. FYI—I'm going to spend the weekend seeing if Harper and I can make a little brown baby with red hair." She held up a hand. "And, before you get your nose out of joint about losing a nurse, I know someone who will fill in for me while I'm out on maternity leave. Then when Harper or Randi Jr. turns six months he or she will become a New Visions baby."

Denise knew she couldn't remain angry with the perky, kind-hearted nurse. The redhead who'd worked at the Walter Reed Medical Center met and married a psychiatrist decided their marriage would lose its newness if they saw each other 24/7. She applied to the center with impeccable recommendations and after a background check she was hired as the medical director.

"Have fun, Randi."

Miranda winked at Denise. "I intend to. Enjoy your weekend."

"I intend to," Denise repeated.

As soon as she finished up at the center, she planned to go home and pack for the weekend. Then she would do what she hadn't done in weeks: pick up dinner from her favorite takeout, eat in front of the television, and then take a long relaxing bubble bath before going to bed.

She was looking forward to Belinda's baby shower. Her cousin was listed with several baby registries, and Denise had chosen a number of items and had them shipped to her parents' address. Boaz and Paulette would bring everything to Paoli in their SUV.

Her gaze shifted to the bouquet of flowers on the edge of her desk. Rhett had sent her the flowers as a thank-you gift for sharing dinner with him at the hotel. When she'd called his cell to thank him it went directly to voice mail. That was three days ago.

Her telephone rang and Denise stared at the phone. The display indicated it was a private call. The center was closed; all of the children had been picked up so she couldn't understand who was calling at that hour. After half a dozen rings, the voice mail feature was activated. Less than a minute later her private line rang, and she answered it.

"New Visions Childcare. Denise Eaton speaking."

"Hey."

Denise smiled. "Hey yourself, Rhett. Was it you that just called the main number?"

"Guilty as charged. What are you still doing there?"

"I wanted to finish the grant before I go home."

"Put it away, Denise."

"What?"

"I said put it away and come outside."

"Where are you, Rhett?"

"I'm in the parking lot across the street, leaning

against the bumper of your car. By the way, when did you start driving a hoopty?"

Heat and embarrassment stung her cheeks. "For your information I intend to buy a new car."

"When?"

"That's none of your business."

"I can't believe you were going to drive...*this* to Philly and back."

"Careful, Rhett. You're talking about Valentina."

"Who's Valentina?"

"My *hoopty,* Garrett Mason Fennell. I picked her up on Valentine's Day, so I named her Valentina."

"Tell me something, Denise Amaris Eaton?"

"What is it, Garrett?"

"Why do women name their cars? It's not as if they are pets."

"You wouldn't understand, Rhett. It's a woman thing. Rhett, are you still there?" Denise asked when there came a prolonged pause.

"I'm here. I know it's very short notice, but I'd like to take you out to dinner."

Denise groaned inwardly. "I'd planned to pick up take-out, then go home and have a relaxing bubble bath."

"You can still do that. I'll drop you off home where you can pack—that is if you haven't—then come back to the hotel and order in. After that you can relax in the Jacuzzi until you turn into a raisin."

"What happens after I turn into a raisin?" Her heart was pounding so hard it hurt her chest.

"I'll tuck you into bed, give you a night-night kiss and wait until you fall asleep. Only then will I turn off the light."

Denise remembered how much Rhett liked watching her until she fell asleep. Only then would he turn off the lamp on his side of the bed. She'd promised to be his girlfriend for the summer, but what she didn't want was for them to pretend all was well and they could pick up where they'd left off what now seemed so long ago.

"Not tonight, Rhett. Maybe some other time."

"I'll see you tomorrow morning."

The phone line went dead and Denise knew he'd hung up. The pain in her chest wasn't because of the runaway beating of her heart. It was heartache, heartache for a man she couldn't trust and for a man she still loved.

It took a quarter of an hour to complete the information needed on the last page of the grant. Denise saved what she'd typed, printed out the pages, then stored everything in a file cabinet and locked it. When she finally walked out of the center after activating the security system, she glanced across the street to see if she could see Rhett. Her car was there, but he was gone.

In less than ten hours she would see Rhett again, and at that time the charade would begin.

Denise walked out of her apartment building carrying a leather tote and a large quilted overnight bag. She wasn't certain whether the gathering she and Rhett were invited to was casual or formal, so she packed outfits for both. Fortunately, the weather had cooperated. Meteorologists predicted sun and warm temperatures for the entire three-day weekend. It was six in the morning and the mercury was already seventy-four degrees.

Less than a minute later a silver Mercedes Benz maneuvered up along the curb and Rhett stepped out. He was casually dressed in a pair of navy linen slacks, a white short-sleeved shirt and black woven slip-ons.

She smiled when he closed the distance between them and reached for her bag. "Good morning."

Rhett angled his head and brushed a kiss over her mouth. "Good morning, beautiful."

She blushed, grateful that her darker coloring hid the heat suffusing her face. It was the same greeting he'd whispered to her whenever they'd slept together. Not only did he look good, but he also smelled good. The cologne was the perfect complement for his personality. It was masculine, yet subtle.

"I'll keep the tote," she said when he reached for that, too.

"What's in there?"

"My wallet with my driver's license and a few feminine incidentals."

"Are you going to need your tampons and sanitary napkins before we get to Philly?"

"No, he didn't ask me that," she said under her breath.

"Yes, I did," Rhett countered, taking the tote from her loose grip, shifting both bags to one hand, while the other cupped her elbow. "I was the only guy at Johns Hopkins who bought his girlfriend's tampons and pads. The wiseass in checkout once asked me if I'd had a sex change."

Smiling, Denise gave him a sidelong glance. "You never told me that."

Rhett helped her into the passenger seat, stored the bags in the trunk, then came around and slid behind the wheel. "That's because I was too embarrassed to repeat it."

Denise buckled her seat belt. "Well, I bought our condoms."

Shifting into gear, he pulled away from the curb. "Lots

of girls buy condoms, because they don't trust guys not to put holes in them with pins or needles."

"That's not why I bought the condoms, Rhett. Neither of us wanted nor needed a baby at that time in our lives."

"What about now? Are you ready to start a family?"

Staring out the windshield, Denise pondered his query. It was one she'd asked herself every time she celebrated a birthday. She would celebrate her twenty-eighth birthday at the end of September and each year brought her closer to when she would be deemed high-risk.

She loved children and eventually wanted to become a mother but didn't want to be a baby mama. More than half the women who'd enrolled their children in New Visions were single mothers, most struggling to make ends meet. Even those who had earned a college degree and were making fairly good salaries had to monitor their budgets closely because it was becoming more and more difficult to support a family of two, three or even four on one salary.

"No," Denise said after a swollen silence. "I still have a few years to think about it."

"Don't think too long, sweetheart."

She turned to look at Rhett, silently admiring his distinctive profile. He held his head at a slight angle that she'd always found very endearing. "Why would you say that?"

"I remember you saying you didn't want to be faced with the countdown of a ticking biological clock."

"I still have a few years before the clock starts ticking. What about you, Rhett? Are you ready to become a daddy?"

"Yeah, I believe I am. Business is good despite the soft real estate market. If I had any doubts before about

fatherhood they were dashed once I saw the little darlings at your center."

"They are precious," Denise said proudly. "I'd like
you to join us when we host our welcome summer party.
We've made it a tradition to throw a party for each season where we celebrate all the holidays that fall within
that season. The kids love the summer celebration because we grill outdoors and they get to splash around in
the wading pools."

Rhett followed the signs leading to the interstate. "It
looks as if we made our dreams come true."

Denise smiled. "We talked about what we wanted
enough, so all that was left was putting it into action.
You wanted to run your own business and I wanted a
career in education."

"How long did you remain in the classroom?" He was
asking a question to which he knew the answer.

"Four years."

"Four years as a classroom teacher, two years as the
director of one of the most progressive child care fa-
cilities in the Capitol district and you plan to set up an
after-school homework/tutoring program for middle-
and high-school students. That's quite an accomplish-
ment, and all before you celebrate your thirtieth birthday.
Speaking of the big three-oh, I submitted your name to
the editor for the *Beltway Business Review* thirty under
thirty rising star. Don't be surprised if you get a call
to submit some paperwork for the thirty under thirty
awards."

Denise's jaw dropped. "No, you didn't."

"Yes, I did, Denise. Don't be so modest. You deserve
the recognition."

"I do what I do because I love it, not because I need validation from a group of businesspeople."

"It's not about validation, baby. It's about you setting an example for those who will come behind you, and because you did it some young girl will believe that she can do it, too. You're blessed, because you have a family of educators as your role model.

"I had no male figures in my life when growing up. I didn't know my father, my grandfather was dead and my aunts were either widowed or single. If my mother hadn't scrimped and saved to send me to a boarding school where I was mentored by their only male black teacher I don't know where I'd be now.

"Although teachers were forbidden to interact with students if it didn't pertain to education, Mr. Evans used the ruse that he was tutoring me whenever we met in the school library. He was a parole officer—a clergyman, psychologist and teacher rolled into one brilliant man who'd spent most of his life in foster care after his father murdered his mother. He taught me to use what God had given all of us—my brain. I was told I was smart, but I hadn't realized how smart until I competed with the other boys whose parents were graduates of elite finishing schools and Ivy League colleges.

"What really saved me in going to an all-boy boarding school is that I wasn't distracted by girls. It was hard as hell to study for a chemistry exam when my hormones were short-circuiting. It took a while for me to catch on that some of the upperclassmen, instead of going home on the weekends, would hang around campus, then pile into taxis and go to a little town where women charged the students for sex. Most of the boys had money to burn, so they literally screwed their brains out. My mother sent me money for what she called my emergency fund."

"And for you, sex was an emergency," Denise said, smiling.

"It'd become a welcome respite from living with two hundred boys 24/7."

Denise found it odd that Rhett had never talked much about his boarding school experience before. The only thing he'd told her was that his mother had sent him to a private school in northern Virginia to ensure he wouldn't be tempted to join a gang that was recruiting boys with the promise of drugs, guns and girls.

"Had your mother known you were sexually active?"

Rhett waited for a passing car, then accelerated into fast-moving traffic heading north. "She found out after she discovered a condom I'd left in the pocket of my uniform slacks. She'd put it on my bed with a note that we had to talk when she got back from work. I was surprised when she didn't go into a rant, because at sixteen she felt I was too young to engage in sexual relations with a woman, but commended me that I'd taken the precaution to practice safe sex. What bothered her was the possibility of my becoming a teenage father. I'd promised her I wouldn't father a child until I married. I knew what she'd had to go through as a single mother and I didn't want the same for my child or children."

Denise didn't want to tell Rhett that he sounded like a public announcement sound bite only because she knew how careful he'd been not to get her pregnant. They'd gone from using condoms to her eventually taking an oral contraceptive. Too often young coeds, away from home for the first time, found themselves pregnant in their freshman year. A few had abortions while some dropped out to have their babies.

Their conversation segued from sex and parenthood to innocuous topics ranging from television shows, movies and celebrity gossip. They'd lapsed into the smooth and uncomplicated camaraderie they'd shared before infidelity and distrust shattered their world and future.

Closing her eyes and settling back on the leather seat, Denise smiled. The sound of soft jazz coming from the vehicle's powerful sound system was incredible. Luxury seating, a navigation system and a surround sound audio system caressed her senses. "How long have you had this car?"

"I picked it up in January. Why?"

"It still has that new-car smell."

"It's my first new car," Rhett admitted.

Denise opened her eyes, giving him an incredulous look. She didn't know his net worth, but it was reported that he'd become a millionaire before he'd turned twenty-six. "What did you drive?"

"Used cars. The first two definitely were hoopty status. I lost a tailpipe on the parkway and I thought the car was going to explode because the pipe left a trail of sparks that made it look as if the car was about to take off. Another needed a catalytic converter and it made so much noise that it set off car alarms whenever I drove past. I managed to upgrade every year, but they were still used. Last year, I decided it was time to step up and treat myself to something new."

"You stepped up nicely."

"Thank you. Let me know when you're going to replace Valentina and I'll go with you. Some salesmen tend to take advantage of women whenever they go to purchase a car."

"I'm going to wait until the fall when the new models come out before I make a decision."

"I'll still go with you," Rhett insisted. The sign indicating the number of miles to Philadelphia came into view. "I'm going to stop so we can eat."

Denise glanced at the clock on the dashboard. It was after seven. It'd taken an hour to go forty miles. Holiday traffic was heavy and slow-moving.

"Okay."

She wanted to tell Rhett that she didn't want to linger too long because she and Chandra would have a small window of time in which to decorate the house before Griffin and Belinda returned to Paoli.

Rhett maneuvered into an empty space in the parking lot of a restaurant off the interstate offering family-style dining. Leaning to his right, he pressed a kiss to Denise's temple. "Don't worry, baby, we'll get there in plenty of time."

She nodded. He'd read her mind.

Chapter 6

When Denise directed Rhett down the tree-lined street in Paoli to the house where Griffin and Belinda lived with their twin nieces, she'd tried to ignore the flutters in her belly. It was as if she'd come full circle. Instead of bringing Garrett Fennell with her to meet her parents, he was accompanying her to a gathering where most Eatons were expected to attend.

She didn't want to send the wrong message, but with Rhett in tow everyone would assume they'd reconciled and now were a couple. And she was certain it would be easier for Rhett because he'd lapsed into calling her *sweetheart* and *baby* as if they'd had an ongoing relationship.

"There's Chandra's car." She pointed to the dark blue sports car parked at the end of the block.

"Where do you want me to park?" Rhett asked.

"Pull up behind her Audi. If we park in the driveway, then Belinda's going to know something's up."

He followed her instructions, parking and cutting off the engine. She waited for him to get out and come around to assist her. With the exception of the men in her family, Rhett was the only man who'd exhibited impeccable manners. He opened and closed car doors, held doors open for her, seated her in restaurants and stood up whenever a woman entered the room. He claimed it was something that had been drilled into him at the boarding school.

Rhett retrieved Denise's leather tote, carrying it while he escorted her across the street to the three-story Colonial set on a half-acre lot. Although he'd visited Philadelphia, he'd never ventured into the suburbs. Large nineteenth-century homes set on expansive lawns and massive century-old trees projected a postcard perfect picture where people could live and raise a family in exclusive comfort.

"This is very nice," he said softly.

"I love this place," Denise confirmed. "There was a time when anyone living in Paoli was identified as the *crème de la crème* of Philadelphia society."

"It still looks that way to me. After all, Griffin Rice is as much a celebrity as the clients he represents."

There had been a time when the high-profile sports attorney had been a favorite of the paparazzi when they snapped pictures of him with his famous clients, glamorous models, beautiful actresses and recording stars. But his electrifying lifestyle changed when his brother and sister-in-law were killed in a horrific car accident and as a legal guardian along with Belinda Eaton had become the parents of their twin nieces.

Griffin settled smoothly into the role as stepfather, and after he married Belinda had become husband *and* father. Now, he and Belinda were expecting their first child. Tests confirmed it was a boy.

Denise led Rhett around to the rear of the house. She smiled when she saw Preston Tucker removing folding chairs from a rack and setting them up under two long rectangular tables.

She hugged and kissed the brilliant, award-winning playwright. "Hey, P.J. I'm glad something pulled you away from your computer."

Easing back, she met a pair of sensual, slanting heavy-lidded eyes that were mesmerizing. There was more gray in his cropped hair than had been when she saw him at Christmas. There was no doubt Preston would be completely gray before his fortieth birthday. She'd been maid of honor at Preston and Chandra's Thanksgiving Isle of Palms wedding.

Preston Tucker chuckled softly. "Chandra would've had a hissy fit if I didn't come."

Denise held out her hand to Rhett, he taking it and threading their fingers together. "Preston, this is my very good friend, Garrett Fennell. Rhett, this is my cousin Preston Tucker."

Rhett, who'd set Denise's tote on a chair, extended his free hand. "My pleasure, Preston. Denise didn't tell me she was related to P.J. Tucker."

"I married her cousin last fall."

"Congratulations. Are you working on something new?" he asked the playwright.

"I just finished editing a new play in which I'd collaborated with my very talented wife." As if on cue, Chandra walked out of the house carrying a box. Preston raced over and took it from her. "I told you not to carry anything."

Chandra sucked her teeth loudly, a habit that annoyed her mother. "It's filled with paper, Preston."

"I don't care if it's filled with air. I don't want to see you carrying anything."

Denise whistled sharply through her teeth. It'd taken her more than a week of coaching from her brother before she was able to make the piercing sound. "Will someone please tell me what's going on here?"

Preston glared at Chandra. "She's pregnant, and the doctor cautioned her about heavy lifting."

Denise did the happy dance, spinning around like a whirling dervish. "You didn't tell me you were going to have a baby," she shrieked, hugging her cousin around her neck.

Chandra Eaton-Tucker pushed her back. "Please don't get too close. Every time I smell perfume or cologne I hurl."

"How far along are you?" Denise asked, taking a backward step.

"Just six weeks."

She turned to Rhett. "I don't think I have to introduce you two."

Rhett smiled at the woman who looked enough like Denise to be her sister. They had the same almond-shaped eyes, high cheekbones, pert nose and lush mouth. The first cousins both had curly hair, but Chandra had always affected a wild flyaway style that suited her free-spirited personality, while Denise's shorter style was more conservative. Mrs. Tucker had tamed her curls by pulling them into a single braid.

Chandra blew Rhett an air kiss. "I would hug you, but

I know you're wearing cologne. You have no idea how good it is to see you again, Rhett."

"That goes double for me, Chandra. Congratulations on your marriage *and* the baby."

Chandra moved closer to Preston, looping her arm through his. "Thank you. I hope you don't let my cousin run away again now that you're aware that she's a flight risk."

Denise made a cutting motion over her throat. "Chandra!"

"Denise!" Chandra mimicked. "Well, it's true."

Preston dropped a kiss on his wife's hair. "Get out of their business, baby," he said softly. "Please, baby," he added when she opened her mouth to come back at him.

Rhett gave Preston a surreptitious nod, discernible only to the two men. "What do you want Denise and me to help you with?"

"You can finish setting up the chairs while I fill the pool."

Denise mouthed a thank-you to Rhett as she took the box filled with party favors and streamers from Preston. "Chandra, I want you to sit while I decorate."

"I'm pregnant, not an invalid," Chandra mumbled.

"Go sit down and don't talk back," Denise said firmly.

"Like damn, cousin. You don't have to get so *hosstile*."

Denise waved her hand in dismissal. "Preston, please handle your wife. Rhett and I will do what needs to be done."

Chandra pulled away from Preston, sitting down in a huff, while crossing her arms under her breasts. Preston brought over a footstool and placed her feet on the cushion, then removed her sandals. Leaning down, he kissed her mouth. "Relax, baby."

It took less than an hour for them to set up the chairs, cover the tables with kiwi-green and chocolate table-cloths and fill the inground pool. It took several tries before Preston was able to get the chlorine to a safe level. Rhett checked the tanks of propane and then hooked them to the gas grills. The men set up the tent, attaching streamers of brown and green to the poles. Deliveries of balloons, bouquets of flowers and potted flowering plants added a festive touch to the outdoor space.

Myles, his wife, Zabrina, and their son, Adam, were the first to arrive. The day before they'd driven from Pittsburgh to Philadelphia, checking into a downtown hotel for the night.

If Myles seemed surprised to see Rhett, he didn't show it when he pulled him close in a rough hug. "Don't be like me, brother. I had to wait ten years before I got my woman back."

Denise hugged Adam. "If you don't stop growing you're going to be taller than me in a couple of years," she teased, kissing his cheek.

Curly-haired, golden-eyed Adam Eaton gave her a shy smile. "The doctor said I'm going to be taller than my dad."

Denise smiled at the eleven-year-old. He'd inherited his mother's hair and eyes, but his lanky frame was his father's. "That's the way it usually goes. Each generation is usually taller than the one before it."

"Even girls?"

She nodded. "Even girls."

"So, if Mom has a girl she'll be taller than her?"

Peering over Adam's shoulder, Denise saw what hadn't been obvious from first glance. Zabrina's face was fuller, and her breasts under a loose-fitting top also appeared larger.

She smiled. The Eatons were about to have a population explosion. First Belinda, Chandra and probably Zabrina. Dr. Dwight and Roberta Eaton would have back-to-back-to-back grandchildren.

"Yes, Adam. Chances are she would be taller than your mother."

She didn't want to ask him if his mother was pregnant, and if she was, then Zabrina and Myles would probably make the announcement after the shower was over, or perhaps even at another time.

Eatons were arriving by the carloads, all bearing gaily-wrapped gifts. It'd been a while since Denise had seen her uncles and their wives. Her great-grandfather came to Philadelphia as a young boy during the Great Migration. Daniel Eaton had worked two jobs all his life to give his children what had eluded him: a college education. Her grandfather, Daniel Eaton Jr., earned a law degree from Howard University and three of his five sons followed in his footsteps, while the other two became physicians. The five brothers married schoolteachers, establishing the criteria for future generations to select careers in law, medicine or education.

Denise waved to her parents as they joined the others on the patio where the noise level had increased exponentially as relatives greeted one another with laughter and excited shrieks. Xavier followed Boaz and Paulette, carrying boxes she knew were filled with her mother's incredible cake creations.

Weaving her way through the crowd, she looped her

arms around her mother's waist. Paulette Eaton had put on a little weight since she'd retired. "Hi, Mom."

Paulette kissed her daughter's cheek. "I heard you and Rhett were back together," she said quietly.

Denise smiled at her mother who'd been a Temple University homecoming queen and was still stunning at fifty-six. Her flawless sable-brown skin, large dark eyes and fashionably cut black hair still turned heads. "We just started seeing each other again. We decided to hang out together for the summer, then see where it goes."

Paulette narrowed her eyes. "You let him get away once. Don't be *no* fool, Denise Amaris Eaton," she drawled. "Not many women are blessed enough to get a second chance with the man they love. And I still don't believe your excuse that you'd fallen out of love with Garrett. Remember, I'm your mother and I know you better than you think I do. You're still in love with him and he's still in love with you. So, stop the foolishness, marry the man and give me a grandchild. I can't stand Roberta now that Belinda's about to give her another grandbaby. She's struttin' around with her nose so far up in the air that if it rained she'd drown."

Denise gasped, complete shock freezing her features. For a reason she couldn't fathom, her mother had always competed with Chandra's mother. Roberta and Dwight had had four children to Paulette's two and all of Roberta's children were married and either had, or would give her grandchildren, while Paulette was waiting for her first.

"Mama, what has Aunt Bertie ever done to you where you have to bad-mouth her?"

"She couldn't wait to call me and gloat when Belinda told her she was having a baby. It was the same when

Donna had the twins. Then when she found out that Myles had a son that took the rag off the bush." Paulette's eyes filled with tears. "She knows how much I want a grandchild."

"What if you never have grandchildren? What then? And I shouldn't have to remind you that you *do* have a son."

"Harrumph!" Paulette snorted. "I'd probably be old as Methuselah by the time Xavier decides to settle down with a woman long enough to marry and start a family." She snorted again, squared her shoulders and walked across the patio, heading straight for Rhett.

Denise smothered a curse. Whenever her mother embarked on a campaign it was always advisable to stay out of her way.

"I've been reading some good things about you, son," Boaz Eaton said to Rhett, while pumping his hand vigorously. "Congratulations."

Rhett smiled. "Thank you, Judge."

Boaz wagged a finger. "None of that judge business, Rhett. I'm not sitting on the bench, or wearing a black robe. I don't know why you and my daughter broke up, and I don't want to know why. But I must say it is nice to see you together again. I never much cared for that other fellow she dated a couple of years ago, but I'm not one to get into my children's personal business, so when she finally gave him his walking papers I was as happy as a pig in slop."

Rhett realized Denise's father had revealed something that hadn't been in Eli Oakes's report. She had been involved with another man, and he knew for certain the man wasn't Trey Chambers. But for some unknown and perverted sense of jealousy it bothered him that she had been with a man when he was hard-pressed to remember all of the women he'd had after they'd separated.

Rhett wanted to tell the older man that he and Denise were together not because they had fallen in love again, but because of his need for revenge. His love for Denise Eaton had defied description, yet she'd fallen prey to lies fabricated by Trey Chambers. It wouldn't have mattered if she'd believed the lies, but sleeping with Trey had been the ultimate betrayal.

He smiled at the man who should've become his father-in-law. Boaz Eaton reminded Rhett of the elegant-looking black men in the photographs taken by James Van Der Zee. He was tall, slender and the rimless glasses added to his overall patrician appearance.

"Denise and I are giving ourselves the summer to see if we can make it work this time," Rhett said instead.

Boaz leaned in closer. "My daughter is a great deal like her mother. She tends to be a little difficult at times. But don't let up on her, son. If she's worth having, then she's worth fighting for."

"I'll keep that in mind."

At one time Denise had been worth fighting for, but Rhett hadn't had the wherewithal to fight the fight. He had been a month from graduating, he had a position waiting for him at a major real estate company with perks that included tuition reimbursement for graduate studies. Instead of fighting for Denise, he'd walked away.

"Welcome back, stranger."

Rhett turned when he heard the familiar voice belonging to Xavier Eaton. The two men exchanged handshakes. "Thanks. What's up?"

Xavier's dark eyes took in everything about the man

who'd at one time been the love of his sister's life. "Not much. Did Denise tell you I left the military on a medical discharge?"

"Yes, she did happen to mention it."

"I was in a funk and wallowing in pity parties until my sister forced me to see that my life wasn't over, that I could remain involved with the military if I taught. I applied to several military schools and colleges and come September I'll begin teaching a few courses on military history at a school in South Carolina. I—"

"Xavier, could you please help your father bring in the gifts from the car, while I talk to Garrett?"

"Good luck," Xavier whispered under his breath as he walked away.

Rhett stepped forward, lowered his head and kissed Paulette Eaton's cheek. "How are you?"

Reaching up, Paulette patted his clean-shaven jaw. "I'm just fine, Garrett. My, my, my, you look wonderful."

"Thank you, Mrs. Eaton."

Paulette's dark eyes sparkled like polished jet. "How is your mother doing?"

"She married a wonderful man last year, and they're now living in Virginia."

"She was always such a lovely woman. When you talk to her, please let her know I asked about her."

Rhett smiled. "I will."

"Now that you and my daughter are together again, can I look forward to planning a wedding?"

"No, you can't, Mom."

Denise had come up behind her mother just in time to hear her ask Rhett a question that made her want to scream at Paulette for the first time in her life.

Paulette gave Denise a too-sweet smile. "If Garrett is

able to negotiate multimillion-dollar deals, then I believe he's capable of answering for himself."

Rhett wanted to tell Paulette he'd just negotiated a deal with her daughter based on revenge, but she'd flipped the script when she invited him to come with her to a family gathering where everyone expected them to pick up as if six years hadn't happened. As if their beautiful, talented Denise hadn't slept with his best friend while professing her love for him.

"I'd say planning a wedding is a little premature at this time. Denise and I have just begun dating again, so we've decided to keep our options open about the future."

"What options are you talking about?" Paulette asked.

"Mom, please," Denise pleaded.

"Don't…" A loud roar filled the air, stopping what would become a rant from Paulette.

A very pregnant Belinda Rice, supported by her husband, had covered her face when she saw the decorations and the small crowd that had gathered on the patio of her home.

Her hand came down as she cradled her belly with both hands. "It would serve y'all right if I drop this baby right now." She glared at Griffin Rice. "You had to be in on this. Riding my behind up and down the road when you know I have to have bathroom breaks every twenty minutes."

Denise reached for Rhett's hand, lacing their fingers together. It was as if they'd turned back the clock and holding hands was as natural to them as breathing.

"For a woman who is expected to deliver any day, Belinda looks so incredibly beautiful," she whispered to Rhett. Belinda had cut her hair and the scooped-neck white tunic over a pair of black cropped pants artfully concealed her swollen belly.

"She does," he confirmed.

Belinda was more attractive than Rhett had remembered, but so was Denise. He'd barely touched her, except to hold hands, had kissed her once and not with the passion racing headlong throughout his body whenever they shared the same space, and yet he wanted her with a ferocity that overshadowed everything that had happened between them.

Denise was right when she'd reminded him of his revelation that he'd felt more connected to her than he had with any other woman. The monies he'd paid to the nameless, faceless women—his mother's hard-earned money—for sex had been nothing more than a receptacle for his lust. The women he'd slept with after he and Denise split up he paid in other ways: dinners, gifts and exotic vacations. Despite the moans, groans and unorthodox positions, none of them had touched the part of him he'd withheld from every woman except Denise Eaton.

Initially Rhett had believed he'd stayed with her out of guilt because he'd taken her virginity. But when he finally recognized that what he'd felt for Denise was an unconditional love that would stand the test of time, he knew he'd made the right decision to continue to see her.

Rhett closed his eyes for several seconds. He'd lured Denise into a trap to assuage a vendetta—something he should have dealt with six years ago. Her family believed they'd reconciled when what they had was a business arrangement. She'd gone along with his scheme to save and expand her business, while he'd sought to take advantage of her vulnerability.

If his mother were to uncover what he'd done, Rhett

knew she would disown him. Once he'd told Geraldine that he was going to set up his own company she'd warned him about storing up material wealth at the risk of losing his soul. "Please don't end up like your father." When he'd asked her what she meant, Geraldine ordered him to leave her alone. It had been the first and last time his mother had spoken of his father.

He had made a lot of money buying out failing companies, stabilizing and then flipping them, but not at the risk of losing his soul—until now. Manipulating and blackmailing Denise made him no better than the man who'd fathered him. A man his mother was loathe to speak of. A man whose name she'd never uttered in his presence.

Rhett gave Denise's hand a gentle squeeze. He smiled, meeting her questioning gaze. "Thank you for asking me to come with you today. It's been a long time since I've felt a part of a family unit."

"That's because the Eatons have always thought of you as family, Rhett."

"What about you, Denise? Can you think of me as family?"

A beat passed. "Where are you going with this, Rhett?"

"I want you to forget everything we talked about at the hotel."

"Come with me," Denise ordered, pulling away from the others to a corner of the patio where they wouldn't be overheard. "Talk to me, Rhett."

Releasing her hand, he cradled her face gently between his palms. "I'm releasing you from our agreement. I won't double your rent, and when your lease renewal comes due it will be no more than five percent.

And…and you don't have to stand in as my hostess if you don't want to."

Denise blinked. "I don't understand. What brought on this change of heart?"

Rhett wanted to tell Denise he wanted what Belinda had with Griffin, what Myles had with Zabrina and what Chandra had with Preston. He wanted to marry the woman with whom he'd fallen in love with years ago, and still loved.

"The day care center," he said cryptically.

"What about New Visions?"

"It's about you providing quality child care for the people who need it most. It's about you making sacrifices in your personal life to make a difference for those less fortunate. I realized that last night when I tried to lure you away from your work to have dinner with me. Unfortunately, I let my ego get in the way of common sense."

Denise covered his hands with hers. She'd never known Rhett to be self-deprecating, and she felt no joy in seeing him humbled. "Thank you for not increasing the rent where it would become fiscally impossible to keep the doors open." Going on tiptoe, she pressed her mouth to his. "I've heard that all work and no play can make one quite dull. If you can assure me that we'll have fun this summer then I'm more than willing to stand in as your date and hostess."

Rhett's smile reached his eyes, making them dance with delight. "I promise that you'll have the time of your life."

Chapter 7

A bartender had arrived and was busy mixing drinks for the assembly, while the caterer and his staff had set up trays of prepared foods at the far end of the patio. Twin grills were fired up to offer grill-to-order steaks, burgers and the perennial hot dogs.

Adam and his twin cousins, Sabrina and Layla, had changed into swimwear and preferred playing in the pool to eating. Chandra, who'd taken the responsibility for co-ordinating her sister's baby shower, wanted everyone to eat and drink before Belinda opened her gifts.

It was as if a permanent smile was pasted on Griffin Rice's incredibly handsome face. He'd become the consummate host, seeing to the needs of the respective grandparents Dr. Dwight and Roberta Eaton and Lucas and Gloria Rice.

Denise sat at the table between Rhett and Preston

Tucker. She saw her mother's gaze on her whenever she leaned closer to Rhett to hear what he was saying to her. Each time their shoulders touched she felt a jolt of awareness race through her to settle in the region between her legs.

He'd offered her an out but instead of running as fast as she could in the opposite direction, she'd elected to spend the summer with him to see if she could recapture some of the magic from their past. If they continued to see each other beyond the summer then she would enjoy it, but if they didn't then she would know it wasn't meant to be.

Her life had become so predictable that if anyone wanted to stalk her it would be very easy for them to monitor her whereabouts. Denise went from her apartment to the center, then back again. The only time her day deviated was when she attended board meetings on the two organizations where she'd become a member.

She'd made it a practice not to socialize with her staff except when it was necessary. At twenty-eight she was younger than most of the staff, and Denise didn't want to compromise her authority by becoming too familiar with them. Age aside, it had been her hard work and a business loan that provided them with the means of collecting a biweekly paycheck.

She swallowed the last of a delicious concoction filled with fruit slices and liberally laced with rum. It tasted like Hi-C, but the effects were lethal. Closing her eyes, she rested her head on Rhett's shoulder.

"I feel as if I'm swimming in the Bermuda Triangle."

Cradling her hand under the table, Rhett dropped a kiss on her hair. "Poor baby can't hang out with the grown folks," he teased.

"You know I can't drink."

"That's okay, baby. I'll be your designated driver."

She opened her eyes and smiled at him. "I think I like you, Rhett Fennell."

"You think?"

"Okay. I know I like you."

Rhett wanted to tell Denise that he more than liked her. He was in love with her. "Do you want to go inside and lie down?"

She shook her head. "No. I'm good. It's just that I have to wait until my head stops spinning."

Rhett looked at her plate. She'd barely touched her food. Releasing her hand, he picked up her fork and speared a forkful of potato salad. "Open your mouth, darling."

Denise complied and over the next ten minutes she permitted Rhett to feed her, unaware of those at the table throwing surreptitious glances their way. The fuzziness in her head subsided and she took the fork from Rhett and cleaned her plate.

There was another flurry of activity when chairs were adjusted to accommodate another one of Daniel's sons, who'd come in from Texas with his daughter instead of his wife, who was recovering from eye surgery and had been cautioned not to fly. Dr. Hyman Eaton went around the table kissing everyone while his daughter, Mia, a fourth-year medical student, hugged and kissed Belinda before resting a hand over her distended belly.

"It's incredible that your father and his brothers all look alike," Rhett said in Denise's ear.

The fourth Eaton brother, Solomon, a Dade County federal prosecutor, had flown up for the day, but was scheduled to take a red-eye back to Florida later that night because he was awaiting the decision on an extortion and racketeering case that had become front-page news.

"They look like their father. The exception is Raleigh, who's laid up with a broken foot. He looks like my grandmother. My dad and his brothers used to tease him, saying they found him on the doorstep and decided to keep him. His comeback is that he's the only good-looking one among the bunch, so he knows he's special. Uncle Raleigh happens to be the only one who can't seem to make a go of his marriages. I think he's now on his fourth wife."

"Damn!" Rhett whispered.

"Ditto," Denise said, laughing softly.

The sun had passed its zenith when Griffin Rice, sitting beside his pregnant wife, handed her gaily-wrapped gifts as she read the attached cards aloud before carefully and methodically removing the paper. The gifts ranged from a changing table, crib mobiles, cartons of disposable diapers, wipes, several bottle sterilizers, countless packages of socks, undershirts in varying sizes, bibs, sweaters, hats, baby monitors, crib sheets and blankets, towels and grooming supplies and a table lamp. The grandparents had shared the cost of purchasing the nursery furniture.

Denise had paid the grandmother of one of the center's children to hand-quilt a blanket in differing shades of green and brown—the colors Belinda had chosen for the nursery. The result was a stunning piece of art. She also gave Belinda the complete set of the Little Golden Books for her to read to her son.

"You didn't have to do that," she chided Rhett when

Griffin thanked him for the savings bond for the baby's college fund.

Rhett glared at Denise for a full minute. "Don't ever tell me what I can or cannot do with *my* money," he said between clenched teeth.

She recoiled as if he'd struck her across the face. "Well, excuse me."

"You *are* excused, Miss Eaton." He pressed the pad of his thumb to her lips, before he angled his head and kissed her. "Sometime that mouth of yours is going to get you into a world of hurt."

Denise saw her brother out of the corner of her eye as he came closer. He was limping, which meant he was either in pain or tired. She touched his shoulder. "Are you all right, Xavier?"

Silky black eyes flickered slightly. "I'm good. I just came to tell you two to take that face-sucking inside. After all, there are kids here."

"FYI—the kids are in the house playing video games. Don't tell me you're jealous, my favorite brother."

Xavier smiled, revealing beautiful straight white teeth. "A little. I'm glad you guys are back together." He slapped Rhett on the back. "Take care of my sister."

Rhett gave Xavier a level stare. "You don't have to worry about that."

"Just don't make me have to worry," Xavier countered, walking away and leaving them staring at his back.

It didn't take an IQ of genius for Rhett to realize he'd been warned *and* threatened. He wanted to tell the ex-soldier that he hadn't been the one to walk out on his sister. It had been her decision to end their relationship. Denise calling his name recaptured his attention.

"What is it, baby?"

"I said I'm going into the kitchen to help my mother bring out dessert. After that we can leave whenever you want."

Rhett nodded. "Okay."

The waitstaff had begun putting food away and cleaning up. Meanwhile Belinda had retreated into the house to lie down. Over slices of cake, pie and cupcakes, Preston and Chandra announced they were expecting and the baby was due two months after celebrating their first wedding anniversary. Myles and Zabrina added to the excitement when they revealed they were expecting their second child, a girl, at the end of September. They hadn't said anything earlier because Zabrina had been on bed rest during her first trimester.

Denise refused to look at her mother, who was shooting daggers at Roberta, who wept openly when she realized she would celebrate the birth of three grandchildren in one calendar year.

She leaned in closer to Rhett. "As soon as I say my goodbyes, we can leave." She wasn't going to hang around and be forced to deal with Paulette Eaton's histrionics.

It seemed like an eternity when she hugged and kissed her relatives. After promising Chandra she would call her, she and Rhett were able to make their escape.

Seated and belted-in with the engine running, Rhett stared at the woman seated beside him. "Give me the address of your place." She gave it to him and he programmed it into the navigational system.

They didn't talk during the ride from Paoli to Philadelphia. There was only the sound of music coming from the automobile's powerful speakers to break the comfortable silence.

Denise stepped out of the elevator, Rhett following and carrying their bags, as she led him down the carpeted hallway to her apartment. She was counting down the weeks until she would be free of the responsibility of maintaining the space.

She'd continued to pay the maintenance on the co-op *and* rent on her D.C. apartment, because she hadn't been able to find someone willing to buy it, until Chandra returned from a stint in the Peace Corps and offered to sublet it. Her cousin had barely moved in when a month later she vacated the co-op to live with her husband.

Denise unlocked the door and pushed it open. The scent of pine and lemon wafted in her nostrils. It was obvious the cleaning service had come by to dust and air out rooms that hadn't been occupied in weeks. Whenever she drove to Philly to visit her parents she'd made it a practice to stay in the apartment rather than in the bedroom in the large house where she'd grown up.

Stepping aside, she smiled at Rhett. "Welcome to my humble abode," she drawled, flipping the switch and turning on an overhead Tiffany-style hanging fixture.

Rhett entered the immaculate apartment. The light from the fixture was reflected in the high gloss of the wood floor. He set down the bags in the entryway as Denise closed and locked the door.

He didn't know what to expect, but it wasn't oyster-white walls and a living room with a white seating grouping with differing blue accessories. The living room flowed into a dining area with an oak oval pedestal table with seating for six. To the right of the dining area was a set of four steps that led directly into the kitchen.

Walking across the open space, he peered through wall-to-wall pale silk drapes to look out on the water. The Benjamin Franklin Bridge spanning the Delaware River was clearly visible from the sixth-floor apartment.

Denise joined Rhett at the window, drawing back the drapes. "I love this view, especially at sunset or after a snowfall."

Rhett reached for her hand. "I don't know what your D.C. apartment looks like, but this one is fabulous."

"The one in D.C. is nice, too."

"Why do you have two apartments?" He'd asked the question even though he knew the answer. Eli Oakes's investigative report on Denise Eaton was very comprehensive. What he hadn't uncovered was her relationship with the man Judge Eaton had spoken of. It was apparent her father hadn't approved of the man.

"I own this one, but hopefully not for much longer. I have a June tenth closing date."

"What if you don't close?" he asked.

Denise blew out her cheeks. "Bite your tongue, Rhett. I've been trying to sell this place for nearly two years. Thankfully I don't have a mortgage, so there's just the maintenance fee. When the bottom fell out of the real estate market, banks weren't willing to write mortgages. Some of them were asking for a third down, and for most people that's an impossibility.

"Chandra, who'd spent two years in Belize as a Peace Corps volunteer, returned home last fall, asking to move in. I told her she could stay as long as she wanted. All she had to do was pay the maintenance. However, that lasted about a month. She'd met P.J. Tucker and hadn't planned to marry him until this June, but he didn't want to wait, so they had a Thanksgiving wedding."

"Where do they live?"

"Preston has a condo in a beautiful historic neighborhood known as Rittenhouse and a country house in the Brandywine Valley."

"If you only have to pay the maintenance, why get rid of it, Denise?"

"I can't afford to maintain two residences on my salary."

Rhett squeezed her fingers. "If the deal falls through, I'll buy it from you."

"Do you need another place to live?"

Releasing her hand, he pulled Denise close until she stood between his legs. "No. I'd use it for rental income."

"How are you going to monitor a tenant when you live—"

Rhett kissed Denise, stopping her words *and* her breath. It was what he'd wanted to do the moment he saw her enter the hotel lobby. In that instant everything he'd felt and believed about her since their separation vanished, replaced by a rushing desire for a woman who'd touched him in a way no other had or probably would.

His mouth caressed hers, as he left nibbling kisses at the corners of her mouth, biting gently on her lower lip before giving the upper one equal attention. "Do you know how long I've wanted to taste your mouth?" The admission was drawn from someplace Rhett hadn't known existed.

Curving her arms under his shoulders, Denise pressed closer, the curves of her body fitting into the hard contours of Rhett's body. He'd confessed that he'd wanted to kiss her when she'd wanted the same.

She'd picked at her food when they'd had dinner in The Lafayette, because whenever she'd stared at Rhett's mouth the images of how he'd used his mouth and tongue to bring her maximum pleasure wouldn't permit her to chew and swallow a morsel without choking.

Denise gasped when she felt Rhett's hardening penis against her thigh. His arousal had happened so quickly that it'd shocked her. Desire brought a rush of moisture between her legs and she pressed her thighs together in an attempt to control the wet, pulsing flesh that made her feel as if she was coming out of her skin.

"Rh-ett!" His name had slipped from between trembling lips. She gasped again. One minute her feet were on the floor, then without warning Rhett had lifted her as effortlessly as if she were a small child, his arms tightening around her waist.

Denise looped her arms around his neck, holding him as if he were her lifeline. But Rhett Fennell wasn't her lifeline but the portal to where she could revisit her past—and hopefully get it right this time.

"Where are you going?" Rhett was striding across the living room.

"Where's your bedroom?"

"Why?"

Rhett stopped, meeting her eyes. "You're going to have to trust me, Denise. We lost six years because you didn't trust me, so tell me now what it is you want."

Denise buried her face between his neck and shoulder rather than gaze into the eyes that were able to see things she didn't want him to see. Rhett had known she'd fallen in love with him before she'd gotten up the nerve to tell him. His "I've known for a long time" had left her flustered *and* embarrassed, wondering if she'd been that transparent.

"I want us to start from the beginning, to pretend we just met and need to get to know each other better."

Rhett smiled. "That's not going to be easy, especially since I know what it's like to make love to you."

Her smile matched his. "Can't you pretend?"

"No, Denise. That's something I don't want to pretend about. Where's your bedroom?"

"It's down the hall and on your right."

Denise needed Rhett to make love to her, but she didn't want him to believe that she was desperate, that she'd been sitting around waiting for him to come back into her life. He'd had the distinct advantage when he'd blackmailed her into posing as his date and hostess and she'd been ready to trade her body to save her business, but not her heart. If they were to start over it would have to be the way it'd been when they'd met as college fresh-men—as equals.

Rhett entered the bedroom and placed Denise on the queen-size bed, his body following hers down. Although the drapes were drawn, light was discernable through the diaphanous fabric. Moving with the agility of a large cat, he straddled her body, supporting his weight on his elbows.

He lowered his head, burying his face against the column of her scented neck. "Do you know how long I've wanted to do this?" he whispered in her ear.

Denise closed her eyes. Rhett had echoed her thoughts. She didn't want to feel him inside her as much as she'd wanted him to hold her. Sex she could have with any man, but it was the foreplay and afterplay that had made making love with Rhett so different from what she'd had with Kevin.

She uttered a small cry of protest when he rolled over. The breath caught in her throat when he stood up and unbuttoned his shirt and kicked off his shoes. Denise wanted to look away but couldn't when he unbuckled his belt and tossed it on a chair next to the bed. His slacks and briefs joined the belt, and with wide eyes, she stared at the muscles in his back and firm buttocks. She gasped again, this time when he turned to face her.

Denise had lost count of the number of times she'd viewed Rhett's nude body, but seeing it again made her aware of how beautifully proportioned it was. Years had added muscle and bulk to his lean frame. A smile parted her lips when he leaned over and kissed the end of her nose.

Rhett reached for the hem of her top, pulling it up and over her head. "Are you all right with this?" Denise closed her eyes, nodding. "Do you trust me not to do anything you don't want me to do?"

She opened her eyes. "Yes, Rhett, I trust you." It was the same thing he'd asked her before making love to her for the first time.

Slowly, methodically, he removed her clothes until she was as naked as he was. Gathering her off the mattress, he pulled back the duvet, placed her on the sheet and got into bed with her. He dropped an arm over her waist and pulled her closer until they were nestled like spoons.

"Are you okay, baby?"

Denise shifted into a more comfortable position. "I'm good, Rhett."

He swallowed a groan. "I'm not going to be so *good* in a minute."

"What's the matter?"

"I'm getting a hard-on, Denise, and unless you have some condoms on hand I suggest you stop wiggling."

"I don't."

"Neither do I," Rhett informed her.

"I thought most men carry condoms with them."

Rhett wanted to tell Denise he wasn't most men. Even when he'd become a serial dater he hadn't slept with *every* woman he'd asked out. The ones he'd slept with were still more than he'd anticipated before turning thirty.

"I guess I'm not like most men. If I'm not dating a woman, then I don't see a need to walk around with condoms in my pocket."

"Aren't you ever spontaneous?"

Rhett chuckled. "Is this your roundabout way of asking me if I ever had a one-night stand?"

Placing her hand over the large hand resting on her thigh, Denise smiled. "Yes."

"One-night stands can backfire. Remember what happened to Michael Douglas in *Fatal Attraction?*" He and Denise had what they'd called movie night. Either they would rent a movie or visit a movie house in Baltimore that featured retro films.

"How can I forget. But I don't blame the Glenn Close character as much as I do Michael Douglas's, because he was married and picking up a crazy woman was his punishment for cheating on his wife."

"She knew he was married when she invited him back to her place."

"So, that makes him exempt, Rhett?" Denise argued in a quiet voice.

"No, it doesn't. You know how I feel about men who cheat on their wives."

"But what about men who cheat on their girlfriends?"

"A girlfriend is not a wife, Denise."

"So, that makes it okay for him to cheat on her?"

"No, it doesn't make it okay. It's never okay once a man and woman are committed to each other."

"Then why—"

"Let's not rehash the past tonight," Rhett interrupted. He pressed a kiss to the nape of her neck. "Please, baby."

Denise smiled, despite her annoyance. Rhett was right. If they were going to go forward, then they had to leave their past behind. "Okay, darling. You win—tonight."

"You just have to have the last word, don't you?"

"If you don't know me by now, then you'll never ever know me."

"Don't go Harold Melvin & the Blue Notes on me, Denise."

She giggled like a little girl. "So you recognize the lyrics. Remember when we used to play name the lyrics or the artist?"

"Yes, and you always won."

"That's because I didn't go to a stuffy old boarding school where all you heard was classical and chamber music. My parents played Motown and Philadelphia soul until I knew the words to every Stevie, Teddy and Temptations song."

Rhett's hand moved lower, his fingers grazing the down covering her mound. "That stuffy old boarding school was responsible for me getting into Johns Hopkins where I met this hot little sister who had my nose so wide open that a locomotive could fit with room to spare."

Denise had no comeback. She lay, listening to the sound of her own breathing until she closed her eyes and fell asleep.

Chapter 8

"Come on, Denise. I'd like to get on the road before we get caught in traffic."

Hopping on her right foot, Denise pushed the left into the mate to the leather sandal. "I'm coming, Rhett. I had to comb my hair."

She'd applied what was left of a no-frizz serum to her wet hair and ran a wide-tooth comb through her damp hair in an attempt to tame the curls that were beginning to dry and swell like rising dough. Hopefully, she would be able to pick up another bottle of what she'd deemed her magic hair lotion at a drugstore chain once they got to Baltimore.

Rhett stood with his back to the door, arms crossed over his chest. He'd wanted to get up early and on the road before eight, but they'd overslept. They'd fallen asleep, then woke at midnight ravenous. The fridge was turned off, and the pantry bare, so they'd gotten dressed and went in search of an all-night diner where they'd ordered breakfast. It was after two when they returned to the apartment and went back to bed.

"Your hair looks fine."

She rolled her eyes at him, unable to believe he could look so virile in jeans, T-shirt, running shoes and a frayed baseball cap he should've discarded a long time ago. He'd showered but hadn't shaved.

"I don't like going out with wet hair."

Rhett angled his head and kissed her cheek. "It will dry before we get to Maryland."

"I know it will dry, but I'll end up looking like a Chia Pet."

"You'll just be a very beautiful Chia Pet," he teased.

"You'll say anything, Rhett, just to get your way."

His arms came down. "Is that really how you see me? That I'm all about coercion and manipulation?"

"We'll talk about it in the car," Denise countered, reaching for her keys. Rhett glared at her, then picked up their bags and opened the door. She locked the door, dropping the keys in the tote.

She knew Rhett was angry because she saw the nervous tic in his jaw when he'd clenched his teeth together. Denise didn't want to begin what was to become their second chance to get it right with a disagreement. The reason their college liaison had lasted for four years was because they were able to talk out their differences of opinion somewhat intelligently. Once they were committed, it hadn't become an off-and-on, now-and-then relationship. It was as if they were married, but only without the rings, license and officiant.

Although they had maintained separate dorms, once

they'd begun sleeping together it was either at her dorm or Rhett's. The only time they did not sleep together was when she went home to Philadelphia and he returned to D.C.

They rode the elevator to the lobby and walked out into the brilliant late-spring sun. The streets of Penn's Landing were bustling with the activity of both vehicular and pedestrian traffic. It was as if after a long, unusually snowy winter, Philadelphians had emerged from their cabin-fever doldrums looking to take advantage of every sun-filled day Mother Nature granted them.

Rhett stored their bags in the trunk of the car, then touched the handle of the driver's-side door and opened it. He beckoned to Denise. "Come, beautiful. You're driving to Cape St. Claire."

Denise's mouth opened and closed several times as she digested his suggestion. He wanted *her* to drive *his* car to Maryland. She couldn't use the excuse that she didn't know how to get there because the vehicle was equipped with a high-tech navigational system. She slipped in behind the wheel, waiting until Rhett pushed a few buttons to adjust the seat to accommodate her shorter legs.

Hunkering down to her level, he ran the back of his hand over her cheek. "Do you need to adjust the back?"

She shook her head, flyaway curls moving as if they'd taken on a life of their own. "No, it's good."

"Make certain it's okay before I program it into the memory for you."

Resting her hands on the wheel, she extended her arms. "I think I'm going to need the back of the seat closer to my spine."

Rhett pushed a few more buttons and the pneumatic lumbar support cradled her back. He tapped another button and the three-position memory was set for Denise's proportions. Closing the door, he came around the car and sat beside her. He touched the Start Engine button, then quickly punched in the route to the house that had become his sanctuary.

It was on Cape St. Claire that he hadn't had to think about anything business-related. It was where he went to escape *and* to renew his spirit. Whenever he visited the covenanted unincorporated community he'd always been alone. Denise Eaton would become the first woman, other than Geraldine Fennell-Russell, who would cross the threshold of his waterfront refuge.

"Do you want me to put on some music?" he asked her as she backed out of the parking space.

"Yes."

Denise enjoyed the feel of the finely stitched leather on the hand-polished wood of the steering wheel under her fingers. The interior of the luxury car was designed for comfort, convenience and to soothe the senses with high-gloss burl walnut wood trim, glove-soft leather and an in-dash six-disc DVD/CD audio-video player.

The stiffness in her body eased as she followed the directions on the screen to the road leading to I-95. "I know what you're trying to do."

Stretching out long legs, Rhett pulled the beak of the hat lower over his forehead, then lowered the back of his seat into a reclining position. "What?"

"You know right well that after I drive your car I'm not going to want to drive Valentina ever again."

"You shouldn't be driving her at all, because you never know when she's going to break down at the most inopportune time."

"She is mechanically sound, Rhett. It's just that's she had a lot of mileage on her."

"I'd still feel better if you had a new car."

Her fingers tightened on the wheel. "I told you I'm going to buy a new one, but not until I sell my co-op."

Rhett gave her a sidelong glance from under the beak of his cap. "Do you want me to give you the down payment?"

"No!"

He raised his head, then fell back against the leather seat. "There's no need to get spastic, Denise."

"I'm not spastic, Rhett. It's just that I don't need your money."

"What if I lend you the down payment and you pay me back later?"

"No, no and no! Why are we arguing about money? We never did that before."

Touching a button, Rhett raised his seat back. "It's because I never had any. Your parents deposited money in your checking account every month, while I had to depend on what I'd earned from work study. It galled me whenever you suggested paying for dinner or a movie."

"We were college students, Rhett. We weren't expected to have a lot of money."

"You had money, Denise."

"Okay. I had more than you. Fast-forward six years and now you have more than I'd ever hope to earn in my lifetime." Denise shifted her eyes off the road for a couple of seconds. "I don't know why, but I feel your offer to buy me a car, or lend the money to buy one, is based on revenge and upmanship. I know you didn't like it when I suggested picking up the tab for dinner or a movie, but I thought you were all right with it when we agreed to take turns."

"I was never all right with it, Denise. Every time you opened your wallet the words to TLC's 'No Scrubs' stayed with me for days."

Denise sucked her teeth. "You were hardly a scrub, Rhett Fennell. Every girl on campus knew who the scrubs were, but some were still willing to put up with them because they wanted a man. Even though my parents sent me an allowance, I still didn't have a lot of money. Xavier's undergraduate tuition was just under twenty thousand a year. He and I were in college at the same time, because he'd enrolled in The Citadel's graduate program. That put quite a strain on my parents' finances, but they made the sacrifice because they didn't want us to begin our careers burdened with student loans. That's why I refuse to accept any money from them to sustain the day care center."

"How did you buy your co-op without securing a mortgage?"

"When I was eight, I was involved in an auto accident when a car driven by a drunk driver jumped the curb, pinning me against a storefront. I wound up with a broken arm and a lot of bruises. Daddy sued the man, and the monies from the settlement were deposited in a custodial account. I was able to withdraw the monies that had earned quite a bit of interest after I'd graduated college. I'd taken your advice when you said the best investment anyone could make was in real estate, so I bought the co-op."

Rhett closed his eyes. Denise had trusted him enough to take his advice about investing in real estate, yet she hadn't when he'd sworn a solemn oath that he would never cheat on her. She'd claimed she believed him, but once the rumor started that he was sleeping with another coed, doubt had become her constant companion. He'd lost count of the number of times he'd tried to dissuade her from listening to gossip, but she wouldn't heed his warning. Then the rumor escalated and what was left of their fragile trust was shattered completely.

"What made you decide to start up your own business?"

Denise's sultry voice swept over him and he opened his eyes. He'd performed his work study at a Baltimore bank, where initially he was responsible for coding data for personal and business loans. The branch manager had promised to hire him after he'd graduated, but Rhett was faced with a dilemma when a headhunter from a major Philadelphia-based investment firm recruited him for their investment banking department, offering incentives such as full tuition reimbursement, bonuses and/or profit sharing. The only thing they wanted was a two-year commitment. He'd felt a particular loyalty to the bank, yet what the headhunter offered fit into his plan to pursue an MBA.

"It was a knee-jerk reaction," he said after a lengthy pause. "I was close to burnout from working and attending Wharton full-time. I'd mistakenly left the research paper I'd been developing for my thesis on my desk at work, and when I went into the office the next day it was missing."

Denise's hands tightened on the steering wheel when he mentioned Wharton. It wasn't until she'd read a profile on Garrett Fennell in *Black Enterprise* that she'd uncovered that Rhett had lived in Philadelphia while he'd attended Wharton School of the University of Pennsylvania. They'd lived in the same city yet they hadn't run into each other.

"Didn't you save it on a disk?"

"Yes, but it wasn't something I wanted made public until after I'd submitted it to my professor. Two weeks later all of the work I'd done was presented in what the banking division called developmental sessions. One of the vice presidents had claimed my work as his own."

"Did you confront him?"

Rhett snorted. "I did, but he claimed he'd been working on a similar strategy for more than a year. When I threatened to expose him, he said he had the power to fire me."

Denise gave Rhett another quick glance. "Please don't tell me he did."

Reaching over, he rested a hand on her right thigh. "Now, baby, you should know I don't scare that easily. I told him to fire me, but be prepared for a lawsuit, because my banking and finance professor had a draft of the paper. He asked me if I wanted to share credit on the strategy and I told him no. I think he was a little shocked at my response.

"The next day I came to him with a typed list of demands—I wanted out of my two-year contract without having to pay back the tuition, and I wanted my bonus in April rather than have to wait until December or early January. And I asked for a letter of recommendation for my next employer."

Denise laughed. "You were really ballsy, weren't you?"

"No more ballsy than the thieving bastard who stole my research paper."

She nodded. "You're right. Did you get what you wanted?"

"Yes. I graduated and moved back to D.C. I found a two-bedroom apartment where I set up a home office in the spare room. I'd always liked real estate better than investment banking, so I used a part of the bonus to buy a foreclosed property. The bank gave me a short-term, low-interest rehab loan and after it was brought up to code I sold it for three times what I'd paid for it.

"It took a while for me to build a relationship with the bank where I'd borrowed money, using what was in my account as collateral. The terms were if I repaid the loan in less than six months or a year, then the loan was interest-free."

"So, you've come to live up to the sobriquet as the Boy Wonder of Business."

Rhett frowned. He never liked the epithet, and disliked it more with each passing birthday. "It all comes down to common sense, Denise."

"I'm sure you've heard that common sense isn't all that common."

A smile replaced his frown. "You're right. Let me know when you get tired and I'll take over from you."

Denise narrowed her eyes at him. "I don't think so, Rhett. I *will* fight you if you try to get me from behind this wheel."

Rhett's fingers tightened slightly on her thigh under a pair of cropped cotton slacks. "There won't be much of a fight, baby girl. After all, I am a lot bigger than you."

"But I have a secret weapon, sweetheart."

"Which is?"

"I'm not telling. If I do, then it won't be a secret."

His hand moved up her thigh, the muscles tensing under his touch. "Will it hurt, baby?"

"The only thing I'm going to tell you is that you will enjoy it," Denise teased.

Throwing back his head, Rhett chanted, "Hurt me, hurt me please, baby."

Denise rested her hand right atop the one on her thigh. "You just might get your wish. Tell me about where we're going and if it's casual or dressy."

"The cookout is hosted by a couple I met last year. She's an event coordinator and her husband is a pharmaceutical company executive. The gathering is casual, and if the weather holds, then we'll probably go out for a sail just before sunset."

"Do you have a boat?"

Rhett shook his head. "No, and I don't need one. I don't come to the Chesapeake enough to warrant owning a boat." He raised his seat back, changing the satellite radio station to one featuring soul music from the '70s and '80s.

Denise felt free, freer than she had for a very long time as cool air caressed her face from the car's vents. She sang along with Rhett, her alto blending and harmonizing with his baritone. She crossed the state line from Pennsylvania into Maryland, following the GPS from I-95 to I-895. Traffic wasn't as heavy and the landscape changed once she left the interstate for a rural road. It was half past twelve when she maneuvered down a narrowed paved road to Rhett's waterfront home. They had made one stop at Graul's Supermarket to buy perishables and other sundries for their brief stay on the Cape.

Rhett got out of the car and came around to assist Denise. He held her hand, while escorting her up the slate path leading to a two-story nineteenth-century Shingle Style house. Painted a cornflower-blue with white trim and shutters, it radiated warmth and charm. Lifting the handle on the doorknob, he punched in a code, disengaging the security system.

Rhett tugged at the curls falling over Denise's forehead. "Please wait here, while I check inside."

She sat on the stone step, staring out at century-old trees, ferns and wildflowers that seemingly grew naturally in wild abandon. However, when she looked closer she realized the plants were strategically arranged to give it the appearance of untamed wildness. There was also something about the house and surrounding landscape that made Denise feel as if she'd stepped back in time.

Glancing over her shoulder, she saw Rhett opening windows to take advantage of the breeze coming off the water. The house was built on a hill overlooking the Chesapeake.

"You can come in now," Rhett called out behind her.

Pushing to her feet, Denise kicked off her sandals, leaving them on the thick straw mat outside the front door, and walked into the house. A cherrywood console table flanked by bleached pine straight-back chairs and a large oval mirror filled the entryway hall. Her eyebrows lifted slightly when she saw the gaslight sconces on either side of the mirror, wondering if they worked or were there for decoration.

"They work, but instead of gas I had them wired for electricity."

Denise smiled at Rhett, who stood near the staircase leading to the second floor. "You read my mind."

He extended his hand. "Come, let me show you to your bedroom, then I'll bring everything in."

"Do you want me to help you?"

He shook his head. "No. I want you to relax before we leave. After all, you did drive down."

She barely caught a glimpse of the living room with oversize upholstered chairs in soft hues of cream and tan as she followed Rhett up the staircase. "How large is this house?"

"It was about sixty-six-hundred square feet, but the new addition added another twenty-two-hundred square feet. Originally there was only the entrance hall, living room, dining room, pantry, kitchen and two bedrooms and baths on the second floor. The architect replaced the two-story porch with a side entrance nestled below gables and dormers and expanded the area to include two more bedrooms with en suite baths. I'll give you a tour after I bring in the food." Rhett stopped at the end of the hallway with a colorful runner spanning its length. "This will be your bedroom."

Denise walked in, smiling. The room was large and sun-filled. There was something about the off-white furnishings that reminded her of the bedroom in her D.C. apartment. "It's very nice."

Rhett rested his hand at the small of her back. "You have your own en suite bathroom. My bedroom is on the other side of the pocket doors."

Tilting her head, Denise looked up at Rhett staring down at her. "What time do we have to leave?"

"Three. I wanted to get here early to give you time to unwind before we head out." He dropped a kiss on the riot of curls framing her face. "I'll be back."

Waiting until he walked out of the room, Denise walked over to the windows. The view was so breath-takingly beautiful that she felt a lump form in her throat.

She tried imagining looking out on the churning waters during a storm or the sky obliterated by falling snow. Swallowing, she tried to relieve the constriction in her dry throat.

Rhett had accomplished everything he'd set out to do, while she was still a work-in-progress. There was the matter of securing the grant for her after-school program; and once that was up and running her next project was to set up a private school for at-risk boys.

What Denise found ironic was there was no allowance for romance in her plan for the future, and that meant she had to enjoy whatever time she had with Rhett. They were given the opportunity for a do-over and she planned to make the best of it while it lasted.

Chapter 9

Denise felt like a kid at summer camp when she discovered the en suite bathroom was designed like a mini-spa. A garden tub with a Jacuzzi, free-standing shower and a sunken hot tub, surrounded by a water-impervious wood floor, was the perfect setting for total relaxation. She smiled. Now she knew why Rhett wanted her to relax.

Walking across the space, she opened the French doors to reveal another set of doors that opened onto a balcony overlooking a sizeable semicircular terrace off the main floor. Moving closer to the edge of the balcony, she rested her arms along the railing and closed her eyes. The warmth of the sun, the cool breeze off the bay and the smell of the water swept over her like a magical concoction, renewing and reviving her.

It had been so long, much too long, since Denise had been able to kick back and relax. Attending family gatherings didn't count, because they only lasted a day or two at the most. She hadn't taken a real vacation since opening the center, and long weekends didn't count. Her entire existence was wrapped up in making a go of New Visions, and she hadn't realized how staid her life had become until now.

Rhett had become a master at buying, renovating and flipping properties, and yet he still took time out to relax. Denise opened her eyes. There had to be something wrong with her. She was working very hard but not very smart. It wasn't as if she didn't have anything to show for her sacrifice—the progressive child care center was a model that she was very proud of. Maybe, she mused, reuniting with Rhett was what she needed to gain some insight into what she'd been doing and needed to do.

Rhett had talked about burnout when he'd attended Wharton full-time while working full-time. Maybe it was fatigue that had made him less than alert when he'd left his research paper on his desk at work. Fatigue that had been the impetus to change him *and* his future after his boss had claimed the work Rhett had done as his. It had been enough to fuel his rage where he'd been able to shake off the complacency and strike out on his own—something he'd talked about incessantly when they'd been in college together.

Even when she'd told Rhett that she wanted to follow in the footsteps of her mother, aunts and cousins to become a teacher, he'd asked her whether she wanted to spend the next thirty years of her life in a classroom. When she hadn't answered he'd continued, asking whether she would consider becoming a principal or even a superintendent.

Rhett had always told her to aim high, and every five

years reassess where she was and where she'd want to go. It had taken less than four years of classroom teaching before Denise knew she wanted to open a child care center. Teachers were hired to educate, and she wanted to blend education with what she'd recognized as missing in so many young children coming into school for the first time—social skills.

Many were lacking manners, the tools to work and play well with their peers and too many were willing to settle disputes with their hands rather than with their brain. The children at New Visions were tutored in setting the table, how to eat and clean up after themselves. There were rewards for good behavior and isolation from the others in their group for negative behavior. A three-year-old sitting alone at a table for three minutes while his or hers friends were engaged in play was akin to a life of solitary confinement.

The benchmark for New Visions was love. Love of themselves, their parents, family, neighborhood and country. Her teachers stressed the concept that if you loved someone or something you protected it. Praise was heaped upon the children like rain soaking the earth in order for flowers to grow. Praise and positive reinforcement were in short supply from parents who were dealing with their own stress of keeping their jobs, while attempting to keep their families intact.

The children at New Visions were her children and her babies, and everyone connected to the center had become extended family. Denise opened her eyes to see Rhett, as he carried and set down the frame of a round rattan table on the terrace below. She stood there long enough to see him bring out a quartet of matching chairs before she closed the doors and retreated to the bedroom. She found her bag and tote next to the door.

My bedroom is on the other side of the pocket doors. His words echoed in her head. He'd given her a choice. Either she could sleep in her own bedroom or share his bed.

What Denise hadn't wanted was a choice. She wouldn't have thought him brash or arrogant if he'd taken her overnight bag to his bedroom only because she wanted *and* needed Garrett Mason Fennell to remind her why she'd been born female. She didn't so much want to make love with Rhett—she needed to make love with him, desperately.

Closing the door, she picked up her bags and carried them over to the dressing area. Emptying the contents, she hung them up in a walk-in closet with racks, shelves and drawers constructed with a shopaholic in mind. Even her extensive shoe collection would look lost in the expansive closet.

Denise hung up a pair of navy-blue raw silk slacks she'd planned to wear with a white silk kimono piped in navy with a blue and white-striped obi sash that was an exact match for her three-inch, peep-toe espadrilles. Despite putting in ten- and sometimes twelve-hour workdays, she always took time to pamper herself with a weekly mani/pedi and monthly hydrating facial and full-body massage. Each and every time she left the salon she thought of her mother. Paulette Eaton had taken her daughter to her favorite salon at six for a mini-day of beauty. Denise had been awed by sights and smells associated with a salon and the first time she stuck her chubby brown toes and fingers in bowls of soapy warm water she was hooked!

She and her mother continued their weekly mother/ daughter spa dates until she left Philly for Baltimore. After conferring with her father, Denise had given her mother an all-expenses-paid vacation to a golfing/spa retreat in Sedona, Arizona, for her fiftieth birthday.

Leaning over, Denise examined her toes for chips in the candy-apple-red polish. Removing the rubber shower shoes from her tote, she slipped her feet into them. Nothing ruined a pedicure like walking barefoot.

She checked her watch. She had less than two hours to wind down from the drive and prepare for the afternoon and evening festivities. Gathering a set of underwear, Denise returned to the bathroom to take a leisurely bath.

Rhett finished setting up the deck furniture that had been stored in the three-car garage. When he'd purchased the house it had been abandoned for years following the death of an elderly couple whose children had relocated to the west coast. Jeff McNeill, one of the partners at the architectural firm that drew up all the plans for his renovated properties, had called to let him know about the house scheduled to be sold at auction for delinquent taxes.

Rhett had cancelled all of his meetings and driven up to see the house. It had weathered drastically over the years and was perilously close to the point where it would have to be demolished. Jeff's recommendation had been to strip it to the bare bones. His plans had included replacing the two-story porch with a new addition that increased the square footage by two thousand. Jeff had also added a pair of French doors opening to a series of terraces to take advantage of the water views. Older spaces had been reworked and expanded, including raising the ceiling in the master bedroom, adding en suite bathrooms and an extra bedroom.

Utilizing the services of his favorite interior design firm, Rhett had given them carte blanche when it came to furnishing the interiors. They had been aware of his personal tastes, and the result had been a home designed for living and entertaining.

The first morning he'd woken and walked ten feet to look out over Chesapeake Bay, Rhett had known it was a scene he wanted to repeat over and over. In that instant he'd known this was a house he wouldn't flip, but live in for the rest of his life. It wasn't a house, but his home.

Moving around the ultra-modern kitchen, he brewed a pot of iced tea and removed the cellophane from a freshly made Caesar salad he'd picked up from the supermarket's deli section. Smaller containers held large cooked shrimp, cubes of smoked chicken and thinly sliced roast beef.

His cooking skills were still less than stellar, but Rhett had mastered the art of cooking breakfast. All he needed was a stovetop grill, because he was able to keep an eye on grilling bacon or sausage, home fries and eggs at the same time. It was when he had to shift from the grill to the stove and/or the oven that he tended to burn or overcook something. And there was never the likelihood that he would go hungry as long as there were stores that offered prepared meals. He tended to avoid fast-food restaurants in favor of those serving cook-to-order dishes.

Rhett stepped back surveying the table that flowed into a cooking island in the all-white and stainless-steel kitchen. Turning on his heels, he went in search of Denise, bumping into her as she walked in. He caught her before she lost her balance.

"Oops!"

"Sorry, baby. I was just coming to get you." He and Denise had spoken in unison. "I just put together something to tide us over until later this evening." It'd been twelve hours since they'd eaten breakfast at the diner.

Denise walked into the kitchen, her mouth gaping in stunned amazement. Stark-white vinyl tiles bordered in gray set the stage for a large space with rows of recessed lights in a ceiling of crown molding. Walk-in freezer, French-door refrigerator, sub-zero freezer, wine cabinet and built-in television, double ovens with warming drawers and cooktop stove and grill made the space a chef's dream. A triple sink at the opposite end of a countertop with three high stools with steel frames was the perfect place to sit or eat, while surveying the activity going on in the magnificent kitchen. Fine custom cabinetry without handles or hardware provided a sleekness and uninterrupted wall of pristine white. The tall, narrow vents over the stove did double duty. They were constructed to look like cabinets but were designed to pull all cooking odors out of the kitchen. The light from a ceiling fixture with ten conical spheres, suspended from steel rods over the dining countertop, reflected off the shiny surface like polished silver.

Her smile was dazzling once she recovered. "Now, this is a kitchen."

Wrapping an arm around her waist, Rhett pulled Denise gently over to the table. "You like it?"

"I love it, Rhett." *What's not to love,* she thought. It was the perfect place in which to plan a dinner party. "The house is immaculate," she said, glancing at Rhett over her shoulder when he seated her. "Who cleans it?"

Rhett sat beside Denise, reaching for the pitcher of tea

and filling a tall glass with the cold liquid. He placed a dish with sliced lemons and another covered dish filled with sugar next to her plate.

"Whenever I know I'm coming up, I call a local cleaning service to let them know what time I expect to arrive. Once I'm here I'll call and they send someone over. There's not a lot to do—dusting, vacuuming, cleaning the bathrooms and occasionally changing the beds."

Denise took a sip of her tea before adding a teaspoon of sugar. "How often do you come here?"

"Not often enough. But that's going to change this summer. My mother and her husband come up at least once a month, so the house doesn't remain vacant for too long a period. Speaking of my mother, I told her that I'd run into you again, and she sends her best."

Picking up a cloth napkin and spreading it over her lap, Denise kept her gaze fixed on her plate. "Tell her same here."

"You can tell her next week."

Shifting, Denise turned to give Rhett an incredulous look. "What's next week?"

"She's coming to stay for a week. Unfortunately you won't get to meet her husband because he has to attend a conference in Dallas."

"What is she going to say about me staying with you?"

"What do you want her to say, Denise? That she doesn't approve of her son bringing a woman into *his* home? Look, baby, my mother stopped monitoring what I did and who I was with a long time ago. I didn't know she was seeing anyone seriously until she called to tell me she was getting married. I don't get into Geraldine Russell nee Fennell's business and she doesn't get into mine."

"Unlike mine," Denise mumbled.

Rhett picked up the salad greens with shaved parmesan cheese and placed it in a bowl at her place setting. "I understand your mother and what she wants."

"And that is?" she asked, spearing several shrimp and placing them in her salad, before spooning the dressing over the romaine lettuce.

"She wants grandchildren."

"So do a lot of parents, but they usually aren't so blatant and vocal about it."

"Lighten up on Paulette, darling. Gerri's no different. It's just that she's more subtle with her hints. She's like, 'Garrett, baby. You know it's not good for a man to spend so much time alone.' Or it's 'Look, son, I'm not getting any younger and I'd like to have a few grandchildren before I die.' That's when I tell her to stop the melodrama. Gerri's not even fifty and she's in good health, so I don't believe she's going to expire anytime soon."

"What's up with parents wanting grandchildren? You think they would've had enough of kids when they had to raise their own children."

"I suppose we'll find out what it's all about once we raise our children."

Rhett realized too late what he'd said when Denise stared at him as if he were a complete stranger. He opened his mouth to correct himself and then decided against it. What he'd said had come from his heart. He wanted children, and he wanted Denise Eaton to be the mother of their children.

"I didn't ask you to come here because I was hoping you would sleep with me," he said instead.

"Why did you ask me?"

Rhett knew what he was about to admit to Denise would either shatter their fragile truce or bring them closer together, because the harder he'd tried to ignore the truth the more it continued to haunt him. Every woman he'd met and/or slept with had become her. He'd searched in vain to find a modicum of what he'd shared with Denise in them—but had failed miserably. It was why he'd begun what had become a revolving door of women coming and going out of his life.

He placed his left hand over her right, holding it firmly lest she flee the kitchen. "I love you, Denise. I don't care about you and Trey—"

"Don't mention his name," Denise practically shouted, cutting Rhett off. "Please," she whispered hoarsely. "This time it's only *us,* Rhett."

He lowered his head and his voice. "You know what this means, Denise?" She nodded, her head going up and down like a bobblehead doll. "This time it's for keeps. And, when I put a ring on your finger it's never coming off. Do you understand?" She nodded again. "Is there anything you'd like to add?"

A strength came to Denise she hadn't thought possible. They'd reached the point where their relationship would be resolved by a lifetime of commitment and fidelity. "Yes. There is something I'd like you to do."

"Just say it, baby, and if it's within my power I'll make it happen."

Denise closed her eyes against his intense stare. "Make love to me."

The request was barely off her tongue when she was swept off the stool and carried across the kitchen. She hadn't realized she was holding her breath until she felt the constriction across her chest. She was shaking, from head to toe, and there was nothing Denise could do to stop the tremors.

She'd wanted and needed Rhett every night of their six-year separation. There were times when she'd caught herself searching restaurants, clubs and stores for his face. Every time she'd seen a tall, black man who looked even remotely like the one to whom she'd given her heart, she'd had to stop and make certain it wasn't him before going about her business.

Men who'd expressed an interest in her and had worked enough nerve to ask her out asked whether she was into men when she turned them down. That had been the reason she'd decided to go out with Kevin. It had been the only time she'd dated out of her race, so she'd seen him as safe. The single physical encounter between them had become a disaster—for both. Unable to fake her response, Denise had just lain there waiting for him to finish. Kevin, sensing her nonparticipation, had aborted the act, put his clothes on and went home. The next time they'd met it had been to say goodbye.

Denise tightened her grip around Rhett's neck as he carried her up the staircase and down the hallway to the adjoining bedrooms. He strode past the door to the one he'd assigned her and into his. She wasn't given the opportunity to view the furnishings when she found herself sprawled over a large bed with a decoratively carved mahogany headboard.

Her gaze met and fused with Rhett's as he pulled the T-shirt over his head, then unsnapped his jeans, pushing them and his briefs off his hips in one smooth motion. Her pulse quickened, her breathing becoming shallow as her gaze lowered to his muscular thighs, and she found she couldn't look away from his enormous erection. But she did close her eyes when a rush of wetness left her panting as if she'd run a grueling race.

This was what she'd been waiting for, waiting for Garrett Fennell to come back into her life and remind her why she'd been born female. All her senses took over when his knee touched the side of the bed, causing the mattress to dip slightly. Her chest rose and fell heavily when he divested her of her clothes. His hands were steady, fingers nimble. She smiled. He'd always made undressing her as much a part of foreplay as kissing, touching and caressing. Holding up her arms, Denise wasn't disappointed when Rhett moved over her, his welcoming weight pressing her down to the mattress.

Rhett's nose nuzzled her ear as he trailed light kisses along the column of her scented neck. He'd fantasized about making love to Denise so often that he wasn't certain where reality began and fantasy ended. But it was about to end—now. She was real and everything that made Denise Eaton who she was flooded his consciousness—her scent, the texture of her skin, soft sounds escaping her parted lips. He lay between her silken thighs, his blood-engorged penis pulsing against her belly.

"Rhett?"

"What is it, baby?"

"Do you have protection?"

His heart felt like a stone in his chest when he heard Denise's query. Although he had condoms he didn't want to use them, because he wanted to marry her and get her pregnant as quickly as humanly possible.

"Yes. Why?"

"I don't want to get pregnant."

Rhett wanted to ask her if she ever wanted to get pregnant, but decided it would open a dialogue that was certain to kill the moment. "Let me know when you want to start a family and I'll do everything I can to oblige."

She laughed softly. "Why do you make it sound as if you'd be doing me a favor?"

"It's not about that, Denise."

"What is it about?"

There was a long pause. "It's about us being on the same page. I have to want what you want when you want it. I can't want a child when you don't."

Curving her arms under Rhett's shoulders, Denise pressed a kiss to his warm throat when he raised his head. "I want a baby, darling. It just can't be now. And aren't you forgetting something?"

"What's that?"

"I have no intention of becoming a baby mama." Denise watched Rhett's expression change from desire to one that had become a mask of stone.

"You claim I've changed. But there's one thing about me that will never change and that is I will never get a woman pregnant and not marry her. Speaking of marriage," he continued without pausing to take a breath, "when do you want to get married?"

Things were happening so quickly that she felt as if she were on a merry-go-round of emotions. It hadn't been a week since she and Rhett had reunited and he'd picked up as if time had stood still for them. It was the same question he'd asked her six weeks before their graduation and her response had been she didn't know. Dating Garrett Fennell had been one thing and becoming Mrs. Denise Fennell within weeks of her college graduation had been something she hadn't been able to fathom at that time. What Rhett hadn't known was that her ambivalence had stemmed from the rumors that he was sleeping with her and another woman at the same time.

"New Year's Eve." It was the first date that popped into her head.

Rhett blinked. "You want to wait that long?"

"It's only seven months away. It's going to take that long to plan a wedding if we're going to do it right."

A smile broke through his expression of uncertainty. "Okay. New Year's it is."

Denise closed her eyes. "Now that we've done enough talking do you still intend to make love to me?"

"Do I have a hard-on, Ms. Eaton?"

"How do you do that?"

"Do what?"

"Sustain an erection without going inside me. Are you taking a pill for erectile dysfunction?"

Without warning, Rhett flipped Denise over on her belly, pulling her up to her knees. "I told you one day your mouth is going to get you in trouble, and today is that day."

Denise struggled to free herself, but she was no match for Rhett's superior strength. He managed to hold her while reaching over to the drawer in the bedside table and removing a condom. Using his teeth, he tore open the packet, removed the latex sheath and rolled it down the length of his penis.

He knew she didn't like this position, because he was able to control their lovemaking. Rhett also knew it gave her maximum pleasure when with every stroke his penis rubbed against her clitoris, making her come too quickly. Repressing an orgasm as long as possible assured her maximum sexual satisfaction.

"No, darling," Denise pleaded.

Rhett kissed the nape of her neck. "I'm not going to hurt you, baby."

She knew he wasn't going to hurt her, but she didn't want it to be over before it began. But it did begin when she felt his hardness searching between the folds to find her wet and ready for his possession. Gasps overlapped moans as her celibate flesh stretched slowly to take every long, delicious inch of him until he was fully sheathed inside her.

Rhett couldn't remember Denise that tight, that small. All he knew was he'd come home. Her flesh held him tightly then eased only to repeat it again and again until the fire between her thighs spread to his, dissolving both in an inferno from which there was no escape. He covered her breasts, squeezing the firm globes gently, his hips pushing against hers as she pushed back against his groin.

Her breathing changed, becoming deeper. Her gasps turned into deep surrendering moans of unrestrained pleasure. Sounds of erotic pleasure became unrestrained screams of ecstasy when Denise stiffened with the explosive rush of orgasmic fulfillment sweeping over her. She lost count of the number of orgasms after three, succumbing to the uncontrolled passion that shattered into a million little pieces.

Rhett's release had come too quickly; he'd thought he could hold back but he couldn't. It'd been too long since he and Denise had been together. It was as if he'd been starving for weeks and someone had escorted him to the banquet table, urging him to eat whatever he wanted. Instead of nibbling he'd gorged until he couldn't move, too emotionally drained to speak.

Still joined, he turned her over, tucking her under him. Cradling her face, he placed a kiss on the bridge of her nose. "This one was for me. The next one will be for you."

Eyes closed, Denise's lips parted in a smile. She ran her fingertips up and down Rhett's moist back. "Wrong, Rhett. This one was for me, too."

They lay together, talking quietly as they'd done when they'd shared a much smaller bed in sparsely furnished bedrooms. It was with great reluctance that Rhett pulled out, moved off the bed and went into the bathroom to discard the condom. When he returned Denise had turned on her side, the sheet pulled up over her breasts. He joined her in bed, pressing his chest to her back.

"I love you," he whispered softly.

Hot tears pricked the backs of Denise's eyes. Rhett loved her and she loved him. It wasn't his love she doubted, but her ability to trust him to be faithful to her. However, time was on her side. She had a little more than seven months to put him to the test.

Chapter 10

Denise moved closer to Rhett when they were greeted by their hostess. Brooke Andersen was tall, thin, blonde, tanned and looked as if she'd stepped off the glossy pages of a Ralph Lauren ad.

Brooke extended her hands, the ray of the sun reflecting off the many bracelets with precious and semi-precious stones on her slender wrists. The size of the diamond in her engagement ring and the channel-set diamonds in the eternity band were a blatant show of grandiosity. It was hard to pinpoint her age. Advances in cosmetic surgery seemingly had frozen time for the nipped and tucked woman.

"Rhett, darling. I'm so glad you could come," Brooke purred like a satisfied feline. "We'll be boarding in about ten minutes." Her bright blue eyes shifted to Denise. "Aren't you lovely? And what a darling outfit."

Denise gave the woman a too-sweet smile. "Thank you so much."

Rhett wrapped an arm around Denise's waist. "Denise, Brooke Andersen. Brooke, Denise Eaton."

Brooke beckoned her husband. "Jim, darling. Rhett has arrived."

Rhett exchanged an amused look with Denise, wondering if she'd found Brooke as entertaining as he did. He'd always found her to be a little over-the-top, but whenever he needed her to coordinate an event for him she would clear her calendar and make it happen.

He and Denise had lingered in bed, dozing off and on. They'd shared a shower before going down to the kitchen to salvage the remains of their aborted meal. He knew it was too late to show up to eat at the Andersens', because the invitation had stated it would be a sit-down dinner; however, Rhett had called Jim to inform him that he wouldn't arrive in time to eat, but would be there before the *Elena Victoria* sailed.

Jim Andersen, dressed in white linen like his wife and most of their guests, made his way toward them. Physically, he was Brooke's counterpart. The only difference was his hair was silver to her platinum-blond. He flashed a toothy grin. "Garrett, I'm so glad you made it."

After Rhett introduced her to their host, Denise took note of the people, the Andersens' home and the yacht moored off the pier. The sprawling Georgian Colonial was magnificent, as were the grounds on which it sat. Every blade of grass in the manicured lawn was exactly the same length. When Rhett had mentioned they were going to attend a cookout she thought there would be lots of people and that it wouldn't be a sit-down affair with a waitstaff picking up and setting down different courses.

When her family members hosted a cookout the only sitting was when everyone filled their plates and they needed someplace to set it in order to eat without spilling the contents. What Brooke Andersen needed was a generous dose of reality. Rhett mentioned he'd invited the Andersens and a few of his neighbors to his house the following weekend. Geraldine would also be in attendance, so between the two of them they would give the supercilious Cape St. Claire residents another version of a cookout.

Crew members were carrying crates to the boat as several other couples were arriving. They were younger and more outgoing. The men tapped their BlackBerries, while their female counterparts were texting or listening to their iPods. Two twenty-something women called Brooke mother and Jim father. More cars were maneuvering onto the property as friends of the Andersen children greeted one another with shrieks and laughter.

Rhett noticed the direction of Denise's gaze. Leaning closer, he dipped his head, pressing his mouth to her ear. "Now the fun begins."

"I hear you," she whispered when two men sporting colorful shirts with Hawaiian prints carried audio equipment down the pier to the gleaming white boat bobbing on the water. The younger Andersens had brought along a DJ.

The fun began as soon as the anchor to the sleek 128-foot yacht lifted, and it moved smoothly on the surface of the water. A bar was set up in the bridge deck's sky lounge that was used as a game room and theater. Between the pulsing beat of music ranging from hip-hop, rock and pop, drinks flowed, and a lively card game was in progress, while crew members circulated carrying trays of hot and cold finger foods.

Brooke, who'd appointed herself Denise's chaperone, took her on a tour of the sailing vessel designed with an emphasis on relaxed comfort. She called the *Elena Victoria* her country house party at sea. The ship was staffed by a crew of nine, with three decks of cabins and salons. There were four guest staterooms, a master suite and tender tucked into the aft that opened to become a swimming platform and dock. She proudly announced that the length of the ship qualified it as a superyacht. The interiors were luxurious. Walnut, teak, a gleaming stainless-steel stair on the aft main deck, ebony-and-nickel-accented oak tables bespoke elegance and a grace of style seen in the finest homes.

Brooke stared at the woman who'd accompanied Garrett Fennell. She was more than lovely. She'd fashioned her hair into a chignon; the style was perfect for her Asian-inspired outfit. One of her friends, although much older than Garrett, had asked her to invite him with the hope that he would be receptive to her subtle advances. But the woman was so disappointed when Brooke informed her that the young entrepreneur was bringing someone with him that she took to her bed, feigning a migraine.

"Jim and I are sailing to the Mediterranean this year without the children," Brooke intoned. "I told him I wanted to see the Baltic and cruise the fjords, and see St. Petersburg but only if there's time."

"The *Elena Victoria* is a spectacular ship," Denise complimented without guile. From the leather-topped desk in the study adjacent to the master stateroom to the carefully decorated guest cabins and pieces of art, the yacht was the epitome of safety, comfort and beauty.

Brooke managed what passed for a smile when the muscles in her face refused to move. "I know Garrett is always tied up with one deal or another, but try to convince your boyfriend to come along when we sail down to the Caribbean for a week before the tropical storm season begins."

"I'll talk to him," Denise promised.

"Speaking of your handsome boyfriend, I see him looking for you. Please apologize to him if I've monopolized too much of your time."

Denise mumbled she would as she made her way over to where Rhett was standing near the rail, seemingly half listening to something Brooke's daughter was telling him. His expression changed when their eyes met. She recognized what he was trying to communicate to her.

Walking over to him, she slipped her arm through his. "I'm sorry to interrupt, but I need to borrow my fiancé for a few minutes." The word *fiancé* seemed to get the woman's attention, and she turned and walked away.

"Let's go up on the upper deck," Rhett said sotto voce, as he led her away from the crowd and up a flight of stairs. The view from the top of the yacht was spectacular. There was a near full moon and without the lights from high-rise buildings the stars appeared brighter, closer.

Wrapping his arms around Denise's waist, he pulled her to his chest while sharing his body's heat. "Are you cold, darling?"

Burying her face against his chest, she shook her head. "No. I'm good." Her top had long sleeves.

"I should've warned you that Brooke's rather chatty *and* clingy."

Denise smiled. "She's okay as long as I don't have to deal with her every day. Speaking of every day, she wants me to convince you to go along with her and Jim when they sail down to the Caribbean in a couple of weeks."

"I'd go if you could get away."

"I can't, Rhett. Our enrollment numbers increase during the summer recess. And then there are employee vacations, so we'll be stretched pretty thin over the next couple of months."

"When do you take your vacation?"

"I don't."

Pulling back, Rhett stared at Denise with an incredulous look on his face. "You're kidding, aren't you?"

She closed her eyes and shook her head. "No. I haven't had a vacation in more than two years."

Grasping her shoulders, he shook her gently. "Have you lost your mind? How long do you think you can keep going without taking a break?"

"I get a break."

"When?"

"Remember, I don't work weekends," she argued softly.

"Weekends aren't enough, Denise."

"They're enough for me, Rhett. I sleep until late morning and then laze around for most of the day."

"When do you shop for food?"

"I do that during the week before I go home."

"How about laundry?"

"I have a washer and dryer in my apartment."

"Do you cook for yourself?"

"Of course I do."

"When?" Rhett asked, continuing with his interrogation.

"Usually on Sundays I cook enough to last me until midweek. After that, I'll either bring something in or order takeout."

"Who cleans your apartment?"

"I do."

"Do you hear yourself, Denise? You cook, clean, shop and do laundry. And that's when you're not at the center. When are you going to make time for Denise?"

She frowned. "I don't know what you're talking about."

"When do you find the time to do what you like to do? I remember the girl who loved going to the movies and art galleries. You used to drag me to every museum whenever they had a new exhibit. When was the last time you went to a museum?"

"I don't remember."

"Of course you don't," Rhett countered, "because it probably was with me. I'm going to give you an early birthday gift of a cleaning service and personal chef."

"No, Rhett!"

"Yes, Denise! I don't want to marry a shell of a woman come the end of the year."

Her temper flared. "Now I know what this is all about. You want me nice and perky when you flaunt me as Mrs. Garrett—"

"That's enough, Denise."

"It's not enough, Garrett. You can't come back into my life and turn it upside down without first talking to me. I'm not a piece of property you've bought, then you have to decide whether you'll either keep it or unload it for a profit. When I marry you I want to be your partner. I'm not some hapless creature who can't think or take care of herself."

"I didn't mean for it to come out like that."

"Well, it did. If I'm awarded the grant, then there will be enough money to hire an assistant director, and that will free me up to take a vacation."

"Why didn't you say that?"

"You didn't ask, Rhett. You just started firing questions at me and—"

"I'm sorry. Will you forgive me?"

"I'll think about it, but only if you dance with me."

Rhett listened to the music drifting up from below deck. The DJ was playing one of their favorite songs. Taking her in his arms, he tucked her curves into his body. They danced without moving their feet, their bodies swaying sensuously from side to side.

"I want to make love to you right here," he rasped in her ear.

"We can't," Denise whispered.

"Why not, baby?"

"What if someone sees us?"

Rhett laughed. "Everyone onboard is an adult. I'm certain they're all quite familiar with copulating."

"That may be so, but I'm not going to copulate in a public place."

"Where's your sense of adventure, baby?" His hands cradled her hips, allowing her to feel his hard-on. "I'm in pain, sweetheart."

"It would serve you right if I jerked you off right here," Denise teased.

Throwing back his head, Rhett laughed loudly. "Damn, girl. When did you get so nasty?"

"You were the one who turned me into a bad girl."

He sobered quickly. "You're right about that. But I have to say that you were an excellent student. You were also a quick study."

Denise buried her face between his neck and shoulder. "That's because you were an incredible teacher."

"Do you think you'll need additional tutoring?"

"A little. But you better get all of the tutoring in tonight because I'm expecting my period."

"When?"

"Tomorrow."

"I'll see if I can fit you into my busy schedule."

Denise shivered as if someone had run a feather over the back of her neck. Rhett was talking about fitting her in. Was he referring to his sleeping with another or other women?

"Who else are you sleeping with?"

Rhett stopped swaying. "What!?"

"Don't what me, Garrett."

"Don't tell me we're going to rehash old crap, Denise."

"It's not old crap. I need to know if you're sleeping with me and another woman at the same time."

"No!"

"Don't raise your voice to me."

Rhett dropped his arms. "When I speak in a normal tone you seem not to hear me."

"I hear you."

"No, you don't, or you never would've asked me something so damned asinine. I told you the first time I made love with you that I've never been able to sleep with more than one woman at the same time. Emotionally I'm not equipped to play bed-hopping games. You not trusting me is what drove us apart. Why are you doing it again?"

Denise realized she didn't have a comeback. She

moved over to the rail, peering out into the water. Why, she mused, couldn't she let go of the past? Closing her eyes, she leaned back against Rhett when he came up behind her.

"I'm sorry, Rhett."

Wrapping his arms around her midriff, he kissed the side of her neck. "Apology accepted. And I'm sorry I raised my voice to you."

She smiled. "Apology accepted."

They lost track of time as they stood together, each lost in their private thoughts. When they went below deck they found everyone in the sky lounge watching a movie. All of the chairs were occupied and those who hadn't found a chair sat on the carpet. Rhett found a spot, pulling Denise down to sit between his outstretched legs. It was a romantic comedy he'd seen before, but he enjoyed viewing it again.

The ship sailed down the intercoastal waterway to Chesapeake Ranch Estates before reversing its course. It was after three when Rhett pressed the remote that opened the garage door. He drove in and shut off the engine, closing the door behind him.

"I can't believe it's so late," Denise said around the yawn she covered with her hand when Rhett helped her out of the car.

"Did you enjoy yourself?"

"Yes, I did."

"I'm glad."

He was glad and she was glad she'd agreed to spend the weekend with Rhett. "I'm going upstairs to shower and get into bed before I fall asleep standing up."

Rhett winked at her. "I'll be up in a few minutes."

The few minutes became forty minutes, and when he

walked into his bedroom Denise was sound asleep. He took a shower to get rid of the saltwater smell clinging to his clothes and body. Denise stirred but didn't wake up when he got into bed with her.

She didn't know how serious he'd been when he told her about the cleaning service and personal chef. Perhaps he'd presented it all wrong, but Rhett knew he had to try to convince Denise to slow down before she broke down mentally and physically.

He'd been there, done that when working and attending classes full-time. There were mornings when he'd had to force himself to get out of bed. The theft of his research paper had been a blessing in disguise. If the greedy bastard hadn't taken it there was no doubt he would still be working for the investment banking firm.

Rhett knew he had to find a way to help New Visions financially, so as to give Denise respite from the sole responsibility of the child care center. He knew she wouldn't accept a check from him outright, but she'd be a fool to reject money from a local company willing to make a charitable donation.

His mind was spinning with ideas when fatigue won out, and he joined Denise in sleep.

As predicted, Denise saw evidence of her menses, accompanied by cramps and a headache. She spent the afternoon reclining on the chaise on the terrace, sipping lukewarm tea with lemon. She tolerated the cramps because her period only lasted three days. Any more than that and she would be forced to take something to alleviate the pain. During the drive back to D.C., she was practically monosyllabic, preferring to sleep than talk.

Rhett, who was more than familiar with the change

in Denise's mood, didn't pressure her to talk. He found a space in the visitor section of the parking lot adjacent to her building and he carried her bags when they rode the elevator to her apartment.

"Do you want me to hang out with you tonight?" he asked when she unlocked the door.

Denise turned and stared up at Rhett. He hadn't bothered to shave and the stubble on his lean face enhanced his blatant masculinity. "Do you want to?"

He angled his head, smiling. "Yes."

"Come in."

Rhett kissed her forehead. "Let me go back to the car and get my bag." He winked at her. "Don't run away."

Denise gave him a wry smile. "I'll try not to."

Chapter 11

Denise was surprised to get up earlier that morning and find Rhett in her kitchen preparing breakfast. When she'd complimented him on his culinary skills, he countered saying his skill did not extend beyond breakfast. Her cramps weren't as severe as they'd been the day before and she found herself in better spirits.

She'd picked up *The Washington Post* that had been delivered outside her door, and over breakfast they talked then read the newspaper as they'd done as students. Denise was always interested in local politics and world events, while Rhett devoured the business and financial section. He left her apartment to return to his. Instead of leaving her house to arrive at the center at seven, Denise walked in at eight. She'd planned to take Rhett's advice and take more time for herself.

They would return to the Cape the upcoming weekend when Rhett would host an open house coordinated by Brooke Andersen. It would also be the first time Denise would reunite with his mother since their breakup.

Denise sat at the table in her office with the center's social worker. After the Memorial Day weekend the center shifted to summer mode. The normal Friday-morning staff meetings were staggered with Denise meeting with them individually, because many of the employees, the teachers in particular, had elected to take either Mondays or Fridays off, giving them three-day weekends.

She and Lisa Brown were going over files on the children the therapist had flagged. "What's happening with Angelo?"

Lisa adjusted her half-glasses. Her smooth round brown face belied her age. "He's wetting the bed again, and his teacher noticed a fresh bruise on his thigh. He claims he fell off his bike. The last report of bed-wetting was when his father returned to the house."

"I thought his mother had a restraining order against his father."

"She does," Lisa confirmed.

Denise massaged her forehead, while shaking her head. "Are you certain he's back in the house?"

The retired social worker was a volunteer, working twelve hours a week to offset fees for her two grandchildren. Her daughter *and* son-in-law had been deployed to Iraq and Afghanistan, and she'd become temporary guardian for twin toddlers.

"I can't say yes with any amount of certainty."

"Have you talked to Angelo's mother?"

"I tried, but she's too afraid to say anything. Remember, it was her sister who made her call the police when he broke Angelo's arm."

"Call child protective services and have them make an unannounced house call. You also have to let them know about the bruise." The center was mandated by law to report what they suspected to be child abuse. "What else do you have?"

"Miranda says Ms. Vance still hasn't taken DeShawn to get his glasses."

"Tell Ms. Vance that we're going to suspend her son until he gets his glasses. That should get her attention. It's not fair the child has to sit out most activities because he can't see more than three feet in front of his face."

Lisa made notations on a legal pad. "Ms. Clark called me to say she's going to have to pull her son out because her employer has cut her hours and she can't afford to pay our fee."

"Have her bring in her pay stub and we'll adjust the fee. The woman can't keep or look for another job with a child in tow." The single mother had come to the center after her mother, who'd looked after her infant son, passed away.

Lisa smiled, showing off the braces on her teeth. She'd waited until she was in her early fifties to correct an overbite. "That's it, Denise."

Denise smiled. "Thanks, Lisa."

"You're welcome."

She exhaled an audible breath when the social worker walked out, closing the door behind her. Denise didn't think she would ever get used to the number of incidents of neglect and/or abuse when it came to children. A number of New Visions children were in foster care, which was a constant reminder of the breakdown of the family structure. Single mothers, single fathers, divorced parents, grandparents as legal guardians for their grand- and great-grandchildren, drugs, alcohol, physical and sexual abuse were becoming all too common.

Pushing to her feet, Denise looped the lanyard with her ID around her neck. In addition to her administrative duties, she was the New Visions storyteller. The children loved hearing her read because she was able to change her voice, affecting different dialects and accents, much to their amusement. Today's title for the two- and three-year-olds was Dr. Seuss's *Cat in the Hat*.

Rhett stood over the conference-room table with the Capital Management Properties urban planner and his assistant—an undergraduate student. The constant hammering and drilling coming from the fourth floor was missing. He'd contacted the contractor to arrange for his team to come in after the offices closed for the day. The contractor had reminded him that he would have to charge for the night differential, but it was worth it to Rhett not to be disturbed by the ongoing noise.

Bill Lloyd had spread the architectural plans for the four-square block of commercial property out on the table. "There are thirty-six storefronts—twenty occupied and twelve vacant."

"How many have valid leases?" Rhett asked.

"Fifteen," said the assistant.

Rhett smiled. "That's more than I would've predicted." The former owner had neglected to renew leases, and in the end had stopped making repairs to his properties. "I want you to put a team together to visit each of the merchants and ascertain whether they want to continue doing business. I already have the architect's report as to structural problems in some of the stores. CMP will make the repairs, renovate and update all of the store-fronts to give them a uniformed appearance. Malcolm, I want you to check with the police to uncover which businesses have been targeted for holdups and burglaries. Also, which ones have a heavier than usual number of people hanging out in front of them. Once the area is gentrified the store owners are going to be responsible for enforcing the no-loitering clause in their lease. Teenagers hanging out around corner stores make them easy targets for drug pushers."

Bill Lloyd pointed to the stores highlighted in yellow. "What's up with these?"

Rhett stared at the brilliant urban planner who'd just celebrated his thirtieth birthday. When he'd taken over Capital Management Properties, Bill had elected to stay on rather than look for another position. "One houses a child care center. I've earmarked the adjacent storefront for their proposed expansion."

"That's a prime location because it's corner property," Malcolm said.

"What are you trying to say, Malcolm?" Rhett asked.

He checked the printout listing the rent for the stores. "Isn't the rent rather low for the square footage and location?"

"No."

"No?" Malcolm repeated.

"No," Rhett said emphatically. "New Visions Childcare is a beacon of hope in a neighborhood where parents need a safe place for their children while they work. I will not increase the rent no matter how prime you believe it is."

"But…but you're losing money on the space."

The seconds ticked as Rhett gave the too-eager assistant a lethal stare. "My money, my space."

"Rhett?" Tracy Powell's voice came through the building's paging system.

Walking over to the wall, he picked up the wall phone. "Yes, Tracy?"

"Your mother just returned your call. I have her on hold."

"Please tell her to wait. I'll take it in my office."

Bill placed a hand on Malcolm's shoulder, squeezing it gently after Rhett left the conference room. "A word of caution. Never piss off the person who signs your paycheck."

Preppy-looking Malcolm Robinson gave his mentor a wide-eyed stare. "Rhett didn't seem to be upset."

"Yes, he was. It's just that you don't know him well enough to recognize it. You could have a very bright future with CMP, because we're a young company that's growing when others are struggling to stay afloat. Don't let your mouth get you in trouble."

A beat passed. "Okay," Malcolm said begrudgingly.

Rhett walked into his office and closed the door. He'd called his mother but she hadn't answered the phone, so he'd left a message for her to call him back. Sitting on the corner of the desk, he picked up the receiver.

"Good afternoon, beautiful."

A husky laugh came through the earpiece. "Save that smack for your lady friends."

Rhett smiled. "You don't say that when Maynard calls you beautiful."

Geraldine laughed again. "That's because he's my husband. Now, why did you call me?"

"I wanted to check to see if you're still coming to the Cape for the week, and also to let you know that I'm bringing a houseguest."

"You don't have to check with me on that, Rhett. After all, it is your house."

"That's true, Mom. Out of respect, I just thought I'd let you know."

"Is there something about your houseguest you aren't telling me?" she asked perceptively.

"I'm back with Denise Eaton."

There came another pregnant pause. "Back how, Garrett?"

Rhett knew his mother was going into serious mode when she called him by his given name. "We're going to get married."

"When?"

"New Year's Eve."

"Have you given her a ring?"

He shook his head, then realized his mother couldn't see him. "No. I'm going to wait for her birthday."

"When is her birthday?"

"It's the end of September."

"Why wait?" Geraldine asked.

"There's no rush, Mom. Denise isn't going anywhere and neither am I."

"If you are truly committed to the woman, then put a ring on her finger. You have no way of knowing who else may be looking at her."

"I'll think about it," Rhett countered stubbornly. He knew Denise much better than his mother did. If he went out and bought her a ring now he knew she would accuse him of trying to manipulate their relationship. She'd committed to a New Year's Eve wedding, and he'd taken her at her word.

"When will you get there?" Geraldine asked.

"We're going up Friday afternoon."

"I have to drop Maynard off at the airport Saturday. As soon I see him off I'll drive up."

"Don't forget I'm throwing a little something and inviting some of my neighbors."

"Have you checked the almanac for the weather?"

Rhett laughed. His mother had more faith in the almanac than the Weather Channel. "What does it say, Mom?"

"There is a slight chance of rain."

"It doesn't matter. We'll just bring everything inside."

"I have to go now. The chef just drove up. Today's lesson is short ribs with leeks and spinach."

"That sounds delicious. Love you, Mom."

"Love you back, son."

Rhett hung up, blowing out his breath. He couldn't understand why his mother wanted him to rush into an official engagement when he and Denise had just picked up the pieces to start over.

Besides, when he bought Denise a ring he wanted her to select the style she wanted, not what he thought she would like. If there was one thing he knew about Denise Eaton, it was that she wasn't shy. If she wanted a ring, then she would make it known. After all, she wasn't reticent when she'd asked him to make love to her.

His private line rang, and Rhett answered the call before it rang again when he saw the name come up on the display. "Thank you for getting back to me. I hope you're calling to let me know you have room for my sextuplets, all who by the way are named Malik."

"Didn't you tell me you have three sons and three daughters, Mr. Fennell?"

"Yes, I did, Ms. Eaton."

"You named your daughters Malik?"

"We call the girls Malika."

Denise's sultry laugh caressed his ear. "You know you're crazy."

"Hell yeah. I'm crazy about you."

"I'm calling to invite you to dinner."

Rhett smiled. "I'll come, but only if we can have a sleepover."

Denise laughed again. "Sure."

"Sure what, Denise?"

"You can sleep over. Don't forget to bring your jammies."

"What time is dinner?" he asked.

"Seven."

"I'll see you at seven."

Rhett was glad that Denise had called, because if she hadn't then he'd planned to call her and invite her to spend the night in his suite at the Hay-Adams. He couldn't wait for the workmen to complete the renovations on the fourth-floor apartment. The space was configured to contain four bedrooms, five baths, a living room and formal dining room and a media room. He'd wanted a full-size state-of-the art kitchen, not the utility ones that came with most apartments. He'd invested a great deal of his personal wealth into renovating two homes, but what good was making money if he didn't take time to enjoy his life?

So many people he'd met hadn't planned for their futures when he was planning not only for his future but also for generations to come behind him. Rhett may not have known his father but what he didn't want was for his mother's bloodline to end with Garrett Fennell.

Pressing a button on the intercom, he buzzed Tracy. "Please call Mr. Tolpin and see if we can meet at one instead of four. Let him know something very important has come up and if he can't accommodate me, then we can reschedule at his convenience."

He released the button, came around the desk and sat down. Stanley Tolpin was his banker and a financial guru. Stanley had a sixth sense when it came to purchasing or passing on a parcel. Rhett had called Stanley because he'd wanted to discuss the hostile takeover of Chambers Properties, Ltd. He'd forgiven Denise for not trusting him, but Rhett didn't think he would ever forgive Trey Chambers for sleeping with his woman.

Chapter 12

Denise opened the door, shaking her head when she couldn't make out Rhett's face behind an enormous bouquet of white and pale pink flowers in every variety. "What did you do, buy every flower at the florist?" she teased, smiling.

Leaning over, Rhett kissed her cheek. "Practically. Don't try to carry it," he said when she reached for the vase. "It's too heavy for you."

Resting her hands on her hips, she watched Rhett cross the living room and set the vase on the credenza in the dining area. "How do you expect me to lift it to change the water?"

"You won't have to. I'll come over and change the water."

Denise stared at the exquisite arrangement. "Thank you. The flowers are beautiful."

Rhett slid the strap to a leather backpack off his shoulder and closed the space between them. Wrapping his arms around her waist, he lifted her effortlessly off her feet. He stared at her scrubbed face, awed that she looked so young even though their birthdays were only months apart. Denise didn't claim the kind of beauty producers wanted for daytime television actresses, but a soft natural beauty that would only improve with age. Wisps had escaped the ponytail, and with her tank top and cutoffs she could easily pass for a high-school coed.

He angled his head, brushing her soft mouth with his. "How was your day?"

Looping her arms around Rhett's neck, Denise buried her face against his strong neck. "It was good." She told him about her storytelling session with the children where she broke character and ended up laughing harder than any of the children. Teachers from other classrooms had come in to see what the hysterics were about.

Rhett lowered her until her sandaled feet touched the floor. "You know you missed your calling."

"What's that?"

"You should've become an actress, because you have a flair for being quite dramatic."

Denise's hands slid down the front of his shirt, under the hem and up his bare chest. "My, my, my," she drawled in a flawless Southern inflection. "Ah had no ide-ah you wah so strong, dah-ling."

Smiling, Rhett caught her hands, stopping her from arousing him further. It would be a few more days before he would be able to make love to her again. The brief encounter had served to whet his voracious appetite for Denise. What he hadn't understood was how Denise had believed he was sleeping with another woman. When he hadn't been in class, working or with his study group they'd been together.

The summer months had been excruciatingly lonely for him. Denise had returned to Philadelphia while he'd stayed in Baltimore. The bank had offered him full-time employment over the summer and he'd taken advantage of the opportunity because he'd wanted to save money. He'd found himself counting down the days to the beginning of the fall semester, unaware that he figuratively had been holding his breath until he'd knocked on the door to her dorm and waited for her to open it. They'd made love around the clock like rabbits before settling into their familiar routine as if time or space hadn't separated them.

"Why didn't you become a drama teacher?"

"If I'd majored in theater and drama, then I never would've met you."

Rhett nodded. "I hadn't thought of that." Bringing her hands to his mouth, he kissed her fingers, then sniffed them. "I smell garlic and peppers."

"You have a good nose. I'm making roasted bell peppers, couscous-stuffed pork chops and a first course of shrimp with a spicy avocado sauce."

"That sounds good."

"Come to the kitchen with me. I have to check on the pork chops."

Rhett sat on a stool at the cooking island, watching Denise as she moved confidently around the kitchen, chopping, stirring, whisking and blending the ingredients for a spicy avocado sauce. The kitchen wasn't large but the way it was designed maximized every square foot. A pantry and a washer/dryer unit were nestled in a corner, while black granite countertops and appliances broke up the white palette of the floor and cabinetry.

"I spoke to my mother today."

Denise stopped arranging jumbo shrimp on a small baking pan lined with oiled aluminum foil. "Did you tell her about us?"

Rhett met her eyes, seeing indecision in the dark orbs. "Yes. I told her we're planning to marry on New Year's Eve."

"She's probably as shocked as my parents that we're seeing each other again."

"If she is, I didn't detect it in her voice," Rhett admitted. He stood up, came around the island, his arms circling Denise's waist. "Everything is going to work out okay, sweetheart. We don't owe anyone an explanation. All I want from our families is their love and support."

Peering over her shoulder, Denise met Rhett's resolute gaze. "We have that, darling." She closed her eyes, moaning softly when he nuzzled her neck. "What are you doing?"

"I'm kissing the cook."

She smiled. "If you kiss the cook before she finishes the meal, then no one is going to eat."

"Do you need me to help you with anything?"

"You can set the table."

"Do you want candles?" Rhett asked.

Denise rested the back of her head against his shoulder. "Yes. There's a supply of tablecloths and liners in the credenza."

"Should I put out wine or water goblets?"

"Both."

Rhett pressed his mouth to Denise's ear before he released her.

Gathering dishes, silver, stemware and napkins, he walked out of the kitchen to the dining area to set the table. He'd stopped, a long time ago, trying to analyze why he'd fallen in love with Denise Eaton and not some other woman. At first he'd believed it was because he'd taken her virginity—that it was out of guilt that he'd continued to see her. It had taken a month, another thirty days, before he'd made love to her again. On the second encounter, his willingness to bring her pleasure while denying his own had been the single most telling act of selflessness. From the very first time he'd slept with a woman Rhett's goal had been achieving an erection, sustaining that erection and ejaculation.

Denise was also different, special, because she was the first woman with whom he'd slept with and hadn't exchanged money for sex. She'd offered him her innocence, love and her heart—precious gifts he'd coveted and treasured.

Never, not even once, had he glanced at another woman when he and Denise were together. And it wasn't as if women hadn't passed him their phone numbers or devised schemes to get him to come to their dorms to study, while others had been bold enough to ask if he would sleep with them.

If he'd been different, if he'd been like some men who didn't have to go looking for sex, he could've slept with a different woman every night of the week. But that hadn't happened because he'd committed to one woman, Denise Eaton.

Stepping back from the table, he surveyed his handiwork. He'd learned to recognize formal and informal table settings when he attended the boarding school, but it was Denise who'd taught him how to set a table. Even when they'd ordered takeout or pizza, he would set the table at his dorm with paper napkins, plates and plastic forks and spoons. It took about two weeks before Denise let it be known that she detested eating off paper plates with plastic utensils when she handed him a shopping bag with plates and flatware and glassware with a four-piece place setting.

Rhett had teased her, calling Denise Miss Prissy, but it had been too late. He'd fallen in love with the girl with the brilliant smile, quick mind, sexy voice, unyielding drive and impeccable manners.

Denise walked into the dining area with a carafe of ice water and another filled with a chilled rosé. "The table looks nice." Going on tiptoe when Rhett took the carafes from her, she kissed his jaw. "I think I'm going to keep you for a long, long time, Garrett Fennell."

"How long is a long time?"

She scrunched up her nose. "I'd say give or take a couple of lifetimes."

"That sounds about right."

Rhett placed the carafes on a handmade oyster-white crocheted tablecloth with a matching liner. He remembered when Denise had bought the tablecloth. They'd driven up to Lancaster, Pennsylvania, when he'd talked about seeing the Dutch Country. He and Denise had spent the weekend touring, eating and shopping. They'd returned to Baltimore with the trunk of her car filled with homemade quilts, candles, tablecloths and jars of jellies and preserves. After he'd moved to Philadelphia to work and attend graduate school, Rhett had found himself drawn back to the epicenter of the Amish country where the appeal of simplicity and community were interchangeable.

"Rhett!"

He blinked as if coming out of a trance. "Yes?"

"You looked as if you just zoned out on me for a minute."

"I was thinking about the time we drove to the Amish country."

Denise's eyelids fluttered wildly when she recalled the weekend that had almost changed her life and their future. It'd been the first and only time they'd made love without using protection. Her menses, which had always come on time, was late and she spent the next two weeks in dread. Rhett, who'd appeared totally unaffected by their dilemma, said that *if* she was pregnant they would marry and he would drop out of college to work and support her. She'd screamed at him, saying she wasn't going to let him forfeit a full academic scholarship because they'd been irresponsible. Fortunately, she wasn't pregnant and after a thorough examination her gynecologist prescribed an oral contraceptive to regulate her cycle.

"Were you thinking of the time when we had unprotected sex?" she asked in a quiet voice.

"No, Denise. I wasn't thinking of that time."

"I'm going back on the pill." She'd called her gynecologist, who'd told her to come into the office. He'd given her several samples to see which brand she could tolerate without too many side effects.

Rhett's eyebrows lifted a fraction. "When will you start?"

"I'll take the first one Thursday. I don't want us to have to deal with an unplanned pregnancy when we have to plan a wedding and honeymoon."

The mention of a honeymoon brought a smile to

Rhett's expressionless face. "Where do you want to go on our honeymoon?"

"It has to be someplace warm. There's no way I'm going to marry on New Year's Eve in the northeast, then hang out at a ski resort."

"You have a choice between the Caribbean, Hawaii or Tahiti."

Denise ran and jumped into his arms, and he swung her around and around until she felt the room spinning uncontrollably. "You know I've always wanted to go to Tahiti," she said breathlessly when he stopped.

"How long do you think you can stay away from your babies?"

"At least two weeks." Even if she hadn't hired an assistant director by December, Denise knew Lisa Brown was more than capable of running the child care center in her absence. The retired social worker had spent her entire career in a school setting.

"Make it three and we'll take side trips to Australia and Hong Kong. I heard shopping in Hong Kong is the bomb."

"I'll see what I can do," she whispered against his firm mouth. Denise kissed him again, pulling his lower lip between her teeth. "Put me down, darling. It's time to eat."

Dinner became a leisurely affair. Denise dimmed the overhead chandelier, and lit a quartet of fat pillars but hadn't drawn the drapes at the window spanning the living and dining area, and the lights in buildings and monuments in the nation's capital provided a romantic backdrop for the two people sitting opposite each other talking quietly as a radio station tuned to soft jazz filled the apartment.

The meal had turned out better than Denise had expected. Roasted shrimp, brushed with hot-pepper sauce and sprinkled with cumin seeds, were placed on lettuce leaves and covered with a spicy sauce made with chunks of avocado, tomato, coarsely chopped white onion and finely chopped jalapeño chiles. She'd added a couple of tablespoons of fresh lime juice and salt, putting all of the ingredients into a food processor to pulse them to form a chunky purée.

She altered the recipe slightly for the couscous-stuffed pork chops when she'd coated them with orange marmalade and dried currants. Denise had gotten the recipe from a parent who sat on the New Visions Childcare board of directors. She'd served warm buttered pita bread and roasted bell peppers to accompany the meat dish.

Rhett patted his flat belly over his shirt. "I think you've got your mother beat in the kitchen, baby."

"Don't even try to play yourself," Denise drawled. "You know my mother can cook rings around me. Even Grandma Eaton had to admit that Paulette Eaton was a better cook than she was, and that was something extraordinary coming from a woman who never took to any of her daughters-in-law. For some reason she thought they weren't good enough for her *boys.*"

Rhett smiled at Denise over the rim of his water goblet. "You don't have to worry about not getting along with your mother-in-law. My mother adores you." He set down his glass. "Now that we're on the topic of weddings, do you want to get married in a church or a catering hall?"

"I'd say a catering hall if it wasn't a holiday. Chances are most of them will be reserved for New Year's parties. What if we marry at my parents' house? It's certainly large enough to hold a hundred people comfortably if we remove the furniture from the living and dining rooms."

Rhett nodded. Boaz and Paulette Eaton owned a large house set on several acres in an exclusive Philly suburb. "Who are you going to get to do the officiating?"

"My father, of course."

"He's going to perform the ceremony *and* give you away?"

"No," Denise said, laughing softly. "Xavier can give me away. Do you plan to have any groomsmen?"

Rhett nodded again. "I'm going to ask my mentor from Marshall Foote Academy to be my best man and my stepfather to be a groomsman."

She thought about Rhett's choice—older men who'd impacted his and his mother's lives. Had his mentor replaced the father he never knew and was he grateful for the man who'd changed his mother's life?

Denise knew if she and Rhett hadn't separated, Trey Chambers would've been his best man. Both had attended the same prestigious boarding school, were college business majors and in a study group together. They'd referred to each other as "brother," were close or even closer than brothers who shared a bloodline.

Trey, who purportedly couldn't be faithful to one woman, had earned the sobriquet Casanova. Denise had been exempt from his charm and advances because she'd been Rhett Fennell's woman. She'd gone to Trey after discovering Rhett's betrayal, staying in his apartment until she'd gathered the strength to return to her dorm. She'd submitted the paper on Statistics and Research Methods and packed up her room, arranging for the contents to be shipped back to Philadelphia. Later that afternoon, she'd gotten into her car and driven home. It had been two days before graduation. Her parents hadn't seen her walk across the stage to receive her degree, and she hadn't been there to watch the man she'd loved receive the highest honor bestowed on the student with a perfect 4.0 GPA.

"Who do you want in your bridal party?"

Rhett's query broke into her musings. "I'll probably ask Chandra to be my matron of honor and Belinda a bridesmaid. If you can come up with one more groomsman I can either ask Zabrina or Mia. I'd probably choose Mia, because she's the only one who won't become a mother this year."

"Speaking of mothers—have you told your mother she's going to be mother of the bride?"

Denise traced the stem of the wineglass with her forefinger. "Not yet. I've decided to tell her in person. Dealing with Mom on the phone is like pulling a wisdom tooth with dental floss."

Rhett chuckled. "She's not that bad, baby."

"You say that because she's not your mother. I love her dearly, but nothing is easy when it comes to Paulette Eaton."

"Do you want me to come with you when you tell her?"

"No. But, thank you for asking." Denise blew him an air kiss. "Are you ready for coffee?"

Rhett, pushing back his chair, stood up. "Don't get up. I'll make it."

Denise waited for Rhett to walk out of the dining area and then got up and began clearing the table. He shot her an angry glare when she entered the kitchen with plates and serving pieces. Things had changed but they hadn't. He'd cautioned her about getting up because Rhett knew she couldn't remain seated. She'd always appreciated his help, but whenever he cleared the table and scraped plates a fork or serving piece would invariably be missing.

"Not to worry about your silver," Rhett drawled facetiously. "I now count the number of place settings, and if one is missing I check the garbage."

"Thank you, baby," she crooned.

He smiled. "You're welcome, baby."

The rain came down sideways and Rhett turned the wipers to the highest setting. The almanac was right when it'd predicted rain for Friday and intermittent showers for Saturday. He'd told his mother the weather wasn't a factor in canceling the soirée because he'd planned for an indoor or outdoor gathering.

He'd conferred with Denise as to the menu for the small crowd of thirteen and then called Brooke Andersen with their preferences. They would offer a cocktail with the requisite crudités and hot and cold hors d'oeuvres on the terrace, weather permitting, or in the living room. An informal sit-down dinner, weather permitting, would be served under a tent on the terrace with a DJ providing musical selections spanning several decades.

The event coordinator had reassured him she assumed the responsibility for ordering flowers, hiring the waitstaff, bartender, DJ and personnel to set up and clean up. All he and Denise had to do was look pretty. Rhett had invited couples he'd met at the few social events he'd attended on the Cape, in addition to his architect, who'd confirmed he would attend with his wife. Tapping a button on the remote device, Rhett maneuvered into the driveway at the same time the automatic garage door opened.

Denise waited in the car as he entered the house to

check around. He lingered long enough to adjust the thermostat and then returned to the garage to escort her inside before emptying the trunk of groceries and luggage. He'd suggested she pack enough clothes and personal items to last throughout the summer months; he was stunned into speechlessness when he stored four pieces of luggage in the trunk of his car.

They'd worked quickly, storing perishables in the refrigerator and freezer before filling pantry shelves with staples. She'd unpacked her bags, putting everything away in the walk-in closet, when Rhett joined her. His hair was so close-cropped she could see his scalp.

Crossing his arms over his chest, Rhett angled his head, staring at the feminine curves so blatantly outlined in a pair of hip-hugging jeans. "I came to ask if you would be interested in sharing my hot tub."

Denise gave him a sensual smile, her lips parting to reveal straight white teeth. "What else are you offering besides a hot tub? After all, I do have one in my bathroom."

"What about a personal masseur?"

Denise assumed a similar pose. "And what else?"

"I'm willing to rub lotion all over your body."

"And what else?" Denise crooned, closing the distance between them.

Rhett dropped his arms with her approach. "I'm going to kiss you, starting with your face and ending at your feet." He winked at Denise. "I just might take a slight detour at a rest stop to get something to eat."

Heat flared in Denise's face like opening the door of a blast oven. "Your offer is beginning to sound very tempting."

"What else do I have to do to tempt your further?"

"I want to go to the rodeo."

Bending slightly, Rhett scooped her up into his arms. "Hee-haw!"

Chapter 13

Rhett walked out of Denise's bedroom and into his. Lowering her feet to the carpet, he took his time removing her clothes: blouse, bra, jeans and bikini panties. His eyes ate her up when his gaze lingered on the slender body with curves that never failed to send his libido into overdrive.

She was slimmer than she'd been years ago, but her breasts, although small, were firm, perky. They were what he thought of as a handful and mouthful. Cradling her face in his hands, he kissed her, teasingly at first before taking full possession of her mouth and increasing the pressure until her lips parted under his sensual assault.

Denise held on to Rhett's wrists as she felt herself being pulled under and down into an abyss of drugging pleasure from which she didn't want to escape. She'd become his and he hers the first time they'd lain together in a sparsely decorated dorm. The room had become their sanctuary where they'd shared secrets and whispered promises. It had been where they'd planned for their future, a future that included marriage and children. They'd pretended they were married, repeating vows to love and forsake all others until death parted them. However, it hadn't been death that had torn them asunder but lies and distrust.

She'd walked around hemorrhaging emotionally. As she'd thrown herself into teaching the bloodletting had subsided and she'd stopped crying herself to sleep. Dating Kevin had become a welcome diversion, because he'd been someone she could talk to other than her family members. Someone who'd filled the empty hours when she hadn't been preparing lesson plans or meeting with parents to discuss their children's progress or lack thereof. He'd been there when she'd needed a date or escort to a social function, and he'd been there when the built-up sexual frustration had become so intense that it had kept her from a restful night's sleep. The single encounter with Kevin had been blatant proof that she hadn't gotten over Rhett Fennell.

Denise had shocked her family and herself when she decided to open a child care center in D.C. She'd almost convinced herself that moving from Philadelphia to D.C. was because research indicated the need for quality child care was greater in that particular D.C. community than in her hometown. It hadn't been until the contents of her co-op were loaded into the moving company's truck that she had been able to admit her decision was predicated on the expectation that she would run into Rhett again. It had taken two years, and now that they were given a second chance at love she would cherish every precious minute of her life with him.

Moaning softly, she undid the buttons on Rhett's shirt, her fingers trembling in her attempt to free the buttons from their fastenings. She managed to get two unbuttoned before Rhett finished the task. Her gaze never left his when he kicked off his running shoes, unsnapped the waistband to his jeans, pushing them and his briefs down and off his hips in one smooth motion and stepping out of them.

Rhett pulled the elastic band from her hair and a riot of curls floated around her face and neck. Her full parted lips, slightly swollen from his rapacious kisses, sensual curls and half-shuttered eyes fired the desire racing headlong throughout his body. He'd had to wait almost a week to make love to Denise again and the respite had tested his patience and resolve not to touch her until she deemed it.

It had taken Herculean strength not to laugh when she'd mentioned rodeo, because it was Denise's favorite position in bed. It had also become a favorite of his because lying on his back while she straddled him prolonged the intense pleasure while delaying his ejaculation.

Wrapping his arms around her waist, he lifted her slightly while walking in the direction of the bathroom. He'd dimmed the recessed lights and opened the French doors, but had left the doors leading out the terrace closed because of the driving rain. Music flowed from concealed speakers. Rhett stepped into the hot tub, and gently lowered Denise until her feet touched the bottom. He sat down, easing her gently down as the warm soothing waters bubbled up around her breasts.

Resting her head on Rhett's shoulder, Denise closed her eyes. "I can't think of a more perfect way to unwind at the end of a workweek."

Burying his face in her hair, Rhett emitted a guttural groan. "Ditto. We can come here every weekend if you want."

"I want," she said, sounding like the children at the center. For the two-year-olds it was "no," and the three- and four-year-olds it was "I want."

Rhett nuzzled her ear. "I told you before if it's within my power then I will make it happen."

"What if it's not within your power?" she asked.

He chuckled deep in his throat. "Then, I'll pay someone to make it happen."

Denise wanted to ask Rhett if that was what he'd done—if he'd paid someone to uncover that she'd leased the space before he bought the land on which the child care center sat, but knew it would open the proverbial can of worms and that was something she wanted to avoid at all costs.

In the past they'd rarely argued, but when they had it was as if they'd unleashed all the hounds in hell. They had gone to their respective dorms and waited for the other to apologize. Three days had become the limit, and when they'd reunited the makeup sex had been explosive.

She gasped when his hands covered her breasts, thumbs moving back and forth over the nipples until they were hard as pebbles. One hand moved down her belly to her thighs. She gasped again when he touched the sensitive nodule at the apex of her vagina.

Denise moved her hips against his hands, the warm water serving to increase the rising heat between her thighs. A long shudder shook her when he inserted a finger between the wet folds, her pulsing flesh opening and closing around his finger.

Rhett hardened quickly and he withdrew his hand, turning Denise around to face him. Holding his erection in one hand, he guided it between her legs, both sighing in unison when in that instant they became one with the other.

Reaching down, he grasped her knees and her legs went around his waist. Being inside Denise without the thin barrier of latex made him harder, his fingers gripping her hips as they slammed into each other. It wasn't lovemaking but mating as the sound of heavy breathing drowned out the soft strains of light music.

Denise held on to the rim of the teak tub, her hips moving against the hardness sliding in and out of her body like a piston. A guttural moan escaped her parted lips when she bared her throat. Rhett had taken her breast into his mouth, his teeth nipping at the distended nipple until she mewled like a wounded creature. One of the side effects of the oral contraceptive was tender breasts, and the pain-pleasure had her close to fainting.

The slight flutters she'd tried to ignore grew stronger and stronger and she tried thinking of any and everything except the delicious sensation of her lover's hard sex pushing in and out of her vagina.

The muscles in Rhett's neck bulged as he tried holding back. "Let it go, baby."

"No!"

"Please, oh please," he pleaded. If he didn't come he was afraid his heart would explode.

Denise let go of the edge of the tub, her arms going around Rhett's neck. She buried her face against the side of his neck, her breath coming in hiccupping gasps. "Oh, oh, oh!" The litany escalated, echoing in her head like a needle stuck in the groove of a vinyl recording.

Rhett pulled out and stepped out of the tub without releasing Denise. Walking on bare feet, while dripping water on the teak floor, he made his way out of the spa, through the bathroom and into the bedroom. He fell across the bed, bringing Denise down to straddle his thighs.

They shared a knowing smile when Denise sank lower and lower until Rhett was fully sheathed between her thighs. Their passion revived, she rode him fast and hard, he bucking like a rodeo horse.

Rhett's heat and hardness responded to the newly awakened sensuality that had lain dormant for years. As her passion rose higher and higher so did his until it exploded in an awesome, vibrating liquid that scorched her mind and her body, leaving her limp, sobbing and convulsing in an ebbing ecstasy.

The rush of his release left Rhett light-headed. Somehow he found the strength to reverse their position, breathing heavily to force air into his lungs. There was only the sound of their labored breathing in the stillness of the bedroom as they lay motionless, reliving the aftermath of a sweet fulfillment making them one with the other.

"Hee-haw!" Denise whispered in his ear.

"Ditto, baby. Dit-to!"

The rain had stopped and pinpoints of light pierced the watery sky as the sun rose higher. Denise, leaning against the door frame, watched Rhett help his mother as she stepped out of her car. It'd been a long time since she'd last seen Geraldine Fennell, but time had seemingly stood still for the tall, slender woman who'd passed her features along to her only child. At forty-six, she looked at least ten years younger. A smile touched her mouth as Geraldine touched Rhett's cheek, Denise finding the gesture loving, gentle.

The glow of loving and being loved had lingered long after she'd forced herself to leave the bed where she and Rhett had spent most of the night making love. He'd kept his promise to give her a massage, followed by slathering her supple body with a scented cream. She'd fallen asleep under his sensual ministration, and when she'd woken hours later she'd returned the favor; it had been her mouth and not her hands that had left Rhett pleading for mercy. The impasse had ended when he'd managed to free himself from her rapacious mouth to ride her until spent.

Denise's smile grew wider. The delicate circle of diamonds on Geraldine's hand sparkled. Her future mother-in-law was now a married woman.

Geraldine Russell glanced around Rhett's shoulder, her gaze meeting and fusing with the young woman who'd enthralled her son in a way no other had before or after her. Denise Eaton had changed. It wasn't the longer hair, but something else, something that wasn't discernible at first glance.

When she approached Denise, who'd straightened from her leaning pose, she saw determination in the dark eyes that didn't waver. She hadn't only matured, she'd grown up. She extended her arms, and she wasn't disappointed when Denise moved into her embrace.

"Welcome back—daughter."

Denise hugged Geraldine tightly, kissing her soft cheek. "It's good to be back—Mother."

Easing back, Geraldine smiled at the girl she'd always wanted as her daughter-in-law. "He loves you so much, Denise," she whispered.

Denise's gaze shifted to Rhett, who was unloading the trunk of his mother's car, then back to the older woman with chemically straightened hair, parted off-center chin-length blunt-cut ends. "He loves me and I love him." A beat passed. "This time we're going to get it right."

"We'll talk later," Geraldine whispered as if they were coconspirators.

The rains had stopped completely, the sun had dried up the moisture soaking the earth and the afternoon temperatures were climbing steadily to the low eighties. Brooke Andersen arrived at the house at three and minutes before a pickup truck bearing the logo of the florist emblazoned on the side doors parked behind her white Escalade. The caterer, waitstaff and DJ weren't expected to arrive for another two hours. The printed invitations had read: cocktails at 6:00, dinner at 7:30 and fun until ???

Denise and Geraldine walked a short distance from the house to keep out of the way of the workers who'd come to erect the tent and set up tables and chairs. Rhett had remained behind to oversee the setting up. The two women sat on a stone bench flanked by large stone planters overflowing with a profusion of sweet pea and peonies. Leaning back on her hands, Denise stared at the calm surface of the water. There was a comfortable silence until Geraldine exhaled a sigh.

"When Garrett asked me to come with him to see this property I thought my son had taken leave of his senses. The house was large, but falling apart. And there were so many weeds I was afraid to walk anywhere because I didn't know what I would step on. He was so excited about buying a house that I didn't have the heart to tell him he was throwing away his money. I was wrong and he was right—as usual."

Denise leaned forward. "As usual?"

Geraldine turned to stare at Denise staring back at her. "When you and Garrett broke up…" Her words trailed off. "When you left my son," she continued, "I was afraid Garrett was going to hurt himself."

Denise felt her heart sink like a stone in her chest. "You…you're not talking about suicide?" Much to her surprise, Geraldine laughed.

"No, Denise. Garrett loves life much too much to take his own. I'm talking about physical pain. He'd become an insomniac. If he wasn't working he was studying. And when he could find the time, he was seeing women—a lot of women."

Denise felt as if someone had put their hand around her throat, squeezing and cutting off oxygen to her lungs. Rhett hadn't mourned their breakup, but had replaced her with what probably had been a long line of nameless, faceless women.

"Everything came to a head when he had a problem with one of his supervisors," Geraldine continued. "What he hadn't realized at the time was it was a blessing in disguise. He left Philly, moving back to D.C., where he stayed with me for about three months. During this time he spent countless hours in the library and on the Internet learning everything he could about the real estate market. After he purchased a foreclosed house, he secured a loan to rehab it and eventually sold it for a three hundred percent profit. It was, like the kids say, on and poppin'. He claimed buying and selling real estate was like crack cocaine. It was that addictive."

She sighed again, this one louder and longer. "I'm going to tell you about Garrett's father. It's something I've never told anyone—not even Garrett, and I want you to swear you won't tell him."

Shaking her head, Denise closed her eyes for several seconds. "I can't do that, Mother. I've been given a second chance with Rhett and I'm not going to jeopardize our future together by keeping secrets. If you don't intend to tell Rhett, then please don't tell me."

Geraldine crossed her outstretched legs at the ankles, staring at her toes painted a flattering raspberry shade pushed into a pair of leather thongs. She'd carried the secret for almost thirty years, and she wanted to unburden herself. A wry smile parted her lips. "I can see why my son fell in love with you, Denise."

"Why's that?"

"You're loyal, caring and selfless."

Denise placed an arm around Geraldine's slender waist. "I love Rhett. I think I fell in love with him at first sight. We've had our ups and downs like most couples, and even when we were apart I never stopped loving him. If you love Rhett as much as I know you do, then give him some peace. Please tell him about his father."

Resting her head on the younger woman's shoulder, Geraldine nodded. "I know I'm going to have to do it."

"Please do it before we officially announce our engagement on my birthday." Denise and Rhett had discussed a timeline for their engagement and wedding, deciding three months was long enough for an engagement for a couple who'd met for the first time ten years ago.

"That doesn't give me much time, but I suppose I'll work up enough nerve before then. Maybe I should give him a special birthday present when I reveal who his daddy is." Her son would celebrate his twenty-ninth birthday August fifteenth. "I'd offered to come and stand in as Garrett's hostess before I realized you were going to do it," Geraldine said, deftly changing the topic of conversation.

"You can still do it," Denise teased, laughing.

"Nope. If I'm going to do any hosting, then it's going to be for me and Maynard. As soon as my husband returns from his conference, I want you and Garrett to come for a visit. I'm taking cooking lessons, so I promise not to treat you guys as guinea pigs."

"What have you learned to cook?"

The two women spent the next forty-five minutes talking about food. Denise revealed the number of meals that had ended in disaster before she'd been able to complete one that was palatable. It had taken her a while to come to the conclusion that she would never surpass Paulette Eaton's culinary expertise, who'd been taught by her mother, and was resigned that she'd become a competent but not a fabulous cook. She was a lot more creative when it came to planning a menu for entertaining. She'd planned the menu Brooke had passed along to the caterer.

Denise had become the consummate hostess, standing alongside Rhett as they greeted their guests with handshakes and welcoming smiles. A black-and-white silk faille striped, sleeveless dress, nipped at the waist and ending at her knees and a pair of black patent-leather Louboutin slingback stilettos complemented Rhett's black linen Hermès suit and white shirt he'd elected to wear outside the waistband of his slacks. He'd also fore-gone a tie for the evening. She tamed her curly hair with a gel, while brushing it until she was able to pin it into a loose twist behind her left ear.

Brooke Andersen flitted around like an anxious stage mother waiting for her child to be auditioned, making certain the waitstaff saw to the needs of Rhett's guests. Her husband ignored her antics as he and a group of men discussed their golf handicaps.

"You look beautiful, Mother," Denise whispered to Geraldine. A light coat of makeup highlighted her attractive features. A narrow headband made from peacock feathers held her hair off her face, while a black silk man-tailored blouse, white silk slacks and black ballet-type slippers flattered her tall, slender frame.

Geraldine flashed a demure smile. "Thank you, Denise. If I'd harbored any doubts about the woman who Garrett would end up with, they were dashed tonight when I saw you with my son at what will be the first of many gatherings the two of you will preside over."

A slight frown found its way between her eyes before Denise replaced it with a slow smile. Geraldine had said *preside over* as if she and Rhett were heads of state. Was that, she mused, how she'd thought of her son? Was he the issue of some prominent black Washingtonian?

What she couldn't understand was why Geraldine was so willing to divulge Rhett's father's identity to her and not to him. Of course she wanted to know who'd fathered the man she planned to marry, but not if he didn't know.

Her eyes lit up when she spied Rhett's approach. He was carrying a flute with a sparkling liquid; she recalled the bottle of champagne he'd ordered the night they'd reunited at The Lafayette.

Rhett handed Denise the flute, his eyes roving appreciably over her body before coming to rest on her face. He found her perfect from head to toe. The four-inch heels were sexy and showed off her curvy calves and slender ankles to their best advantage.

"I had the bartender fix that for you."

Hoisting the flute, Denise saw a dollop of dark syrup in the bottom. "What is it?"

"It's called a kir royale. It's made with crème de cassis and champagne. The cassis is made from black currants," he explained when seeing her puzzled expression.

She took a sip, holding the liquid in her mouth for several seconds before letting it slide down the back of her throat. "This is good." The cassis was a sweet contrast to the dry champagne. She took another sip. "I think I've finally found a cocktail I like."

Rhett leaned in closer to her. "Don't let the fruity drink sneak up on you."

Denise brushed a light kiss over his mouth. "I'm not driving, so I figure I can have a couple of these babies." She kissed him again. "Will you save me a dance, darling?"

Rhett angled his head, smiling. Seeing Denise totally relaxed, smiling and outgoing filled him with a pride he hadn't known existed. She'd become the perfect hostess and assuredly a perfect wife and mother. Even Brooke had complimented him on Denise's menu choices. She'd selected buckwheat blinis with sour cream and caviar, spicy shrimp crostini, fresh salmon tartare croutes and spicy pork empanadas with a chunky avocado relish. Asian-inspired hors d'oeuvres included fresh herb and shrimp rice paper rolls with peanut hoisin dipping sauce, sushi rice, wonton wrappers with herbed prawn and a tangy lime dipping sauce and salmon caviar sushi rice balls.

A carving station with rib roast, turkey breast and grilled plank salmon, along with grilled vegetables and salad greens, had been set up for buffet-style dining. The dessert menu included tiny chocolate cups filled with white chocolate mousse, mango and mascarpone cream, kiwi raspberry and lime mousse and sweet tartlets with fillings ranging from cherry and almond, citrus ginger cream and summer berries.

Entertaining on the terrace under the tent created a fairy-tale atmosphere with baskets of colorful flowers. The view of the Chesapeake in the foreground was awe-inspiring. Japanese lanterns, suspended from the poles holding up the tent, would be lit at sunset.

"I'll save more than one dance," he whispered in her ear.

Denise found it odd that she and Rhett were the youngest couple in attendance, most of the others ranging from their mid-thirties to fifties and possibly sixties. Again, when he mentioned those he wanted as groomsmen in their wedding party the men were older than him. She didn't know his D.C. social circle, but she was willing to bet they, too, were older than Rhett by at least a decade. And it wasn't for the first time that she wondered if he connected with older men because he was looking for a father figure.

Couples had set down their drinks and tiny plates with hot and cold appetizers to dance to the monster Black Eyed Peas hit "I Gotta a Feeling." Denise and Rhett exchanged smiles and winks, then joined the others. The DJ alternated upbeat tunes with slower ones, allowing those wishing to dance a respite to eat and drink. It was only when everyone sat down to eat that the music changed to softer relaxing instrumentals.

It was close to midnight when guests reluctantly took their leave, thanking Rhett and Denise for their generous hospitality, while reminding them to keep their weekends open during the summer so they could return the favor.

Geraldine had retired to her first-floor bedroom, pleading fatigue because she'd gotten up hours before dawn to drive her husband to the airport two hours before his scheduled flight.

Denise, standing barefoot in the bathroom slathering cream on her face before she removed it with a damp cloth, saw Rhett's reflection in the mirror over the vanity. "It was a wonderful party."

He came closer. Droplets of water shimmered on his wide shoulders from his shower. "You were wonderful."

Lowering her head, she splashed water on her face, nearly choking when she felt his erection pressing against her hips. "Can't you wait for me to wash my face and take a shower?" she asked, patting her face dry.

"You don't need a shower, baby."

"No, Rhett!" Her protest came too late when he picked her up, carrying her back into the bedroom.

Everything became a blur when Rhett made love to her with an intensity that stole the breath from her lungs. His tongue journeyed down her body, tasting every inch of flesh while branding her as his. She opened her arms and her legs when he moved up over her, welcoming him inside her. Denise struggled, but was unable to hold back the moans of erotic pleasure that became screams of ecstasy when she stiffened with the explosive rush of orgasmic fulfillment. The screams faded to surrendering whimpers of physical satiation as she closed her eyes and reveled in the rush of Rhett's release bathing her still-throbbing flesh.

They lay together, limbs entwined until Rhett pulled out, rolled over and gathered her against his body. Minutes later they slept the sleep of sated lovers.

Chapter 14

"Mom, will you please stop crying."

Paulette, dabbing the corners of her eyes with a tissue, narrowed them. "Are you getting married because you're pregnant?"

Denise threw up her hands. "No, you didn't say that," she whispered not to be overheard by those at a nearby table at her mother's favorite D.C. restaurant.

She'd called her mother to let her know she was driving up to Philly to see Belinda and Griffin's infant son, but Paulette had informed her she and a few of her sorority sisters were going to New York to attend a Broadway show and take in the sights. She'd promised to come to Washington to visit with her before returning to Philadelphia.

Sitting up straight in a huff, Paulette squared her shoulders. "Well, are you?"

"No, Mother. I am not pregnant." Denise had punctuated each word. "I'm not getting married until December. If I were pregnant, I wouldn't wait that long."

Eyelids fluttering wildly, Paulette smiled brightly. She pressed her palms together. "I hope you're going to ask your father to do the officiating."

Reaching in her handbag, Denise removed an envelope, pushing it across the table. "I've written down some things I'd like to incorporate into the ceremony and reception. Rhett and I will officially announce our engagement on my birthday and will exchange vows New Year's Eve. Because most catering halls will probably be booked for the holiday, I thought having it at the house would be the perfect venue to combine a wedding while welcoming in a new year."

Paulette rested her hands over her heart. "Thank you, my darling. You don't know how happy it makes me to hear you say that. Your father keeps complaining that the house is too big for two people, that he wants to downsize and moved into a townhouse like Dwight and Roberta. But I'm constantly reminding him that we're the only Eatons in Philly with a house large enough to accommodate the family whenever they get together. Now that Belinda and Griffin have a new baby I doubt if they're going to be doing that much entertaining. By the way, did you get to see the baby?"

Denise nodded, smiling. "I did. Oh, Mom. He's adorable."

"He looks just like Griffin."

"I agree," Denise said. The baby boy, who'd been named Grant in honor of Griffin's late brother, was all Rice. It appeared as if the only thing Belinda had done was carry the boy to term. When she'd asked Belinda if she was going back to teaching in September, the history instructor still hadn't decided whether she wanted to stay home and raise her son and nieces or hire a nanny to care for the baby. Although Griffin worked from home there were occasions when he had to go out of town on business.

"All I can say is that in another twenty years he's going to break a lot of hearts. Now, when are you going to shop for wedding gowns?"

Denise didn't think she would ever get used to her mother jumping from one subject to another without taking a pause. It was as if her brain functioned faster than her mouth.

She indicated the envelope, which Paulette hadn't bothered to open. "It's all in that envelope. But to answer your question, I'll probably start looking in November. I'm not going to deal with countless alterations and fittings if I gain and lose weight over several months."

Paulette surveyed her daughter with a critical eye. "You are a little on the thin side."

"Remember, I always gain weight during the winter." She closed her eyes, smiling. "I have grits at least once a week from November to late March. Come April 1, I swear off grits and the weight comes off."

Paulette was saved from asking any more questions when the waiter arrived with their dining selections. She glanced at her watch. "I have three hours before my train leaves." She'd taken the train from Philly to New York, then from New York to D.C.

"Don't worry, Mom. I'll make certain you get to Union Station on time."

Denise didn't tell her mother that she had to go home and prepare for a fund-raising event for later that evening. Although she would sit on the dais with other board members, she'd asked Rhett to accompany her.

Rhett got out of the car, handing the keyless device to the valet. He reached for the jacket to his tuxedo, slipping his arms into the sleeves, and then came around to assist Denise. When he'd arrived at her apartment to pick her up he'd found himself unable to speak. Her obligatory little black dress was exactly that—little. Strapless with an empire waist and ending several inches above her knees, it displayed an inordinate expanse of velvety brown skin. Matching silk-covered stilettos with ties wrapping around her ankles directed attention to her smooth bare legs and groomed feet.

Resting a hand at the small of her back, he pressed his mouth to her ear. "If any man looks at you sideways I'm going to kick his ass," he said, smiling.

Denise stiffened before relaxing against his splayed fingers. "What's this all about?"

"Your dress, or the lack of it, *baby*."

"There's nothing wrong with my dress, Rhett."

"So you say," he mumbled. A swell of breasts rose and fell with each breath.

They walked into the mansion where the organization dedicated to raising funds for college scholarships for disadvantaged high-school students had contracted to hold their annual dinner dance.

"Denise."

She turned when she heard her name, smiling at one of the volunteers. "Yes?"

"They want all of the board members seated on the dais *now*."

Denise rested a hand on Rhett's lapel. "I'll see you

later, baby. I told them to put you at a table close enough to the dais so I can flirt with you during the boring speeches."

Rhett resisted the urge to laugh when Denise turned her heels and sashayed, her hips swaying sensually in the revealing dress and high heels.

"When did you and Garrett Fennell hook up again?"

Teeth clenched, Denise leaned to her left. Whoever had arranged the seating had sat her next to Trey Chambers. Good-looking, smooth-talking Trey had been blessed with the charm of a pimp seducing women into his lair and the morals of an alley cat.

"That is none of your business."

"What I don't want to believe is how you can take up with him again, knowing he can't be faithful."

"Again, that's none of your business. Now, if you don't take your hand off my shoulder, I'm going to hurt you."

Trey dropped his hand. "What's the matter, Denise? Are you afraid your boyfriend is going to say something?" His voice was so low the woman sitting on his left couldn't overhear what he was saying. "It's funny he never said anything when he came to my apartment and I told him we were sleeping together."

She went completely still, unable to move even if her very life depended upon it. "What did you say?"

Trey's eyes filled with contempt. For years he'd stood in Garrett Fennell's shadow. There weren't many black students at Marshall Foote Academy and for some unknown reason the instructors had always compared his grades to Garrett's, and he'd come up short. Very, very short. He'd had to study around the clock and bust his ass while Garrett had earned As without opening a book.

It had been the same at Johns Hopkins, but things had changed when he and Garrett joined the same study group. Garrett had become his unofficial tutor, helping him when they had studied for exams and editing his papers. He'd hated Garrett as a boy and even more so as a man. He hated his confidence, smug attitude *and* his brilliance.

"After you found that naked girl in your goody-two-shoes boyfriend's bed, you came running to me because I was your precious Rhett's best friend. You kept asking me why he would sleep with her when he had you, and I told you some men are dogs like that. But you neglected to ask me the most important question, Denise."

"I asked what I needed to ask," she spat out. "And that was how you could hit on your best friend's girlfriend when you knew what I'd been through."

"Remember, Denise, you'd broken up with Garrett *and* because you were no longer sleeping with Garrett, I saw you as fair game."

She rolled her eyes. "To you, any skirt is fair game."

"Whatever works," Trey drawled. "What I couldn't believe was your naiveté. When I started the rumor that Garrett was sleeping around you swallowed it hook, line *and* sinker." He stroked the nape of her neck. "You never asked how that hooker got into Garrett's room," he crooned. Denise slapped at his hand, but he tightened his grip on the back of her neck. "I made a copy of his key and gave it to her. What made the ruse so easy was you were so damned predictable. I knew you always went to Garrett's dorm on Wednesdays, because his last class ended at six. So, when you walked in on Bubbles she gave you an award-winning performance."

Twin emotions of rage and relief surged through Denise as she tried to process what Trey had just revealed. She'd wanted to tell him he was lying, but couldn't. He'd set her up. He'd also set up Rhett. But why?

Grabbing her forehead, she counted to ten in an attempt to control her rising temper. She reached for her evening bag. "Don't ever come near me or speak to me as long as you live." Denise pushed herself in a standing position, and on trembling legs managed to make her way off the raised stage without falling. She didn't see Trey wink at Garrett sitting at a table a short distance from the dais when he, too, stood to follow her.

Rhett, who had crossed his arms over his chest, lowered them. He'd sat silently, watching the man who at one time had been as close to him as a brother. But that all had changed when Trey told him that Denise had come to him distraught because she'd found a naked woman in his bed, and in her grief she'd asked him to make love to her and he had.

Trey had been one of the Marshall Foote students who'd gone with him on what they'd called their "panty raids." There had been times when Trey had given him money to buy sex when he'd run short on funds. They'd become brothers in every sense of the word, swearing an oath never to hit on the other's woman. It was easy for him to keep his promise, because once he'd begun sleeping with Denise Eaton he'd never looked at another woman.

Pushing back his chair, he wove his way through the tables set in the ballroom, stepping out into an expansive area where formally dressed couples were filing into the mansion. "Did you see where Denise Eaton went?" he asked the woman sitting at a table checking tickets against a computer printout.

She pointed to a door to her left. "She's in there."

Taking long strides, he reached the door and turned the knob. It opened and what he saw made his blood run cold. Trey, who'd grabbed the area between his legs, was on the carpet writhing in pain. "You bitch!" he hissed between his teeth. Tears were streaming down his face.

Denise stood over him, one hand curled into a tight fist. "I told you not to touch me!"

Rhett kicked the door shut, closing the distance between him and his childhood friend. He rested his foot on Trey's neck. "If I ever hear you call her a bitch again I will kill you."

Trey shuddered violently. "She kicked me in the balls."

Leaning over, Rhett increased the pressure on the hapless man's throat. "She had a good reason for kicking you in the *balls*. I'm only going to warn you this one time—stay away from my fiancée." He removed his foot, his eyes dancing wildly when he looked at Denise. "Let's go!" Cupping her elbow, he led her out of the room. "Miss Eaton isn't feeling well, so I'm taking her home," he informed the woman at the table.

"Rhett, please slow down," Denise pleaded when he forcibly pulled her along with him.

He gave her a warning stare. "Please, don't say anything to me until we're out of here."

"Slow down now!" He shortened his strides, permitting Denise to keep up with him.

The valet seemed shocked when Rhett told him to bring his car around. He gave the young man a generous tip and peeled out of the parking lot on two wheels after he and Denise were seated and belted in.

"I don't know what kind of game you're playing, Denise, but it has to stop. You let some man feel you up, then when you decide you've had enough you kick him in his groin. Do you realize I was a minute away from crushing his windpipe?"

"For your information I didn't let him feel me up. I'd warned him if he didn't take his hands off me what I'd do."

"Why didn't you just get up and change your seat?"

"I needed to hear the truth, Rhett."

"What are you talking about?"

Denise told him everything. "What I can't understand is why he'd felt the need to break us up."

Rhett hadn't realized he'd had a death grip on the steering wheel until he felt the tingling in his fingers, indicating he'd impeded blood flow. Never had he wanted to hurt someone as he did Trey Chambers. He'd lived for twenty-eight years without having or wanting to fight, or defend himself using his fists, but that had all changed within the time it took for Denise to relate what she'd been told.

He placed his right hand on Denise's knee. "It's okay, baby. I'll take care of Trey Chambers." What he didn't tell her was that what he'd planned for Trey would devastate him more than a beating.

"No, Rhett. I don't want you to take care of him."

"What *do* you want?"

"I want you to leave him alone. He can't hurt us any longer."

Rhett chuckled despite the seriousness of the situation. "I think you hurt him enough." He gave Denise a quick glance. "Damn, girl. You should register those stilettos as a lethal weapon."

Denise sucked her teeth loudly. "He's lucky I didn't stomp on his package."

"Ouch! Remind me never to piss you off."

She smiled, covering the hand resting on her knee. "You don't have to worry about that. I would like to have your babies."

Rhett blew out a breath. "I guess that means I'm safe."

"You're safe as long as you don't mess up, Garrett Mason Fennell."

Rhett sobered. "I'm sorry you're missing your fundraiser, because I don't trust myself not to go back and finish what you started. I promise to send a generous donation in your name."

"Rather than send a donation, why don't you establish a Garrett M. Fennell college scholarship? You're one of D.C.'s success stories, and whether you want to acknowledge it or not, you are a role model."

"You know how I feel about that, Denise. Parents should be role models for their children, not strangers or athletes."

"You're preaching to the choir," she said in a quiet voice. Geraldine said she'd wait until Rhett's birthday to disclose his father's identity, and Denise hoped she'd keep her promise.

Rhett turned down the street leading to Denise's apartment building. "I know we talked about announcing our engagement on your birthday, but I've changed my mind. What do you say we go shopping for rings tomorrow?"

His query surprised Denise, because they'd agreed to a short engagement period. "What made you change your mind?"

"It was something my mother said about commitment. She told me if I was truly committed to you, then I should put a ring on your finger."

"Ring or not, Rhett, I've always been committed to you."

When he'd heard Denise was staying with Trey, Rhett thought she'd gone to him for emotional support. However, when Trey had opened the door wearing nothing more than a pair of briefs, proudly informing him that he'd been a fool to give Denise up because she was a freak in bed, Rhett had felt as if he'd been stabbed in the gut. Three days. It had taken only three days for her to go from his bed to the bed of his so-called best friend.

"I know that now. Can you forgive me for not staying and fighting for you?"

Denise moved as close to Rhett as the seat belt would allow her. "I forgave you a long time ago. I had to or I wouldn't have been able to get on with my life."

"Unfortunately, it has taken longer for me to get past the need for revenge." He'd forgiven Denise, but didn't believe he would ever forgive Trey. Rhett gave Denise a quick glance. "Even though you're dressed for a night of seduction, I'd like to make a quick detour."

"What are you doing?" She gasped when he unexpectedly executed a U-turn, the squeal of tires leaving skid marks on the roadway.

"I want to take you to see something."

It was another twenty minutes before Denise realized what Rhett wanted her to see. He pulled up in front of a four-story town house blocks from Dupont Circle. A brass plate affixed to the front of the building identified it as housing the offices of Capital Management Properties, Ltd.

Rhett disarmed the security system, escorted her into the building and through a modern lobby with gleaming marble floors. He punched the button for the elevator for the fourth floor.

Leaning against the opposite wall in the elevator, Denise saw a glint of amusement in Rhett's dark eyes. "You've done well, Garrett Fennell."

He winked at her. "And I'll do even better once we're married."

"That's going to happen," she said confidently.

"I know it will." The doors opened on the fourth floor and Rhett stepped out, holding the door for Denise to follow. The tall windows were covered with butcher paper, while naked bulbs hung from the exposed ceilings. He beckoned to her. "Come, baby, and see what will be *our* home."

Denise was confused. "Home?"

He took her hand, leading her around a ladder, sawhorses and other workmen tools. "The offices of CMP occupy the first three floors. This floor will be configured for personal living space. Let me show you the floor plan."

Denise stared at the large architectural rending of what would become a four-bedroom, five-bath residence with a state-of-the-art modern kitchen, home office/library, theater and exercise room. She pointed to the master bedroom. "I like that we'll have his and her bathrooms." Hers would have a bidet and Rhett's a urinal. "It looks...wonderful."

Rhett heard the hesitation in Denise's voice. "You don't like it?"

"What's not to like, Rhett?"

Reaching for her shoulders, he pulled her to his chest.

"Why do I feel that you're not on board with this? Would you prefer living somewhere else? Perhaps in northern Virginia or in one of the D.C. suburbs?"

Denise cradled his face between her hands. "Forgive me, darling, if I look as if I'm not excited about living here. Nothing could be further from the truth. I love this neighborhood. In fact, I'd tried renting an apartment in a town house around the corner, but it was too pricey for my budget." She leaned closer, brushing a tender kiss over his firm mouth. "We're going to have a wonderful life together. It's large enough to entertain and have an occasional houseguest. And when daddy Fennell decides to work late he doesn't have to concern himself with getting stuck in D.C. rush-hour traffic. All he has to do is come upstairs, have dinner with his family and then go back to the office."

Rhett stared at Denise under lowered lids. "We can wait a couple of years before we start filling up the bedrooms with children. I know it would make your mother happy if we started right away, but I'm going to leave that decision up to you."

She scrunched up her nose. "Let's wait a year. If I decide to change my mind, then it'll be sooner rather than later."

He lowered his head and kissed her with all of the passion he could summon at that moment. Trey's revelation had opened the door to their past, but served to put to rest all of the doubts that had plagued him for years. Denise hadn't slept with Trey and she knew he had been faithful to her.

The twisted cretin may have gotten by with his subterfuge for six years, but he wasn't going to get away unscathed. Rhett would make certain of that.

Chapter 15

Denise sat on her bed, legs crossed in a yoga position, with the cordless phone anchored between her chin and shoulder. "I don't care about your belly. I want you in my wedding party."

"I'm going to look like a beach ball in a gown," Chandra argued softly.

"What am I going to do, Chandra? Zabrina probably will have delivered just before Christmas, so she'll be recuperating. The only one I can count on is Belinda. I still have to call Mia to see if she'll be available—providing she doesn't get pregnant, too."

"Mia's not even dating anyone, so I doubt if she's going to get pregnant. You definitely can count on Belinda and Mia. Zabrina is questionable, and my due date is January twenty-eighth, give or take a week. If I go into labor and spoil your wedding Aunt Paulette will never speak to me again."

"Don't worry about my mother. I'll handle her. And even if you do go into labor, there will be enough doctors in attendance to deliver your baby."

"Bite your tongue, Denise Amaris Eaton. I will not have my father delivering my baby."

Denise laughed softly. "Let's hope you don't have to eat your words. But seriously, Chandra, I want you to be my matron of honor. I haven't begun looking at gowns, but I'll probably choose one with an empire waistline, so your gown will be similar to mine. We can have a Jane Austen–inspired wedding."

Chandra's laugh came through the earpiece. "I don't think you'd want me to expose my chest. I told Preston that for the first time in my life I'm willing to do a centerfold layout. My *girls* are off the hook!"

"What did he say?"

"It's something I can't repeat on an open phone line. But I told him to enjoy them before my belly takes over."

"Are you big?"

"No. I'm getting thick in the waist, but so far no belly." She sighed heavily. "All right, I'll be your matron of honor."

Denise closed her eyes, whispering a prayer of gratitude. "Thank you, cuz."

"You're welcome, cuz. I'm honored you asked me. Now tell me, what does your ring look like?"

Denise held out her hand and described the exquisite diamond engagement ring featuring a cushion halo with a round cut center stone, three rows of micro pavé diamonds on the shank and surrounding the center stone.

"When are you coming to Philly so I can see it?"

"Tomorrow. I have to come up for the closing on the co-op. If you're not busy maybe you can meet me for dinner."

"Call me when you're finished and I'll come and pick you up."

"Why don't you and Preston come down here a weekend? We can hang out at the house on Cape St. Claire in Maryland."

"I'd love to, Necie, but Preston's still working the final edits for *Death's Kiss*. He's planning a short theatrical production before filming begins—"

"It's going to be a movie?" Denise interrupted.

"Yes. Griffin just negotiated a movie deal with a major Hollywood studio. Griffin insisted on complete literary control on behalf of his client, or he was going to take it to an independent studio. He gave them twelve hours to come back with a yes or no. It took only three hours for them to agree. Literary control has been something Preston has wanted for years."

"You know my father calls Griffin a legal hustler."

"Whatever works," Chandra drawled. "His hustling got my husband what he wants, and when my baby is happy I'm happy."

"I ain't mad at you, cuz," Denise drawled.

"Thank you, Necie. As soon as P.J. Tucker comes up for air we're going to take you and Rhett up on your invitation to come down and hang out with you guys. I overheard Mom talking to Aunt Paulette about not putting on a family reunion this year because Belinda's still recuperating from sixteen hours of hard labor and Myles says the doctor doesn't want Zabrina to travel long distances."

"That's okay. I'm taking some time off in the fall to

look for a gown, and during that time I'm going to make my rounds and visit with everyone."

"Is your gorgeous fiancé coming with you?"

"I don't know. Right now he's fixated on some deal that has him getting up out of bed to talk on the phone in the middle of the night. I'm so exhausted that I told him to stay at his place until whatever he's working on is resolved. Unfortunately, I don't do well on three hours of sleep."

"Right now I sleep through everything," Chandra admitted, "and that includes thunderstorms. Don't forget to call me tomorrow."

"I won't. I'm coming up on the train, so maybe we can eat somewhere near the station. My treat."

"You treated the last time. I'm…"

Denise hung up, cutting off what she knew would become a rant from Chandra. Once she deposited the check from the sale of the apartment into the bank, not only would she have more disposable income but she would also amp up her anemic savings account. Unlike her fiancé, who'd paid as much for her engagement ring than she planned to pay for a new car, she had become more discerning when it came to her finances.

Leaning over, she placed the receiver in its cradle when it rang. She picked it up without looking at the display. "Hello."

"What's this I hear about my favorite sister getting married?"

Denise frowned. "Why do you always refer to me as your favorite sister? Does Daddy have a secret love child hidden away somewhere?"

Xavier's smooth baritone laugh came through the earpiece. "Dad may be a badass on the bench, but I know he's not so bad that he would risk cheating on our mother, who probably would make his life a living hell."

A smile replaced her frown. "Mom is worse than a dog with a bone when she becomes fixated on something."

"I hear you. She's going to love playing the role of mother of the bride."

"I've decided to let her have her wish and go along with whatever she has planned. The only thing I'm going to do is show up and exchange vows with my new husband. I'm certain Mom told you that Daddy is going to do the officiating, so I want you to give me away."

There came a beat of silence. "Are you certain that's what you want, Denise?"

"Of course it's what I want, Xavier. Who else is going to give me away? Besides, everyone in Philly knows Paulette Eaton is the consummate hostess and puts together some of the best parties in the city. That's why she's on all of the social registers of every bougie African-American couple and organization."

"You know how I feel about her fake friends."

"You just don't like them, Xavier, because they're always trying to set you up with their daughters."

"I've never had a problem finding my own women."

Xavier was telling Denise something she already knew. All of her friends in high school and college had wanted her to introduce them to her brother. What most hadn't known was that he had a jealous mistress—the military. Denise didn't know what it was about putting on a uniform, standing in formation and marching for miles with more than sixty pounds of equipment on his back that her brother found rewarding. He claimed it turned boys into men, girls into women, while building character.

"I'd always thought you would get married before me."

Xavier laughed again. "I'm glad you're marrying Garrett, because now the pressure is off me to give Mom a grandchild."

"Give me time to enjoy being married before I start pushing out grandchildren. Right now there's an Eaton population explosion with Belinda, Zabrina and Chandra."

"True. But all the babies are Aunt Roberta's grandchildren."

"I'm still not going to bow to pressure and have a baby because our mother wants to be a grandmother. Now, tell me, dear brother, are you going to give me away?"

"Of course I will. I'm going to hang up now because the truck with my bedroom furniture just pulled up."

"How's the new house?"

"It's nice. I'll call you later in the week. Love you, baby sister."

"Love you back, big brother."

Unfolding her legs, Denise slid off the bed and walked over to the closet to select an outfit for the next day. Closing on the co-op had been a long time coming, and once the title was transferred to the new owners that phase of her life would be behind her.

Her next move would be from her current apartment to the fourth floor of the town house near Dupont Circle. The contractor projected completing renovating the space by early fall. Then there was the task of decorating the apartment. She knew it would take time to select what she wanted in each room, then she and Rhett would have to wait for the pieces to be delivered. Denise didn't expect to have every room decorated for quite some time, but Rhett had asked her to decide on the furniture for the master bedroom suite so he could move out of the hotel.

She'd tried imagining, and failed, getting up in the morning to go to work where she only had to ride the elevator one floor or take one flight of stairs to her office. Rhett would never have the excuse that he couldn't get to work because of bad weather or traffic jams. She also couldn't complain about him bringing his work home, because his home and his office were in the same building.

Rhett pumped his fist in the air in triumph. Chambers Properties had pulled out of the bidding on the commercial property near Baltimore Harbor, resulting with CMP coming in with the lowest bid. His prospectus included building several middle-income rental units and a nearby shopping center with stores ranging from supermarkets, boutiques and a sporting goods shop to a movie theater with two screens.

"I heard Trey and his father are looking for investors."

Rhett hadn't known what to expect when he'd returned his financial planner's telephone call, but it was not the news that CMP had the winning bid to a parcel of land he'd had his eye on for years. "How much are they looking for, Stanley? Is it doable?" he asked after hearing the figure.

"Hold on, Rhett, let's crunch a few numbers."

The rapid tapping of keys came through the intercom as Rhett waited for the financial guru to work his magic. "If I'm going to take over Chambers Properties, then I want total control."

"You read my mind, brother," Stanley said, chuckling. "I can make it happen if you're willing to sell off your latest acquisition."

"Not happening," Rhett countered. "My fiancée has her day care center on that parcel."

There was another tapping of keys. "What about putting your house in Maryland up for collateral against a short-term, no-interest loan?"

"Make it happen like yesterday."

"Give me thirty-six hours to get the loan approved. Meanwhile I'll contact Chambers and let him know that I represent an anonymous party willing to invest in their company."

"I want to ink this deal before the end of the week." He and Denise were scheduled to spend the weekend with his mother and stepfather.

"Hang up, Rhett, and I'll call Chambers."

Punching a button on the intercom, Rhett disconnected the call. He pushed back his chair and paced the width of his office. For some reason he was too wound up to sit and wait for Stanley's call. In fact, he'd waited long enough to exact revenge on the man whom he'd trusted like a brother, a man whose deceit had kept him from the only woman he'd ever loved.

He and Trey had been, as people would put it, thicker than thieves. Their friendship had begun in boarding school and continued throughout college. Although Trey had inherited his father's good looks and charm, he had always struggled academically. Rhett lost track of the number of papers he'd rewritten for his friend, or the countless hours he'd tutored him for an exam. He'd told Trey he was blessed to have a position waiting for him at Chambers Properties. What he hadn't told Trey was he doubted whether he would've been able to hold down a position outside of his family's business because he preferred socializing to studying.

Being academically inept hadn't stopped the indulgent only child from concocting a scheme that would've worked if Rhett hadn't been so in love with Denise. Even after he'd blackmailed her into dating him again, he realized he'd never stopped loving her.

He had promised Denise he wouldn't hurt Trey. He knew she was talking about physically hurting him, when his intent was to cause psychological pain—namely humiliation. The man had to pay for stealing six years of his life.

His private line rang and, taking long strides, Rhett picked up the receiver before it rang again. "Yes?"

"We're on for Friday morning. I told Trey Jr. that I would meet with him, his father and the board at ten o'clock. We'll discuss the terms of the takeover, take a vote, then sign the necessary documents. I also told Trey, without mentioning your name, that you had a prior engagement and will join everyone at the luncheon following the board meeting. The only thing I'm going to tell you is that I don't want to be anywhere close to that restaurant when the fireworks begin."

Rhett smiled. "Don't worry, friend. There won't be any fireworks." And there wouldn't be. It wasn't his style. He'd executed one other hostile takeover, resulting in little or no casualties, and he was certain it would be the same with Chambers Properties, Ltd.

Denise walked out of the bathroom, a towel wrapped around her head, turban-style. Rhett had decided to change their sleeping venue and had spent the past two nights at his suite in the Hay-Adams. It was very different not to have to make the bed, clean up the bathroom or cook. His suite was on the top floor, which offered unobstructed views of the White House.

Rhett was in bed, talking quietly into the tiny microphone attached to his cell phone earpiece. The television was tuned to a station featuring a local D.C. news program. She crawled into bed with him, supporting her back against a mound of pillows on the king-size bed. She liked the suite because the French doors opened onto a small balcony.

Dinner had become a romantic affair when they'd ordered room service. She'd lit candles while Rhett found an all-music radio station featuring classical selections. They'd shared entrées of goat cheese and basil ravioli with spicy black olives, tomato sauce, capers, pine nuts and shaved parmesan and sautéed sole with parsley potatoes and lemon caper sauce.

Swinging her legs over the side of the bed, she walked over to the thermostat, adjusting the temperature. Although the space was icy-cold, it didn't seem to affect Rhett, who had left his chest bare after pulling on a pair of cotton lounging pants. He lifted his eyebrows questioningly when she met his gaze, pantomiming rubbing her bare arms. Nodding, he returned his focus to his phone conversation.

Denise knew she had to compromise, or her marriage to Rhett wouldn't survive its first year. He was a businessman, and that meant he would spend hours in meetings, on the phone or computer. Rhett had promised not to conduct business at home after eleven at night. The exception would come when they moved into the town house where he would have access to his office 24/7.

Rhett managed to concentrate on what Stanley was telling him even though he'd found his mind straying.

Denise had emerged from the bathroom in a revealing black lace midriff top with a matching pair of bikini panties. She came back to the bed, moving closer and resting a bare leg over his.

Everything was in place. The meeting for his take-over of Chambers where he would hold the controlling share of the decades-old real estate corporation had been confirmed. Stanley would negotiate on behalf of a CMP holding company, which made it virtually impossible for Chambers to identify the players. But then even if he knew that Garrett Fennell was his mysterious inves-tor he doubted if Trey could afford to turn away monies needed to keep his company afloat. The next step was filing for bankruptcy and financial ruin for the family and the company's shareholders.

He reached for the television remote, increasing the volume when a special bulletin flashed across the screen. "Stan, let me call you back." Rhett ended the call, staring at the large flat screen. He heard what the newscaster was saying even when he didn't want to believe it. Someone had assaulted Trey Chambers Jr. and left him for dead. When his father was notified of the attack, he'd collapsed and was transported to the same hospital where his son was undergoing emergency surgery.

"You didn't!"

Rhett's gaze swung from the screen to Denise. Her eyes were large and filled with unshed tears. "What are you talking about?"

Denise slipped out of bed as if in a trance, backing up when Rhett reached for her. "Don't touch me!" She hadn't realized she was screaming. "You promised me you wouldn't hurt him."

Ignoring her protest, Rhett pulled her up close in a

punishing grip. "How many times do I have to prove myself to you, Denise? When I told you I wouldn't hurt Trey Chambers I meant it."

"Why is he in a hospital fighting for his life, Rhett?"

"I don't know, baby. It's not because of anything I've said or done. Do I dislike Trey Chambers? Yes. But not enough to have someone beat him and dump his body in an alley. There are other ways of making him pay for his sins without resorting to violence."

Denise went completely still. "How?"

"That doesn't concern you," Rhett countered.

"What do you mean it doesn't concern me? Are we going to start keeping secrets from each other even before we're married?"

"Whatever goes on with CMP is *my* business, Denise, and I don't intend to involve you in it."

"How dare you..." The hotel phone shrilled loudly, preempting whatever Denise was going to say.

Rhett released Denise and reached for the receiver. "Fennell," he said, identifying himself. "Calm down, Mom. I can't understand a thing you're saying if you don't stop crying. Okay, I'm coming." He slammed the receiver in the cradle. "Get dressed. My mother wants to see us."

"Now?"

"Yes now." Rhett had slipped out of the lounging pants and was searching through a drawer for his underwear by the time Denise was galvanized into action. It took five minutes for her to slip into a pair of underwear, jeans, T-shirt and running shoes. Damp curls hung around her face, and she managed to grab her handbag before Rhett took her hand as they raced out of the suite.

Chapter 16

Only the slip-slap of tires on the roadway shattered the silence inside the car as Rhett exceeded the speed limit during the drive from D.C. to Falls Church, Virginia. He could not have imagined what had happened to trigger his mother's histrionics. The sign indicating the number of miles to Falls Church's city limits came into view.

Denise bit down on her lip, wishing Rhett would ease his grip on her left hand. He drove with his left, while holding her fingers captive in his right. It was as if holding on to her would keep his anxiety at bay.

She'd tried imagining why Geraldine had called, asking to see not only Rhett but her, but was unable to come up with a plausible reason. What Denise did not want to entertain was the possibility that something had happened to her husband. Geraldine and Maynard had recently celebrated their first wedding anniversary and…

Her thoughts drifted off, dissipating like a puff of smoke. She closed her eyes and when she opened them again Rhett had turned down a winding path to a cul-de-sac with a sprawling Shingle Style bungalow set back from an expansive manicured lawn. He maneuvered into the circular driveway to a home ablaze with light.

Denise always waited for Rhett to get out and come around to open the door for her, but tonight was different. She was out of the car before he cut off the engine. The front door opened and Geraldine stood in the doorway, waiting. The car's doors closing sounded unusually loud in the stillness of the warm summer night. The hoot of an owl and the incessant chirping of crickets serenaded the quiet countryside.

She waited for Rhett, and hand-in-hand they approached Geraldine Russell. Her hair, held off her face with a wide headband, looked as if she'd combed it with her fingers. The T-shirt she'd put on backward over a pair of cropped jeans was evidence she'd gotten dressed in a hurry, or in the dark.

Geraldine kissed her son and the young woman she'd come to think of as her daughter. "Thank you for coming so quickly." Even though she had Maynard, she'd felt as alone and frightened as she had at sixteen. She opened the door wider. "Please come in." Denise walked into an entryway, Rhett following, and she closed the door behind them.

"Where's Russ?" Rhett asked, looking around for his stepfather.

"He won't be joining us."

"What's going on, Mom? You called me in hysterics asking me and Denise to drop everything and come here, and now you tell me your husband won't be joining us. Did he do something to you?"

Geraldine rested a hand on her son's shoulder. "No. Maynard Russell would never hurt me."

"Where is he, Mom?"

"He's in the bedroom. I told him that it would go better if I was alone with you and Denise to tell you—"

"You're not sick?" Rhett asked, as fear filled his eyes.

A hint of a smile broke through Geraldine's expression of uncertainty. "No, I'm not sick. Come in the kitchen. I just brewed a pot of coffee."

Denise lagged behind, staring in awe at the living room filled with light from diamond-paned windows or light screens. Antique runners on gleaming wood floors imbued a sense of warmth and richness, and artificial light diffused through colored panels and skylights were reminiscent of the style attributed to Frank Lloyd Wright.

The smell of freshly brewed coffee lingered in the kitchen as Rhett wrapped an arm around Denise's waist and led her over to a breakfast nook, seating her on a cushioned bench seat at the rectangular oak table.

"Sit down, Mom. I'll bring the coffee."

He poured coffee into delicate china cups for his mother, Denise and himself, placing them on the table already set with place mats and serving pieces. The silence in the room was deafening when he opened the refrigerator for a container of cream. He sat down beside Denise and opposite Geraldine, watching her under lowered lids as she added dollops of cream to her coffee until she achieved the shade she sought.

"We're ready." It was his signal for her to talk.

Geraldine stared at her cup. Overhead light glinted off the older woman's flawless dark face. "What I'm about to tell you should've been told years ago." Her head popped up, her gaze steady. "I've lost count of the number of times you've asked me about your father, and I never could work up the nerve to tell you, Garrett, until now."

His hands tightened around the china cup. "Why did you change your mind?"

Picking up a napkin, she blotted the corners of her eyes. "I don't want him to die without giving you a chance to meet him."

Rhett leaned forward. "Is *my* father dying?"

"I don't know. The last news report was that he'd suffered a massive heart attack." Her reply was a whisper.

Suddenly it hit him, the realization rocking him to the core. "Is Trey Chambers Sr. my father?" Geraldine nodded as tears streamed down her face unchecked. Rhett got up and sat next to her. Reaching for a napkin, he wiped gently at her tears. "Tell me about it, Momma."

Geraldine broke down, sobbing inconsolably. Her son calling her Momma was like going back to a time when she fought to keep her son safe, to make sacrifices in her life so he wouldn't repeat her life and that of his grandmother's.

"I was sixteen when I met Trey for the first time," she said after she'd regained control of her emotions.

Rhett and Denise listened, stunned as Geraldine told of working part-time at a restaurant to earn money to help out her single mother and save enough to pay for her senior prom. She had put off plans to attend college part-time because her mother's asthma had made it more and more difficult for her to work.

Trey would come to the restaurant several nights a week and sit at Geraldine's table. "He was the foreman at a construction site in my neighborhood, but what I hadn't known at the time was his father and uncles were in the business of buying up properties in low-income D.C. and Baltimore neighborhoods. Some they renovated but many were left to deteriorate. He would leave me tips that the other waitresses would have to work a week to collect.

"First there was the money, then gifts like gold earrings, a silk scarf, a shopping spree where I would select beautiful lingerie and cashmere sweaters. When I asked him why he was spending so much money on me he said it was his wish to make me happy. Of course, he being older said all the things I wanted to hear. What I hadn't known at the time was he was dating another woman in his social circle. I'd become the plaything across the tracks that kept him occupied when his fiancée was busy with her Jack and Jill and sorority meetings.

"Everything came to a crashing halt when he told me that he had to get married to save his father's company. In other words, it was to be a marriage of convenience. What I hadn't known at the time was that his girlfriend was pregnant and they'd opted to marry sooner rather than later that year. The day I discovered I was also pregnant was the day my mother died from an asthma attack. The social worker from social services arranged for me to live with my aunt, who'd never married or had children. She asked me once who the father of my child was. I was too ashamed to tell her, and she never asked again. I dropped out of school and went to work while Aunt Audrey watched my son."

Rhett closed his eyes, digesting what his mother had revealed. "Why," he asked, opening his eyes, "did you enroll me in Marshall Foote knowing your former lover's son was also there?"

Geraldine's eyes narrowed. "It was the only way I

could make him pay for his deceit. I knew he would send his son to the boarding school, because he'd been one of four students who'd integrated Marshall Foote back in the day. I wanted him to see that I'd moved on, and that he'd given me a gift that was priceless. When he saw me with a young boy whom he knew had to be his son I thought he was going to pass out. I could see him mentally doing the math, and I told him Garrett was *my* son, would never be his and I had no intention of messing up his so-called perfect life."

"What did he say, Mom?"

"Thank you."

Rhett blinked. "That's it?"

Geraldine gave him a tender smile. "That was it. I read later that his wife had filed for divorce and Trey was already looking for her replacement. It was apparent Trey could not remain faithful to any woman."

"Like father like junior," Rhett mumbled under his breath. "Do you know if senior told junior that we were half-brothers?"

"I don't know. That's something you're going to have to ask him when…or if he survives."

Rhett, still numbed by the news that he and Trey Chambers were brothers, placed his hand over his mother's. "Have you told Russ?"

Geraldine grew teary again. "Yes. I had to tell him."

"What did he say?"

"What he always says. He loves me." Blowing out her cheeks, Geraldine stood up. "Let me go and get my husband. It's time I introduce him to his future daughter-in-law."

Denise waited for Geraldine to walk out of the kitchen, then moved to sit beside Rhett. He took her hand, threading their fingers together. She didn't say anything only because she didn't know what to say, knowing it would take time for Rhett to come to grips with the revelation that his brother had systematically planned to destroy his happiness.

She rose to her feet when Maynard Russell entered the kitchen, walking into his outstretched arms. Russ was only several inches taller than his wife. His light brown skin was still smooth; dimples and a sprinkling of freckles afforded him a boyish look. His graying sandy-colored hair was cropped close to his well-shaped head.

"We finally meet," Maynard said, kissing her cheek. "Gerri has been bragging about her beautiful daughter and I agree with her. You are lovely."

Denise nodded, pressing a light kiss to his jaw. "Thank you, Father."

Maynard glared at Rhett over her shoulder. "You call me Russ, while this beautiful child calls me Father. Son, you've picked a real winner."

Crossing his arms over his chest, Rhett winked at his mother's husband. "What can I say? We've got impeccable taste when it comes to women."

"No lie," Maynard drawled. "You guys must be exhausted, so I want you to bed down in one of the guest rooms. Everything will look clearer in the morning."

"Come, darlings," Geraldine crooned, leading the way out of the kitchen. Rhett and Denise exchanged a glance, then followed.

Trey Chambers Sr. survived his heart attack and sailed down to his vacation home in San Juan, Puerto Rico, to convalesce. It took Trey Jr. longer to recuperate. The assault had left him with a concussion, six broken ribs, a broken nose, fractured leg and cheek.

Rhett found himself spending hours in his brother's hospital room, waiting for him to surface from his heavily drugged state so he could ask questions and put their past to rest. He had Stanley Tolpin contact the board members of Chambers Properties to inform him that his client was still interested in investing in the real estate company. Instead of a takeover, his client now sought a partnership.

"Mr. Fennell, Mr. Chambers is lucid and can speak to you now."

Rhett popped from the chair like a jack-in-the-box. He'd spent the past hour in the hospital's solarium, reading. He smiled at the nurse. "Thank you."

He hadn't realized how fast his heart was beating until he walked into the private room to find Trey sitting up in bed. Most of the bruises dotting his face were beginning to fade. A two-week stay in a hospital room had robbed his olive complexion of its natural rich color.

Standing at the foot of the bed, he and Trey engaged in a stare-down. "How are you feeling?"

Trey ran a hand over his hair. "I've been better." He closed his eyes. "Just say better than the other day."

"What happened?"

"I got my ass kicked."

Rhett's impassive expression didn't change. "Why?"

"I owe gambling debts."

"How much do you owe, Trey?"

"A lot."

"How much is a lot, *brother*?"

Trey closed his eyes. "You know?"

"Hell yeah, I know. What I want to know is when did *you* know?"

Trey's chest rose and fell heavily. "When Dad found out that you were graduating at the top of the class and I was near the bottom he let it slip that the son of a high-school dropout was smarter than one whose mother had graduated college with honors. That's when he told me you were his son. I'd always been jealous of how easy it was for you to get As, when I was lucky to get a C. Then, when you'd managed to snag one of the prettiest, most intelligent black girls on campus I knew I had to mess up your perfect world."

Rounding the bed, Rhett sat on the chair next to the bed. "It looks as if your perfect world has imploded. I'm not going to pay off your debts. I'm willing to make Chambers Properties a partner of CMP. *Your* father will be given a generous retirement package, while you will be demoted. I will pair you up with someone who knows the ins and outs of the real estate business. You will be evaluated at the end of a year and, based on your job performance, I'll decide whether to keep you on or fire your ass."

"What about my debts? The moment I walk out of this hospital someone will be out there waiting for me."

"I don't want to know who you owe. However, I'm going to send someone to see you and you'll give him the name. Then, he'll negotiate with your loan shark as to how he wants to be paid. The first thing you're going to put on the table as a bargaining chip is your Thoroughbred."

"No!"

"Yes, Trey," Rhett countered heatedly. "It's betting on something with four legs that put you in that bed, and if you don't want to end up in a box six feet under, then you will sell the horse. My person will have you sign a power of attorney, giving him the authority to sell the animal to pay off your debts. Tell me now if you agree with what I'm proposing, because when I walk out of this room the deal will be off the table."

Trey nodded. "Okay."

Rhett leaned over, patting his shoulder. "Hurry up and get well, brother. You're going to have to work for the first time in your worthless life."

He walked out of the room and bumped into Denise. She'd called to tell him she would meet him in the hospital's visitor parking lot. "I know I'm early, but I didn't want to wait downstairs."

Rhett angled his head and took possession of her sweet mouth. "Let's go to the Cape."

Denise rested a hand over his heart. "You want to go tonight?"

He gave her a tender smile. "Yes, tonight. It's been too long since we've had a quiet evening at home."

"How long has it been, darling?" Denise asked.

"Too long, baby."

And it had been. Since Geraldine's frantic telephone call it was as if their cloistered world had been turned upside down. He'd spent most of his free time at the hospital, and when he went home to Denise it was to fall asleep in her scented embrace.

He loved her, loved her more than he could've imagined loving a woman.

He'd waited six years for her. But now he was counting down the months, weeks and days when he would claim her as his wife. Denise Eaton had tempted him not once, but twice, and both times he'd succumbed to the woman who'd captured his heart forever.

* * * * *

He has long
learned not to trust
women...but then
she came along.

KIMANI ROMANCE

AlTonya
Washington

AlTonya Washington

Self-made developer Gage Vincent learned long ago not to believe the words of a beautiful woman. But he thought Alythia Duffy was different. Yet how can he trust her after he finds out that she is bidding for space in his hot new skyscraper? Will Alythia be able to prove to him that she is the special woman meant to share his life?

"Washington is an excellent story-teller, and readers will enjoy the surprises around every turn of this tale with a storyline so novel it's difficult to forget." —*RT Book Reviews* on *PROVOCATIVE TERRITORY*

Available April 2014
wherever books are sold!

HARLEQUIN®
™ www.Harlequin.com

KPAW3510414